A great book I would highly recommend for anyone who likes tales of the middle earth. This book is filled with wizards, gnomes, and Catholic truths. I had to admit I am not one who reads a lot of fiction but this is an enjoyable read and release from the modern age of the loss of faith. I also have read his novel Never Leave Your Monastery. Both stories are an entertaining and enjoyable release from the reality of humanism-cancer that is in our holy Church. I suggest you relax, take a deep breath, and take a trip to the underworld with Father Harry. It is a much lighter approach to the troubles in and outside of our Church. If you like Tolkien then you will enjoy this book.

Todd M.
Grand Rapids Michigan
Jul 4, 2019

other works from H.G. Potter

THE DEEPTRACKER'S GUIDE

THE BLADETONGUE SAGA

NEVER LEAVE YOUR MONASTERY

REALMS OF
WHITEHAWK

The Fall of Nystol and Other Tales

Realms of Whitehawk

H. G. POTTER

H.G. Potter

ISBN: 978-1-7325499-2-0

Interior Art Designs by H.G. Potter
Cover by younesselh @fiverr.com
Bookman Old style 9
sp=11.2

The Nomads of Sardu

Great signs have been appearing. I know, it could all just be the torments of my own ceaseless mind, an overzealous storm stirred up by hopeful imaginings, or just vain superstition. One must never dismiss such possibilities. But these were uncanny, these were come as signs indescribable, alignments of planets, protean shapes in the clouds, stars that blazing fall to earth. They intend something momentous, a shift in the destiny of things. They portend some threat returning from beyond the known world, or from beyond even the grave. I tracked the phenomena closely and presented the collected data to a local astronomer.

He drew down from his shelves a certain tome which he called a *galactocriticon*, and thumbing through the decaying leaves found the desired planetary entry. He read it aloud and gave his interpretation of the phenomena: that the likelihood of divine favor upon my proposal certainly should not be dismissed. Even so, he said, planetary omens were not absolute enough for taking risks. Terrestrial signs must also be weighed. Better to wait and hold off from any immediate change of plans.

Two garden cranes took an Eastward flight just at the same time as were walking into the rose garden and considering the importance of terrestrial omens: he did not notice them, but assured me, let the proposed expedition be dismissed for the time being. Studied caution, he warned, should be the rule in all such discernments.

Had misread the signs? I suspected, but said nothing.

It was because of something else, something uncommonly propitious, that both te priest and the astronomer soon changed their minds. It involved myself, an indication unmistakable, a true omen. Should I think of this as no sign? My knees, after having been useless for twenty years, as if of their own accord, mysteriously and quite miraculously have healed.

It happened the morning after long and prayerful supplications to God about the undertaking. I awoke at dawn and simply leapt out of bed, without a second thought, completely oblivious to pain or crutches. It were as if I were a youth again. I walked freely without the slightest imbalance.

Upon examining the miracle himself, they have agreed that we must set out on the expedition at once.

Things will therefore be made ready now. A certain devout brother has already resolved to quit his daily affairs here in Whigg and accompany me. We will hazard the journey South across the Whitehawk continent, to finally arrive at the howling plateau of the Sardu wilderness.

As an Abbot I always attend to every particular thing, as God desires of me, never letting down my shepherd's guard. Even so, heresy has all but consumed our beloved monastery of Whitehaven, and I cannot help but to assign at least partial blame to my own leniency. Therefore my resolution is final.

Here will I record an account of this travel, and surely it may be the last thing which I communicate to those who have been my friends. May it be a useful reference for future pilgrims, or anyone who would seek the lost library.

May God in his mercy send angels to protect us.

Day the second

Much preparation done today. We have located a better chart in the library. I think that the donkey Atlas will suffice for the load. Kruth used to say that the creature is immortal. What an imagination. We will go for a little ways and camp tonight upon the plain of Karkor.

Day the third

Evening is come and camp is again underway. The warm fire is a haven from the cooling airs of dusk. The flames flicker with a poetry, a solitary light in a vast and bewildering night that hurries to overtake the prairie. Kar was a far more beautiful land than I would have guessed. I was sad to have left it.

There are no monks save us from chores. Crickets are the only chanting *creatures* in this valley, their monasteries of tall grass and mulberry hedges. This is how the ravine of the Washir ends in the West. Night birds add a delightful refrain; reminiscent of some regale in which I had once delighted as a boy.

Today the hot winds from Kithom came upon the ridges of the Hermit Hills and we tired quickly. We did not even finish a second league.

We set camp early, careful to descend into the cool valley, not pitch in some a high place. All the more wisdom, for it's too easy to be spotted on the ridges. Since I have a few moments of twilight, I can now look after this journal with a more complete explanation of things.

We have been in the saddle two days, and we already sense remoteness from the walls of Whigg. We will be crossing shallows not far from the great rapids of the Washir. Then we must enter into the unwatched paths of the great middle forest, Chyldeshire.

Fourth day

I have been rash. It is a foolish and desperate trip we have undertaken. Although I have brought along a trained guardian-monk who excels at the open-handed combat, we have with us no formally trained military escourt. Perhaps God wants us to put our trust in Him and in prayer rather than the sword. Eventhough the Edolunt Rangers patrol these regions, I fear that, not far off, there prowl outlaws, bandits, or other dangerous kinds, barbarians and mountain savages, or worse, subhumans whose occult lair is below these very places.

Just today we halted by a human skull resting in the ashes at some abandoned camp site, perhaps left by horgrim or cannibals, or carnivorous trolls, who knows. I hastily performed a burial for the poor soul.

The huge barrier of the Hermit's Hills will also pose difficulty. We had expected to go as far as Kithom and the Yezez country without trouble. We are willing to go farther than any other tome-hunting expeditions in which monks have ever gone. It seems like a boyish dream to me now.

Can I reasonably expect to keep alive in these wilds from day to day? Should we turn back while we have the chance?

Reckon this: a seeker of high lore, powerful scion of a mythic race, a great name, also holding the office of Arcavir, had for a long time urged some kind of mission to Nystol and her rumoured library. But he would refuse every request from the clandestine archivist's guild for funding. In order to avail the cause I had to look elsewhere for patronage.

I found other parties interested in this endeavor besides him. I have a great desire to at last secure the ancient writings of legend. When the gnome refused, the Librarians of Regulum were nevertheless eager to accept my proposal.

Also, certain scribes at Whigg were ready to offer me considerable funds and even a reward.

They have their own motives, which, I trust as Abbot, be not unwholesome, for who would dare? It must involve matters are of high import beyond my keen.

It used to be that the Abbot of Whitehaven was the highest of all leaders, spiritual and temporal, "The Godmouth". Now this office is considered merely titular, although few realize that the actual power of Eldane over all the Furth was never recinded, but remains.

It is better to play a servant that knows little or nothing. Worldly princes will disregard me and I can lead God's Church in earnest. So I eagerly accepted the down payment.

I am ready to put my skills at last to the test. If we do make it as far as Astodan, the vaults under Nystol, then nothing will bother me, for by the grace of God it would surely prove that nothing can stop us.

The Arcavir is also a collector of high lore. But he has now retired from his tome-seeking and went into a possibly centuries-long hibernation, (it seems the slow march of ages can become wearisome even for the fey-races).

To him I have no further obligation, unless there be counted an obligation to the archivist's guild which he founded. They will be permitted to make copies of whatever we bring back, if they have the time and coin.

Last week, upon having obtained to the Arcavir's abandoned Torgrith tower, the guild found a few important works preserved, as well as the magic silver ring which the creature left.

There was nothing else there that could bring further light to the darkness of these mysteries, neither any record of explanations for the strange success of the heresy which we struggle against, nor a single theologic tract to disprove the heretics, and no clue of other rumored conspiracies, only whispers linked to the eldritch ruins of Nystol.

Sleep beckons and already I lack the strength to complete the extensive journal descriptions of the terrain which I hoped to accomplish. I would rather leave this explanation as a kind of last will and testament. Anything can happen out here.

Day Eleven

As anyone who has made it across the Furth continent will tell you, overland travel is far more treacherous than any travel through the trap-laden tombs and troll-tunnels under the earth. Even so, we have been making good time slipping through bandit territory quickly and unnoticed, as it seems.

Most of our strength is spent by the time we pitch camp. Therefore I seek your forgiveness for my negligence in keeping these records

There comes to me now some swell of strong inspiration.

I no longer fear to reveal many things.

I am Cromna, monk and Abbot. In my youth I became a monk at Whitehaven, but later was sent to the Monastery in the Dry Blood Sea, which became my home for years. I returned to Whitehaven and was elected Abbot.

Now I am a man exiled from there. Those halls were once a sanctuary of the righteous, of devout hymns and incensations rising heavenward. Now, as almost over night, the heresy has metasticized the sacred precincts into a vile den of iniquities.

After fleeing that place of foul lies, that stage where perversions of the truth masquerade as enlightenment, I secured help. I evaded the pursuit of the wicked. "Insolent" they called me, one who dared to oppose their enlightenment.

By the aid of angels I escaped them, even so within a widow's mite of my life. I then took ship, hoping for a better place, possibly the Monastery of the Weeping Brotherhood in the Dry Blood Sea. But later I would hear at Regulum that they too have embraced the heresy, even more completely!

Somehow surviving a terrible shipwreck, I made it through to the shores of Osring, and came to the border of the Nine Feudatories. Then was I driven by the Spirit to the Friars in town of Whigg. That is my story so far.

I let pass two circling years sojourning in Whigg, learning as much as possible under the Arcavir Kruth, living at the very edge of society, relying on the help of many other fine guild members.

Before I find another house of prayer and take up a sacred life again with brethren, I will do all in my power to expose the heresy of the monks I once trusted.

I am certain that Our Lord wishes me to alert all believers to the weird doctrines that have brought so much grief as of late to our ancient way. Heresy masquerades as truth, worming its way into the sacred confines of the inspired intellect, and it corrupts every aspect of true faith.

I at least hope to stifle it.

I will seize from them the fuel against which their infernal ardor blazes: the books of the ancients. I expect that by now they have burned all sacred books in the monastery, and they are probably spreading their darkness, going through the stacks kept for centuries at the rock-oasis of Vath. I heard them swear that they would.

Like termites going through a dying tree they will destroy any leaf or bark that does not support their twisted labyrinth of deception.

Next they will enter into Nystol's ruins in hopes to seize the eldark codices left there, but I will have made it there before them to rescue the most valuable texts. Precious leaves are thought to be left there, but no one will dare enter that place.

The land of Nystol has been cursed, like that one forgotten city by Galilee's shore, Corazain, a town cursed by Christ himself for failing to hear him. Nothing grows there, it is burned out. Nystol has been under a similar curse. All the land to the South is reported to be fertile and green, but the Sardu plateau on which the towers rest is become a barren hell.

Like the fig tree that would bear no fruit, such must wither in the face of the unapologetic light.

We ourselves are in great danger. I should not expect to return or ever see the inside of a monastery again, nor perhaps even the steeples of Whigg.

Therefore I will dispense from the archivist-guild's rule (namely that anonymity should cover anything we write). Instead I leave my name recorded here. In this I only endanger myself, no one else. I must do this because I remain a monk and even more so I am an abbot as well.

I too am their priest, albeit exiled, but still by God am I charged with grave responsibility, and so I must explain these many things for the protection of other monks as well. I do so not for my own brethren, who have already forfiet their souls, but for any other monks who might come into contact with them and their deceptions.

My responsibility to Kruth's guild does not eclipse this.

Any Ammouric monk will consider seriously an Abbot's warning. So if you find this journal upon my corpse, clutched in my bony hands, please bring it securely to one of the northern monasteries such as Whitehaven.

Monks, you see, are particularly susceptible to this new and weird heresy.

As member of the guild I am susceptible as well. I also warn any untrained and unauthorized monk, especially anyone who has been a monk but only few years, who may happen receive this record: maintain the rule even for this and do not read further than this page without permission from your abbot, (unless of course, you suspect that even your abbot has gone crazy with all the unholy teachings).

Otherwise fear God and reserve these things for the eyes of the elect only.

Child, you will do far more for the sake of righteousness by disciplined obedience. It is not in your hands alone to save the world from the coming darkness.

Learn this: that it is for such an end that my companion and I set out on journey to Nystol, and entertain no doubt whatsoever that I am chosen by the Furth High King himself. Soon I must retire to my blanket. I will write more on these things another day.

Oh, I should mention my group before I sleep. I have been traveling with the very same monk (he is also a guild member whom I may not name), the same who availed me escape from the heretics. He is a kind and ready soul who has helped me ever since that time.

I also bring along pack animals, (the donkey Atlas being the best, a smart beast who can carry many tomes). We are getting very close now.

There is good cause to suppose that we both might reach the Astodan caves alive and enter into the corridors which are said to twist down into the basements of Nystol.

Who knows, there might even be stored there a copy of *The Golden Pages of The Wind*, or even the mysterious *Vortex Poem*. When it comes to ancient papyri, I know that straight stalks can be found planted among the twisted tares of Sorcerer's scribbles.

Twelvth day

After a brief exploration of the bush country on the outskirts of the Canyon of Hermius, we came across men who had come up from the basins below. These two were herders, Kutaal nomads armed with sabres, of the tribe of famous bladesmiths who wander this part of the world.

They stood at one of the occasional wells just beside the main route into the mountains. They did not introduce themselves to us, but kept to their own business, bringing up buckets of water for their herd.

Our horses were spent and needed water. We stood in the baking noon-day sun and thought a moment how we might approach them.

Their own goats, a small herd, began to encircle us, nibbling on our tunics and trying our boots. We were glad with the tunes of much whinnying.

(My companion was not familiar with goats, having come from an island, but only with sheep).

"I find these creatures, distended and horned, very strange... rather weird in fact." said my companion. "As if a perverse version of the sheep."

"They are rather shameless." I commented. "Perhaps their owners are the same way, for they watch us and are amused."

"And they seem not to care, abbot. This one here has attempted to make a treat out my cincture-rope, and now is eyeing our packs. Tribesmen use the creatures to hinder travelers from easily passing through.

Perhaps an offering would encourage these nomads to herd the creatures away. We have a skin of wine left. If they do not comprehend our tongue, they would doubtless be persuaded by "the fruit of the vine" which clearly cannot grow here."

I consented and we gave them some wine as a gift of passage. There was much laughter and play with the animals, and this resulted in easing the tensions among strangers.

The nomads could not hope to ignore us further and they drove the aggressive goats away from us, smacking the behinds with the long branches. They did not thank us or answer or acknowledge us in any way other than to brandish the wine sack before squirting a red stream into mouth.

We pitched camp not far from there and the sun has already dipped below earth upon its celestial wheel.

Thirteenth day

The nomads returned in the late morning. After some hesitation, they approached to speak with us. Perhaps that was their custom. Or perhaps they hoped for more of that Aquilaran wine.

We offered our salutary introductions in Latin, but they did not return it on account of their rough knowledge. They were not without minimal proficiency in the Oruscan Greek however, the only shared tongue of which any in those regions had slight recognition. They immediately gave their opinion of the old abandoned towers, fore-guessing the purpose of our journey: The ruins of Nystol.

They teased us with insult as is their custom. The translation is exact.:

"Foolish maidens, you are come for the ruins up there, on the mesa of Sardu? They are forbidden to outlanders. They are shunned. It is a place where shadows lurk. Do not go there, let the bricks and stones be."

"You have brought yourselves but you are not good enough." added the other. "You have not any others?" He shook his head in disbelief

"...and you hired no trained war-party? Most outlanders coming this way and seeking that place pay warriors for strong protection. They always bring many shield-bearing men. You must turn back, and not go. You listen and you will know why: tall snout-heads patrol region not far down river, the devilish hyena-heads. Some spot them moving in southernmost reaches of the canyon, the approaches to mesa. They carry ash spears and sharp stone weaponry. They have killed many...but that is nothing compared to the other dangers."

"Other dangers?" I asked. (Any thumb-bit of lore I considered worthy of looking into). Hyena-heads are an old legend of unreliable gain. The ancient Greek explorers of the east called the same *cynocepheloi*, dog-heads, but there have been few other accounts besides the fabulous.

The native tribes popularized it in order to make foreign princes wary of crossing their lands. It seems to be some barbaric tribe that dons the hyena's head for armour, for they must hunt down and slay a hellish hyena with their bare hands in order to be initiated as warriors.

"Not only them, but there wander shadowy spirits upon the mesa. To meet them is worse than death."

"And that is only for those who make it." The other nomad interrupted, "...most travelers pass by and most travelers never find the ruins. Many come, but ruins are never reached. They die while looking for the passage. The desert takes them...or the hyena-heads track them down. Blame the remoteness, blame the highness so steep and far above in climbing; nor are the ruins easily marked from below with your eyes."

While listening to him, I noticed how he glanced at my boots. He tried changing the subject and began speaking instead of their donkey, explaining how proud he was of the fine animal.

It was obvious to me that both were hoping to seem unsurprised, as if visitors were common in these parts. Surely they were trying to keep a secret.

The first nomad, his face covered with an immense shaggy beard, perhaps owned the animals. The other, who may have been his son, doubtless worked hard. My companion urged me with subtle looks to push for more information.

"Make you journey far and wide and you still not come near the ruins," the bearded one warned, "for those are ruins hidden from us. There is only one way. . .you follow paths that only certain trained one is able to remember . . . a man who knows the narrow defiles, a scout who is close friend of the desert. There is one who does this thing. One, not any others. He is trained guide and good survivor, living two years on earth with terrible danger near his spirit. He does not say many things, the Zerbi will show you why. He is dwelling in secret tent, but we are requiring you have good pay for him. Only he guides, other fearful-walking nomads despise the ruins."

"We do not want to involve another guide." I said. "All the reward can be yours if you take us now. You are not fearful of the old stories, are you? Do all the Kutaal and Sardi tribes despise that place?"

He looked at me askance, nervously, shifting his eyes here and there. For a moment he held his speech, and finally consented.

"In earth's dawn, say the grandfathers, some monarch, accursed be his name, enslaved our people. Thousands went into chains, thousands to work and make free the giant stones from within mountain. Later, many massive towers they build, and now those stones also lay there. Stones are fallen, and grandfathers say they are huge, like the huge trees which grew in age-time of titans, before the deep waters swallowed many peoples. Some of our fathers used to dare and used to go up and to bring back bronze pieces, pieces they were breaking off from the colossal statue. But returning they spoke of ghosts and hyena-heads, so they did not return there and did not bring back more bronze.

Some temples remain where the alien gods dwelt, the demon-gods, they are broken but standing. There are many strange monuments of nether-princes. Monuments which exalt the glory of wicked masters. All those now lay about, they are banished from our talk. They are whitening like bare bones now, like goat bones in the desert, when day fades into night, and they are wrapped up in the red vines and in shadow."

"Also..." the other hesitated, breaking in as in an unspoken disagreement, (doubtless fearful that too many things be revealed), "the crumbling roads and bridges are dangers. Not for me, I am not about to take you to Sardu cliffs, not for any the livestock or the riches you make trade with." In their nomadic tongue he muttered some rebuke to his fellow but the other in replied with words that fell on deaf ears. I looked hard at him and frowned.

"...do not direct eyes at me," he said, "not me as one who may lead any there...the sandy desert takes many man, and if not that, then the rocky mesa leaves your bones for vultures. No, it would be death!"

"We must go to this place," I explained, "there are others who seek to retrieve the learning of their own ancestors, and it is said that some important things remain beneath the ruins. Perhaps you will convey us to the guide you mentioned."

"We will take you to him, but do not expect to persuade him. He is Sardi, of the tribe Naar, and he knows us. We will do this for you...but now first you make happy trade of ass with us."

"The ass is not for trade." I said. Atlas the donkey was invaluable. The creature was rumoured to have been made intelligent by means of the gnome's magic. He had seen many things and been on many adventures. He was also world-famous, or infamous, for having lost most of *the Black Books* by attemping to stubbornly cross a mountain ford during a downpour. Is it because of him that 80% of Whitehawk history is missing? His presence on the current journey was considered penance. I was insistant that the donkey be kept. I frowned sternly. "Never this beast...!"

"Then you gift fancy oxhide boots to us."

My leather boots were new, not even broken-in. Nevertheless, this was it, this was for what I had waited, waited for so many years. So I passed them off and recieved the nomad's miserable goat-hide sandals, which, I suppose, are more like what the Apostles must have worn on their many journeys into strange lands. At least the sandals fitted.

In the morning they would come for us, and we were to follow those two nomads, together with their goats, into destiny.

Day Fourteen

The sun is upon the horizon.

We've mounted our pack animals and have descended on a rocky trail with our nomad guides, perhaps some two thousand measures into the floor of Hermius' Canyon. I mounted my horse and put my packs on the donkey Atlas, and tied the animals together.

The old donkey was disagreeable. As if in retribution, he seemed very unmindful of the steeply dropping ledges as he carelessly bolted about. The animal was so overconfident; we must surely be about to slip off the trail falling to a dreadful end a thousand measures below. The pack-horses are not much better. Even if those creatures are accustomed to such terrain, it gives the rider little consolation when balanced so close to a precipitous drop. They are skillful animals, and may somehow have understood this quiet game at our expense. They doubtless have their pleasure in it.

In a few hours we will have arrived at the encampment of the nomadic tribe on the canyon floor. Unlike the dry bush country above, it will be mild and shady down there.

Since there are no breezes, the horse flies found us and offered their menace with infernal buzzing. In my opinion they are little demons with wings. They did not even go after the nomads, whose heads are well-wrapped in turbans.

Our horses splashed through the river to reach the large nomad-tents.

We came about and rode to the far edge of the encampment and arrived at a poor little tent. It was a small round tent, the tent of a reputed Nystol-guide; a rather shabby tent, made of old skins tied together, and in a lonely, separated place.

The goat owner went into the tent alone for a few moments and then came out again. He invited us to enter the smokey interior.

We saw an elderly shaman, bald and gazing with dreamy eyes,

sitting cross-legged. He was perhaps in his nineties, and a very young man, his hair long and uncombed, sat with him. The shaman was obviously the one who had hung up strange objects such as lizard heads and a number of feathers, and many skins decorated with magical glyphs, as well as various bowls filled with perhaps herbs, incense, or any number of weird substances I could not identify.

The nomads introduced us not as monks, but as "trusted travelers" for they did not recognize our monastic habits. After all, it has never been heard that our kind had ever gone so far abroad. They did find our habits curious, (under which we had made provision to wear leather armour).

At once, after introductions, it became apparent that the boy was apprentice to the old shaman. I began to question this gaunt young man known as "the mesa guide." He did not answer and it soon became apparent that he was unable, and that, in fact, he was speechless.

"In order to find the entrance into the accursed library, one must follow tunnels underground, within the mesa, is that true?" I asked.

The boy nodded in affirmative. The leader nomad who had brought us, the bearded nomad, spoke for the young man, interpreting the weird sign language.

"Will this boy inform us..." I asked, "why does he not speak? Who or what maimed him? Or has he no natural sppech ability?"

When this boy-guide heard the nomad's translation of this, he shook his head emphatically. Obviously the dread of giving information on an identity still held its forbidding threat.

"He has never revealed it..." explained the nomad who had brought us, "and he would not reveal it, if he could reveal. We only know this: he disappeared for an entire winter. He went to be guide for many horsemen, for shield-bearing warriors. He returned alone without ability for speech,as one literally scared speechless, permanently, and the warriors, each one, had their bones lifted."

I never did discover if this mutilation were actually real, or if it were just a way to get us to feel pity so they could ask for more. As a man of God I could not be rude and demand to examine his mouth.

There is a legend that certain long-living wizards have survived and haunt the Deadly Hills and parts of the canyon. According to this, the wizards of Nystol would always cut out the tongue of anyone foolish enough to try overcoming them by force. It was an eye-for-an-eye retribution against the five kings of the ancient world who originally exiled the wizards to Sardu. They had attempted to put an end to spell-casting by "cutting out each spellwise tongue."

"...bones lifted?" I asked.

"A *terriculum*, it is the cthumis tree, a type of, how do you say?...scare-away-man? Skull and bones tied on the bare pole-tree to make warning... The boy has swift feet and knows every wild place, every rock of the canyon, every hill of desert sand. One day men pay us for his knowledge, for expedition. On third day boy goes to river near the tiny water-flow to wash and to drink. It was a place not far from the entrance to the secret tunnels that lead into mesa, and up into Nystol. When he is coming back again from river, every strong warrior he finds cut apart and piled in bloody heaps. He not say more than only that, afterwards he become always speechless, no one knows why.

He has been now in a bad way and will not take a big war-party, not any longer. He knows how big-war parties leave many tracks and campfires. The hyena-heads always find out, they always thirst for killing. He is brave but you must do what he says, travel on foot when you reach plateau, no horse...and he will be guiding only when sun is sunk down, when there is night.

It is likely that the hyena-heads are gone far south to Mullith, it be season to make war with the Vri. If so, if not tracks of hyena-heads, you will make it, but if not, he will return to safer territory and not go to Nystol."

"Perhaps you have kept some of the old scrolls and books of Nystol yourself?" I suggested, "They are treasured, you know." And I added rather imprudently. "if you do, if you have kept any here, we can pay good coin."

"Our people, they are not trained to make words on paper. Many say making signs on goat-skin be devil-work. We rely on magic way that each has been given, but we have no magician lord beside this one shaman...him, and he is too old to remember, so many spells and curses he cannot utter. I think that is why some power cut out the tongue of his apprentice, to destroy magic word-saying. There is not any high one with most powerful magic...and this guide would not make signs to tell of magic things even if magic things, like writings, were left here."

There was a pause while the boy sat there on his goat hides watching us. He had a glint of keenness in his eye, and he was skinny and somewhat worn looking. He studied close our faces, our gestures, it seemed, looking us over with curious eye. The old shaman could care less for us, and by the distant gaze of his dreamy eyes he must have been elsewhere in spirit.

"Will you then be our guide, boy?" I asked, "I have plenty coin."

"But not for coin," said the nomad, answering for him, (it was rather apparent that he looked after the poor guide and received a considerable cut of his bids). "Our kind do not much be going among ruled townsmen...you must offer a number of goat and then he will guide. It is best hope for to make of good living he need. He make risk of his own skin as the guide. He does not accept many request for this, so offer many goat or he is about to refuse."

We had to make an offer, though we did not own any goats.

"Ten goats..."

"Not enough...do you think this is not deadly work? Many have died. Fifty head is good."

"Fifty? We have not enough. Just thirty will cost us all our coin..."

"Thirty-nine is low, but we accept."

"I did not offer that yet..."

"I heard from the wise they offer the very same amount to nomads, whenever they go abroad. Less would be insult. I am glad we do not hear less is offered. It is almost a right number, but you are new to our ways, so we give special low price, thirty-nine, you agree. Not many do this. You are in good deal, very fair. We Kutaal are too generous to outsiders, we must cease being that way. Our wives will be angry."

So what they required was promised. I did however require in turn that my boots be returned. The other two nomads will also accompany us as far as the end of the canyon.

By nomadic arm-clasping we closed the deal and they went off to make preparations and meals.

We bade farewell to a certain brother and guild member with instructions and monies to purchase goats about the sacred cliff-city Vesulum up the canyon eight leagues north, and to meet us again back there in no longer than two weeks.

As collateral the nomads have our two pack horses after coming to the furthest reach of the canyon and they will care for them until we return, if we return.

So practical and deliberate a folk are the Kutaal nomads. How was it that ways so strange and foreign to what I am accustomed are part of this life? They know nothing of monks or scribes or imperial librarians, or even of written law of the tablets and the men who twist it. Their only worry was the hyena-heads, or other humans all the more, the goat-thieves and vicious gold prospectors and various mean-hearted *gazalir* wandering in the Canyon.

The journey is to take two and a half days traveling south, leaving the Yezez desert-valley and entering into the higher zones of the sub-plateau.

Day Fifteen

After packing our tents it has become clear that the nomads are now treating us differently. Perhaps they have lost every trust afforded well meaning strangers as regards us, and having obtained our payment, they count us among the doomed. They did not reveal their names when we inquired, but clammed up or cast a downward glance.

Whether this is out of some custom, superstition, or unspoken fear of magic, Perhaps we should not even hope to learn.

The two herders will not go all the way. They plan to relinquish the party when we reach the end of the canyon, where the wilderness of Kedemoth begins.

They know the land and can fight, and though they are very guarded, they have become very talkative again and treat on many things as to how we should travel in the desert. One, for example, showed us how to extract clean water from the canyon floor.

We made several attempts to persuade them to stay on. They were not to be persuaded. They will part ways come nightfall.

The donkey Atlas has been acting strange. His ears twitch in an unusual pattern and he refuses to lay down for rest.

"To be earning much coin as helpers on mesa-expeditions would become bad luck, would hasten death..." they say, "only trained guide may go all way."

Day Sixteen

Much of the same today; the air is getting very dry as we near the high desert, but the canyon walls keep us cool and there are occasional trees. There is no more water left.

If we have some divine assistance, we might be able to avoid the waste-desert entirely, treking instead through the cactus forest of Kedemoth.

One incident involving the nomads deserves mention before continuing. On the last night before their departure, we had arrived at one of their oft-used camp sites (in an area the guide assured was safe). We lit up a small fire underneath a huge rock overhang. We were roasting and eating some small orthopods seized from the diminishing river.

The leader-nomad, not waiting till he had finished swallowing, spoke:

"You wifeless travelers, (he would call me that), what do you seek in that place....treasure? Powerful magic?"

"I cannot say what is my purpose, friend," I answered, "but it is thought that there are things left up there which describe the entire history of the Furthreaches, as well as sacred things of days long past. I wish to collect these, whatever remains, and bring them back to be copied and stored in the library of the emperor. There is one book of utmost importance, which must not fall into the wrong hands."

"You are seeking *The Black Books* then?"

I was stunned that he would somehow know that. I checked my chew on the orthopod and stared at him, speechless.

"These are famous books." he explained. "Many who have come have mentioned it...

"*The Black Books* are valuable, yes," I admitted "and they surely are useful for learning the history of certain lands, ancient kings, and relics. Since Nystol's magic is gone, only relics left over from the ancient world remain, and they yet retain powerful magic. The books describe their elemental powers. This must be controlled by the Church. And there are other books I am seeking which are even more precious to men of faith."

"There are other things written in them." he said, brooking no disagreement.

"There are some things which I must not speak on't." I admitted.

"There be what Sorcerers seek. You have brought evil with you. A bird follows you, one who is dark, a vulture. He is afraid and keeps distance. The winds speak to me, they say he is the eyes of a warlock, one who knows big magic. I have seen him many times flying."

"If that is true, he cannot come near," I said, "but will look for a chance to snatch the book if we find it. There is a Sorcerer shadowing us, whom the men of these lands call the Warlock of Yeth. We have dealt with him in the past. He cannot work magic against monks."

At the name "Warlock of Yeth", the speechless boy, our guide who was sitting with us near the fire, looked up with eyes wide, alarmed, and something like dread came over his face. He started making protests by arm gestures, as if to shoo away an evil spirit. Fear turned to anger, he grunted angrily several times trying to talk. He looked like he was about to get up and flee, relinquishing our agreement.

"Tell him that the warlock cannot harm him." I ordered, "Tell him there is no danger because we are men of God. The warlock has been made weak before us. He is punished...Only his familiar, a vulture, watches from afar, a useless exercise."

The leader nomad took hold of the speechless boy's flailing arms and spoke to him with charged words, (and also, I suspect, he reminded him of the great need of new goats).

"He has fear of this warlock, it is the spirit-man, many say. Our grandfathers also spoke of this sorcerer, he envy many others and think himself cursed, he haunts the canyon and the Deadly Hills and the Yezez. They say that he goes by the name Arizel, though they were uncertain. Why we must believe that you have done this punishing to great warlock, feared of numberless days long past? You are not wizard. What kind are you, wifeless, or are you a woman guising as a man? Your eyes say not even kill in battle yet. You read too many book. Are you priest of Ammouri?"

"No, just a monk seeking out lost *volumina*. Now listen, tell him quiet down. Who knows if any hostiles come round this part of the canyon hunting game at twilight. Did we not see an old campfire someone left earlier, with unknown tracks? Inform him this: We smashed the old warlock's power just weeks ago in Vesulum with old-fashioned "God-magic." Tell him that Eloniah did this."

The boy guide looked puzzled when he heard the name. He did indeed recognize the title The Eloniah. It is famous in the few lands accustomed to keeping the old lore. The leader-nomad translated these things and the guide began to calm down. He at last continued his meal.

Our campfire crackled and glowed more fiercely...

"You be friendly with dwarf-shaman, the Arcavir called The Eleusinion?" asked the leader nomad.

"We are...and I am surprised that any so distant from Whigg would reckon: the secret name of the guild-master is unexpected."

"He is become legend. He saved our fathers during the wars with the Kalar Maurob, during an age now past, taught them to fight. Men say he is enchanted, a gift to tribes from the good mountain-father. Where he is gone? You go with him recent days?"

"We are cut off from the power of The Eloniah now, and we must rely only on our own wit. Without him we would never have made it, but I tell you this, none but your great grandchildren might see him again, for he has withdrawn from the world. The time grows short and we are hunted men. It is not safe to inform you of more, not here in the open. The nether-brood have big ears indeed. Demons unseen may also be eavesdropping nearby. There is danger ever present and the powers ready themselves. The Eloniah taught us of these things....I have many plans, many tricks of escape to avoid hyena-heads or other hostile ones when we get into the defile."

"Not for you to be coming up with plans, saying, we do this now, we go here, do this plan." said the nomad, rather sternly. "You do everything that not-with-tongue mesa-guide indicates, you not question him. He has one good plan which is best if enemy tracks you down, sniffs you out."

I could not think of how to answer such a strong injunction. Here was a man that could not write, lived a primitive existence, and he was informing me that my skills and knowledge would avail us nothing.

"You do not think it would be wise to have several plans?" I asked. "Each of these many could be considered, and the best one chosen in each different event."

"No. Not that way."

"Why do you demand that?"

"I tell you story of why...and you listen good. It is story of animals that haunt the Canyon, Fox and Cat who live and hunt in Canyon. Fox make boast to Cat: "I have many ways to escape enemy hunters, a whole bag of tricks, hundred ways to escape." Cat say: "I have only one way, but I manage with that one way many-many time." Just at that time they hear cry of a pack of hounds coming toward them, and Cat immediately scampered up an yew tree and hid herself in the boughs. "This is my plan" said Cat. "What is your plan? Which one you do now?" Fox first thought of one way, then of another, and while he debated to himself the hounds came nearer and nearer, and soon Fox in his confusion was caught up by the hounds and soon killed by hunters. Cat, who had seen the whole thing said: "Better one safe way than an hundred on which you cannot reckon. So now you know. You just let mesa-guide be as Cat. If you do this you will succeed, if not you will fail. You are after the accomplishment of dangerous enterprise, urgent works, we do not disbelieve it. This far beyond the short-seeing of our ignorance, our simple ways, our goats, but we not so simple as our lives seem. If before this I had knowledge of how important your quest to hinder dark power, I would before say: all nomads help him!"

The old nomad was right, his earthly wisdom was something not to be lightly brushed aside on account of its rustic origin. So I too, by his simple fable, have become convinced that this world is filled with many dangerous spiritual killers who lay traps for the soul. There is only one way, not many, to escape them. It is the tried and true way of our ancient discipline.

"Your help is providential," I said, "God is watching over us. The Eloniah himself told me that the route to the tunnels of Astodan which lead to the summit of the Sardu Mesa is almost impossible to find. Perhaps we shall return with warriors instead."

"Tomorrow," he observed in a reflective tone, no longer eating, "we go back to our goats and our wives, to those things which give comfort. You, however, you do not much rest, not much take comfort. Not for you, not much easiness, as long as the doings which The Eloniah has asked of you are left undone, even if it costs the shedding of blood. This I know, our fathers commanded it. The Eloniah alone remains, he is the key-holder, sent by the All-spirit, who guards against the power of the abomination. You go hire warriors if you need, our tribe wait two moons for you."

There was a silence. A troubled look remained on the speechless boy's face.

All listened to the coyotes yipping in the distance.

"There is too little time. What we do, we must do quickly."

The Kutaal nomads do not say good night. It is thought bad luck. So does superstitious custom have hold over them.

We will not use tents tonight but will sleep in blankets under the stars. It will be our last chance for slumber during the dark hours.

Day Seventeen

This morning the nomads bade us farewell. They promised that they would pray to the All-spirit for us. We also passed over our pack animals to them as agreed, for the animals were weary anyway. We kept only the donkey Atlas, in hopes of loading him down with crumbling books.

One donkey, that is all, one beast of burden to carry the burden of the world's learning, in order that the darkness of ignorance might not swallow all peoples and keep truth locked away. In the balance the world is suspended as if on a string over the abyss.

All choices which a single soul makes in his entire life, if looked at together, are a labyrinth leading to the inner chambers of eternity.

The problem is that would-be heroes, who go into labyrinths, can perish, miserably lost in those labyrinths. They fail of starvation in some dim corner of a dead end, having gotten disoriented without any knowing guide or map to follow, and unable to detect the slight breeze of air, or discern good water from bad water, aye, he fails at what is most crucial.

On the other hand, others do know the right way, how to navigate this world's maze, but they may not have the resolve of will to follow it out.

This is why Eloniah has sought out knowledge on behalf of the race of men. What might be found yet to increase our knowledge of the blessed Allfather?

Are there not sacred doctrines to teach us what manner worship is pleasing to the Creator?

Could we also forever lose such ancient lore to the dusts of Nystol, or the fires of the heretics?

The crypts of Astodan, rumoured to lay beneath Nystol, are where the Sorcerers entombed themselves away from the Maharim barbarians, clutching their precious tomes. It is called "an accursed ground." But men in their folly never cease to covet what is left there upon the chests of those lifeless lords, locked under bony fingers, some occult power enclosed within the bindings and the indeciferable writing, words forever lost to human memory.

However among the weeds one may sometimes find a rose.

On account of these things, with regard to his appointed task, the special donkey accompanies us, a donkey who is to bear the load of mundane learning on his back upon our return from Nystol.

The nomads have promised they would take good care of the pack-horses and I was consoled having days earlier spotted much ungrazed river bank awaiting them upstream.

We passed by the colossal head of some ancient monarch there, tipped as if fallen down, but from where? It seemed chiseled of old Authapian style, the visage of some forgotten Hegemax.

I proposed that it was antediluvian, for why would men bid a monument be so placed? Nay, the stupendous flood waters deposited it at nigh the same time the beautiful canyon was formed.

The narrow ways through the Canyon twisted through great rock walls where the water or uplifted mountain rock had made many small overhangings.

It was in these dusty places that we would camp and warm our bones near the fire during the day, within seeing distance of the river, buzzing with dragonflies, where Atlas cooled himself in shade provided by occasional trees.

We will doubtless sleep hard during the daylight hours and will rise at twilight to pack our blankets.

Day Eighteen

The guide knows the path so well that he can work with very little light. We have entered the wilderness of Kedemoth and its defiles. He has forbidden campfires.

At one point, during a starless night, the guide suddenly signaled and halted our march through a little grove in a wide area of a cactus-forest. He knelt down near to the ground and was examining what most likely were foot or hoof prints, though I could not really make out what sort. We stood and listened for a half hour, but we heard nothing.

The boy guide pulled a little white bird from out of a pocket. The creature seemed lifeless. Holding it in his hand for sometime he breathed upon it. It suddenly stirred and was soon fully awake. The guide cast the creature into the evening sky and it flew off. We travel onward.

Nineteenth Day

This is what I remember from the nineteenth day, the day of both disaster and grand revelation.

In the morning the speechless boy drew many pictures on the ground and made many hand gestures, and we guessed at his meanings. We had little chance of guessing right, save that the tracks he had seen were indeed hyena-heads, recognizable by the shape of the long clawed foot.

The enormous tracks were perhaps only several hours old, and merely retreating would not assure avoidance of their war party. These hyena-heads were accompanied by other deep imprints, what seemed armoured bipedal creatures, but anything more we could not ascertain, save that it was obvious that they were on the hunt.

The party had been patrolling even into the Canyon, which they never do, though it is one of the main routes to Nystol.

Suddenly the earth shook and the air hissed with sounds of bestial evil.

"Turn about!" My companion yelled. Although still crouched, turning my head I saw towering an enraged beast standing on its hind legs, a devilish hyena-headed humanoid rushing upon us, his fanged mouth agape. He seemed gigantic in stature and he was clad in leather banded-armour.

There were perhaps four others just behind him.

In several quick movements he went to hew me down with a club that was once a small tree.

I reached for my own weaponry, but could not ready the sword quickly, since I had to roll away instead from the impact of his massy club which would have smashed all my bones.

Then, before I had recovered from the roll, the hairy creature grabbed me and put me in a head-lock under one of its huge hairy arms.

"Flee!" I bellowed, but it was too late. The hyena-head had struck me again. I expected that it would next bite into me as if I were a deer it had caught. Instead the hairy beast pulled me up and struck me down with its claw so that I was tossed to earth and went out, as if dead.

The next thing I remember was that my hands were cruelly bound while I was being pulled along in a captive march. In front of me, also bound in ropes, the speechless boy-guide and my companion were spared and as captives were being taken somewhere. Whatever was reason I could not garner, perhaps to sacrifice us to their demon-gods.

With a glance behind me I saw the two nomads with whom we had contracted.

Obviously they had not gone far in return before they also were captured by the hyena-heads. Several other creatures of this strange beast-tribe now marched beside us and struck with a whip when we lagged.

We were hostages of strange and unpredictable, perhaps even semi-intelligent creatures.

"What will they do with us?" My companion guide cried out. Immediately he was struck; brutal force by one of the guarding creatures.

With terrifying canine howls they goaded the other men and treated us roughly. Were they were planning to keep us alive for fresh meat at some later time?

After ascending the canyon for some span of time, they conducted us along a ledge, a steep drop of perhaps a thousand measures into the canyon waters below.

The hyena-head then seized me and was ready to hurl me down upon an outcropping of jagged rocks. That would have been the end, for he lifted me above his head so as to fling me off the precipice.

In a moment other hyena-heads had seized the remaining captives and were terrorizing them with equal taunts. It was just an entertainment for them.

I am writing these things now as I reside in the chambers of "the Moho", the ruler of the hyena-head domain, Graanak. We have been taken here into these sandstone combs at the bottom of Hermius' Canyon and have been hostages of the hyena-heads already several weeks.

The creatures do not speak an intelligible language by human standards, but nevertheless are able to grasp the intentions of human word. They are not without some semblance of intellect, and are wise enough to rely on a leader with a much greater intelligence and learning than they could obtain themselves.

Having consented to their demands, I have updated this journal which they returned to me, and, provided I complete the translations of the accursed books which they have presented, I may do as I wish under their watch.

Although I am their slave for now, I hope not to be leaving too soon, or be executed all of a sudden, for there are many things in this place which can be found no where else. I mean writings of high import.

Hopefully, Atlas is wandering out there somewhere in the Canyon, safe from harm, waiting for me, or designing some plan with his donkey-brain to furnish our escape. When the moment is right I will take back what these beast-men and their Moho have stolen, and return.

At this time however I am too busy translating, doing what they command in order to avoid the whip. With this captivity we are thusly and rightly chastized for our sins, especially our worldliness. It is a mercy.

Even if I were to complete the account of so many recent events and revelations, they would appear far too obscure in meaning for anyone who has not examined the crucial nature of the background lore.

Therefore, good reader, generously consent to wait and read the interesting books and rimestocks which the Moho has commanded me to translate, foolishly supposing that he can use it.

I will describe only a few things of what transpired shortly thereafter. Upon the dawn of our third day of captivity they tortured us.

I will not mention in what manner so as not to plague your dreams or cause undue trepidation in anyone who wishes to venture bravely into these lands. The good Lord provided me more stamina than ever expected I possible.

No doubt this also is grace, for they obtained naught of what they sought. Our screams could not be heard beyond the thick sand-stone walls of those tunnels.

Afterwards, barely conscious on account of having passed out for pain, and bruised, bloodied, and weak, they marched us into a chamber furnished sumptuously and well-lit by many torches. They knelt us before "the Moho" who turned out to be, to my dismay, a human. We found ourselves kneeling like slaves in front of a false monarch. It was obvious by the arcane cut and trim of his robes that he was some sort of Sorcerer, also being a young man with long reddish locks and a goat's beard, perhaps the same whom the nomads had called "the Warlock of Yeth."

One other man, a sturdy warrior in heavy leather armour and ring mail, armed with a double-bladed axe, stood by him as personal guard. Exactly what kind of human being is content to live among a monstrous race such as the hyena-heads I cannot guess, but the creatures seemed to fear those two humans, and the Sorcerer especially, so they obeyed his every order. He knew immediately that I was a monk.

"What a great gift from the powers, to deliver a monk into my hands. What were you doing out in this wilderness of the canyon, monk? Shouldn't you be looking after the prayers to which you are obligated?

"Whatever sort of man are you," I replied, "if you do not mind seeing your fellow humans treated thusly by beastials. It is my duty to serve you not, for I am a free man. By the command of God Almighty, have you any righteous fear of what is holy? Then I say release us now or soon discover the scourge of divine vengeance."

"I do not have any fear, good monk, and that is why I am able to remain here and command an army of these hyena-headed creatures who obey me as to an absolute master. Now I recommend that you cease from pious and superstitious warnings and tell me your business here. Afterall, I have done you a service and allowed my hyena-heads to rough you no further. The outlands are dangerous for a monk."

"I could advise you of my purpose, wizard, but what is it to you? What fellowship does light have with darkness?"

"No fellowship, but truly does one seek to cancel the other. Even so, you have tread with infidel feet upon the sacred homeland of the hyena-heads without even thinking to ask permission. You have insulted them with the most profound insult one could offer in their custom. Were it not for me they would have torn you limb from limb and already eaten you raw. Nevertheless, these creatures are not without tolerance. If you serve me in the way I desire, you may win your life back. I do not care if you have some superstitious belief in an ancient deity, a deity that must be obviously displeased with you since he is allowing me to keep you my prisoner. He may even bring me some benefit now.

"Here is your only chance. You will notice over in the corner there by the candles a treasure chest containing a stack of books. They were brought here from Nystol by the hyena-heads, who alone were fearless enough to venture into the vaults under Nystol. They contain rarities, preserved not long after those great towers burned on that ignominious day four hundreds of years ago. I am a Sorcerer, yes, and learned in many secrets, but I cannot translate that horde of books, since, eventhough I possess certain skills with various languages, those tongues are too old and rare for me to recognize.

I wish you to translate them for me. I know by the habit you are wearing, monk, that you are from that Monastery in the Dry Blood Sea, and doubtless not only do you have knowledge of Oruscan Greek, but also of Saturnian Latin, Gohhan and Akaratic. You will be fed well and treated humanly in your cell, and even allowed sometime for fresh outside air. When all the books are translated, you and your companions will be free to go, or even join my cause if wisely you are persuaded.

Some books resting there, monk, must contain a variety of spells, yes. However, as everyone already knows, verbal spell-casting no longer has any activation, so there is no need to translate any spell book. What I crave are those historical accounts, details concerning the placement of certain relics, ancient magical items still potent, known to have been of old endowed with elemental power. You realize this, don't you? Although the Hyperstatic Rift destroyed the efficacy of verbal components throughout the four worlds, nevertheless any physical object infused with arcane structure was not contaminated by the rift, and retained operative magical integrity, since their superstantial mode was permanently fixed in materiality and did not alter with the spin of the terrestrial vortex.

Nor is it that only is needed. Especially do I want that small handbook you see on top of the stack. It is more valuable than any grimore. It is, I am sure, written in subterraneous Latin by a certain being. Translate that for me so that I can refer to it during my perilous journeys beneath the earth. In so doing you will save the life not only of yourself but of your miserable companions as well."

He rose from his throne and walking over picked up the little book from the stack. He then approached me and bade his hyena-heads to unbind me.

There he stood fast before me.

In his hands was a book with semi-decayed leather cover. Even so, I immediately recognized its design: a priceless copy of the *Enchiridion de Rebus Subterraneis* (Handbook on Subterraneous Matters) by long-living Kruth the Arcavir. This work had been recorded as missing for nigh one hundred years. The being himself wrote it in a long past era, along with his Bestiary, collecting its information over a period of some three hundred years.

The gnome, when he was still with us, remembered his labor of hundreds of years passing and yearned to recover the missing book, but being himself our guild-master and all that he is, he was not only unable to locate the original Latin manuscripts, but he also could not even find any later translations.

Nevertheless, certain evidence, such as extensive quotations in other works, had suggested to Archivists that it was still extant, possibly in private collections. So you can imagine my most visible reaction.

"So then you do know what is this book. I can tell by the look in your eyes that you recognize it. You perceive its rarity. Of course, you will accept my offer, won't you? It is not unfair, rather it is even generous. Is it not? You monks are known to be stubborn and paranoid, always on the look out for the devil. I am not asking you to trust me, only to accept a reasonable hope for yourself, and for myself. Although I do not believe in your superstition, something nevertheless warns me to avoid having the blood of an Ammouric monk on my hands. Therefore have pity on me and yourself, for I cannot protect you and your friends from these hyena-heads if they see that you are of no avail to me, for they are brutal indeed, and smart, as you have learned this morning."

I reached out and took the precious book into my hands, perhaps the only part of my body that my beastly torturers had left unbruised. By this signified that I accepted the Sorcerer's offer. What other choice did I have? It is not a sin to translate a non-magical book. Would you have me allow the others to die? But pray that God have mercy on my soul for having aided a Sorcerer.

Paging through the vellum codex I recognized minuscule being Ulthoran, therefore several hundred years old. It was one of the oldest copies, complete with all the commentary. The Sorcerer knew that that I knew he could not read the Saturnian Latin and many gnomish sayings, and that the artifact was useless to him otherwise, a strange book left in a desert cave that he could never hope to use. I was not only to translate the *Enchiridion* and *Bestiary*, but the stack of other works as well. These "Foundation Texts of Astodan" were many, and it was a hard decision not to present certain ones to you.

I have only included those writings which bear directly upon the mystery of iniquity that is presently being investigated: how Nystol fell and what will come of it all. These include the following: two works of history entitled The Nagamaud Amulet, and another disturbing work, *Demonstrationes Daemonicae,* or "The Demon Proof" being a philosophic dialogue from the days not long after Nystol fell. There are also Kruth's own records of Nystol's fall drawn from Voethius' *Decline of the Eldark,* which some have entitled "*The Last Days of The Magi*" describing the Hypostatic Rift by means of the only known eye-witness account. Also here you will read *Turris Mirabile Wyrd,* or "The Tower of Wyrd", another eyewitness account of journey through the deep earth and eyewitness testimony of the great host which sacked the arcane city.

Interiorly I was in a state of disbelief that such long sought-after codices had actually survived and I had been the one to come upon them. It was a good thing too, eventhough I expect never to see the great Arcavir again. Kruth the gnome had been very active throughout the early ages of the world.

The being himself had written the original, (how amazing it is to relate), over a millennia ago, during the time of the famous campaigns of a great general and empire-builder, Hermius the Conqueror. Then again he added to it after the Atlantean wars, and again worked on it of and on through subsequent centuries. Sometime after the fall of Nystol he added the most important material.

Kruth's fragments from the first period are the earliest that remain. Through all his many years of wild adventures, somehow he had kept the original text safe. These early fragments he set down in Saturnine Latin, a form similar to the old Rumilian.

Centuries later, during the close of the fourth world-age, the common usage of Latin had been forbidden and relegated to the underground. Kruth, though he could barely identify the accounts written by his own hand, begrudgingly translated his original text himself.

On several occasions he found himself wondering over the meanings of certain sentences. "My memory can barely reach back that far." He would often say. He translated the words, (back then he thought his usage was up to date), into what has now become an archaic style of our language.

At that time he added the copious notes and inserted the texts of the many other discoveries on his tome-hunting adventures. Nevertheless certain works which he would have cited from memory could not be reproduced.

Today the collection is exceptional and he would be very excited. We find available a good number of the appropriate excerpts from texts that were only a short time ago thought irrecoverable.

As far as the corpus of Whitehawk literature goes, we can be certain that the cataclysmic fall of the many-pinnacled college of scrolls, Nystol, and the burning of her grand libraries, especially the Tower of Manihord, caused the greatest possible loss. All higher thought available from the early worlds vanished. Innumerable chronicles and annals, epics and odes, bestiaries and philosophies, even music and chants, medical and thaumaturgical texts, apocalypses and histories, all perished.

On the other hand the great burning destroyed many unsound writings, incredible and seductive works of evil mind, grimories of the blackest magic and scrolls summoning ancient horrors, things which would have proved very harmful to the welfare of mankind.

Recently there has developed a great new interest in searching for lost masterpieces. They are sought regardless of whether they represent any lasting worth. With the recovery of the Khnu inscriptions and the *Foundation Texts of Astodan*, much of what scholars had thought cryptographic and obscure in Whitehawk literature has been re-evaluated.

A great deal is now understood with considerable clarity. Such is the case with the obscure *Narthecium de Legendis Nodosis*, (The Arrangement of Knotty Legends) a tract to which which my master himself often alluded; a post-flammam history which he thought would, if somehow recovered, be very useful for elucidating the mysteries of the fall. So it is that many old things are now highly valued, things which before would have been forgotten and thought unnecessary or outdated.

Like men themselves, some books tend to gain our human attentions when they are found to be slightly rotten. The handbook included a great deal of outdated marginalia referring to a number of sources and histories on Whitehawk, as well as instructions and archeological charts useful for excavation at the Nystol site. It also contained his many revisions, especially the citations from the *Narthecium.*

That same treatise had once been translated from Subterranean Latin by the Gorric scribes under Arabel Escorvus. It was completed as late as the end of the last century.

After much searching I acquired copies of other commentaries and undertook to present them in appropriate paleo-syntactic form. I wanted them to read in way comparable to Kruth's saga-style.

I have attempted in all places to represent the condition of the original manuscripts, as well as the typical gnomish vagaries of Kruth's writing style. It should be kept in mind that the gnome did not see himself as writing religious literature. The constant theologic allusions must be attributed to the great faith of those early ages, which now he no longer takes for granted, a sentiment you will find expressed in his furthsay.

His first intention was for the recording of practical information bearing upon deep-trakers, banishers, quest knights, and other "men of action." These would have included men of quest like his companion the famous Duke Ikonn, whom he assumed would not have time for fanciful turns of phrase when endeavoring to raid tombs and carry off the treasures of pagan kings.

This new publication however I have arranged for the archivists, the Metahistorian, and Archeologue.

There is the introductory letter from the Arcavir, which must be read. It is sometimes known as *Kruth's Admonitions*, or *The Gnome Epistle*, and remains unmodified with the exception of a few minor historical clarifications.

In this compilation, my intention is to offer the reader a taste of Metahistory. This discipline encompasses many oddities. Principally it is the study of sub-reality hidden within obscure legends. In effect, this mode seems to have been nascent in the original work. By necessity my master had to explain the histories of the upper worlds in order to reveal the causes of the state of things below.

All we had to rely on was the weird and incoherent Metahistory of the pagan seer Mercurius Yod. Then we discovered the *Narthecium.*

Where before there were found only citations to verse numbers, in this edition I have inserted my translations of the entire passages in question. In the instances involving poetry, elegaica and grand epics, I thought it best to preserve Kruth's translations from the Oruscan Greek, since his knowledge of that language was first hand.

All of the many poetic and historic works which my teacher cites were at one time available in his personal tower-library located in the ancient hills just outside of Whigg. Since he was rarely home, few who succeed in climbing up that far ever actually managed to gain admittance into the tower locked with locks inextricable.

When my teacher wrote his first edition, in the time before the Endarkenment, he had expected his readers to know the great variety of names and places. As an aid for those who are unfamiliar with the continent Whitehawk, I have added an appendix, as well as a list of places, terms, and history, partly drawn from an old *Zonarium* of unknown authorship, (probably a humble monk who did not wish to glorify himself by adding his own name to the work, but who is nevertheless the foremost authority on Whitehawk geography).

The source-manuscript collection was re-arranged by Hanno Escorvus, without Kruth's editing, for since we never dreamed that the *Enchiridion* would be found, the project had to go through yet another overhaul. Access to such an ancient codex completely illuminated many mysteries.

Nevertheless, I have chosen to allow most his primary format to remain.

As for my plight as prisoner of the hyena-heads and their Moho the Sorcerer, of how I finally accompanied him into the dangerous corridors of Astodan with six of the accursed elylinth volumes of *The Black Books of Melancholia*, and how we (almost?) saved the world from darkness, and why I placed this treasure horde of books on the back of the donkey Atlas and sent him off into the wild, these details I must save for later, after you realize the implications of all that is involved.

Indeed, by reading through this gnome's horde of lore you will learn how the collection was brought to the Moho's den in the first place.

When I last saw the Arcavir Kruth, months before I undertook this expedition, he had indicated his preparations for withdrawl from the world of men might be nigh. He promised the guild that a scroll-letter would be sent if any emergency occurred, especially in the event that he was compromised.

Such a letter did arrive, and it was the last he sent to me. He insists that our secretive archivist's guild must continue on, even though we are almost useless without his knowledge and throne-sight.

I have placed this here which now should be read by those who have the responsibility. It is for all guild members to ruminate upon, and it serves to orient the initiate on certain crucial issues.

ABBOT'S DREAM

The Fall of Nystol occured ninety orbits of Calduin passed, reckoning from the time of this compilation. It was the greatest catastrophe of its time, not for Nystol's administrative size or the reach of her magistrates, like some massive empire quickly crumbling, but on account of the vast arcane influence which that famous city of mages exerted over all Whitehawk, and of the suddeness by which she was no more. The tatooed barbarians who razed her did not fathom their deeds. They did them as unwitting avengers. With the aid of unsolicited treachery at her subtern gate they ushered in an iron retribution for a wicked age. It was a nemesis long overdue.

The ruins, high upon the mesa of Sardu, even to this day have a secret but very real seduction upon the hearts of men, stirring their imaginations, all of which in turn amounts to a clandestine war against civilization.

Of that great fall, which few could have predicted, its story is in danger of being forgotten, as the many peices of the puzzle must be connected, for the war is real, but unseen. The investigation and consequent implications are far too formidible a subject to relate in a short treatment. A mere summation would require that I cheapen what has been costly, for all have risked their lives, and some have lost them. Therefore I have collected for you all the principle sources for that enigmatic research, brothers, for I myself am too old and my mind is weary, being unable to fully embrace the labour, or to recall every subtle nexus.

The prophecy under which all these things are compassed can clearly be understood. It is a lesson that obviously you still resist, and it already has come to pass and hastens to fulfilment. The Time of The

Harvester is nigh. Do you not remember the old hermit who first announced these mysteries to us? Everyone deemed him a raving lunatic. No longer is he so adjudged. The world is on the verge of the All-war. Will you persist in your doubt? Soon it will be too late to change your course.

I am not a prophet of doom. Quite the contrary... however I do affirm this: tribulation must come first, there is no sacred victory without it.

Here in Whigg I have accepted a guest, brother Orbian, refugee from the Monastery of Weeping Brotherhood in the Dry Blood Dunes. He was among those long-suffering and exiled monks who witnessed inexplicable things, bizarre distortions of truth, expressions of the fierce struggle even now upon us—what the ancients called the *enantodromion*. Along with the several others, he has given testimony to the vile heresy that infiltrated his monastery. In the end it drove him from his own land and people, and from his own brother monks. The same heresy has now invaded your own beloved Whitehaven, but you resist my warnings and say it is not so.

I beg you, brothers, weigh these matters cautiously and pray. Here is the second purpose for provisioning this collection for you: that it might goad all of you monks and help you return to Reason. Why do you so readily tolerate the heresies of The Red Ascetic in your midst? -simply because he has been elevated to the Godmouth? When I was with you, and sat as Godmouth for all Whitehawk, did you ever hear me teach you anything along the lines that he has? It is outright heathenry. Make no mistake, the Red Ascetic is *The* Dark Shepherd.

Do you not see that, by tolerating these things, the mystery of iniquity is at work in you? Be not afraid. Know that it is not entirely your fault. The tentacles of this conspiracy stretch through centuries and reach out from ancient times.

Now we see those tentacles taking hold of the kings. Of the great inheritance upon which our ancestors founded the civil order, none of the dominions currently remain free, save for one: Ael's Lot, city upon the Vastess Ocean. The monarch there holds fast her family's castles, unmoved on her throne, refusing to depart in the least from the ways of her ancestors and yield to an alien religion.

All the other Maceonid houses across Whitehawk have not only faded in glory, but are hurrying towards dissolution. The times run like the sun in his Autumnal day declining. Swift Hyperion's steeds draw down the shining orb athwart the rim of the Western reaches, and the blue heavens that once embraced the happy noontide of our world slip away forever like a passing dream. The shadows grow tall.

Uncontested goes the last flicker of illumination, vanishing beyond the flood, and twilight presages the tyranny of eld Night upon the lands. How many more years will be granted to your beloved Whitehaven monastery before all things have taken place? You must make plans. The barbaric masters in clerical vestment have already infiltrated many churches on the continent.

Be of good cheer, for those of you monks who hold fast to the faith, I say to you, God himself will deliver you.

I know that you think me an outlandish fanatic. I am not so. The sages of old affirm, as does scripture itself: someday, not only these lands, but all the furth will be consummed in a deluge of fire, as was Nystol herself, and as someday will that Whore of Babylon also blaze, that "Lazaria" who even now flaunts herself. Know that it is just recompence for sin. There I go again, sounding like a prophet of doom. I beg you, my brothers, ponder these things. All this war in Heaven will unleash ever more profound revelations.

The famous stag-rider, Kruth the gnome; him I have never encountered. Nevertheless some insight and knowledge from him passed by way of secret messengers.

We possess a letter recapitulating ominous signs found in a certain codex which he has deeply researched. The tome was lost for ages, a powerful relic, and it even came into my possession for a while. When I realized the importance, at once I knew that the original would be sought by wicked men, so I planned to have the monks make a copy of it.

Trusted labourers could not be found here in Whigg. As it turned out, I myself was the monk whom God had chosen to work the ink.

You see, it may sound as a tale bizarre, or like some epic dream, but some nasty humanoid monsters captured and enslaved me in the desert catacombs of Garmsir not far from The Deadly Hills. For months they kept me alive in order to sell me on the market. But the Lord's angel was watching over me. Apparantly monks are undesirable as slaves and fetch only the lowest bids. They were stuck with me. Therefore instead of brutalizing they hoped for some way to make coin off me.

I convinced them of the value of a monk for the copying of manuscripts, as you will hear explained in my journal.

This collection includes all my own archeologic accounts drawn from the histories of Sardu and Nystol. They are proof of the conspiracy and of the secret hand of Nystol. Think not in terms of days, dear reader, but rather centuries, as sound monks do. Conform not to the spirit of your time.

Orbian and his crew were not alone in their conviction

concerning what they saw. People long vanished from this surface world join in testimony with them. Even the great philosophers of old, giants of the mind, could accept talk of wizards, gnomes, dragons and all the rest, and many things otherwise thought unworthy of serious students.

Several events described in these pages are well attested by ancient authority. Our interest is the Fall of Nystol, of which no eyewitness accounts, other than what's found here, are extant. The few others who survived to tell of the catastrophy did so depositing their story in the ear of the gnome, who in turn conveyed all of it to old Budderham in the Vale of Chimera and deposited it in the Nautilus library. It is the only place were one can be absolutely confident that the word would be long kept safe and uncorrupted.

The Arcavir Kruth, the gnome in question, was last sighted in our time, at the opening of the final age of the Whitehawk continent. It was he, assuredly, who, whenever he was not busy harvesting the work of bees or growing leaf for his pipe, first preserved these rare accounts.

He kept himself cooped up in his famous Torgrith tower, during the waning-time of the Nine Feudatories. Later, when men began to distrust his race, he abandoned the tower and left a letter and all the other writings behind for us. At last he went into hiding on account of *"the magnitude of darkness that prevails in this final age of men."*

It was in order to learn truth first hand that Brother Fragga and I hazarded a perilous journey. We endured a very dangerous canyon-land to reach Nystol's eldritch ruins. All this is recounted in *"The Nomads of Sardu"* It could hardly be called a collection worthy of monastic copying, and the adventure was nothing like what the gnome told, but it nearly cost us our lives.

Therefore we monks request of the Christian soul reading this, (you who in future years might somewhere come across this copy after we have passed from earth). In return for our labor we beg you pray for our souls, pray that a quick passage be ours, to speed out of purgatorial flames, and at last into Eternity.

I also charge and beg of you, with the strength and power that the truth can bring to bear, whosoever you are, being in possession of this book (perhaps you own it, or are borrowing it, or keeping it for another), you should quite freely and purposefully never mention its existence among a gathering of the uninitiated.

Nor should you allow just anyone to read or copy it. And especially let there be no commentaries published on it. The lore it contains is adverse to certain principalities. Powerful minds who hold exalted offices of governance may seek to trace its whereabouts.

Please examine *the Gnome's Epistle*, so that you may reckon some important things catching you up with the way things are in Whitehawk. "*The Demon Proof*" is a most pristine record left from the ancient world, and should drive home the point and make you most keen on many matters. Also there is *Dialogue with a Stranger*, which will familiarize you with the clandestine operations of the guild, and with the Antichrist. Then you will study the basics concerning the Fall of Nystol in my translation of Orbius' *The Great Burning and Banishment*, an old proem once required of school boys to memorize, now all but forgotten. It begins the Nystol cycle proper, and it is best if those accounts be read in the order I have placed them, although it is not necessary.

For the believer this is not doom, but we look forward to it. The crucified one will be revealed for all to see. When the end is come, all the world will see the one whom they peirced. Those who are wise confess with scripture: someday, not only the furthlands, but all the world will be rolled up like a scroll in an instant.

There will be a warning first, and a Great Abandonment. Whosoever has prefered the darkness, and comprehended not the light, they will flee into the prisons of the abyss forever. My brothers, pray in reparation for the blindness of the perfidious ones who have ravaged our lands and betrayed The Furth High King. May He make His messengers, terrible of aspect, visible to them.

So be thou heedful of all these things, for this book will be nothing but an erksome invitation for those unwary sheep who are content to remain grazing mindlessly on the wide paths. Such paths require little effort and pass through the open fields of this earthly life, where they may graze unconcerned for the shepherd's voice and great destiny, and remain unprotected from the wolves.

For the goats among us this book will become as a thorny tree, as the buds seem sweet, but the thorns are many, and there will climb into it many who are self-satisfied in their learning and they will voice harsh criticism and contempt.

The remnant flock, the sheep of disciplined and charitable disposition, on the other hand, will find great satisfaction and wonder growing here and there in the rocky hills and narrow pass of these writings.

I therefore bestow the Ammouric Benediction *de corde* and an Indulgence of 1000 orbits of Calduin on those who read all these accounts with humble intention and are encouraged with an earnest zeal to frustrate the powers of darkness.

Watch thou and stay alert, for thy adversary sleepeth not.

The
Gnome-Epistle

Valiant and worthy members,

Read this letter aloud to guildsmen in a remote chamber, secure from eavesdroppers and spying *homunculi*. This discipline is essential, "as protocol requireth."

A certain insight has alerted me to matters of concern for our cause. These things are urgent, and I cannot intimate all that is necessary with just a simple note, so I write a full letter in detail. You must destroy it afterwards.

It was evening on the ides of November just past, when, without the usual Bamusk tea, certain metaphysical revelations rushed into my soul. I had been slipping into a certain human weakness, eventhough I am not all that human. I had, slowly and imperceptively, become dull of mind and had not been amiss, forgetful of the "wakefulness" that scripture prescribes.

That evening, worn out from chopping wood, I retired to my chair. My eyelids were already heavy, pressing to shut, and I had not yet even opened a book. That's something dangerous for me when it happens early in the evening. You see, numberless years can slip by for a gnome were he to drift off into some enchanted dream. We therefore do not go to bed until late, and we rise early, lest many hours of sleep induce strange phantasms in the nocturnal mind.

I had wanted to do a little study, which usually turns out to be quite alot, more than I need. So I roused myself and went to the window to let in some crisp air, and subsequently fetched some leaf for my pipe.

I hoped to do a little copying as well. Although I have a certain distaste for that seeming endless labour, no matter: to copy out a translation of the great scrolls was something I had been putting off. You see I had acquired these certain scrolls fom Old Budderham. He passed them along to me last year so I could copy them into a codex. Apparently the owner is long deceased, and the scrolls are so old, that they had nigh but a century left in them.

The work was overdue. My evening plan was to get started on them. The excitement of reading such a work was high, and that alone would keep my mind active, my eyes open.

But something unexpected transpired that night. It was something most would ignore, as it is a rather common incident. Let me not fail to be exact on the circumstances and context of my contemplations. I had just opened the scroll and was at work translating, and I came to a hithertofore unknown and mysterious passage: "*The Light from beyond entered so that the elect might see and perceive, and make all things ready for the final contest.*"

The verse struck me powerfully. It rung with ominous tones like a magical sword. There was something about it I could not place.

The hours of sun and moon circled round, and the glint of stars filtered down from the celestial dome. The candles had melted down an hour ago and left miniature mountains of wax arisen on the desk.

I pulled the chair closer to the glowing furnace, the fiery pit and chimney. On that verse I ruminated. There were various alternative translations possible so I took some moments to toss in a new log. When it comes to sacred things one should always ponder why they present themselves at the time or moment that they do. The warmth and radiance effortlessly defy the all-embracing reign of Night.

Something, I could not at the be certain what, seemed amiss. How curious was that sense. I reached out to bang my pipe against the chimney, to empty the ash, but at once I halted. I placed the pipe down and listened. November's cold wind howled around the tower.

I dismissed this be-puzzlement and turned to look after a delicate task; breaking open the final seal of the series of these very unusual old scrolls.

The seal-wax, dry from a thousand years, crumbled.

The soft *bembus* leaves I slowly unrolled. The hand writing was exquisite: Hyrcanthine majuscule of continuous script with a Gohhan gloss in cursive at the margins.

At first glance I did not recognize the text, but first assuming it was just a commentary, soon realized the words of power written within. They were admonishments of the Furth High King, long lost exerpts from the *Golden Pages of the Wind*!

Almost too excited to stop reading, I at last asserted some self-control and paused. I put down the scroll and went to pray the hour of Nocturn passing, giving thanks for such an unexpected treasure. Afterwards I returned immediately and another hour, it seemed, (perhaps more) slipped by translating. I came across a gloss on the reign of the Emperor Echecrates. I began mulling over certain metahistoric insights, possible conspiracies hinted at, all sorts of things too obscure for me to list for you here.

Visions floated in the back of a gnomish brain, visions of the things that were, the things that are, and the things that will come. I returned to the sacred text. The last lines of that final scroll ended with stupendous poetry.

Logs crackled and sparked happily, as if they knew. May one describe burning timber as somehow happy? I wanted to undertake such a high task slowly and savor the work, so I closed up the scroll with a slow and most careful intention lest any damage come to the text. I was very late and I must rest so as to continue tomorrow.

As my fingers were kneading the delicate bembus, I happened to glance down at something of unexpected motion below me. There was a flash, a small something darting forth, then a pause; a breathing omen: lo, a living creature, there in the midst of the eldark books!

A furry being with four tiny claw feet had scampered into my abode. It emerged nonchalantly from the shadows and boundaries of the nocturnal world. In my excitement I had stayed awake much later than usual. He must be a regular visitor at that hour, a stealthy burglar rather. He was not aware of my presence.

This uninvited guest at once approached the piles of books stacked by the chair. He did not notice me, seated there, one like a king ofr knowledge who must hold fast his throne.

Oddly, the creature had startled me...never my usual reaction to such little ones. How strange that it stirred a sense of intimidation mixed with violent thoughts. I glanced, it seemed inadvertantly or instinctually, to the burnished brass poker set close by the chimney, there between the chair and the iron grate. It was good and hot.

In the struggle to keep warm up here in the Hermit's Hills at night, I stir the coals often, but that is not why I thought of it. Its always in the back of my mind that I can grab the poker quickly and strike devastation at any intruder, eventhough bandits have never bothered to climb up this high. Of course you never know.

In some dire altercation, God forbid, the poker may become like a flaming sword of Wrath. But why this mad thought now? Why feel so threatened as to go against a minor forager with it?

My finger twitched, but I stayed myself from fear, I did not grab the brass poker.

The creature poked around my haven which was still aglow from the blazing hearth. The little thing was unaware that I had detected his intrusion. The glow of cinders revealed the features of this otherwise unseen visitor, this lesser beast who now dared enter the story. Fiery reflections danced his otherwise black eyes, demon lights from another world. His fur was hoary and white as snow.

I never let any sort of natural phenomenon unhinge or shake me, but this incident, this sight, at this moment and place, was different. Something was being communicated to me.

How is it that any forest denizen would climb this high to the bare outcrop of frost-laden hills way up here this time of year? I wondered and watched. A reasonable answer would have spared me the beginning of suspicions. So uncharacteristic a thing for mice ...was there to come some great change in weather then? Why would a creature from so far away, down in temperate zones, pilgrimage to search for food at such an elevation when there is plenty to be had below?

The possibilities were of uncommon magnitude indeed. It was at that thought, there in the chair, that I froze. I froze as if one being dead.

A wandering varmit... does this common mouse, a species of *ponfit*, require further description? I gazed, again searching my mind to be rid of any possible fictions. This whole matter, this sense of intimidation: I should dismiss it as nothing but a feeling, stirred by the merely unexpected.

Perhaps some contagion caused the aberration, the weirdness of its presence. Irreconcialiable explanations and cryptic suspicions began to form a maze within me. Whatever it was, there was nothing I deduced as natural as to the cause: a stray rodent hinting at some dire mystery. Oddities of fancy danced in my gnomish imagination, clandestine mentalities, unfinished meditations, all this welled up in me at once.

Among the sentient races of *elphim*, any of those operating as an established Arcavir will find things rarely ever straightforward. Many are the years spent in solitude. The mind can become unbalanced up here.

Suspicion does not lead to imaginings, but rather imagining leads to suspicions. True enough...

As for me, you know that I am of gnomish descent enough to be called a gnome, although I have been mistaken of a small human. Although we have many similarities, our brains are not susceptible to exaggerations as are the fallen race, and we can see things that they cannot.

Now, after much reflection, I no longer doubt that the *ponfit* was in fact an agent of espionage. Yes, espionage, and a minion of ancient Night. You all surely have heard that a certain spiritual entity still haunts Whitehawk and has even taken up residence, one who is filled with spite and whose radience is darkness.

On occasion, this principality of melancholy has been allowed to control lower animals. Name the dreadful spirit what you will, the mind who learns secrets, or who strikes with invisible arm, "Nimrul," "the Archdeceiver," "Nazageist," it is the same one who devises the wars of entire worlds and plots the burning end of ages. That very intellect also could send forth this little beast, an apostle of Night.

Did the mouse come to intimidate me? Was this a cynical reminder? Was there an implied message, namely, that we who love sunlight yet dwell upon a frail surface? It is, after all, true that beneath this visible world there broods an unknown over which men exert negligible influence. The Sons of light must not fear.

Even though I am of an ancient race, and I once had great familiarity with the caverns, knowledge of many things subterranean has been lost to me. A few things I suppose have been purposely forgotten. Many have been the years at this post on the earth's surface. Perhaps I am exhausted and must eventually go to sleep for a century or two. Too many orbits of that planet Calduin I have spent upon the surface, teaching the sciences and the various sources of knowledge for civilization. Someone had to do it, and I am the last of gnomish descent.

Far too much was lost to learning after Nystol's libraries burned, it was a veritable "bibliocaust." I could not simply pass into the twilight along with the elves and let the race of men flounder, so I stayed to complete these labours.

Now one could simply dismiss that little creature, as anyone would. It darted and came quite close. He quizzingly sniffed my socks. Into the flickering shadows beneath he slipped. There in shafts of shadow he halted a moment under my ankles. A cold draft came through and I wanted a sweater. I kept still, unmoved however, and I watched, with stillness as do cats when they spot what they crave.

Suspicions began to gnaw. It started first as vaguely

apprehended whispers echoing in the chasms of my mind. Surely, there could be no mischievous intent in the creaturely presence of this mouse. On the contrary, being the lone inhabitant of rather inaccessible hills, should I not enjoy the company of small furrys?

This mouse was not without charm as he directed his curious nose here and there in the usual manner. Other mice lately have been about the cedars in the valley below. I see them caught in the beaks of the White-hawks. Many of those birds return there all fattened from their raids into Whigg, town of many-steeples. (And not all are dinner for the hawks, mind you, for the cats of those streets are many, and execute whatever carnage Nature bids them).

Even were I to become delighted with such a tiny guest, I should never let down guard, nor forget that any animal may become "possessed by demonic entity." Yes, its true, even animals. Think of the snake in the garden. So I must ask; does the specimen seem to search with unnatural abandon?

This one had climbed up far beyond the boundaries of normal mouse-territory. Up here in the highest reaches of barren hills, near where the stars in their fixed motion glide, mice may tarry not long in the frost. If any of them happen get past the snows and rocks, the snowy owl will take them in his talons for lunch.

Would not the tiny brain of this mouse, in order to get here, have detected the risks, especially the presence of hawks and owls? It is aerial death. This mouse hazarded death anyway. That was the very thing; a striking calculation which I suspect a mouse should not be capable of-…this was why I was become silently alarmed.

All his exploration was for the purpose of something other than cheese or crumbs. I tell you it was indeed for another cause. It was reconnaissance. It was a scouting mission for the sake of a most unholy war.

He reared his head and sniffed drafts of air. Satisfied, he moved on to the next thing.

One would expect that he would keep ample distance from the crackling blaze. The tiny beast, that possessed entity, neared it anyway with his poke-about quest. He ambled into position to claim one of the many old manuscripts. It was a codex which, in my thoughtless obsession with other works, I had laid aside. It rested on the stony rim.

This diminutive spy operated in a shameless manner, unaware of my observation. He began nibbling on the volume's cover. This particular book featured a binding of fine pigskin that guarded finely wrought verses, a skin which hinders elements and mold, but not mice. It was a collection of magical epics, tales of wonder from one of the pagan ages of the world.

The manuscript was to become a massive eating-project for the minuscule belly. This codex had been one of the many sources for my research. It included exhaustive commentaries on the elemental planes, the worlds above and below, the mysteries of the cosmic order.

Creatures such as this mouse (and the many-legged mini-beasts as well), are actually living sarcophagi, the devourers of refuse, and that includes anything of moribund knowledge. Consider them either the exacters of divine retribution, or the demon-hand of darkness claiming what is its own. In reality they combine these duties, a dual purpose. Otherwise, explain why it is that they always seem to have a taste for those unclean pagan writings, the remnants of the old worlds.

You know that works like those have become very hard to find; perhaps it's a good thing indeed.

I write these things on books mindful of the considerable implication the opinion holds. As I am sure that any archivist-guild member is already aware: certain arcane remnants and magical tomes have caused a magnitude of evil to awaken. Ancient horror now lurks throughout your beloved Furth realms again.

Mind you, guildsmen, never esteem heathen writings as highly as the holy books, though the latter may be found to be inadvertently stacked upon the former. Your human forefathers have long taught the sacred trust. Holy books, copied by monks age after age, are more than mere mythologies. They are the vessels of a wisdom which the righteous confess to be divinely revealed, and their pages live forever. Whatever wisdom the ancients knew only darkly, the living word brings in full brilliance.

They are to be reserved for the sanctuary, or the libraries of the righteous. Is there anyone, even in the celestial courts, worthy to open such books and read them? Men do not consider the holiness of God in this age.

Worldly things we will easily loose, but the divine instruction can never pass away. Even if almost no one harkens to the Word anymore, the Truth abides. The Monks of Whitehaven and Friars of Whigg have an interesting tradition on this. For a book that is blessed and considered holy, the monks do not number the pages. Afterall, one does not measure holy inspiration. Each decorated page the angels remember; every illumination is a delight for the soul. It's a custom that makes sense to the monk, after all, the holy book should glorify God, not men and their ideas. For the interest, knowledge and edification of men monks have made and preserved them, but the words themselves transmit something of God himself.

Not so with those *other* tomes and scrolls, all the ones left by the many scribes and sorcerers, the men of the hopeless epochs. Those writings, if you trust, do not provide the proper food for souls. Desperate and hungry for acquiring every secret knowledge, men began numbering the pages so that they might notice if a page went missing. Great labors for naught, *nequiquam*! Such works must by necessity rot away. Beautiful phrases to hear, as they do glimmer in the pagan poetry, but like marble and whitened sepuchres, within they are bloated by worms and rot. Ah vanity!

With a shout and a gesture I interrupted the rodent's pigskin dinner. He sped away in a flash, just as celestial fire flashes forth the very moment the sun slips from the horizon, from the east rim all the way to the western horizon. Aye, that fast was the little menace gone, back away into the obscurity of Night's borderlands.

Should such vast armies of subterraneous devourers always be considered a result of natural causes? Or rather should we ask if their race has been claimed under the scepter of some principality? Granted, such a notion seems far-fetched.

What follows therefore may seem to be the melancholic thoughts of the feeble-minded and insane, but I have the confidence of some 1200 years of health. I testify that gnomes can suffer from no serious mental maladies. Our thoughts do not run the same as the thoughts of men.

Even so, you should remember, that although I am quite ancient, one of the Arcavirs, nevertheless my memory, being injured by all the bloodshed and mortal wars I have witnessed, does not reach back very far at all, not much further than the eighty or so years of eldest mortals.

Beyond that there are only glimpses, fragments of the past. I can barely remember my adolescence nine hundred years past, and although a youthful joy remains in me, it is now has been tempered by the council of wise teachers and much experience.

In my early years I visited Egypt, a distant land accross Vastess Ocean-sea. and the stories they told concerning mice infestation were almost enough to make one worship cats like they do. This is of no slight significance, for although the *ponfits* are small, be warned that the growing race of rodents is not caused from the natural result of the earth's goodness. Something unnatural is going on.

The same may be said of ravens and crows, those dark flocks that blotch twilight's horizon, for they also have increased everywhere, searching on black wing for rotted meat. All these then, believe thou me, are in frank estimation hordes possessed by undead minions of that infernal ghost.

The rodent retreated in order to wait securely in the dark narrows here of the Torgrith tower library stacks. I imagine that later the little beast and his stealthy companions will return in the dead stillness of sleeping hours to complete the mission.

It is likely, given the importance of the tomes stored in the tower here, that the principality has instructed them to feast and bring final ruin to the bindings!

These undead spirits who spread oblivion will attack this small library after I am gone. If they do not finish off the books, there are the Natural elements in time that will. As if books and scrolls didn't already have enough enemies!

My first teacher, Duggan, a dwarf-scribe, spirit of good will, described the process, for he was in the business of rescuing forgotten vellums. New archivists, he said, must eventually replace the tired archivists of many years, (and these new monks are often of lesser vision, keeping but with scant wisdom). After many circling years, they tend to overlook certain difficult or seemingly fantastical books.

Like youths who confidently dismiss the dreams of old men, they pass it by in favor of verses that are trimmed of archaism or fancy. In their scorn of anything but hard facts, accomplished monks and "serious" students rarely examine a certain "outdated" codex, since much of the author's perspective seems naïve for word choice, and so librarians deem it as one not worthy to be recopied or specially preserved. It is stored, (imprisoned rather), below, in a rough dungeon-like chamber.

Perhaps in time water or heat will weaken the pages. Mold will make an entry. Corruption of its irreplaceable contents results. Perhaps half-way to final dissolution, an odd and curious searcher of more modest study happens upon it.

Excited that he has found a rarity, he might even copy parts of it or quote from it. Satisfied with his partial knowledge he puts it back where it was, but having been disturbed it is now in more fragile condition. Soon the mindless devourers will discover new cracks. They will worm their way through its binding and pages.

An age comes and goes.

The original text will become a matter of speculation and doubt. If the work had presented eyewitness accounts of wonders or real heroism, these records will soon likely become subject to the most rigid and pusillanimous skepticism. If scribes recover the work partially, they will look upon its depiction of a noble past as imaginary, not arisen from the integrity of the righteous, but from primitive ignorance. Its pages are more for the childishly gullible. What once was considered history will now be considered only myth, or at best legend. Only fragmentary quotations in other books will remain.

Even more years uncounted pass. The very order of the world is changed. No one has even noticed.

New languages have arisen. Finally, even the extreme remnant pages of the old mastery pass into dust.

I glimpsed futility in the flash of my mind's eye, the futility of my own effort mirrored through time. Be comforted, it is no intolerable thing. I have made a new resolve to accept that "all is but chaff."

Many sacred texts were set down by ex-wizards who became monks or priests after the time of the quickening, in the days when Nystol faltered. Therefore certain sacred invocations may sound like arcane spells. Among these are very important prayer tracts of Ammouric thaumaturgy, collections of transcendent formulae, incantations for clerics, or monks with their unceasing chants. As such, they alone the Soothfold deems permissible.

Note well however, if you come across anything similar but not authenticated, in the name of our patron St. Dismas, list it as condemned and seal it.

Next concerning the genuine *arcana*: magical books and grimores which have survived, and even any others of recent authorship, take care that you mortals avoid them, since they may retain residual effects: *relinqua*.

The original integrity of the arcane systems has been compromised, and the structure of reality, altered by the quickening, no longer supports a righteous use of *arcana*.

Wizardry in its pure form is defunct. Any magical casting requires forbidden commerce with evil archons. Any who use conjurations or summonings justly earns condemnation, both in this life and the next.

Not a few, I hear, assert that this is an onerous restriction, but I insist upon it. I have seen with me-own eyes the great damage that mortals have done both to themselves and others by traditional casting, especially sorcerous illusions and summonings.

If humans crave travel in the dangerous underworld to search for mysteries, let them rely on mine *Enchiridion*, not magics.

The good stuff which you remember from the old sagas, such as those famous wizardic spells, do not even take anymore. I am permitting you alone to examine those verses however. Should not everyone be thankful that the old restriction has again been decreed upon mortals throughout the furth, in accordance with the All-law?

It is law and divinely so.

A disobedient generation has made lawless magics more popular than ever, therefore the age must hasten to its consummation.

If you are tempted to join the crowd of those who store up Hellfire for themselves on this account, remember that by no means can 'a good work' arise from what has been deceptively titled 'white magic.'

This might be thought a burdensome teaching. I ask you, however, did the Furth High King deign to recommend his white-robed paladins preform arcane spells? Did he not rather command them to work miracles, which can accurately be called a transcendent magic? In so doing with great zeal they went as burning messengers throughout all the lands of the Furth, even standing before the ancient Maceonid kings and offering them the white robes as well.

So did all the kings of that age renounce wicked alliances and renew their lives in baptism.

To the Furth High King all knowledge, power and authority in the terrestrial, astral, and etherial spheres, aye, in all spheres, is given. Well, to put it planely, He is the King of All Creation. Mysteriously, he deemed it best for the dragons and demons to remain, albeit hidden from sight, so that men, by struggling against them, might become better in spirit by virtuous discipline. But this is not done resorting to craven magics, into mediocrity of spirit, as in the hopeless epochs.

Some of you used to joke with me over this, asking how I, a gnome, someone who is constantly casting spells and administering every manner of enchantment, can sit here on this quasi-throne and forbid mortals the same freedoms...such are the exaggerations I must endure.

My magic is very limited. And I affirm again the original answer: the gnomes came into the world this way, and we are what we are. Humans, on the other hand, are born having the required paraphysic faculties entirely collapsed, and their arcane mind inoperative.

Think it over this way: magical effusion is proper to my essential being. A man of gnomish descent can be no other way. On the other hand, if your first parents, who were living in the Akaratic state, Eden, or whatever your clan calls it, had not committed the Archsin, doubtless you would have retained certain comparable powers.

Nevertheless they consented, they gave heed to the old dragon, and took on a spiritual malady for the whole race, and that's just the way things are now.

Do you think it a terrible situation? Allfather already had the restoration of your race in mind, even before the great transgression.

Ammouric transfiguring can make you mortals even better than you would have been had the primordial couple never lapsed. If only the slumbering masses of men would awaken to this! Awake, O sons of men, the great and terrible day is upon you!

So I still stand by my unpopular claim: magics must be forbidden. To allow humans access to the preternatural fonts and the superstantial vortices without proper intellective and volitional healing would be catastrophic, as furth-history has shown. Because of the Hypostatic Rift, the cancerous side-effects of casting spells is now sevenfold magnified.

Only elemental battle magic is permissible, but how one might access it, since the source-fonts are closed, I cannot avail you with. No gnome or elf has any familiarity with it. Might old Budderham know someone who could find you the wizard rumoured to have discovered how to circumvent the collapsed vortex?

As I mentioned before, examination of certain select wizardic teachings has been permitted to some, and surely this will benefit human knowledge, provided that the Guild member has been taught how to discern which verses are sorcerous and which are heretical, which to be used as demonstration and which to be rejected.

All those years of training as archivists are to that skill especially. Indeed, this discipline should be restricted to the elect, and to the initiated such as yourself.

There is said to have once existed grand monuments of mortal wisdom. As a Tome-hunter, extracting precious texts from dark tombs and underworld libraries should be your first concern and quest. Be wary, and never descend without those properly trained by The Guild as Deeptrackers, Banishers, and Wyrmslayers; they are worthy helpers indeed. Always defer to the maps of the Arcavir.

There is much yet to be done, and many ancient texts of forgotten sciences are waiting to be recovered. Hark to me, I know that somewhere there yet remains words written on *bezebus* leaf by the grand masters even pre-dating the Gohhan papyri.

Those eld sages were much greater in mind and spirit than your own generation can envision, Just think, they did not even have access to all the lore in *The Golden Pages of the Wind*, like you do now.

Nevertheless you can see how their scrolls lasted so very long. . . the works of the Elthildor, and it is told that even the letters themselves glow with the radiance of true knowledge!

Even so, when the fatal day dawned, not even the lesser share of their Eldark writings could be saved. The great conflagration of Nystol snatched them away forever. Nigh all the glory of the passing worlds, the thoughts of eldritch days, went along with them. All went up in devilish smoke.

The wizards and sages who once wrote and re-copied them vanished as well. Now they are the stuff of what poets dream, or of what bards longingly sing, and even their memorial lays also hurry to slip into the dust of ages. No doubt even our own humble records, me-own labor of history, must someday disintegrate as well.

Unseen spirits, some for help and others for hindrance, continue to dwell undetected among us. Certain familiar animals of the lesser gods, concealed in the dark, listen, watch, and wait. It is not wrong to hold certain species suspect, for just as a saint may load a donkey with holy books, so can a conjuror pile the same donkey with works of perdition.

Some may laugh and call it unreason, but such laughter will ring hollow if the crops fail.

The righteous need not live in fear. Remember all the revelation you have received concerning the Furth High King, and keep the memory of him alive by partaking in the established Ammouric rites, for though his return seems delayed, in this way you will be supplied with every refreshing help. You received this message not only from me, but from the traditions of your fathers and grandfathers, going back uncounted generations, whose testimony it has been me-toil night and day both to recover and to guard.

The magnitude and power of the Ancientmost is indescribable. In former ages he was known to have put an end to wars over the entire earth. There is no reason to think that he will not someday do so again. At the very sound of his voice the great earth shrinks away.

I ask you, will he not again bring dismay to our arrogant adversaries, will he not *break their bows, snap their spears, and burn their shields with fire*? *...Although no one has ever seen him, who would dare refuse such a being honour, or the glory due his name*?

This prolonged stay of mine on the surface has of recent seemed to have been a fruitless enterprise, for although many things change and improvements are made, the wretchedness of human nature remains the same. This truth was brought home to me even this very day, before I sat down to write this.

A couple of peasant boys from Whigg must have actually spent a good part of their day climbing up to this remote crag, no doubt having heard the rumours, of a tower, of a gnome, of magic. I observed unnoticed from the garden as one picked up a stone and smashed mine door's little peephole for no other reason than entertainment, or to break in, or just nastiness.

I could have used gnome-magic to exact punishment, but instead I secretly followed them to their home with a view to involving their parents and seeking reparation. When I confronted the parents, they interrogated the older child "Didst thou do what I forbade, that ye climb nar the hill? And didst thou cast a stone to shatter the glass of yon tower-door lookout?"

The boy wagged his head in denial. "Nay, I know naught of it." (A small sin gave birth to a much greater sin). The smaller boy, unperceiving a lie and standing near, said, "Yea, surely remembrest the deed thou must. Verily witnessed I truely as thou did, and broke apart the Arcavir's peephole?"

So it is, and how painful that someone so young should actually lie.

So are humans upon the earth. But I am grown weary. These then are me-last instructions, which you should share with initiates of The Guild who have not met me. It is for their sake that I have gone into all these lengthy explanations and considerations, unnecessary for the experienced like you.

Here in the *foruli* I have left the rescued scrolls and other manuscripts in the order of presentation recommended. Please also do not fail to include as much lore from the *Narthecium* as you can. I have placed hawk-feathers in the pages where revisions should intrude upon the fragmentary text.

The scrolls are protected by a glyph of warding that will dispel once the signet ring is replaced on the seals. If somehow you have been able to open one of them without employing the ring, you know what that means and what must be done.

I trust in your skillful foresight and knowledge of the new techniques, so make the changes as you see fit.

I have prayed over it and slept on it, and have awoken with undiminished concern of the gravest kind. I know of things that are beyond your keen and I have the authority to take the extreme measures.

Therefore I must leave quickly, even before the snows have melted. I must hasten to an undisclosed location. It stands to reason, after the mouse incident, that a *homonoculous* or some other remote *automata* will be sent next. The fact that the adversary has, after nigh two millennia of our strict secrecy, discovered the location of Torgrith tower, this beloved seclusion, (and has already sent scouts to assess the holdings), leaves me little choice.

I fear that his vampiric mind has employed brutal terror to extort such intelligence from one of ours. Please try to ascertain his source by the means we discussed.

As for the mice, any further like-minions must beware. I have summoned forth the snowy owl from a nearby hill. He will be perched here watching, (and rather sated I imagine), when you arrive. He is more deadly to mice than hawks who prefer larger prey. Nothing can get past the eyes and ears of so amazing a creation.

My gnomish magic of varhithril (moisture-shielding) dissipates during lunar eclipses, and I am told that one may occur this month. I cannot re-cast the spell from afar and the cold airs up here will penetrate the stonework if I am long absent.

If Finbar comes to you with this message late, the works may already be in danger. I have instructed him to bark twice upon finding you if he has been delayed more days than he can remember.

I know that you do not travel abroad often, and I am asking a great deal that you travel in secret. Do not fear, I am giving you our beloved donkey Atlas, who is not as ignorant or as stubborn as his kind is reputed. He knows the way if you get lost, and he can carry a load of many books. A useful quasi-mind has the beast, and he can even sense if a tome has slipped off his pack.

If you are somehow compromised or captured, the animal will finish the journey alone. Please, he is not a metamorphed human as some have rumoured.

Also you will find with this letter instructions on how to communicate with Atlas, but they might not avail much. He has not "said" anything to me for several centuries and bears a considerable grudge, ever since I ruined his reputation for his slip in the mud and losing several volumes in a mountain downpour. Regardless, I think that he would enjoy such an important trip. His longevity is brought about by paramorphic cancelling and needs to be renewed with fairy-barley every ninth equinox. He always remembers the time and location of the field but prefers to be accompanied just in case.

He will care little to communicate with humans.

I authorize you to go ahead and take the journey East across the hills through Kithom and beyond into Sardu: Nystol's ruins brood like a slumbering viper there waiting in the bosom of the Furth. I have repeatedly warned you of the risk that such an expedition proposes, but you are determined, as your last letter imparts.

Along with this scroll I have enclosed in Finbar's tube a few extra coin to procure supplies for anything unforeseen. I do not have enough for you to pay mercenaries but they would not help anyway, after all, I assure you, they would flee the haunted corridors of Astodan at the first apparition.

The cactus-forest of Kedemoth is very dangerous, but there are Kutaal nomads in the region who have found a secret path up into the necropolis Astodan. To undertake such a grave risk however, I leave entirely up to you and your associates. It is not encouraged from me as Thronekeeper of the Guild, but I cannot restrain you indefinitely.

The loss of your head to some ogre would be a great blow to guild-operations, so please be extra careful. By no means should you continue if the presence of strong hostiles is detected.

Friends, we have spread the word throughout many lands and have been rejected and persecuted by the powers that be. Our reward is merely this: we restored Whitehawk. Now we are betrayed however, but have done what the Furth High King willed. Many are going underground, and even some furth-guardians can no longer remain. It is doubtful that I will be in contact with your kind again, at least not in your lifetime. A new time is come.

Have faith, the lawless one shall be unmasked at the afore-destined time...

I have found a strong hart grazing outside of Whigg and will be riding the beast to some wild and uninhabited place in the remotest furthreaches where it is very quiet and where the air is cool and mild, and where I can sleep deeply for many years. I have already toiled two decades past the setting of mine interior sun.

May the Ancientmost and all his host protect you and guide you.

KE

The Demon-Proof

Memnos himself has commanded me to write this on behalf of the great Epinanaus. You will not believe what I will tell, not at first, but after I do reveal all, you will believe. I am wasting the few days left for me repairing for my transgression by writing these things, for that is how the sage of Sardu dies. It is in part a confession of all the erroneous doubt that led to my undoing, first as a scholar and senator, and later as a hermit. All that's of little account until it is viewed within the greater wreckage of civilization. What I will communicate to you is nothing less than the forces work the demise for our civilization.

Only an examination of the unfinished researches of the renowned Epinanaus can illucidate the dark mystery that was born of the ages, for his antiquate history alone is all that is left of those days.

Let the words reveal the dimness of my soul, nay of every soul, and all the civilization that was under destruction before the holy one delivered it unmerited Unto the True Knowledge. These are the various trials and follies from the time before I relinquished my former course and steered for the eternal passage instead.

In those days, the time of my youthful corruptions in the great cities, an unhealthy curiosity tyrannized over me. I loved many gods, and many books, and through these things I hoped to exalt myself in the eyes of the scribes and pharisees of this world. So I entertained a thirst to record the vain histories of men and unravel the iniquious mystery of the powers of old.

One year I was elected as tribune in my beloved Regulum, and weeks would pass until the fasts of the Hyperlyptic Alignment concluded and oaths could be uttered, so I retired to my coastal villa near old Allapis.

On a certain clear night, when a strong breeze blew upon Vastess Ocean and many stars were dotted like milk-spray across the celestial dome, I went with the dog along the lane of sumac trees. I happened to arch my back to look straight up above.

After a moment of viewing the heavenly bodies, I noticed stretches of star clusters in the Constellation Perseus blinking in and out in succession, and then also in Capricorn. Something substantial was moving across the stratosphere. I strained my eyes. I could discern the silhouette of vast featherless wings outstretched, gliding upon that high ring of breezes that the elves used to call Elmalmere-lok.

The civilized conceit that such beasts are mere fiction was finally extinguished from my mind. The sighting I took to be a sign from the gods. The old beasts of yore still prowl the worlds, but are hidden from sight.

That very night there came an unexpected pilgrim knocking at my door, seeking food and shelter. It was a monk from the Monastery of the Weeping Brotherhood, that mysterious isle of desert seclusion located in the Dry Blood Dunes.

Some power, I know not what, urged me welcome the wayfarer. I could have him stay a few weeks and assist me in copying certain books, and even add to them, drawing from the fragile urn of his memory. In that clay vessel, everyone admits, some monks preserve nectars of good tale which were forgotten, not to mention rare histories.

So, if the divine race wills it, let the winds whisper the truth of things in my ears; of what was, of what is, and even of what might come.

Open thy mind for the sake of recording things which may pass entirely from human familiarity. Rare is the codex or rimestock in our city that men have saved from Time, devourer of all things. Therefore I hold nothing back and favor no powerful princes as I recount the passing of ages and struggles of men in this world.

How should one unthread the secret warp of ages, all the generation since Anathron the first man? Are we not struck with wonder, how the furthworld entire has so passed over the lapses of centuries, and there now remains little of what was...

The Christian monk who came to me that night carried in his mule-packs a number of priceless codices. He presented them to me, saying that he had heard in the Bibliothek Rumiliad that he might find work from me in making copies, since I am a well known collector and the last of the Rumilian librarians.

Notably, he carried with him Epinanaus' famous long lost work: *The Twilight of the Republic*. He described how difficult it was to choose which books from his own great monastic library to take with him, to save rather, since the heretical monks of his own order had determined to rid the monastery of any writing that points to right doctrine. Nefarious, he said, were those monks who, by means of artful rhetoric, made novel teachings appeal to the otherwise truly religious and devout. In their success, they designated that many precious books must be destroyed, including pagan writings. The sight of the desecration drove the faithful monk from his own beloved desert monastery.

He was an outcast who held onto the old ways. So we had something in common.

I myself once was a great voice of the worldly city, Regulum, mighty governor of Illystran provinces, in the days when it was safe within the walls. Those days have fled away, and it is now better for men of good will to live apart from those workers of corruption and sin who dwell in her dismal streets.

My own loyalty even now remains with the Regulian Principality, for six hundred years Empress over all Maceonid kingdoms.

Let me confess the sadness that upon me now comes. My own nation's achievements, though glorious, hasten to their undoing. How is it that such native might as our own could be so quickly undone?

Such a doom as this, I reckon, the powers have spun like wool from a blemished sheep in the warp of our past. It entered into the fabric of our ways long before the century of glory had commenced. In the loom of the cosmoid the seers behold doom's weave interwoven, and fear to say it, lest they be labeled "prophets of doom.'

You already know the warp. Herein you may discern the causes, the weave, if you endure in the study.

The very ruins of the Old Hegemonies are just shy of my scope. They stand not far off, for in this little shore-side villa, upon my desk, the pages of a great text are caressed by the evening's seaward breeze.

It is strange how on this very night when I begin my undertaking, the moon becomes reddish under some numinous eclipse. The gently crashing waves roll upon a shore not distant. The ocean's resounding calms my soul.

In those days I had been summoned to appear before the Imperial Hegemax Bolgud himself to answer charges of conspiracy. This suspicion was of course built on lies which in turn were built upon deeper, more "rational" lies, which in turn were built on some assumption or conviction crucially mistaken. No doubt some evil gnome had his ear.

I was said to be an outspoken opponent of the impious new regime.

Some had accomplished enormous interference with our cult of the imperial gods. They had turned our sacred shrines into feasting halls and our liturgical rites into drinking parties, ignoring the austere customs of the ancestors and tossing out all traditional incantations.

All manner of depravity and vice reigned in our temples.

"I have come before thee, great Hegemax, and serve at your pleasure. If you will, do accept my unworthy head lowed down and forgive my tardiness." I bowed before his curile seat in the Hall of Venerable Maceon. There was a brief silence, which lasted far too long as he stared down at me.

"Accept your head? Should I not remove it from your torso? What if that were my pleasure?!" he snapped, "My pleasure!? Obviously my pleasure means little to you, since being without much pleasure yourself, little motivates you to be on time before this assembly. What of pleasure, you say? You have not yet joined us in the righteous bacchanals and solemn rites of Venus, tribune. I cannot imagine that you would think yourself above the gods, with all your austerity."

"Your Magnitude, I must keep myself from partaking in such pleasures which the gods have deemed restricted, in accord with the true understanding of ancestral wisdom."

"It is also forbidden by the gods to hold in contempt your lord's wishes. Where is wisdom in that defiance? Do you imagine that you may dictate morality to the senators? Do you say that your flesh need not be satisfied? You are a liar. You even lie to yourself. You hide behind the so-called wisdom of the ancestors because you are afraid of letting yourself live, truly live. You spend your time reading books and scrolls as if the mind would show you what's true. The moment to live is now. There is no worthy reflection, what is past is gone forever, and the future is nothing nor can it be known. You must find "salvation" in the time-stopping ecstasy that only our devotions can give you."

"Has not my loyalty to the imperial seat been to your satisfaction?" I asked, "Why must devotion to the old ways, the blessed codes of Ptoleus and Zorcades, be a burden to the state? Have I not in every way carried out all your commands, save to participate in rites which I hold to be in need of reform?"

"You think they are beneath the dignity of our people. No, councilor, your thoughts are imprisoned in the old regime and the glories that can never return. You learn many things, but you have no true pleasure. No pleasure that can transform you, which can make you a demigod in *the state of Cathartic Titan* -which I myself am about to reach!" His face turned red with rage. "The Red Asceticism now rising will never fade from the world, it has been long in the making. Miserable superstition has too long shackled men to wretchedness and made them unable to live."

"It is the sublime peace of wisdom that I seek, my Hegemax, not the pleasures that lower men to the level of the beasts, without love and the consolation of true friendship. Do you ever consider the sad and abused state of your many pleasure-slaves?"

"You dare accuse the Imperial Hegemax of not caring?!" He bellowed. "I am most kind. I could have you ripped out of your skin!"

"Forgive me, Son of the Principate, perhaps I have spoken without proper restraint. Consider that I do not fear death, and so I speak freely and do as the gods see fit. Let me narrate for you a little fable writ by a famous priest of far away Delphi, the man Aesop: A jar of honey happened to tip over. Out spilled the golden delight. A swarm of flies settled to immediately disgorge themselves. So sweet was the feast that the flies couldn't pull themselves away. Soon this became literally true, as their legs stuck in the mire of spilled honey and held them fast. The flies were in despair of ever escaping. They bemoaned their fate, crying: 'Oh how unhappy we are -for a brief bout of pleasure we must now perish.' So it will be with those of your sect who wallow in the decadence of the new carnal licence. Nature's laws shall somehow hold you fast. How appropriate it is that for the new imperial shield-device you had your praetorians depict the black swamp fly against a red field."

"You dare prophesy our demise?!" He bellowed.

"I have said what I have said. We who pursue wisdom know that the pleasures of this life distract us from truth. It is what we spend our time preparing for, entry into the upper world, the aetherial realm of the gods. There by the power of our contemplation we shall be enveloped in light and withdraw forever from the turmoils of the flesh. We shall merge with the soul of all. This is why I may not participate in the rites of your mystery-cult, for I make no provision for my flesh."

There was a most disturbing silence. The dreadful prince looked over his assembled court, to see if anyone would speak. Finally the Bolgud himself made utterance.

"And that is why, fool, you are accused of conspiracy. Your "philosophy" is an elaborate conspiracy to keep men under the yoke of superstition. My informants tell me that you are counted among the pernicious fold of so called wise men, what is it they are called? The Eldari? A secret society of the Kutaal meant to subvert the mental health of the citizenry. So have you secretly hoped for my demise ever since I took the curile seat! How do you answer the charge?"

The emperor took a deep draught of his wine and thrust out his great cup for the slave to refill. I took a foolish chance to give so bold an answer.

"I hope and pray that the true gods will draw you out of ignorance and bondage to pleasure, into the light of reality, and wisdom of the republican system. May they grace you to know the freedom of your own human life, and the acknowledgment that your body is a sacred vessel not to be abused. It is true that I walk with the Eldari, but our discussion is only upon knowledge of the good."

A look of distant sadness seemed for a moment to betray the Bolgud's inward thoughts. It was as if he suspected or even knew that what I had said was true, and secretly desired my peaceful walks with the Eldari. He was deathly afraid to ever give heed to the warnings of the wise, as if such actions would topple the worldly power he had so recently, after so many years of struggle, at last acquired. His sadness turned to resentment and envy against the simple joys of the wise.

"Republican system..." He smirked with contempt. "Enough, stubborn old man, you have not heard a word that I have said. I might as well be a fly on the wall. I am your Hegemax. I am your divine lord! You will pour libations to my divinity and pleasure yourself on the slaves that I send you. That is the good!"

"You are not a god. Nor are you acheiving the lasting good, but only ephemeral goods. You merely convinced the Regulian populace that the traditional ways of disciplined life which they once kept were clever means for subjugation. Then you promised them what they thought they craved: a utopia, but when that didn't sound real enough, you promised a utopia of pleasure, under the aegis of the Red Ascetic. Now that you are Hegemax, do you concern yourself for the good of the Regulian populace? Or is your concern for your own good, and thereby set up tyranny? Our sinful people deserve such a master. I will obey my Hegemax in all things save any sinning against our ancestral gods: I will never utter falsehood by refering to you, mere dust like the rest of us, as an immortal deity. No, you are my Hegemax, godlike, but not a god. Nor will I offend the divine gift of bodily delight, prepared by the beneficent maker. I will not commit carnal acts in the name of an erroneous ideology."

"Then the state must execute, since that is your pleasure. I do command this because I pity you."

So ended his rampage against the scribes and philosophers. He announced to everyone that, were he less nice, he should have me executed. By Regulian law it is not possible to have a magistrate executed on such grounds. Moreover, at that time I was an esteemed member of society. In those days, the Red Ascetic, whose magic had kept him alive for four-hundred years, had still not fully consolidated his political hold over the hegemony, and he might have feared the populus would turn on him. So he prevailed upon the Hegemax to spare my life. I was publically shamed and went into exile. There is no doubt however that, in these years today were I to use the same words and provoke him so, I would have been executed on the very day.

Within these pages you will find much that I must confess, good friend, and an entire secret history my pen will lay out. I do so hoping for wisdom, for an answer, for both myself and the darkening world, or rather that conspiracy that has made me its dupe.

𝒳 𝓍s𝓆 i◡

The history of Epinanaus begins with this introduction from one of the scholasts:

It was in Regulum, the city of earthly delights, that the history of the conspiracy was first recorded. It is the first known history and concerns only the northern aristocracies, and by the time these very passages are in their first revision, only broken gestures of sorts will have been comprehended.

Let us imagine how this history is sown inwardly together from sundry fragments. In origin one Epinanaus of Asosmos set it down, the magistrate of the Pellemant and the pontifex of the hill cults of the Timoh region, (a very important responsibility, though unmentioned in any of his works).

I have read through Epinanaus' collection with great care and courtesy to the delicate papyrus, as well as the first revision, found by the tomb-raider Kruthulus, a manuscript centuries old and partly devoured by Time, left in the remnant basements of a library in Ancient Rises of Nystol. They were forgotten, in the place where once of old many a sage and adept assiduously kept pristine texts.

Urguard and Orusca, bright cities founded by Itrurian colonists, Allapis the vanished empire of the Atlantean hegemony, and our own city Regulum, of Latin origin, though they might seem long established, are but an afterthought of the gods. The streets of Nystol, Vesulum, and Authapis are much more ancient. Those realms were never abandoned by the original inhabitants of the land, and their libraries of strange languages, whatever remains of them, have been closed off to the curiosities of men by Time's judgement. But through an unusual caprice of the gods this text came under my hand and I shall present.

My hope is to append unto Epinanaus' work the recent fragments and recoveries of Kruthulus who entered Nystol's labyrinths of spirit-infested libraries in the fifth year before this *scriptolem*, and recovered the only translation of these ancient histories from the Oruscan proto-script, along with his famous excavation notes. Here then is the only surviving history of the old order *The Twilight if the Republic* told by Epinanaus of Asosmos.

Anonymous Commentator
(very likely Epinanaus himself)

Epinanaus:
The Twilight of the Republic

May it please the Father of All that Epinanaus of Asosmus, his servant, here sets down a history of the Republic for preservation, lest the frail memories of men lose knowledge of how the world past unfolded, and how the free Republic governed the furthreaches, be it in exploit of war or abundance of peace, or in failure of both want or of excess. Be it writ in hope that the grave slip of free civilization into disastrous tyranny be recalled, especially the warp of centuries unfolding and so unto due course by the will of the gods bring to restoration all confidence. Know thou therefore how the realms came into conflict and by what secret discord became they the prey of the fell races.

The lore of Maceon and his sons has been entrusted to me by Annio, scribe of Vesulum, a sacred town of the Kutaal. Annio is he who recorded it with precision on Outhapian papyri. He did this in the days when he had audience with Jah Thal, saga-sayer of the first order of Ammouri (the Kutaal descent) who could recite by memory the story of the five tribes and foundation of the All-Law.

The work that was not destroyed, (the migration of the second tribe, the sons of Elod, into the northern coasts of the High Gohhan Sea) is recounted in detail. Jah Thal had received these stories from his father who had in turn received it from his father and so back for uncounted generations.

The recording by Annio was left unfinished, but the inquisitions of the Red Ascetic came the following year. Thal was imprisoned. He had voiced a lack of interest in defiling his body with unholy pleasures. In the end, he and his entire house were buried alive, and all his memory perished with him.

Annio, upon hearing tidings of an inquisition, hid well his transcripts, being wise to the hatreds of the Red Ascetic.

On this I spent all the remainder my inheritance. I employed nigh all my wealth to acquire those precious books from Annio. It seems that some evil god does not want the lore to be heard. Oh that the *Lay of Xilmuria* writ in full was not forever lost, the rimestock being impossibly scattered. Most of it must have simply vanished into earth.

The terrible bloodshed unleashed by the centaur raiders in the Andolyn mountains was the principle incident of our loss. The famous half-horse men are usually associated with the southern lands, the forests and hills of Illystra. They are seen patrolling their conquered domain Mahanaxar and terrorizing enslaved humans, or slipping into the foothills of the Antelynk range, like bandits waylaying travelers and looking for booty and glory in war. These kind are armed with either bow or spear, but their favorite weapon is the whip.

The centaurs stole the books and captured my servant Hepthe. A man of solid character, Hepthe had been captured in the wars as a youth and for two years labored in servitude on my lands. Being thus later stolen from me he did finally escape his captors, those savage beast-men centaurs. Lost in the East, Arraf, after many years he took service in the Army of Hermius the Conqueror, later recovering the thirty-third tome. As I herein recount, Hepthe would return to me years later, bearded and weather beaten, with long whitened locks, a wild man taught by formidable adventures.

The severe mishap, the centaur ambush that was our undoing all those years ago, will not rest in my memory. We were deep in the cedar forests of Echorias heading southward and east to Nystol, for the Rumilians had granted us monies to journey to distant Nystol that we might hire scribes to make several copies of the Illystran books. This was in accord with the treaty signed by all the civil lands, a treaty made with Nystol during the Ataluran Wars: every kingdom and principality must at once submit all their precious and ancient writings to Nystol for copying, (paid for by the owners!) The war-magics of Nystol had crushed the terrifying Ataluran tyranny, where the alliance of Maceonid sword could not. So the many kingdoms were more than willing to fulfill their side of the bargain.

An unusual set of tomes bound in black elephant hide was also entrusted to us for this purpose. Slave-girls and monks copy such valuable works in fine handwriting and the artisans of Luz and Xasbur illuminate them with elaborate traceries.

My new boots caused me discomfort, for I had not yet been broken them in, and there were few stops. Our guards were the Pikeman division of the 3rd Regulian Legion. They did not even have full leather boots but instead wore those special military sandals which prove better for a long hike in hot weather. They carried all their equipment with them on back frames, and wore their typical banded armour.

The mounted officer was a Vrynth noble of the Rumilian militocratic family Arvidae, (his full name escapes my memory), but he was well mannered and exacting in discipline (I had heard that he had attended the same nomotorium as myself). He often would ride ahead to reconnoiter with the two hawker-scouts (since it was well known that these forests were entirely dangerous and unexplored, and rumoured to conceal a bandit army. Nevertheless the path departs from the Serrian Way in the north where it begins to deteriorate. Often taken by pilgrims to Vesulum, it is the oldest known road through the Antelynk range. For this sake it is patrolled often by Edolunt Riders, especially during the festival season. The road crosses the Washir and passes through Aquilaris and the forests of Echorias, where it climbs the foothills of the Andolyn mountains and turns south to run the pass of the Vale of Chymera, finally turning into a mere forest path.

The uphill route into the Andolyn Mountains exhausts even the Hurth-horses of the Echorian Mountaineers. We took many breaks, for it was not considered a high priority mission by the Hegemont. The trail is deficient of reasonable campsites. On two occasions, since the upper forests became exceeding rocky and steep, we made a hasty camp on the path. It took us a whole day just to descend the first major foothill, with the pack-mules constantly halting and turning back, and we could not yet even see the distant Andolyn mountains looming high into the atmospheres.

It was during the noon hours of the following day, when we were nearing the falls of the river Murmrik with the Echorian-verges below that a sense of being irretrievably distant from the civil order crept into me. The bird cries were different, more musical they, and the crows now were seen with greater frequency, bearing wings larger than northern kinds, and they kept just ahead of the party, cawing loudly.

I took the noon meal with the Rumilian officer and the high of rank. My talk turned toward how darkly thick the ground-brush and grasses were in these hills, easy for concealing foes. The officer said nothing, being a neophyte, but the old leathery-faced centurion spoke up, agreeing.

"Bloody-handed bandits," he said, "oft like foxes laying in wait for pilgrims, their archery being most deadly, swift death for the unwary. But there are worse dangers here."

"It is not possible," the neophyte officer claimed, "that any half-provisioned band of forest thieves would dare go after a detachment of the famous 3rd legion, no matter how fast of foot or bow-shot."

With stern brow the old centurion, forgetting rank, he offers a look of trepidation.

"So few of well armoured men there are in this detachment...Aye, and I suspect it were not merely the typical cheat of senatorial coin."

"Do you think that our numbers are insufficient?" I asked. "Even to keep back a band of outlaws?"

"It has never been this way," he muttered. "They have never sent so few into the high Echorian wilderness alone. There is something amiss, I tell you. There are black motives among the syndicated gentry, whispered plans, sinister things of greed or other sin. We are an offering, we are not meant to return."

Surprized, the young officer paused his eating and looked at the centurion. Being gentry himself perhaps he knew that it were true, or at least suspected as much. It seemed he had suddenly put a few things together in mind, that he had just discovered why he had been chosen. He starred off elsewhere with the look of one who has been given a death sentence.

The centurion could be speaking in earnest. It was to be a lengthened journey through perilous and uncharted regions and we should have been augmented more troops. The sergeant had some scouts go ahead and search out the rocky path which passed through the over-grown ruins of eld Azerdon, a route which has been held by outlaws in the past.

Thirty light infantry marched in two columns. Picture the glint of the forest sun blessing their helms, (their diamond-shape shields slung over back) Little do they percieve how swiftly death is nearing. How like shadows and dust we men. If the flesh recoils at such slight injury as a pin-prick, how will you, oh hero, hope to persevere Mahark fire or Ataluran sword-slash? Should not then every man make preparation to soon breathe his last? Consider, I pray, how great the confidence in these men to soon see again their wives, children, and homes. Yet that very day will deny them even of again seeing the sun's gentle decline.

The next thing my memory keeps is pulling on my boots on in the morning; there is a sense of being watched, someone notes, and that encompasses my mind. We make ready to pass through the ruins only a furlong distant, in order that we might make Fort Flammelstag in the Chymera valley by the third hour.

For almost half the previous day we've heard strange horn blasts some distance off the old forest path. Yet the commander and other officers take no cautionary measures.

Then as the sun arises in the morning, pack mules and hirelings and troops cross a grassy forest opening. We are at once hear horn blasts on all sides, and next bestial roars of an hundred unseen enemies.

Of the Regulian soldiers, some are spooked by the haunting war-cries of the savage. At first they look about perplexed, unable to spot the enemy. Of a sudden they fall beneath the hurled axes of the savages before they could even muster a line and unsheathe their short-swords.

The mounted officer in his noble cape and raiment, the neophyte, is immediately struck with many arrows. He and his horse fall to earth, they crash into the brush.

Many of our lackies and supply troops, seeing this, flee into the woods. The centauri are waiting for them with nets. One centaur, eager for war, races toward the legionaries makeshift formation, some of whom are still struggling to throw off their backpacks, while others stand fast and ready their pikes and swords. The galloping centaur is impaled by a well placed Regulian pike through the neck, it was the first engagement less the centuar's advantage of surprise. But the point is to no avail in diminishing the morale of the enemy. In the chaos a line of centuars rushes in, and a beastly lord gallops up and succeeds in divesting the same pikeman of his helmeted head.

The two men next to me, hired muleteers, both at once are struck by arrows. One dies instantly. The other lunges forward with only his dagger but is straightway trampled by two horse-beasts. The forest keeps pouring forth centauri, their torso tattooed over with colorful designs of savage aspect.

Seven or eight of the remaining infantry form a circle and with a poorly formed shield wall fend with their pikes while the swift-hooved centaurs circle round and round loosing shafts of death. It was clearly to become a massacre. Having grabbed the short-sword of a fallen soldier, I could not determine what last intention to make, to die in war, or, not being a soldier, to flee and die alone starving in the wilderness. The speed and ferocity of battle were things still unknown to me, being a mere indentured scribe.

Before my mind directs itself out of confusion, a centaur's club must have knocked me unto the head, compelling my frame to the ground.

I do not know how long I was knocked cold, but my sight returns and I look up. From the grassy earth I watch two book-laden donkeys moving off into the wilderness. Then the blackness overtook me.

Not until hours later does an awakening come for me, when the sun had curbed his steeds now descending. My face and hair steeped in blood, my companions are dead or have lost contact, the soldiers are laying about on the grasses and boulders, cold and dead, and there is now only myself. Great dread fills me.

As a blessing for the many slain I offer my prayers to the gods and cover handfuls of earth over those stripped by the ambushers. I am able to notice that those who were seriously wounded but not at once slain were tortured by the savages while they lay bleeding to death. (their Atlantean armatures, loricas, swords and blankets were also taken). And all this is a tearful thing to see.

I am strong enough to make way to the house of the old Buderham in the foothills of the Andolyn mountains. The old man cares for me and the after the third day we ride back to the trail in order to bury the dead.

Two days afterward that, when my recovery from wounds is certain and my horse found, the Edolunt rangers that keep Fort Flammelstag ride out with us to search river beds for the mules bearing the precious books.

The Regulian Principate tolerated such provocations less and less, and finally retaliations were administered. Even so, the centaur bands became more and more bold and finally waged war openly on all humans, claiming for themselves all the arid grasslands of Mahanaxar and part of Echorias. All this could easily have been avoided by honouring the treaties, but those with financial interests in expansion prevented it. We were as bait, as the sinister beaurocrats calculated, acquiring a *causa belli* against the Centuar tribes. And how cynical those wicked nameless plotters, simultaneously stirring the indignation of the people while ridding themselves of political rivals in the military, a ploy that cunningly kills two framexes by means of one arrow stealthily sent.

With much of my fortune lost and no longer favored by the lords of Vrynth, old Buderham offered to train me in the way of the Ammouri, provided that my submission to him in all things be absolute.

After seven years of training, my thanks to the Patriarch was heard in the Citadel of Ammouri. However, I publically declined adherence to their superstitious faith and refused the priesthood. The next seven years saw me in Azerdon teaching Neoplatonism and working as an Eldark thaumaturge instead. Suddenly the All-Being called me to desert seclusion and contemplation of the deep mysteries.

Would that the One might soon draw my spirit out of the shifting dusts of this world. Retired life now continued in a peaceful hermitage east the southern Canyons of Hermius, just north of Garmsir, in this place known as the Well of Souls. It is so titled because our blessed water is a refreshment for thirsty souls in the desert, not because there is an actual well containing souls, at least not that I know about.

The lapse of three years had slipped by. They were mostly spent on gardens and contemplations. My only contact with others was this: every new moon I am brought news of the distant wars, and this compels me to write tractates against the errors of the Red Ascetic.

The Red Ascetic and his bizarre cult play no little role in the unfolding of this secret history. Let it be understood that the Red Ascetic himself was once an Ammouric Knight, who along with me studied and later strove against the old faith. Nor does he deny this, but in his commentary on a certain rare work he highly values, *The Utterances of the Dead*, he claims that illumination has released him. He has been liberated from the shackles of "the superstition of Patriarchs."

The Red Ascetic erected himself as sole spiritual arbiter. He rejects the ancient teachings concerning the right of free souls in lawful harmony. He promotes the despising of the succession of royalty established from time immemorial. He is now drawing entire nations down into black Dis with him. He profanes and twists our ancient truths learnt of genuine authority. Only a handful of ancestral families from Ammouric clans hope to preserve in secret the primordial doctrines.

Only these reversals of order can explain how it is that a band of rustic centaurs dared to attack a Regulian line within the imperial regions of influence. The Mahanaxaran King no longer patrols his lands, infatuated as he is with Red Asceticism, "the Unknowing" and the "pools of Emptiness." What is more, his love for the strange Sorceries of Nystol and their libraries has compelled him to issue a most novel decree. Contrary to ancient restrictions, the princes may speak with the dead and even take unto themselves the infamous occupation of Sorcerer. Such erroneous interpretation of sacred law has even fooled those rare and well-intentioned scholars.

For example, there is an order descended from the Eldark, it is the ancient circle of the "long robes of Azerdon," of which only three souls remain. Two of them, Zuphagen and Adeuces, have taken oaths to the Red Ascetic, and the third who refused, Arizel, was left in a maniacal state near death. He had purposely burned down his entire library, envious that any other should learn his supposed arcane secrets after his passing. Though barely able to rise, this Arizel disappeared into the wilds of Mahanaxar. The three had been meeting in Azerdon, it has been reported, to discuss the situation of Nystol and make plans. Neither Adeuces, Zuphagen, Arizel, nor the Red Ascetic could agree as to how and when the state of "Cathartic Titan" is reached in the human soul (or is it the body?). They spent many months debating this and plotting their plots.

Yes, the arcane art was permitted to a very few for a time, (lest the old abominations prevail entirely). But men began to abuse it. They began designing illusions or speaking with spirits and turning power toward themselves.

As time passed, Arizel also masterminded the destruction of the libraries in Nystol. He put his hope in two strategies: the designing of special incendiary bombs and the cooperation of the Mahark barbarians. The two methods did not fail him. The Great Burning was accomplished. Yet he did not foresee the survival of so many various "Foundation Texts." fragments of Nystol's waxing, but dangerous sorceries indeed.

Yet much more remains to be told. My account shall not neglect to unfold it. The famous 33rd tome may indeed hold the key to the undoing the rise of the great heretics like the Red Ascetic. The spirit Ambrosius, diviniton and oracle of the All-Knower, when asked (by certain half-learned men), how the knowledge of a heretic like the Red Ascetic could be so luminous replied thus:

"How is it that he can have the key of knowledge who doth deny the author thereof?"

2

Here in the desert hermitage new depths of meditation concerning the unbegotten reality had of recent given me much consolation. I had endured the crucible of the Second Quietude, at last, after years of concentrated work and study. My preparation to enter the veil of the remote Third Quietude was near complete. One night, as the supreme hour approached for this interior bliss, there was a sudden knocking. Someone was at the hermitage door, sole entrance of that little adobe cottage.

Such a clamor was a powerful disruptive to the fabric of reality, my meditative state. A fear flashed through me: understand that the soul enters a delicate transition at this advanced stage. The sages warn that any disintegration of silence could all but tear the superstantial realization! (Of course you recall that true metaphysic assures us such a disaster is impossible).

How could any unnecessary being thus disturb me so? To that question no answer came to mind. The noise jolted me back into the waning sub-realities of the transient world. Of course, the ritual demands utmost attention. My response was not to ignore but to answer the knock with a commanding tone.

"Hold; wait ye a few moments you must..." (I no longer had familiarity with my own voice; that also unnerved me).

The ritual ended. My slippered feet carried me to the door, to discover what sort of uninvited guest would dare disturb, for all know that the few inhabatants of that barren land dwell there so as not to be disturbed. Even so it is not permitted a hermit to treat anyone dismissively. It is our custom to first welcome and dine guests, then ask questions; but these were dark days...

So I open the door of my hermitage. I see a slight man with near-Eastern visage, his eyes cast upward to the heavens. He lets down his glance from the above and looks upon me standing there in ceremonial dress. He presented a wild, untamed expression, as did his array; unshod and outfitted in camel-hair. He was aged roughly in latter middle years, and stood like an ancient, as if suspended in time. He was of formidable bodily frame, and the sun had darkened and thoroughly wrinkled his skin, but yet his spirit shon luminous by facial expression and from radiant eyes. He immediately bowed and, esteeming him a poor suppliant, I raised my hand to grant blessing.

"I will bless you of course, now. But you must then depart at once, unclean one. For I have nothing else to offer save water or tea."

I lifted my hand to make the nine-fold sign for benediction but to my dismay he immediately motioned away so as not to receive it.

He stood with an unusual confidence for a transient, and it was incredible to see a man dare refuse the blessing of a 7th level sage of the Eldark.

"It seems you are a wanderer of many wildernesses," I said. "Perhaps too much so, for I do not often receive men of another fold..." This ragged loner, desert storms etched on his face, stood there as if he were some god disguised as a man. So I awaited his explanation, whether he sought refuge, star-wise direction, or victuals.

Perhaps indeed one of the gods roamed the earth disguised as a beggar to in order to deem men worthy or nay. With a peculiar and rough expression of words he now opened to me his purpose.

"I have come from far across the desert waste, kind sage, on pilgrimage unto true understanding. I have just this night heard from wayfarers that you are just, renowned among hermits, and that you might take travelers in for a spell. I am in pressing need, for the desert night is some cold."

His bright blue eyes darted about in a worried manner. Brushing aside his wild mane, he added:

"They said that you are a high sage, and I glean by your well-combed beard and dress it should not be doubted. I myself have sought a life of simplicity, but I am driven by the spirit to announce the day of righteousness come."

"You are an Ammouri?"

"I am, and I have wandered far and wide. Forgive my disturbance of your silent contemplation. I thought to offer some toolwise instruction to avail in building your Solomon's temple."

"Our cultic traditions are not at peace, but the one sternly contradicts the other. Wise was Solomon to build the temple of his deity in absolute silence, as the Eldark say. But your faith has rejected important axioms of wisdom. You should return some night when I am away camping in the hills gathering berries. You are clearly no savage, so you are welcome to use the hermitage any time when I am gone, provided you wash regularly. You are doubtless a God-fearer. As for tonight, I am sorry...discussion is not possible."

I began to close the door, but he placed his fingers upon the lintel and spoke.

"Please...since when have the Eldark failed the practice of hospitality? Do not your Neoplatonic scriptures command you to receive the alien? Surely you confess that all men are made in purpose of like dignity, for the All-being's delight?"

"We do teach a doctrine approximating that," I answered. "Although be informed, the All is indifferent, the All has not delight as men conceive it."

"Will you turn away one of his own children?"

"We are sentient beings who adhere to law. Your kind do not carry this wisdom, nor the succession of righteousness in law."

"But would the divine being not, in generosity, invite those who are outside into his house, as if children adopted? Will not your deity take note of your abandoning me to the night and darknesses of desert, to grow cold and be devoured by framexes? Will the judger of souls not avenge this strictly?"

To this I knew no certain answer. Indeed the Eldark also did teach this, in the primitive and symbolic way of seeing the Godhead as a person. But it is not found in the Neoplatonic wisdom.

"I think the divine essence cares not for the anguish of us sinful men, for how could pure spirit gaze upon our corrupt flesh? Nevertheless, perhaps if I deny a stranger the lesser gods will be disturbed and my heart will be tormented and I will be punished, as the myths warn. Therefore your point is well met, worthy of consideration."

"And what a benefit of company I will provide."

"What benefit, unknower?"

"I have stories to tell, and a certain wisdom to expound that would not be averse to a Neoplatonic sage. Kindness covers many sins."

Now I considered this for a moment.

"It is in sooth against custom...however...I confess that it is true, the desert night is ruthless and cold. Therefore you should come in till morning. But hold, these are strange times, and it is night, so I warn you in a way my ancestors would not have comprehended or thought necessary: remember pious fear and offer no violence to a welcoming host, lest the gods instead turn on you with sevenfold fury. There is here a bowl for washing."

The powers seemed not disagreeable. I gestured a welcome and sat him down near the fire where it was enough warmth for him to rest. My eyes picked out a strange yellow dust on his fingertips as he offered them to wash. To this day my heart repents that I had not encouraged him to identify it or say anything of its meaning while I was pouring the water. I did not remember to ask later and forgot about it, forgetting till the dreams of my old age and the writing of this account have reminded me. I have suspected that it be the yellow pollen of desert croccus, but now it is impossible to have any certitude.

"Many thanks..." the stranger said, apparently quite relieved, "I came once before, years ago...your memory must surely recall. . ."

"I do not. Perhaps you are thinking of a time when old Epinanaus dwelt here, but he has committed his flesh to the earth and gone to the One."

"It is a name that I somehow recognize...but now I must admit ye this: It were not cold airs that concerned me enough to seek shelter from the desert night, rather it were freezing airs."

There was an abrupt silence, as he wished me to consider his words.

"Your meaning intends something hidden...do you suspect that we are not alone? Why do you not speak plainly?"

"I have enemies, and words are known to echo easily in the desert, especially when the wind is freezing."

"Your wording has an obvious exaggeration and seeks another meaning, for the breezes are everywhere mild tonight. I glean that you are a traveler "upon the spirit," as they say, so my guess therefore is that you speak of the things of the wind, and of freezing inhospitalities, or powers that have no warmth and whose freezing nature does damage to the mind."

Suddenly from just outside the dwelling I heard a great howl. It was not a framex. It sounded more like a dire wolf; a howl truly frightful.

"What kind of beast has been trailing you?" I asked, now rather alarmed. I reached for my only weapon, the quarterstaff. "If it gets in I will punish it dearly, and if it does not retreat, it will die."

"What mean you, sage. What has caused you this upset?"

I looked at him with incredulity.

"You did not hear that with your ears?"

"Did you hear something? I heard nothing."

"What do you mean?! How could you not have heard it? You must be almost deaf, or..."

"Ah, no doubt the desert wind howls and plays tricks on your mind."

"The desert cannot trick his own child. If that is so," I warned, "then it is best that you depart from here. If you say it were the wind, then you will be unafraid go out there."

I looked and saw that my strange guest had suddenly fallen asleep. As I waited an hour or so for him to awake, I heard the howl again. This time it was out beyond the fence, not so close to the dwelling. It was surely some kind of dangerous beast. I opened the door and saw a man standing not far off partly in shadow. His face was not bestial, but gentle.

"Who are you?" I asked.

"Just a man who hopes to obtain comfort from the night's cold." he said. "Your guest; he didn't tell you did he? I am his slave. He makes me sleep outside. He is embarrassed of me. Will you bring me a blanket?"

"We shall see. I will not permit a man to be left outside like a dog. I must talk with him first. I do not know if you are some bandit. Remain where you are and I will return."

I returned inside and closed the door. The sound awakened my guest. At once I demanded.

"Who are you and what is your business in these parts?"

"hmmm? I am a pilgrim to Argunizial, good host. May I learn also who you are?"

"I am Epinanaus of Asosmos, scribe of the Pellemant and Archsage of Eldark mysteries. But you have not in full answered my question, and I demand an answer. Pious pilgrims do not keep slaves, and if you do not tell me the truth at once about your identity and business, this quarterstaff will be the next interrogator."

"Do be rash, friend." He said. "There is no need for alarm. I have no slave with me."

"You have no slave? Then who is that man I just saw outside?"

The "pilgrim" stood up.

"There is no man outside."

"Again, you are false." I said, quite irritated. "Just as you were false about the howling that we heard."

"That YOU heard. You must be having hallucinations."

Then suddenly again I heard the frightful howl. It must have come from the man, or else a beast accompanied him. The guest just looked askance at me.

"You stand there and tell me that you did not hear that? I know in certitude that I am not mad. But I just met you. I have no reason to trust you. Beware, if that man outside dies from exposure, I will call out the Edolunt Riders to track you down. Nay, perhaps I will blow the Gruu-horn and summon them this very night, for it is illegal to impersonate a pious pilgrim. If you are not frank with me at once, you will be arrested."

"No, please," he said. "Do not call the rangers. I will be frank with you. I did hear the beastial howling. Yes, I am sorry that I was not forthright. I did not wish to alienate you by the strange circumstance of this visit. The howling is from a starving beast which trails me."

"And the man?"

"There is no man."

At once I stepped forward toward him aggressively, so as to threaten with my ashen staff.

"Please put down your staff. I tell the Truth. The howl that you heard, that was a beast. But the one you saw, that was no man."

"What?" I said. "Not a man? How can that be? I saw a man with my own eyes and I spoke with him. He requested a blanket. I wish to have him come in. I will not permit slaves to suffer."

"Good sage, that is commendable; But hear me, you must by no means invite him in, or you will jeopardise your own soul, and at the same time cause my demise, for I say to you: that is not a slave. If anything I am his slave. That is a creature whom you heard howling. And as I said, that is no man."

"What sort of creature? Your answer had better be a good one."

"They are unmentionable," he said in a near whisper "so I mention them not, and I suspect that he inspires my brain to fancy many unknown dangers on the night air. But a spirit may be able to manifest in physic force. I fear his cruel assault and still do, at least his hands, or claws rather. By a relentless fury, such a creature can drive a man to real madness. I came here for this reason: there are no Ammouric shrines to sleep beneath around here, so your dwelling must do. I must have protection of a pious dwelling, even if not full in agreement."

"I never hear much of spirits anymore," I said. "We hold that such things be a primitive myth. I wonder if your Ammouric doctrine has caused you the same madness that the rest of the civil world suffers from: a strange fixation insisting upon the correctness of doctrine, even to the shedding of blood. But please do not ask me to accept that the poor man outside there is a demon in corporeal form. You will put me in dilemma, for if you are merely under delusion, a man could die in the cold."

He stared at me as one who is in both rage and fear at once.

"I TELL YOU. HE IS NOT A MAN. HE IS A DEVIL.!!!"

I was soon very concerned that I had made some poor judgement in estimation of this stranger and should not have let him in. The worried look he returned did not much comfort me. Perhaps this wanderer was indeed wild, but was he insane? After an uncontrollable silence I pointed out another concern.

"I am sorry, stranger, but a certain thought about your story concerns me. Although something about you seems familiar, I know that if you were a pilgrim and stayed at hermitages before, you would surely have brought offerings this time, as is right custom. Even a desert flower would have sufficed."

He responded with the typical saying.

"The Eldark surely fear the gods and would not turn even a foolish suppliant away. . . I am a man who is being hunted, and in my panic I forgot."

Suddenly we heard the howl again. The stranger covered his ears as if it brought him an accustomed agony in hearing it often.

"That howl I have had to live with hearing every hour for the past few years. He wishes to remind me how I have become a slave of the devil."

I explained to him that I could not accept the doctrine that posits demonic powers, but only gods. He claimed that the demons and devils are not just for stories, but real fallen entities, spirits turned of malice. In our Neoplatonic opinion if anything is like that, it must be understood as abstraction: the only genuine evil is to be found lurking in men's hearts, or in the forests of the brain, such as what error-filled superstition constructs. On this exception he vehemently disagreed, citing several of the superstitious Ammouric texts, of which we also have familiarity.

"They were created at the beginning, pure spirits," he argued.

"That is not written in the holy texts." I countered.

"But it is your own! Your Eldark traditions also teach the lore." He countered in turn.

"One must distinguish our oral tradition from what the eld texts intend. The war between demons and angels is merely a morality tale, unworthy of scripture. Nor have I ever seen a demon."

"Just because you do not see them, does it mean they are not there, or that they are abstracted? Can you see the air you breathe? Yet it is undoubtably around us and moving within us. These beings are invisible minds, but no human thoughts have they!"

This argumentation was, in my esteem, uncanny and caught my attention. In my youthful days as a plantation owner I had often asked my slave if it were possible for him to see the workers of the harvest "really and truly cutting the stalks in those tall sunflower crops," for the work went too slow indeed. The house-slave's answer was always the same: "...but dom, just because you can't see them (the workers), does not mean they are not there...else wherefore do the seeds in your cakes arise, out of air?"

I was beginning to think of him as not insane. However some concern for the man outside remained in me.

"I will therefore not invite him in, as you request. However I will offer him a blanket. That is just. It is not too cold. He will survive."

"NO!" he cried, even getting on his knees to me. "Don't you realize, that if you give a gift to a devil, it is almost the same as inviting him into your home? Please do not."

I pushed him away.

"I will not be told how to treat guests in my own house, or to whom I may give gifts. Your proposition that the man I saw was not a man is not something that can be proved. I will not live under the tyranny of your superstitions."

I grabbed an old Kutaal blanket from the hutch and stepped outside onto the poarch. I saw no one. I stood a moment and waited. There was silence. The silence was terribly broken once more by the howl, desparate and remote now, even perhaps as far as the foothills of the great mountains. It sent a chill up my spine. I set down the blanket rolled it up on the poarch. I stepped back inside and closed the door. The stranger was still agape with trepidation.

I spoke with him more, but saw fit not to pry or ask his very name. While this went on my thoughts turned up an unexpected plethora of old memories. My ears recognized something in his voice and my eyes saw past the shaggy beard. To my utter dismay I became aware of the fact that I somehow had some previous acquaintance with this man. Then suddenly it dawned on me. He was the head slave of my former life! (He did not at first recognize me, perhaps because of my shaven head).

I did not wish this revelation unto him until I learned that he was not resentful, and why he claimed to be enslaved to a devil. I tried to steer my questions toward his past, and mentioned the slave-war, hoping he would confess either hatred or forgiveness.

We talked on into the late hours. I was keeping my revelation hidden, and tending the cinders.

Hepthe was his name, no longer the youth once known to me, but quite worn and wrinkled by years of wandering. He told how he had come to a constant sense of distrust. He feared blades in the dark. A rejecter of the Regulian reforms, he was a wild man with an uncut beard, wandering the earth and calling men to renounce civilization, to cast off the sinful customs of the age, and make straight the way of the Lord.

So I revealed to him my own name. I was shocked because he could not put it together that I was his former master. I mentioned the fearsome ambush of the centaurs all those years ago, but I would not in full relate my own story unto him, of how of my own life unfolded since that mishap so long past.

He recently left off sojourning in the southern wastes among the Zerbi nomads in the Deadly Hills, ten leagues east and south of Nystol's rise. Uncertain as to how he might react, I finally revealed to him that I was his long lost master.

To my surprise he was glad to learn my identity as his former master, and that my condition was good, for he had feared that I was slain in the wars. He cried out and grasped my knee. My years of having treated him with kindness and generosity in his servitude had not been in vain. Most Regulian slaves would have at least maimed their former masters if given an oppurtunity. Nevertheless he would never trust me as an equal friend. He watched me closely. Did he suspect that I might again attempt to subject him to servitude? He did not know that we who take on the Eldark cord could never again return to worldliness and treat an intellective being as property.

He often went back and forth from the door-peak and glanced out the hole, feigning concern about the slave outside, suspicious that he were being watched. Someone or some thing must have been, for later we heard the howling deep in the night again.

Hospitality for the man Hepthe was a meaty fare (desert hare stew) together with some dandylion wine. My comfort and sage-taught courtesy in this way gained of him new trust. This however was not enough. From his pouch he produced a package wrapped in fine linen, which, unraveling, displayed a thousand little twinkling nuggets of incense.

"Please, let this incense of highest origin be offered up," he said "else I will not be at ease or safe from any spiritual aggression. There walk angels of evil in the night. If wisps of smoke from this kind do not wrap like holy armour about us, I shall have a great deal to dread."

"I am even now burning the best incense from Luz to fortify our spirits? Therefore take heart."

"But you are an Eldark..." he countered boldly. "I however am an Ammouric and have much different requirements as affords pneumatic protection."

"You exaggerate. Devils, if there be such powers, can easily slip past such incense."

"They cannot, they must needs flee. It is a special proportion of frankincense and other aromatics, the prescription of St. John. It is terror upon them, they cannot remain."

"How are you so certain?"

"The principles of your own philosophers affirm it: nothing contrary can occupy the same space: *nihil contrarium in eadem re.* Where the Goodness itself resides no evil can remain."

"A misapplication of the axiom, since spirit is not a spatial reality." I said. "However, if you must, you may burn it upon the skyward ledge above, but please do not profane this sacred home with your superstitious faith."

"I am not offended by that statement, since it comes from one who remains asleep. Our faith is not superstition, though it seems so to many who are of uncircumcised heart. I give you this assurance: that the crucible of The Furth High King thus burning with fragrance pleases the divine nostrils. No spiritual entity stained with the privations of unreality can prevail to trespass beyond the threshold."

"Yet I still may need to invite him in, if the man knocks."

"DID YOU NOT HEAR ME? I SAID, HE IS NOT A MAN. If you do that, we shall both perish!

"I have never been troubled by devils, for they do not exist." I remarked.

"Of course they have not troubled you. What interest do lions have with old bones, whitened by too much desert sun. There is fresh meat to be had."

"Freedom has made you arrogant." I snapped.

Hepthe did not understand or even acknowledge my skeptical discipline. After he lit the incense in the little brass crucible he sat down and continued our discussion with greater ease, but I noted something which he had kept hidden under his cloak. He kept close his short sword. He spake the words of a man who knew no home, not fully describing his wanderings.

"If you wish to stay here," I said, "You must describe your wanderings. I will record them in my journal. This will be in exchange for room and board."

Nor during his whole stay did I ever see the fingers of his right hand cease to rest upon the minor hilt of the Gohhan dagger hanging upon his waist. I did not care, even were he a bandit, I was glad to have had some company.

The night revealed galaxies. Sleep overcame us.

3

Several days pass, during which the philosopher grows accustomed to his barbaric guest. The howling is still heard, several times an evening. The blanket he has left on the poarch remains untouched.

"You promised stories and historic accounts in exchange for your stay here," I said. "It has been several days now and I have only heard anecdotals and trivial adventures, or else howlings at night. I now require that you treat on all which you know, for it is evident that you have knowledge of things beyond the common keen."

"I gather that you are a private man," he said, "and not devoid of wisdom. Soon the time of the half moon will make things safe. I will tell you all that you can bear, especially on certain historical events, those which interest the righteous. However, pray, leave me to work the garden for another day, since I cannot disclose all at once and must fore-measure my words."

Over the next several days, he imparted to me, with great care, a synopsis of *the Black Book*, the thirty-third volume, which he memorized for four years while awaiting execution in the prisons of Gohha on the coasts of the Kalar Maurob. He had long since resigned to joke with himself about what he called *The Black Book of Melancholy* "because of the bitter-sweet consolations which memorizing the tome bears upon me throughout the years."

The very work of those literatures are worthy of epic verse, rimestocks, whether they are separated into tomes or all copied into one huge black *volumen*. It is recorded that the text appears for a brief time, a few years, and is glimpsed by the learned, added to, and then lost again for centuries.

These writings I therefore endeavored to set down, assiduously applying to his every word, but as you will learn, it all came to naught.

After completing several rolls, I provoked him by suggesting that all the ancient work we had been so labouring to record was, after all, "down right useless...."

There was an uncomfortable silence. I opened my mouth again to explain my words.

"A curious history, these your Ammouric texts, if it should be called even that, good for the idle and disturbed melancholic, be assured: the rodents and worms will someday digest them well."

"I take exception to such an ignorant comment, friend," he retorted "and I expect more from the wise, especially an Eldark."

"We Eldark are beyond worldly caring. We understand how all things pass...the Neoplatonic sages have illuminated our scriptures with their reason and insight. Yes, all are past, never again to occur, and these very things, which in the *Black Book* have been kept by memory, have served only to make my fingers numb and my wrist ache. There is no beneficial learning they pass down, not as you might find in a medical or engineering text. Even an erroneous philosophical work would serve greater purpose. These writings now recorded here are merely the ravings of zealots, outcast poets, and feeble old prophetesses."

"You have not the key to their meaning, and you make yourself sound ridiculous in the sight of angels." He snapped. "So that you will learn aright how useful and important such writings are, I will demonstrate how they impact upon the living. I will, in two days, expound upon the most complex and dangerous of all disclosures, namely, the history of the imperial conspiracies."

At this I was silent and could not well respond, for inwardly I rejoiced with great glee. I knew that he had been seeking to avoid relating dangerous research, and had wasted much time by merely delving into obscure antiquities instead, reciting poems and enigmas, but omitting more serious and revelatory lore. Now, however, he had taken my bait.

Each morning I would awaken Hepthe before dawn under gentle

compulsion that he join in meditations, and that he beg the aid of the angelic wheel of Timeless Memory; one of their vain superstitions which I suspect may hide some half-truth. I kept requesting that he pray not even a minute grain of right knowledge be omitted from his treatment. So although we shall never recover the originals, my account shall at least give the closest re-telling.

It took several hours for his memory to relate all this entirely, and there were many lapses of time in which he said nothing but stared off into space and into galaxies, and these lapses of course I have omitted. Another day passed.

"So...since you will not, then shall I begin it?"

Hepthe looked surprised at my pressing petulance. We were at the kitchen table after supper. I could wait no longer. It was a moment he did not expect.

He did not answer, but only looked at me with unexcited expression, trying to hide his agitation out of courtesy. So I pressed further anyway.

"We can begin by examining those great alterings of which we are certain: the turning point in the history of the state: the assassination of the Emperor Florians. It is admitted by all to be the point in history when Regulian Principate became even greater in its sway over Illystra. Of course you are not blind to this."

"I have changed my mind. I no longer wish to talk about it, or anything else of doings in the past, especially not the Principate. Your provocations the other day unbalanced my judgement. I must retract my offer concerning those imperial matters. I have no certitude of their truth anyway."

"You know I do not speak openly about what is forbidden. My word is irreproachable, Hepthe. What you say shall be set down in writing and preserved secretly for future generations. You will be long dead before anyone bothers to read it. Nevertheless, if you choose to take with you this wisdom to the grave, surely there it must forever remain."

"If I tell now what I must, then very soon my body will be found lifeless and cold, for there is an evil upon me. On the other hand, if I do not speak, there shall most likely come no discerning generations in aftertime that may have the wit to learn of it. So I shall therefore burn in hellfire. Therefore I am doubly doomed. To tell it will surely mean death to me, but to keep silent will be the second death and woe to many."

"Again you are exaggerating, Hepthe. How could any hostile enemy learn that you are the source? You said that you have been carrying this burden many years. The creature that howls at night is waiting for you because, like all preditors, they seek wounded or weakened prey. Give it to me and I shall set it down in ink and the torment shall relinquish you. You will regain your strength. Do not fear enemy minds. You will be long gone, again traveling, and these writings I make...you and I shall hide them away in the dryness of the desert's cliffward caves, if it would comfort you."

"Your desire for this is too great." He said "The powers can pick up patterns of speech from afar. I came here to tell you but one thing, and that must needs wait until I hear the trumpet. You see, in the spiritual dream that comes to me on certain nights, I hear a trumpet blast, a blast that also signals the final time, a blast which only I can hear, a blast made by angels. The sound of the horn always awakes me, reminds me of what is expected of the elect. Therefore I may reveal it when the sun passes into a new week, for then that devil must leave this zone."

"You said before that it would be at half moon. Now you are blaming your imaginary demons again."

"It is a Vecradian Devil, according to a manual I examined. Had I not been so great a sinner I might be able to banish the sinister thing by just lifting my hand, like other Ammouri. But as things stand, it is the merciful and divine will for me to be thus tormented for my offenses in this way. If the love of Christ does not drive me onwards, that thing will surely tear at me in hopes to cause me despair. It was the Red Ascetic who made it possible for these entities to clothe themselves with monstrous bodies. Let us speak no more on't."

"Speak no more? Please...do not humiliate me further!" I began to beg.

The man's head sunk down to the table, and he did not lift it again until several moments had past.

"Very well, I cannot keep you from what would be best not to know. I do this because you are an unbeliever, and therefore the prophecy shall have little effect upon you. You are vowed to speak it to no one, but only write it in the book. If you break your word, I cannot protect you, for I myself have forfeit protection. I will first offer you this: in the days before the emperor was assassinated, that bloody event and so sad a thing, a bloodshed that so fascinates common men, some important things were being talked about, things that could change all the civil lands."

"What sort of things?"

"Hopeful things; now troubling to recall."

"Such as—?"

"Such as how societies of Regulian and Rumilian nobles were once very hopeful that their differences could be solved, and peace brought to all Illystran lands."

"So, is that not the typical talk of rhetoricians and men who seek many votes?"

"Not in those days," he said. "Of what else yester-wise I will not say further. Even that news, a seeming change to goodwill, I suspect was not truly genuine. Few histories remain which can seriously testify any real hope for true peace through our own mortal effort; I say it is a thing beyond us mortals."

"I have heard that there did arise a strong hope for peace in the Empire," I remarked. "And as you say, an end to civil fratricides and calamity."

"A hope, perhaps," he said. "The bleak kind of hope a fisherman has after his nets remain empty for days on end. If it were genuine, true enough, I cannot say or judge, since eventhough I remember those days, I myself was not in the know. I was but a slave, still a beardless youth, Aye, I was your slave, remaining untaught."

"Yes..." I said, looking down. "And your servitude, Hepthe, I pray, was not without mercy and humane treatment..."

"Not according to the common perception of things."

"I am certain that you were old enough to remember it so. What is more, do you not see that I myself am different? I am willing to take you in without requiring the sweat of the brow, but only the memories your brow conceals."

"You are not different. To say such a thing reveals a man of some remnant insensitivity and conceit. However I am now your own accomplice in this for having pointed out your flaw, and having accepted your sanctuary. How could I not? Moreover, need I ask, what know you of servitude that you speak thereof?"

"Nothing," I said, a little embarrassed. "Save how to order it according to sound principles of production."

"For that I wager that even the Neoplatonics will see you burn..."

At this comment we laughed outrageously together, the master and his ex-slave, if not equals in law or memory, then at least equals in strange humour. Then he continued:

"But tell me, do you recall those years as well as I do?"

"Probably I do not." I said. "However, does not *the Black Book* prophesy that in those days peace was possible by the adoption of the law codes based on the old Alban founders? The people had sincere trust in the senatorial body and military enforcement... and those old Ammouric superstitions were still held in high regard. Not for any real belief in religious matters, mind you, but rather because most people thought that the codes reflected a common foundation for all right action."

"There are still some few who adhere with vigor to the religious truth," he explained. "Especially those who have encountered the opposition from out the depths ....but of those years I do now recall something of interest...things I did not understand at the time, but now they make passing sense. I recall how it was widely, perhaps foolishly, thought that even those provinces and border kingdoms, the ones which had slipped into a fanatic adherence to the Red Ascetic, (how bizarre his doctrines), could be eventually be won over through diplomacy."

"Yes, that was the common sentiment." I stated somberly, "But think about this: it has long been suspected that the assassination itself succeeded through a conspiracy. The planning involved cooperation of at least two factions: Praetorian Guards who were somehow linked with The Red Ascetic cult, and the other faction, officials hostile to the Emperor's plan for removal of the legions from the kingdom of Mahanaxar. But if such factions existed, common opposition does not seem sufficient grounds for imputing conspiracy."

"You of course cannot deny that they did operate in common opposition. Do not play innocent with me. *The Black Book* is a record itself of an even vaster conspiracy, dating back many ages, of which the assassination was only a part."

"And you hold that this is demonstrable?"

"No, it is not demonstrable, for if it were provable by historic investigation, it should be considered a failed conspiracy. But this one has notoriously succeeded in its goal and anticipated after-effects. Only a fool would believe or disbelieve otherwise.

"Your logic is circular, Hepthe."

"That is merely my human ineptitude. As such it has not much to do with something larger than me or my logic. See me as a broken vessel unable to hold back the overflowing wine of truth. Consider it this way: those skeptics, the same who have discounted the existence of conspiracy, scoff at the roaring waters all around them and proclaim that there is no river, that the presence of waters is "mere coincidence." Their grasp on reality is as tenuous as their blinding ideology. Now learn this: it has long been suspected in the popular mind that there must have somehow been courtiers secretly devoted to the Red Ascetic. It is whispered that the Red Ascetic at that time had secretly placed his hierarchy of priests and adepts not only within the Praetorian guards, to attend their cultic needs, but other important intelligence positions of the Principate as well, including the imperial cult and the academies."

"So...what was his purpose?"

"Their infernal wisdom would have taught an erroneous doctrine, the hell-philosophy of the Red Ascetic, and especially this ruthless principal: that any means whatsoever might be used to gain the advantage and power for the sake of "integration.."...It seems that any means whatsoever were indeed used. Somebody slew the emperor and the mysterious assassin was never found, save for one Vistonn, a nobleman. Do you recall?"

"Yes, he was held as suspect."

"And within a day, he was set free without much questioning. Is that not so?"

"You have learned it correctly," I said. "A great and influential land owner was next accused, and then the imperial lictors and tribunes themselves became suspect. In turn they implicated certain senators and evidence of a so-called wide-spread conspiracy grew."

"What about it?" I said. "The council of twelve tribunes and judges were appointed to lead official investigations. Did they learn anything of the puzzle? Not enough to interest anyone."

"It was enough to interest some." I remarked. "I do recall what they did to mollify the people: to everyone's dismay they concluded that no conspiracy against the Emperor had existed. But now enough of this running over old ground and feigning that you are unable to divulge. Tell me the knowledge that you have for so long withheld."

"I do so at my own peril. Nevertheless my life may not long continue now, and someone else must therefore receive these things, if that howling devil does not seize me first. However, be warned, the burden which this knowledge carries is great, why else would so devastating a minion be sent upon my flesh and seek my life? He will someday take me at last, take me to some horrible place in this world of darkness; but the Lord, I know, will rescue me, provided I am faithful even then.

"Then tell, and fear that no avenging spirit shall put out the lantern you have lit. Even when you are dead after a long life, I shall use the flame to light other lanterns."

"Listen close then...you recall how during those years the people understandably weakened in their confidence of the public governors. Further problems and government scandals soon followed, rumours of conspiracies and plots abounded."

"I was there...it was a troubled time."

"Then do you recall the war and its demoralizing impact?"

"The senate was being pressured to undertake a protracted war in distant Mahanaxar against an army of sun-worshiping centaurs."

"Is that all you know?"

"More... the rival city, grand Turnopolis, the eastern principality, had been suspected of encouraging those chaos-workers. In the following weeks after the ambush which changed my life and yours, three entire Regulian legions, sent to investigate allegations, vanished in the savannahs of Mahanaxar! As the anarchic situation dragged on, the people became cynical and irate, and occasional riots had to be put down."

"Aye...but at the same time new corruptions among the aristocracy were uncovered. The wealthy land owners had begun indenturing their debtors. Did you know that? It were not long before the institution of slavery would be re-established. I was in danger of becoming a permanent slave. Fate would intervene."

"How would fate intervene?"

"A day of reckoning was being prepared. Florians' successor, Emperor Bolgod, had a juvenile temperament. He was thought by most to be power-hungry and ruthless, and later even corrupt. His poor appointments to the Offices of Judgement seemed to confirm this suspicion. Many saw that as a fateful trend."

"The people were badly behaved, Hepthe," I admitted. "They deserved the rulers they got. Perhaps the Ammouri have a point; it were not fate, but rather chastisement."

"If not fate, it was fateful...or rather...fatal in result. Though they seemed not too bad, as humans, they lacked wisdom of governance...unsound laws were passed, contrary to traditions of the pious fathers. The most morally repugnant, for example, legalized the exposure of unwanted infants to die in the wilderness of the Andolyn mountains, an old Atlantean practice, which even your ancestors consistently taught was heinous to the divine race."

"But after Florian died and anarchy was ruining the state," I observed, "it almost seemed natural to me that the Red Ascetic should become a magistrate."

"You voted for him?"

"I foolishly confirmed his appointment to consul. I was away in my country villa and had no idea of the unrest."

"Then you should have considered more deeply the import of your office rather than the profit of your farm."

"You are still sore at me for your servitude?"

"Not for my own difficulty and indignity, but I bear an unhealing wound for my fellows. Please, do not apologize. All this brings back painful memories. I do not know if I can continue."

"You are my guest. I require of it of you. Don't you see? You have become as educated as I am."

"Aye, however be advised: I am become more educated than you, enough to realize that such learnedness means little. Nevertheless I shall humour you...

After you left, years passed and the war in Mahanaxar became old news. The people of the principate grew familiar to the yoke of the many corrupt officials. Even the wealthy began to enroll in the cult of the Red Ascetic. Emperor Bolgod himself had entertained the crimson prince several times at banquet. By his priestly allure and hypnotic gaze the morality of first the court, and then later the people, little by little, corroded into pride, greed, sensuality, and shameless behavior of lewdness."

"Was all this part of the designs of the Red Ascetic?"

"Aye; uninterested in learning wisdom, the youth set their hearts on abandonment to pleasure and vice. Beds of ivory, eventually taking up certain occult philosophies which supported their choice of evil living, allowed free reign of their lust. When a wise old senator warned them how the law was sanctioning vice, he was silenced. *Populus vult decipi.*"

"It is true, the indifferent masses do wish to be deceived, as it seems. I could never understand why."

"So as not to be challenged," he explained. "So as not to hazard an uncomfortable life as an expenditure for Truth."

"These ideas are interesting, and surely morality is something that law should guard, for the maintaining of social control, but, my friend, truth can be understood in many ways."

"So you are an expert on Truth?"

"I worship the gods and submit to the wisdom of seers, Hepthe."

"What of the Truth that is himself living truth?" he asked, pointedly.

"Have you really been persuaded by such cowering faith?" I asked, hoping that he would realize his distortion.

"I have."

"It is a vain superstition, devoid of reason," I remarked sternly. "...fit for slavish minds only. The sublime deity, pure spirit, does not incarnate as lowly human flesh."

"The flesh, the body, is not lowly. We shall one day be changed, yes, stripped of this failing body after long obedience of prayer and fasting, but in exchange for another body, a body by divine spirit made alive, an imperishable glory. Ours is the faith of slaves, but now it is mastering even the earth entire."

"It has not mastered the earth, nor can it, as you can see: all the Furth is sinking into darkness because the gods were neglected."

"Darkness always precedes the day. In right faith no darkness can reside, and in time to come, darkness will seem as daylight, and the mind will not remember thoughts of woe. Even now we partake in a righteousness that surpasses the righteousness of the high Eldark in centuries long past."

"What teaching of devils! How you describe your faith is not what I have heard. Your prelates have stained their hands in blood. In the long years of the Ammouric hegemony, how many were executed for heresy? What sort of holy men would you esteem them?"

"Our doctrine does not render men holy. It only afords them to make holy men of themselves, a thing which your wisdom-laws cannot do, no matter how much effort you make to fulfill them. But it is difficult for an earth-bound mind to learn such ways of sublime truth."

"How can anyone? Certainly not with such arbitrary and contrived doctrines as your priests propose. If you wish to reform your faith and make it acceptable to reasonable men, why don't you change such absurdities of belief?"

"What has been revealed on high we men have no power to alter. It is true that we are unreasonable, even fools, just as a lover becomes a fool for the sake of his beloved. Our wisdom is not of this world. Therefore we put off all vainglory and boastful extravagance, all vices and wicked living, wise speculations and the worship of idols. See how much you struggle to learn the rudiments of spirituality with your philosophic axioms of meditation? All these diagrams of the heavens you make, struggling to get hold of some little secret which is neither here nor there. Our heavenly father has given us insights beyond imagining, real nourishment of the next world."

"No wonder a devil pursues you. You have no experience of such things as I attain to. Enough; let us continue with the history of the conspiracy."

"I do have an experience, an experience to know that you are not yet ready to receive the dreadful history which I am burdened with."

"What experience?"

"You would not believe it. Nor will I cast my pearls before the swine."

"I will respect your word. Tell it."

"Let us return to the history of the conspiracy."

"We must, but first tell me of your experience, for it seems to bear upon these things."

"Very well, I warn you to keep it close, for when the angel finds out he shall cast fiery glances about us. Not long after I escaped the Prison of Gohha, I set my face to the work of living in accord with the Spirit. One day in the empty wilderness a grand vision was given to me. My awareness was resting in the Spirit, and of a sudden, certain powerful holy ones appeared before me, wearing garments whiter than snow, and whose visage shon brighter than the sun, and crying out I fell down to worship them, but they said, "Only the one who sits upon the throne receives worship." They brought me to a high mountain and took away the covering of flesh that veiled my sight. Looking down again I perceived this entire world as it is seen according to the spirit. It had become so ensnared in darkness as to be covered over by the massive web of some demonic archon who seemed much like a spider sucking the life from the many souls it ensnares. Lesser demons accomplished its every bidding. But there were many holy angels as well who were guiding souls away from death and hell, from the pleasures of the flesh that chain us to this darkened realm. I asked, "Will the earth ever be free of the evil power?" The angel looked at me and answered "This earth is passing away, but it is for you to announce that souls may be freed from the illusion of the flesh, for many are deluded. If you will accept this call, you will be pleasing to the unspeakable One who sits upon the Throne. Know that he has chosen you for it." Then I replied "But I am a condemned thief, and a man of envious eyes and bloody hands!" He replied, "That is true. You must pay for your crimes, and there will be sent a devil who will not cease to vex you. In the end he will drive you to ruin, but provided you persevere, you shall not perish forever in darkness. As for your eyes and hands, they shall be made clean." Suddenly there came a blinding light into my eyes and bright interior burning of great pain. Time did not pass as we are accustomed. Then I was shown a shimmering stream that welled up from a spring in the mountain and I drank from its gurgling waters, and at once I was taken up far into the seventh heaven. There I saw and heard things that no man may utter. That is the vision, the purpose of my life. I come as a messenger."

"That is a tale of high imagining." I concluded, smiling.

"It is no tale. It is my experience. You think it a delusion?"

"Only if you still fear death."

"Fear death? One should not fear it, that is true, but the flesh cannot be disrobed until the time has come. It is written, mere flesh cannot inherit the kingdom of the Father. My spirit must endure persecutions for now. Perhaps I fear not of death but rather fear the pain that being born into the next world requires. More likely it is this: I dread that in my hour of trial the evil spirit might achieve an advantage against me. Who is he who is ready to meet the exalted majesty divine and face the inscrutable judgement? I have been a sinful man, sinning out of weakness even since my great vision. The worldly glories still attract me and I cannot put to death my carnal nature for very long. I confess; I...I have also met travelers and have stolen many jewels and coin from them whilst they slept, even striking one of them down after he awoke. Oh what remorse for a wicked deed is done...! It is sheer perplexity, like a Judas! I hear that winged devil laugh and prepare new tortures. Most of all however, the entity wants to destroy me for the knowledge I possess. Retribution: it waits not far off, listening, trailing me wherever I go, howling, waiting for me to slip up and tell everything."

"What measures therefore shall we provide against your imaginary foe?"

"Let us beware, you and I, not any further to contend for one over another in easy quips when we offer rebuttals, for the satan always wins, persuading by whispered intrusion, wherever weakened charity has left a sounding hole in righteous conversation. I have no more to say now."

"But you must explain many things...as promised."

"I did not promise. But now I am weary and do not judge it safe, and I may easily slip in speech."

"Very well...tomorrow we shall go in the morning to the hills to gather berries and find water. You can tell me what you know there, it will be safer."

Indeed that is what we did on the morrow, for I awoke the man early in the morning and we tied the baskets up and went off. His hands were to be a great help for me in harvest time.

During the hike up into the great hill, which I bade be made in silence, I could not help but have a private chuckle for myself over his stories about the aerial spirits and his one crucified deity. At one point during the hike, while occupying myself with trivial thoughts to alleviate the strenuous climbing work, I imagined a ludicrously shaped black devil grabbing him, the same way a monkey grabs a human head. I broke out into a fit of uncontrollable laughter. I even collapsed to the ground and threw my head back, and rolled upon my back weirdly overcome with the hilarity of the thought.

"What is wrong?" He asked worriedly. "Why do you laugh so great a laugh? What has made you so mad?"

After some moments, having mustered as much self-control as I could, I merely claimed to have incidently thought of some parable involving a monkey chasing a woodland creature.

"Which parable?" he asked.

"It is of no account, Hepthe. Let us go."

"Such laughter is a sign of the evil one." he remarked sternly as I turned away.

His remark was ignored. After reaching the summit and working for several hours upon the crags picking the berries, I bade him sit and drink desert flower-milk and partake of the cheeses. So we began again.

"You had remarked that we should not exchange quips and sayings merely to counter one another. We must be humble to arrive at the truth." I said.

"Aye, and we must remember, even in those days of the Ammouric hegemony, both your old Eldark forms and our Ammouric ways were often scoffed at and even considered impious and perverse. Noble and upright men, both Regulian and Rumilian, after some time, removed from the city and went to dwell in country villas or join monastic groups in the desert."

"Yes, certainly that was what I hoped to do at the time. Think of it: the memory of the youthful and confident emperor so brutally slain has an impact that is still known. Many even now, by gleaning inquiry, try to discern the facts of the tragedy.

Those who make any progress soon find themselves in a labyrinth of contradictions too deep for them to contemplate. It seems that certain senators and magistrates may have been involved in destroying evidence. No historian, save perhaps the imperial annalist, doubts that a conspiracy was at work, designed by the highest elements of society and somehow involving the Red Ascetic."

"I have found that is truly the case." said Hepthe.

"There are many things rumoured to be written in *the Black Book*, the work which some have taken every hazard to possess, and which you say you used to keep hidden in a wild place, and consult only very late at night. Those writings, (eventhough the greater portion of them seem fairy tale, the stuff of your Ammouric superstition), I do confess, when understood in the proper context, having consulted an allegoric key, (and so having been purged of their unreason), truly do they convince at what seems to be a conspiracy of shadows. They suggest something more profound and long-evolving even than the assassination of Emperor Florians, now so many years passed. Perhaps I can add what you have learned to the marginalia, if you would tell it to me, after all, you saw everything."

"Very well." Hepthe said wearily. "Consider the life of the reputed imperial confidant Vistonn and the actions of Epinanaus his known killer. For a long time, you know, Epinanaus himself was thought to be involved in the conspiracy..."

I thought it strange that Hepthe used the name Epinanaus; he used my own name and even seemed to be referring to me, for also am I a historian.

"Think on this:" he said "you must recall that at the time of Epinanaus' death, in the months just after the assassination, three-years before the great burning of Nystol, there had been a violent upheaval in the politics of the Allapian coast, not far from Regulum.

You recall, of course, that the two principle clans of the city were in competition for control of the state: the Reguli, descendants of the ancient Roman kings, and the Rumili, the conquered Maceonid tribe which tradition holds had lived there from the beginning. The Regulian Hegemony was not yet fully consolidated. The ancient Rumilian nobility, also said to be derived from the Maceonids of the early furth, still traced their own theocratic patriarchies and were keeping in check most Regulian reforms.

Much of the old wealth was in the hands of the families that dwelt on the Vrynth hill, wealth passed down from the Atlantean line of overlords, a dynasty long defunct, but sharing with the sons of Rumil.

The senatorial governance of the territories was now chosen by rival guilds, some of whom shipped huge quantities of Ardevi grain on barges down the Washir river, the river which separates the city in three parts, to the sea. The Regulian guilds were mostly sea-faring.

You know these facts already, but remember to repeat them if ever you make written record of my testimony.

One spring these Regulian ship-guilds claimed that their rivals, the Rumilian sea-haulers, had, in a night raid, burnt their trading barges. The barges had been docked throughout the Washir delta, the very boundary of influence. The Reguli quickly retaliated.

The resultant violence was far too exaggerated to have been spontaneous. It cramped the composure of the noble families, who were in fear even for their lives. On this account the senate declared martial law and imposed it for many moons.

Mercenary protection from abroad had to be hired. It was a situation which drained many noble families of their wealth."

"I also understand that around this time, with all that going on, Epinanaus suddenly appeared in Regulum, with his volumes of history which he had been editing during his distant self-imposed exile, a thirteen year stay, here, at The Well of Souls, Hermitage in the Yezez desert."

"That is right, but word soon came from relatives, even before he reached the city walls, that his father had been arrested in the fray. Upon his entrance into his native city, he quickly discerned how the Reguli had taken over the state chambers. They were proscripting rival families and holding public executions. Florians had been trying to resolve the crisis, the parameters of which were far from clear, and hoped to temper rival factions under his own hand.

Both guilds were also known to be using underworld elements for reprisal upon one another, so Florians set about arresting certain reputed thief-masters, key players in subterranean trade.

Dangerous power-vacuums suddenly were noticed in the underworld, especially the vast Regulian catacombs. "Who is in power today?" –thieves and many other nefarious kinds would ask. Surely it is well known that any stable authority in Regulum must prepare satisfactory arrangements with the powers operating beneath the streets.

Florians had hoped to put an end to such corruption. He had begun to take measures against the thieves. Within days Emperor Florians would die from several well aimed shots of an Ataluran bow...sent from an unknown hand."

"So is it really true," I asked, "that, after the emperor's death, criminal elements, corrupt governors, senators, and praetorians, had a free-for-all? I understand that they had succeeded in the entrapment of Epinanaus' most aged father Cephilaus and had designs to seize Epinanaus' ancestral Hypatrid plantation."

"Is it true, and Epinanaus' father, bless his noble head, went on trial under the trumped-up charge of having spread seditious talk among the commoners (in order to inspire mutiny against both rival guilds)."

"In truth, he had only opposed over-taxation promoted by the guilds and the horse-masters. Correct?"

"You are correct. As for Epinanaus, he himself had many old enemies from the ancient clan-wars. These clans had, in his long absence, taken control of magisterial positions by subversive alliances with certain Regulian tribunes loyal to the Red Ascetic. Then Epinanaus himself, venerable historian, was implicated for assisting the reactionary politicals known as the Growling Dogs, men who had adhered to the doctrines of that famous Greek philosopher Diogenes.

Even though Epinanaus was thought to be an inactive member of the party, he was charged with other less serious crimes. These in total normally carried only the punishment of cheek slappings, but your "gods" did not smile upon him in those dark times.

He appeared before the Senatorial committee of Royal and Noble Inquiry, an old Rumilian jurisprudence that had been allowed to keep its title. He was sentenced very strictly after the encouragements of Vistonn, a "watcher of the courts" and an influential member of the Echecratid family, of the old Regulian line, a man still under scrutiny for his suspected role in the Emperor's assassination.

Already a self-appointed court had indicted, tried, and secured the execution of many so-called "mutineers, rebels, and heretics of the Hill Cult."

"These men were in reality merely political dissenters, right Hepthe? Men who had refused to accept bribery as a means of political discourse?"

"They were indeed to become pawns in a deadly game," he said. "Epinanaus was a piece occupying a key position. At a critical moment during Epinanaus' trial, which all records reveal was rigged and illegal, this Vistonn character, a long standing critic and adversary, had taken out a very long pipe and begun to stoke it, billowing smoke profusely."

"A thing well known to be rude," I observed, "and that should never be done in the presence of a Vrynth noble, or any noble for that matter."

"Never... no, never. So right there Epinanaus angrily rebuked him, publically shaming the man as "half-gob spawn" and a "brute" and tearing at him with cutting words. Vistonn drew his horse-sword, for nobles could not lawfully be disarmed unless in the presence of the Emperor; and running forth he impaled the incredulous and terrified Epinanaus, the long sword tearing through the man's tunica, slicing the guts, and another strike peircing the thorax and arteries."

"Was everyone certain that this was Epinanaus and not some hired double? It would have been wise for Epinanaus to have cheaply hired a double, having been gone so long, no one would recognize a difference."

"There is no doubt that it was Epinanaus who died there."

"How exactly went his last moments?"

"Torrents of blood rushed out of the man and his knees gave way. He began spitting up blood. It was pitiful."

"This should be counted for sacrilege as well as murder, should it not? After all, the senate is held as a sacred body and the chambers of the senate have been consecrated to the divine beings."

"Yes," he said. "Even the Ammouric law must consider this a crime of the highest order."

"I know the story, albeit not in such great detail. I always bothered me; aye, it is wholly inexplicable to me how a man of known virtue, a cleric governed by righteousness and seasoned in the sanctifications of hermit life in the remote deserts, could possibly have betrayed both his reason and piety to a momentary burst of whimsical rage over some issue of politeness, so deeply insulting someone to drive that person to an act of bloody madness."

"Who can say what really motivated him," Hepthe said. "Unfortunately for Vistonn, a guard appointed by the high court was on duty nearby. He was readily armed, and immediately acted to dispatch the man to Tartarus with swift-flying arrows.

"Our famous author Epinanaus however was still alive, though fading quickly. He did not die immediately. The blood vessels in the neck were torn but his esophagus remained intact, allowing him speech. Covered with blood, Epinanaus begged that his scribe, his most trusted servant, Hepthe, myself, be brought to him. I was rushed in from the senatorial antechamber immediately.

"As he lay during the many moments it took for him to give up the ghost, he granted the remainder of his wealth to the Echecratid family of Vistonn as reparation, an act later criticized by some as suspect.

"Then he called upon one "Ambrosius" the Ammourid, an Agathodaemon, or "selvic spirit," who, wearing a ritual lion mask, as superstitious witnesses allege, appeared for a brief moment floating in the air and spoke strange blessings over him."

"A strange Ammouric apparition; certainly to be discounted by serious men and those who pursue wisdom."

"Suit yourself. I saw nothing, but I noticed the commotion die down after the apparition was said to have appeared. It is believed that Epinanaus had not long before, in rage over having to accomplish some chore, forsaken the faith of the Ammouri. Who knows…"

"Wisdom was not entirely devoid in him. Why did he return to Regulum anyway? Was he hoping to restore his status as a Vrynth noble?"

"I believe he was, but he never said it to me. On the point of death he regretted his perfidy. In his final command, he bade me possess the histories that he had kept and written, volumes for which the nobility had long awaited. I was to find some way to deny the public reading or copying of the documents, and to keep them until, in his words, the nobles had "repented of their guilds and greed," and even until, as he said, 'the time comes when a man walks into the city and can find someone doing reparation to the divine race.'

Indeed, Epinanaus in his last moments prophesied to them all, saying that they would first come to a time when 'no Regulian could explain the primordial Aaphian ruins.'

I wondered aloud. "This chastisement Epinanaus claimed was for the good of the people? It was a judgement that was not accorded to him by rank of nobility."

"He did not care for noble privilege in his last hours. He seems to have rightly understood that it was all vanity. In a thoughtless act of wrathful passion, Epinanaus cursed the Regulian Principate, ordering that all his collections from the ancient libraries be destroyed and that his histories (now only 7 of the original 14 are preserved) be hidden away, so that 'the populus might suffer historic absurdity knowing nothing of their origins, devoid of historical knowledge for a period of 100 years, or until the offending generation has perished.'"

"It would seem," I observed, "that this punishment would not have the desired effect, since, as would be expected, other Regulians should later arise and write histories of even more advanced insight."

"Your reasoning on that point does not maintain however," Hepthe explained. "We know that Epinanaus alone had achieved access to ancient works and histories, rarest manuscripts which he realized had already been destroyed or lost during his own lifetime!"

"So they were of highest value afterall. Surely you did not obey him..."

"I was, as it seems looking back, obedient to my master in all things, so I did not even stay to participate in the burial rites. Immediately before I could be put under the charge of another, I undertook the journey to distant and lofty libraries of Nystol which rise out of the wilderness of Kedemoth in the Southern provinces. Dry winds can keep undamaged any vellum and papyrus there for uncounted years."

"Now, wherefore you became the new possessor of those tomes," I speculated, "tomes which are said to contain secrets of the same profoundity as regards the ancient conspiracy. You didn't know that they would never make it to Nystol? I warrant that, as an ancestor of the clan of Excorvus, you saw fit to deposit what remained of the texts not in Nystol, for it was too dangerous a journey, but in the house of Old Buderham, in the Vale of Chymera, is that guess right? How pleasant and secluded is that green valley of the south Antelynk range, and a seldom visited place to boot."

"You have guessed well." he responded, noting how glad I was for my cleverness. "It was the only perceivable option. For, as it is mentioned in the annals, the Mahark savages of the icy northern wastes had at that time been raiding, and had even crossed over the Andolyn Mountains."

"And on that account I take it that no guides would hazard the dangerous path to Nystol."

"Exactly...Old Buderham, grandfather of the Ammouri, (at that time 190 years old), promised me that his men would undertake the journey to Nystol in the Spring, the time when the Mahark raiding parties usually return North and it is safe again. Of course never was this accomplished, thanks be to Heaven. Nystol, the grand queen of libraries, within five years would be destroyed. All record of the ancient histories of the Five tribes would have been lost, as well as Parhassius' *Atlantean Invasions, The Voyages of Rumil, The Conquests of Hermius,* and many of the *Epics of the Ammouri."*

"And where or in what sort of preservative container worthy of centuries have the histories of Epinanaus been kept?"

"Epinanaus' volumes Old Buderham preserved in a great nautilus shell. He kept them for a period of years until his death. Then they were returned to Regulian Allapis during the Reign of Emperor Echecrates, who ordered them re-copied into books. Soon afterwards, it is believed, the originals vanished, were stolen, or given away."

"That is astonishing! Now I am realizing...now much beginning to make sense....But wait, I myself am Epinanaus, am I not? What is going here? I am the great historian. But you have just described to me my own death."

"I have described the death of your double, Epinanaus; one which we had prepared for you without your knowledge. Even in death he played his role well. No one doubted it was you. We awarded his family with great wealth for his sacrifice. You see, Epinanaus, we who fight for freedom and righteousness, we had developed our own counter-conspiracy. It involved securing your survival, for being an intellectual and historian the long-expected tyrant-emperor would have executed you first. To preserve you we acted, so that you could write the history of the free republic, and preserve it for a resurrection, and an insurrection, in the years when the Empire must wane."

"Ingenious..." I said. "And so it has not been until some thirty years later that the forgotten tomes came to Gohha, into your possession. I cannot process all that you say. It is getting late and we have many berries yet to pick. There is much to think about. I am slow to do a slave's work. I would rather listen to these curious testimonies and theories."

"Picking berries is work that even the prophets did." He said "Now we also are granted it."

"As it appears..." I admitted "But return to the assassination for deeper examination. There is a matter of some considerable doubt concerning Vistonn's murder of Epinanaus."

"Perhaps we shall speak of it again." he said "I however need food. Let us not too long meditate on things that we can do nothing about."

"It is true that we can do nothing to change the disastrous state that the world has come to."

"Trust that the divine being shall someday intervene." he spoke imparting a peaceful confidence.

"All things will come to ruin," I said "that is my consolation."

"That is spoken as one who has no hope. But now come, show me that you can work hard and I will consider you at least virtuous in earthly ways, even if you have not the strength to labour as a slave."

Certain things next transpired when departing from the highlands loaded down with berries, but I cannot here relate, since the history must be completed. Our next conversation was that same night. We heard the occasional unholy howl. Hepthe spoke:

"All was accomplished on the pretext of familial rivalry and rash offence taken at insult. However other reasons are hinted at by some very perceptive Rumilian women, whom I may not name. Though often vague and unexplained, they point to a conspiratorial desire to silence the only man who may have known the identity of the Emperor's true assassins.

In order to explain this suspicion I must return to the assassination of the Emperor. The Emperor had been visiting the port town of the Washir Delta, Octum in the province of Eregion, and was in procession on his white horse in the arena when the three arrows from an Ataluran bow struck him, two in the chest and one in the head."

"That is what all those who remember it in agreement confess." I added. "The people present, who had been rejoicing at the sight of the beloved Emperor, found their joy turned to terror and every soul went into confusion. Screaming out in horror they spread the word, "The Prince of the Gardens is slain! Bloody hands have done their work upon the Emperor! Let the grim spirits of sorrow wail!"

"That is the popular account. Many witnesses agree that the arrows came from different areas, and all seemed to strike in quick sequence. It not an easy task for a single bowman."

"How so is it not easy?"

"To load an Ataluran bow and pulling it back is not easy, even for an expert."

"You know this?"

"I used the Ataluran bow when I was with the Sand Pirates of The Dry Blood Sea."

"They say that, at first, most assumed that several assassins had shot from the perimeter of the arena, and possibly one from the pits below stage. Most of the guards immediately searched through the arena's corridors and found no one suspicious. The Emperor, mortally wounded, was rushed to the castle on the acropolic height where he soon expired. Is this correct?"

"It is correct. However note that Praetorian guards realized that the arrows which had struck the Emperor's chest came not from within the arena but from the Tower of Dil, (overlooking the arena nearby). They searched through all the chambers. One Praetorian would later say that he saw Vistonne eating roast chicken at this time, feigning to be unaware that anything had happened.

For several hours the authorities were perplexed as to where the assassin could be hiding."

"Did they not question the librarians and workers in the tower?"

"They did, and Vistonn was soon reported as missing. They later apprehended Vistonn in the town forum while he was watching a performance of a juggler. Vistonn had then been put under watch and was required daily to report to the high court in Eregion."

"The province where the assassination had occurred."

"Yes, which also causes one to suspect."

"And was Vistonn imprisoned?"

"He had not been charged with a crime, supposedly, because they were still gathering evidence, in accord with right custom."

"I imagine, for what its worth, he was considered innocent by Rumilian code."

"He was, but he feared that the angry mob would seize him if he were not guarded. He begged the court insisting upon his innocence and loyalty to the Emperor, repeating "it is imperative that I attend to legal work against my own rivals who are seeking to undermine the state.""

"What did that mean?"

"It was very strange...who can say."

"So he was allowed to attend his court cases?"

"Vistonn was largely rather respected by all, and so he was granted the freedom to attend the Senatorial Hearings on Noble Inquiry, but under constant surveillance by the imperial guards who could control the masses."

"And it is then, in court, that he would finally be slain by Epinanaus, as described previously."

"After a lapse of eighteen sessions. Although he was known to have once been a Legionary and had worked for several years as a Praetorian Guard, it is known how he had found new work in the Tower of Dil as a stone mason."

"A strange choice for one of noble extraction."

"Very strange, are you kidding? No one knows who gave the

intelligence that Vistonn had been the assassin, but since, moments after the shooting, an Ataluran Bow was found in the utmost level where he was said to have been repairing stonework, the tip was taken seriously."

"And the charge against him still lingered?"

"A real charge was already unofficially in process. The people were made certain of his conviction because Vistonn was soon discovered to have lived in Kalar, the closed land of the east, for several years, and was a renowned and outspoken devotee of the Red Ascetic."

"Therefore he surely must have been hostile to Emperor Florians who was an Ammouric Knight as well as a Prince."

"You are perceptive. But there are several problems with accepting this version, that Vistonn was the only assassin and was driven by red ascetic-madness to slay the Emperor. First, consider how difficult it would be to kill a mounted rider with a bowshot while standing hundreds of feet above. Though Ataluran bows are renowned for their accuracy, it would seem more reasonable for an assassin to prefer using a dagger in the night or to administer poison. Secondly, consider the lapse of time that transpired between the moment when the Emperor saw that in his body was lodged a death dealing arrow-

"The moment when he cried out 'I am betrayed!'"

"Yes...and the final supposed third or even rumoured fourth shot."

"Did they recover a fourth arrow?"

"Yes, but it missed its target and was slightly different from the others, and seemed to have much dust on its shaft. Anyway this moment was equal in length to the time it takes to blow a war horn twice with barely slight pause, which is exactly what happened when the centurion riding nearby saw his lord thus wounded. To load a heavy Ataluran bow, aim, and fire it takes three or four times as long.

One of the great mysteries I have discerned surrounding the assassination was the disappearance of the Emperor's body. Before physicians could arrive to accurately confirm the cause of death, the Praetorian Guard left with the body, bound for burial near the imperial palace. The official record published by the Lictors reads as follows: "The Emperor received arrow shots to the head and to the torso, fired from above, and died within moments. So let it be written." Such is the account that now holds popular opinion, that some conspirators, men unhappy with the Emperor's policies, secretly informed by certain unnamed senators, slew the great man but were unable to fully realize their coup. However, the public has no real understanding of the more sinister elements at work within the matrix of conspiracy, a conspiracy which involves all manner of subtlety on a level deeper than thought possible."

"Please, Hepthe, tell me how you came to learn of all this, for your knowledge of things surpasses what a poor hermit such as me could ever hope for."

"Why do you hope for knowledge? Do not your Platonic meditations satiate your soul?"

4

"There are mysteries that I must discern, Hepthe, and these things are somehow wrapped up in the wicked conspiracies of this failing world. I wish it were not so."

" It is so. You should discover them, for many other souls beside your own are at stake...However, I have told too much, and may find myself at the door of death because of it. I should return soon to my travels. If you want to learn more, you must inform me how it is you began to investigate such hidden things, afterall, for all I know you have become a wizard. I will not sleep tonight if I fear your story is contrived. As you know, even angels can be purchased for a price."

"Nay. You must first provide more, Hepthe. Tell me what you know of the lore of the Dry Blood Dunes, which you mentioned as so deeply rooted the other day while gathering sand onions, for there is much that remains unclear in our pagan records, and the fate of the monks there touches upon these mysteries."

"Very well, I will tell the foundational story that I heard from one of the wandering survivors. There is a mention of your Neoplatonism in it so I think you will be pleased. Surely it will earn me tomorrow's breakfast."

So did Hepthe begin:

"Once there was a monk who found a little dragon in an orchard. Its wing was broken, so he brought the dragon up to the monastery, and asked the monks if they would take-in the beast. At first the monks refused, citing the law, but having pity they accepted the dragon and took him in.

The dragon was put to work carrying water from one level to another by means of lifting buckets with its long neck, for the monastery had several stories. And there were many other tasks for which he was useful. The dragon eventually grew and functioned as a lift for older monks, or he availed to pluck fruits off the superior branches in the orchard. He was able to learn the pious ways of the monks and in a sense imitate them. After some years he became an adult and was able to fly away, but he lived inside the basements of the monastery instead, keeping the monks warm in the winter.

One year the Bishop of the realm, having come to the monastery for his annual visit, discovered this irregularity and demanded that the beast leave for the mountains, lest the people of the town discover and become alarmed. So the dragon left at night and flew to the mountains. He did not forget the kindness of the monks. Sorrowed he greatly and missed the monks, and he longed for the cheerful monastery, growing lonely at Christmas. Even so, he made a comfortable lair for himself, but not resting his head upon piled gold like other dragons were after doing, perferring instead a wholesome simplicity.

The unfortunate time came that the majority the town below the monastery rejected their ancient faith and chose to adopt heresy: stealing from the poor, enslaving visitors, forbidding marriage, outlawing art and music, and teaching various fictions. At last they raided the monastery and seized the jewel inlaid chalice, the six golden candlesticks, and the silver bookstand from the altar, and they even burned the sacred books. Many monks they murdered, hanging them from the edge with ropes.

Only half the monks survived and they fled. They took refuge in a cave within the mountains, for the winter was cold. There they soon realized that they were not alone. Another denizen was lurking in the dark. So they encountered their lost dragon, and from him they begged for asylum, which the dragon, so delighted, granted. When he heard from them of the injustices of the townsfolk, the dragon was determined to burn down the entire town, and was about to fly off to do so. But his friend-monk prevailed upon him to restrain. Instead teach the heretics the Truth, wherefore although they often spoke of God, they no longer believed in the power thereof.

To this end the monk devised a plan. He boldly went off alone into the town and announced to the people that they were wrong about God and such evil customs and fictitious cult which they had adopted. He said that God had bestowed his true power on him and he could prove it. So the people asked how in thunder he could so boast. He said that he, a mere monk, was so filled with the true power of God that he could tame the powers of hell and subdue one of the dragons in the southern mountains. The people laughed at him as he went off.

He returned a couple of days later with the dragon striding humbly behind him, on a chain. The people were amazed and glorified God. However the heresiarch their leader came forward, and seeing this was enraged. He said to them all, "You will see the power of hell, for I will return riding the most feirce of all the Red dragons, Scourg, and he will vanquish this lesser beast in aerial combat. Then you will know that my teachings, although new, must be heeded." So indeed did the heresiarch, whom some suspected a wizard, go off to fetch the red dragon.

A few weeks later he returned riding the red dragon Scourg on featherless wings flapping, and he challenged the monk and his dragon, which was bronze. Yea, verily, they did launch into the sky and make aerial combat.

The red dragon was most skilled at aerial assault and incendary warfare. He sorely wounded the bronze dragon, tearing at him and breaking his wing, and the bronze dragon fell to earth and was stuck in a cleft of earth.

But the monk prayed earnestly to God, who granted him the power of the wind, and he raised his arms, and lo, a great hot wind came from the East. It blew upon the red dragon Scourg as he was soaring aloft in triumph, and it struck full on. His wings could not resist the force of the blast. Thus did Scourg tumble in the upper atmosphere, desaulting in air far beyond the western approaches even to the rim of the world, and by the power of God, he was not seen again.

The noble bronze dragon, who had fallen in aerial combat, men called Gnotus, which means knowing, for they went to him and learning his speech found he was wise. He bled from his wound and could not arise. He did not die at once, but being stuck in the cleft was fading from his life for nearly a century. His blood flowed out every day continuously, and slowly turned the earth to a crimson hue.

The entire town was eventually abandoned and the farms dried up, for God saw fit to punish the infidelity of the people whom he had given a second chance, but instead they turned against the bronze dragon and rooted for the red, delighted in his wickedness. On this account the hot breezes from the East which had banished Scourg did never cease, and the heavens never again let the rains there fall. And lo in a few years time all the land around was turned into a desert of crimson sand. The faithful monk kept the dragon alive for many years, bringing him underground water and nourishment for as long as he could.

One year the famous scribe Morpheus Memnos visited the monastery searching for an ancient manuscript to confirm his researches. He heard the story of the bronze dragon from the monks and bade the faithful monk take him to visit the beast. He found Gnotus still alive after many years, stretched there in the place of the cleft of rock where he had fallen. The scribe was deeply moved and dedicated the remainder of his life to recording the dragon's teaching. The dragon bade the scribe to write down the prophesies that he uttered, for the creature had come to wisdom by meditations alone in the desert night under the stars. So it was done, Morpheus Memnos recorded the entire system of the wisdom of dragonkind, which was was strikingly similar to the teachings of ancient Neoplatonism.

All the brothers wept when the dragon Gnotus at last expired, for the dragon had always reminded them of God's power. Every year they would weep on the passage-day of Gnotus, or whenever they spoke of the creature. But these were tears of joy, since although there could be no feast day, they esteemed the beast as a sacred relic to be treasured. From henceforth were they called the Weeping Brotherhood.

Even so, on account of punishment for heresy, the land was becoming a vast desert, crimson in colour from the Gnotus' blood: so arose the Dry Blood Dunes. The only dwellers left were the faithful monks way up on their tall isle of rock, and the heretics below in huts, for although some important men had repented because of the just chastizemrnt of God, they also eventually passed. Over the years the bronze dragon had been forgotten. Most of the townsfolk, remembering only his fall from the sky, had returned to their former theological fiction and false freedoms.

Sometimes the monks in their pity would invite the unclean heretics up for feast days of Saints, and as time passed, this custom became regularized. It was unwise, for while in the course of feasting, befriending as companions, the heretics eventually persuaded some of the monks concerning their erroneous beliefs, that they should be tolerated. Within a few short years such beliefs went from tolerated, to accepted, and from accepted to promoted, and finally required. The Monastery of the Weeping Brotherhood had been infiltrated with false doctrine and alien dogmas. In a single day the heretic monks seized the Abbacy. Only a third of monks remained faithful refusing to part in the least from the religion of their Fathers.

War in the Monastery followed, and many monks on both sides were slain, including the monk who had originally found the dragon.

Although the faithful monks were victorious in every battle using their staff technique, the treachery of one who had posed as loyal finally got them caught by the heretic powers. Some monks the heretics executed by hanging off the cliff, but most they expelled to the desert, thinking they would die there anyway.

The surviving monks traveled to the Cleft of Gnotus, paying veneration to the remains of the legendary "humble dragon," and there they found the lost book of the *Prophecies of Gnotus*, or *Meta-prophecies* recorded by Morpheus Memnos who also had died there one year working in the cleft, being forgotten, an old man dedicated to recording the wisdom-prophecies.

So did the exiled monks decided to take the bones of Morpheus Memnos back to Sardu for burial at his famous home, and the book of prophecies as well, which they intended to deposit in the library of Hennsooth in Nystol. But as they approached Nystol from the East, lo, they saw from a distance great swags of smoke arising, for the city had been razed by the barbarians...!"

"...Well told, lord Hepthe. Your tale gives much for pondering and was a delight to hear. I had always wondered about those famous events, which seemed most unclear until you delineated them."

"It may be delight, but it is no fiction. For some the fact of it brings sadness, as it is a sacred tale, but also one that is not allegory. I have often wondered about how the meeting and combat with Scourg fits in with another narrative that I heard some years ago. It was an account that claimed Gnotus was captured and the dragon-tribunal put him on trial within the Chasm of Yaa in the East for his attempts to teach dragonkind the way of the wise, and to forbid them requiring human sacrifice. There are other stories that have been told, some of which survive only in oral tradition. The exiled monks of the Weeping Brotherhood however have made this story famous. Many of those monks still wander the Furth and record their account in various kingdoms."

"Indeed, I have myself heard that several do travel about with their mules burdened by a number of valuable codices. I shall now tell you the things I have heard, many of which you may already be familiar with.

"You realize of course that at one time I myself was an ignorant monk of the Ammouric orders, not an enlightened suppliant to the many gods and hearer of celestial wheels as I am now. There came a time when the cruel penances of your crucified Nazarene and the Ammouric disregard for the wonders of Eldark magic truly pained me, so I left the fold and returned to the old and glorious religion of my parents.

"My investigations into these mysteries began sometime before that enlightenment of mine, when I was still enthralled to the weird customs of your man-god. I was studying with the Friars at Whigg in those years but had returned to my ancestral home by the foaming sea for a summer respite. There called upon me one starry night a certain foreign monk traveling abroad needing shelter. The gods often disguise themselves as such so I did not dare refuse, as I have with you. He said that he had traveled an exceeding distance, from the Monastery of the Weeping Brotherhood in the Dry Blood Dunes.

I invited him to stay until the late summer fasts. He told me many things about the wide world. He was offering his teaching services to anyone wishing to learn the ancient scripts.

On account of his wandering he had entered our neighborhood Argodis, which is near some of the old Allapian Ruins, and had heard of our family's renowned hospitality. This man carried with him a locked copy of the original books and researches of blessed Epinanaus, texts which had been hithertofore unknown at Whigg.

Now, when asked why he had left his monastery, he explained that the cultic doctrines of the Red Ascetic had worked their way into the monastic discipline. They had taken over the minds of his fellow monks. The heresy is anti-intellectual and involves a fanatical hatred of philosophy and other higher learning and a sort of blind allegiance to the singular divine will..."

"...which they themselves profess is not sent of the Ammouric seat of the Godmouth, and is without accompanying angels or powers. Accursed heretics!" Hepthe added.

"Must ye speak such vehemence against heretics? At least they superstitiously confess one omnipotent man-god, the Nazarene, like yourself and the Ammouric fold. We polytheists chuckle at your schisms, monotheists should know better than to strive against each other."

"Did you not hear what they did to that monastery? Christ said that he came to bring not peace, but division. The pagan delusions are less reproachable than monotheistic heresies, aye, save in your case since you know better. But the old pagans at least were seeking the Truth. Heretics of our time, on the otherhand, confess to have faith but deny Truth and the power thereof, the Church and her traditions. But do not stop. Tell me more of this peculiar heresy."

"Yes...their "supernatural imperative" requires that all books suspect of what they deemed error or heresy, that is philosophy and poetry, even those teaching virtue and chastity, be destroyed by burning. Apparently, the deluded monks had raided their own library! Many of the ancient books rescued from the Nystol inferno were again in danger, as they were seized by hands bent on their obliteration. These and other valuable works, to the helpless dismay of the abbot, were indiscriminately piled up to be burned as tinder. These tinders were not to keep the brethren warm in the cold desert night, no indeed. They were collected to fuel the burning of seven hated Alethedox monks condemned to the stake!"

"....Alethedox?"

"It is a word similar to "orthodox" in Greek, but means "taught of truth" They were true to the high authority and Truth of the Soothfold, that is what the seven titled themselves in order to attempt a united front against the heresy. They were those monks who attempted to refute the heresy through disputation and proofs of demonstration. But all the rest of the heretical monks were far beyond Reason's influence, believing themselves to be in possession of a new orthodoxy. In a fanatical whirlwind of cultic zeal they did burn the bodies of those poor faithful monks."

"...and so sent them upward," added Hepthe "aye, but they had no power to molest the souls of such stalwarts."

"As you say....now this surviving monk, having escaped, was he who was visiting me, the only alethedox brother left alive. He had fled the great monastery in the night, taking as many precious books as he could pack on two camels. He later explained how one camel had been lost along the way in a dreadful sandstorm known to the nomads of that region and called "The Aerial One."

I insisted that I be allowed to examine those remaining works. In return I promised the kind monk that I would make an excellent copy of the legendary history. I would need over two years time. I offered him supplies and a donkey in surety, and promised him that in the months that he was due to return from the sacred Council of Vesulum (headed by the Soothfold), he could retrieve them. He agreed and parted from my company after some weeks.

Now it was on the subsequent event of what seemed to be an apparition of an ancient hermit, which I myself thought in my delusion that I beheld during the Festival of the Dead, when I resolved to waste no time writing a translation of the ancient book. Of course, I don't really believe that the very spirit of Epinanaus called me from his infernal place in Dys. I do not entertain the imagination that the phantom was seeking to lift his dying curse. However, if so, may redemptive spirits release him.

Abide me to explain the different sources which have been included in this account. The first is the fragments of Epinanaus himself. This is complex, so apply your mind...

When first the labor of copying called me, leave needed to be obtained from my employers, the Rumilian Scribes who kept the library of Regulum. Unknown to me was that there were certain other fragments from Epinanaus's most important source, the 33rd tome of *the Black Book*. They had only shortly before been found by Holernus, Archischribe of the Pellamant Library of Regulum, and these were fragments which were stuffed into a little known book of ancient biology.

"--the fragments of the original translation of the last Saga sayer of The Kutaal, Jah Thal a bhir?" Hepthe asked, excitedly. "They are writ in the original proto Oruscan characters!"

"Such manuscripts are indeed worthy of your outburst." I said "Other testimonies were intentionally excerpted from the text. The fragmentary manuscripts were sent on their first journey to Nystol, because, it was believed, they possessed doctrines "too sacred for the idolatrous eyes of Sorcerers." So reads a gloss written in Greek of unknown hand. There is naught else known of its pedigree. I have found the fragments very important. They are especially useful in their descriptions of your strange worship, the faith of the Ammouri.

Secondly, I found much information about the Illystran epics from Arizel's *Commentaries on the 22nd Book*. Arizel, you may know, was not a real sorcerer, but a famous and genuinely mad "cult cleric." When this lunatic magus Arizel of Azerdon feigned to renounce the practice of sorcery, he took up the study of the ancient monotheists. He envied their spiritual gifts. He especially studied the writings of the Ammouri. The Worship had long been despised in the palaces of Azerdon."

"I have heard of him. A wizard of the worst sort is he. The knave believed that by learning the sacred text which described the curse of the Allfather upon the giants, drow, and rebel nephilim, that he could thereby subordinate those spirits to his mastery."

"Apparently he did not subject himself to the rigors of Ammouric superstition or authority. Like Shahi Nuzzib and later the Red Ascetic, he designed his own heretical version of their beliefs. Arizel studied the doctrines with great zeal."

"A fictional research, and in truth, a conceited one. Did he not resurrect the old fables of Gohhan pagans, devotions according to his whim?"

"I do think so. Even at that time, most of what he could find remaining were second hand accounts, synopses, fragments."

"Is that on account of Nystol's burning?"

"No, the Ammouric histories were, on the whole, preserved from the bibliocaust. Rather it were robber centaurs who would steal off with the volumes, works once treasured as a prime source by Epinanaus. Now these books contain much concerning the rites and deeds of the Ammouri. The barbarous Centaurs of Mahanaxar finally realized the scale of their happy robbery of those books. They knew that they now possessed at least one copy of the most precious of Ammouric songs, and so sent message to the troubled Arizel notifying him of the scale their treasure, the 22nd book, worth its weight in gold, (he was their only possible buyer, since no one else thought it so valuable).

Gleeful to obtain the goods he had so long coveted, the old man took the long trip to Mahanaxar. There was only a handful of attendant slaves to carry his litter. The hardships of the trip almost finished him. By the time he arrived on the fly infested plains of Mahanaxar, his slaves had abandoned him. He had only a horse and two weakened guards left. His coin for the purchase of the work had already been exacted as toll by a formidable patrol of hill bandits. Nevertheless he was determined to somehow bargain with the centaurs. When the centaurs in question tracked him down and discovered him without enough coin they whipped him and almost finished him off, as is their custom in dealing with men.

Somehow Arizel's identity as a prince was confirmed. He made a deal with the centaurs in order to obtain the desired book. Arizel, perhaps by his reckoning of the star charts, as rumour asserts, knew that the turning of the age would soon be upon the Ancient Rises of Nystol. Through his augury and communications with underworld figures like the kleptarch Gulathar, Arizel found secret knowledge of a diabolic design. It was a plot aiming at destruction for the famous Nystol, long planned for and in the final stages of preparation.

The barbaric Maharim, a horde of chariot and horse riding nomads from the hinterlands, of fierce aspect and painted torsos, had found a way to endure the high desert encompassing Nystol. Like other barbarians, their ferocity is displayed in that many of them enter combat without armour or even a shirt. On their chariots they tie the heads of their slaughtered foes. It as a sign of war prowess. For this new campaign untold booty was promised them. All they had needed was a treacherous agent.

Arizel, once trained in Nystol, but now an avowed and twisted enemy, had paid a great chest of gold to win that role. Arizel offered to disclose the plan to the centaurs. When the time came, he would announce to the Maharim a centaur alliance, and would give them a part in the planned Mahark sack of Nystol and its subsequent plunder. The Maharim would be forced to agree or else the final stage, the treachery, would not unfold. The centaurs agreed and Arizel won the book.

In the end, the centaurs themselves never made it to look upon the Great Burning of Nystol. "Arizel the Mad" escaped, but with his madness having increased through guilt and the wrath of the gods, he came to so horrible a mental state of despair that he mutilated his own flesh.

As for Arizel's treasure chest of gold which "won him the right to betray the civilized world," legend claims that it is cursed with a glyph of insanity. Not able to undertake the long labours of translation, Arizel spent his last years dictating the Commentary on the twenty second book. After he passed away, the text was stored in Azerdon and later recovered by Rumilian Scribes. Various important extracts and quotes from the original have been used by me. For a third derivation of extracted verses I have been provided with The Foundation Texts, (Krithusel's Fragments).

When Nystol was engulfed by flame and its vast libraries of magic scrolls went up in smoke, many of its sorcerers were burned alive, and the aeon truly ended. For a hundred years no sorcery vexed men, nor did any dare enter the haunted ruins rising far above the desert wastes.

(Gloss found at end of this leaf: It is said in another place that

Arizel, Adeuces, and/or the monk, had come up with the sinister plan of
burning Nystol when residing at the Monastery of the Weeping
Brotherhood and witnessed the book burnings, however Mercurius Yod
assigns guilt of Nystol's demise not to them, but to Nuzzib.)

Then one Krithusel the Eleusinion, a dwarflike being with a
curly beard and a daring sense of adventure, entered into the forgotten
crypts of Nystol and found vast sections of half burnt scrolls and books.
His most important find, for our purpose, was a singed copy of a
collection of favourite Illystran verses, a *florilegium*, as well as several
other valuable works probably written by the scribes of Morpheus
Memnos, great Sage of the ancient world. Was this an original tome of
the infamous "*Black Books*"? These were attached to Epinanaus' history
in appropriate places by Olusius. (The greatest number of verses, of
course, come from Epinanaus' Anamnesis of Hepthe concerning the
33rd volume, which may indeed be the famous Neoplatonic
Meta-prophecies of Gnotus the bronze dragon!)"

"You speak of many things demanding deep study," Epinanaus
"and you have gleaned much that most scribes overlook. Therefore I will
submit to your request and divulge my entire story which prove the truth
of your research..."

Hepthe soon told about what became of him after the ambush of
24 AF, which I witnessed and have already described, (and which I
assure you treasonous elements had prepared within the Imperial
ranks),

So Hepthe revealed all that had transpired:

"I knew beforehand the likelihood that demonic powers would
somehow eventually gain entry and extract information from me, I never
entered any houses on my journeys, but only monasteries and
hermitages which are protected. I also took the precaution of imbibing a
potion designed by the thaumaturges of Vesulum which can mask
certain areas of the brain so that the *diabolus* will not be able to access.
So I have done it, and now I will pass this final thing to you, a thing
which that devil could not extract. You alone will remain with it after the
assassins come for me.

What I saved concerned things I saw shortly after our infamous
day of being ambushed all those years ago. The centaurs took the mules
and me carrying the tomes east and south to the vast grasslands of
Mahanaxar, naked, bound about the torso with chain and kept alive on
sollick lizard flesh. They used several volumes as kinder for the evening
campfires. Each night a few pages they tore asunder and burned, and at
one solar setting they amused themselves by coercing me to cast my own
books into the bonfire.

These same savage centaurs, some forty of them, drank

themselves into a frenzy and planned war games and fought with each other while the sun sank beyond the western shores. My feet were sorely scarred and the centaurs handled me as if I were captured game.

These were not the worst torments. The horrid horseflies of Mahanaxar brought me to the point of insanity whilst they stung my face and back freely under the sweltering heat. On the ninth sun fall, after all day spent jogging with an brass coil around my neck, one of the centaur masters saw fit to beat me harshly for daring to speak.

This centaur called 'Orgo of the swift council', being a creature of high intellect and of some savage charm, with lyre did he sing many a song of the high plains. Of centaur-battles he sang, and the worship of planets which sail the heavens. I memorized his favorite ballad. It is an ancient poem from the savage Orcodon Paenisula in the tropical East. The Spartans, the only men brutal enough to settle in colony in those monster-infested lands, had conducted many wars against the native inhabitants. In one song, the Spartan King Sopoliton sings of how after being blessed by the gods with victory in war, he in turn lost his beloved horse Dandylon, the most beautiful horse in the world:

Let me tell you of my steed Dandylon
Who drinks from the river Eurotas
Cooling his mane beneath the shady cypress
Let me speak of his long waiting
Untold of the beastly Gyrops
Who dwells in the caves of Kakon
Who drinks from the river Eurotas
Who sings the song of our longing
Who bewails the death of our brothers
And grows the beard of long living
Dandylon danced on the banks of the river
Tall mighty and proud,
Dandylon shed gold from his eyelashes
when he beheld the setting sun
As the sun sunk upon the pillars of night
Dandylon startled in sleep and neighed
Gyrops tore at his flesh afrenzied
In the dawn I came a mightily
Eyes weathered in the Bacchanal of night
In the dawn I came sorely
Upon the steed Dandylon lacerated and dead
I saw bees feasting on his carcass
upon the steed Dandylon once fair
Who drunk from the river Eurotas

For whatever reason, the centuar Orgo loved this rhyme, and I would sing it for him, and his brutality would cease. Then one day I foolishly offered to write it down.

The centauri roam the lands lawlessly and live by ransoms pressed upon the plain folk, and learning nothing of writing they keep their life and history upon the winged words of evening song.

Now my offer was taken therefore as insult. For this Orgo beat me senseless. After all the bitter pain had passed, starry Night covered heaven's dome with her tresses.

All the horse-beasts had slipped into sleepy oblivion, but cool breezes stirred the thunder-footed centaur Orgo, ever-restless, awake. So uprose this one and seeing me his captive, laying there in ruin, perhaps knew something of remorse or pity. He flung a wineskin unto me, something which before they never had afforded me. Mayhap chastened by the thought of his own earlier ferocity and cruelty towards me, the heavenly powers put it in his bestial heart to leave a way of escape for the prisoner, and he offered only this word:

"A captive once, I myself had been, so now likewise unlock yourself, human, secretly escaping by use of my comb. Give thanks to great Valherc, son of Ulthuring, gladiator of the Uriod, who was once my liberator. Now my debt to him is paid." So he spake and letting fall his hairpin and comb to the ground nearby, the centaur returned to his slumber aside the dying embers of bonfire.

I did prevail to free myself with the hairpin that very night, for I was certain that they were saving me as an offering, a sacrificial victim for the planet Saturn, which was to rise in two days.

Divine protection did fall upon me, for the centauri do each day sleep off their wine late into morning. Away from them and far off I ran. Only the horseflies would catch wind of it, and they too would not stir until towards noon.

The next day the Sun mercilessly cast noon shafts of punishment upon the earth, but I was free."

Rénu

"That is no little accomplishment, Hepthe, or divine grace. Were all the tomes destroyed?"

Hepthe looked at me as if I had not been listening, and did not answer, but continued the story of how he was restored to civilization.

"I met a traveler on the road and found by inquiry the way out of Mahanaxar. I made way to the Ancient Rises of Nystol, a high wind-swept mesa lost in the unearthly deserts of The Dry Blood Dunes and Kedemoth, some thirty leagues to the south and east of here.

Never have my travels before taken me there, but many say that sorcerers and adepts still do there reside partaking of Ethereal draughts, foolishly savoring life spans extended into centuries. They do not rightly reason that such designs offend the All ruler, and that by living beyond what is allotted by "the gods" they risk falling into ways of injustice.

To such a place most mortals will not venture, even the strongest of warriors. I knew that I must go there regardless, lest the memory of the past be forfeit forever, and all our efforts unto republican restoration fail. One thing brought me confidence: while escaping the centaur band I had stealthily reclaimed the thirty-third tome.

It was soon afterwards that I learned of the fall of the republic and the assassination. I was hoping to offer the surviving tome to the Library of Forgotten Worlds, that I might receive in return no little sum of coin whereby to avoid servitude.

At Nystol they fed me well and I slept in silken sheets. However, the next day I retracted my offer under the shocking discovery that the Thesprotean adepts of Nystol were communing with the dead at the Pool of the Ghost king Narcissus, the Grecian lord of legend, a suspicion not without real foundation. So I instead kept the book, fleeing back to the merciless desert in fear for my soul. The pool, it is said, reflects mysterious images which captivate the human spirit. I realized this the moment when I spotted one initiate gazing into the pool, frail and with seemingly soulless eyes. That moment I resolved to have nothing more to do with the place. While in polite discussion with a notable adept. I asked for conduct across the desert. They refused. I asked for a camel. They remained silent. So I fled at the first possible instance of unguardedness.

I should not speak of what troubles the years brought me between the day I left Nystol and my expulsion from the nomads of the Deadly Hills."

So went Hepthe's account of the years that transpired in his new freedom. There lingered in me some suspicion about this man, my guest, a stranger, a wanderer upon the broad earth. Survival in Kithom and the parched deserts was a minor challenge for him. That was clear enough. Had he thrown in with the sand-pirates of the Dry Blood Dunes? Nor did I dare ask him what became of the *Black Book*, but I suspect he sold it to regain his freedom.

The late hour arrived and I set out the straw mat for him. He stretched out on it for the night. It was then that I spotted something alarming. There was a tattoo painted on the inside of his arm: nothing less than the triple-headed snake-pattern of Master-thief Godiun Foute!

5

There was a knock on the door. Six knocks to be precise; an event unexpected.

"Do not answer, Epinanaus." Hepthe warned. "Who's to say if it is not an assassin, one who has at last tracked me down and has come to make quick work of both you and me with dagger or crossbow."

"I do not scare so easily."

"Have you ever seen an Ataluran rim-dagger? In obtaining the knowledge I have given you, we are the last vessels of hope for the old republic."

"Do others know what you know? I suspect, Hepthe, that you know it be no assassin, but the poor man we have neglected these past few days, who has come no doubt near starvation. He howls like a beast to keep predators away from him, predators who detect that he is weak. Is this how you treat your slaves, Hepthe? Did your years serving under me teach you so little of human decency and kindness? I will answer the door. I will defy your fear and superstition. You who accept hospitality from me must not encourage others to ignore the laws of hospitality which all civil men accept."

"Epinanaus! I say to you, IT IS NO MAN! Do not open."

So I opened the door, and there before me stood a man, apparently, and one who did not look in any way hostile or wicked, but whose face had a kind expression. Unshaven, he was garbed as a primitive, in skins, like some caveman. He glanced at Hepthe, then back at at me.

"Has my master not seen fit yet to forgive my failures?" he asked in a soft pleading voice. "I am in great need of food and shelter, friend. I have eaten all the local mushrooms and berries; nothing is left, and your blanket will not shelter me from the coming storm. Please have pity on me....!"

"No Epinanaus! Do not invite that pit-borne devil in here or give him anything! I forbid you to even speak with him further." Hepthe spoke sternly. "Do you not realize what that creature can do?"

The ragged man looked at me with worried eyes.

"My master punishes me, friend. He has lost his right mind. It has been this way many moons now. He thinks that I am assassin waiting for the right moment, or that I am one who is somehow involved in a conspiracy with someone called the Red Ascetic. I do not even know who the Red Ascetic is! Do I look like a devil? I am just a simple man of Rumilian descent, a carpenter originally. Do you not hear him, good sage? He cannot even admit that I am just like both of you. He is clever in this, convincing even a sage to cooperate in such cruel enormities now for many nights. He is truly mad. However I am loyal, even as a slave. I am loyal and attend to my master no matter what, for that is our way."

"Lies he speaks Epinanaus! I say to you, this man is really a devil. He was sent from the very underworld city of Dis to harass me. He's a Vecradian Devil come to administer strict justice for my sins. God allows it. Do you not know that a devil can take on the likeness of men? What sort of man could just survive on his own for a week in that desert? Look at him. He is not starving. He is a wolf in sheep's clothing! Let him stay out there with the framexes."

"Enough!" I said, "I have had enough of your bizarre Ammouric superstitions."

"So you will let him in? Then, Epinanaus, I say to you, if you do you will soon be pleading for our Ammouric superstitions. But it will take a *selva*, a priest, to exorcize this place, and they are hard to find. One must go all the way to Vesulum. Do not be a fool, Epinanaus. Not only will you defile this hermitage and put your own soul in the hazard, but the restoration of the old republic will get out of reach. You know it and I know it; if the old republic is not restored, if laws inculcating virtue in the citizens not enforced, the world will grow dim again. The assassination of Emperor Florians was only the beginning. Nations will soon find themselves in great conflict. Then the prophesied All-war must commence, culminating in an entire age of ignorance and darkness. Is that what you want? Let this devil in and he will make sure your histories are never finished. This creature has the power of mind-search, he can obtain all that is kept in our minds, all information involving the counter-conspiracy, including highly confidential things I have not yet revealed to you. But in order to do so he must be invited in."

"Do you really expect me, Hepthe, a man of reason and superior education, to accept such hogwash? This one standing before us is flesh and blood, a man in need of help. How can you be so cruel?"

"If you do not believe me, Epinanaus, then ask him his name."

"What is your name?" I asked, turning to the ragged slave.

"As long as I am treated as an outsider," he said, "does it matter what is my name? I am nothing more than an animal to you. But you will always remember me." He turned so as to walk away back into the cold night.

"Wait," I said.

"Epinanaus, let him go," Hepthe urged. "You have chosen well. Do not second guess. Devils will not give their names for fear that an exorcist use it to banish the thing back to the abyss."

What Hepthe said made sense, but the feeling of pity was still with me. His use of the word "abyss" however caused me to pause. The whole concept of abyss, or void, is something that we Neoplatonics and Eldarks reject. To my knowledge, even the Ammouric theologians do not accept it. There is only the "non-void." So this ignorant reference to something of completely outlandish cosmology suddenly irked me. I wanted to resist Hepthe.

"Wait, poor man," I said before he stepped off the poarch. "Come, stay here for tonight. We have wine, warmth, and bread. It is okay, come."

He turned back and looked sharply at me. He immediately stepped across the threshold.

After that I remember very little.

The entity morphed into its true form, a hideous devil with horns, entirely black. He grinned and spread his featherless bat wings which enshadowed all about. With his claw-hand he smote me down. He approached Hepthe and grabbed the man's head with his huge talons. Hepthe started shaking as the devil drew from his brain all the information he was seeking.

While the thing was concentrating on this theft, I took it as my chance to check him. I grasped my quarterstaff, a blessed instrument, and stepped toward the enemy to strike. Before I could even make a swing, the creature's black tail, long twisting and rope-like, having terrible little spikes, wrapped around my neck as if it had a life of its own.

The coils squeezed so that I could not take in air. I dropped the quarterstaff and tried to tear it off me, but to no avail. The thing was too strong.

Shortly I passed out. The last thing I saw was the creature reveling, his bright white fangs grinning, his sinister white eyes rolled back in glee, as it sucked up information from Hepthe, laughing.

mzáᵠⲧⲩ

The next morning Hepthe awoke me.

"Do you realize what you have done?"

I said nothing but only looked down.

"The alliance of free peoples is completely compromised now, Epinanaus. It shall not recover for decades, rather for centuries...aye, perhaps never."

"Where has the devil gone?"

"Who knows...with the information he copied he now has the identities of all our informants...probably to Regulum he has flown, or

Tyrnopolis, or perhaps first to the Dry Blood Dunes. He will easily find a way to have Imperial agents discover our operatives and promptly execute them. Who knows, he can go anywhere now. Before this he was limited to only following me because his knowledge was so scant. It is by knowledge and information that these *diaboli* make way, that's how they are transferred, by various branches of knowledge, like a serpent moving about a tree, and by the seed of sin within the fruit that is forbidden."

"We must pilgrimage to Vesulum to find a *selva*." I said, at a loss. "A *selva* can perform a banishment ceremony for us, can he not?"

"A *selva*'s power is effective on the believers who surround him. He certainly can banish any power, but the thing will in short time return and take residence in its former host. As it is written "*Some demons can only be cast out through prayer and fasting*." Therefore it is not sufficient merely to believe. You must believe strongly and you must live the faith. Then they can't touch you. So, are you a believer now?"

"The demon I saw is proof enough for me that there are entities opposed to the good. But what entity would be opposed to an impersonal good that is merely an abstraction or substance? No, these oppose the God and Father of All, the true lasting good from whom all good things derive. So rebelling does a spiritual creature turn black with evil and hatred, making an abyss of his own soul."

"Eventhough you are a fool, Epinanaus, you are only so because you have not believed. But now, after all this, you are starting to believe. You are probably the last man who can keep this crucial information."

The risk of keeping his company had been well worth it, but there can be some assurance now that those histories will be no more, even though the surviving volume with its grave implication is still within reach. To shelter a man so driven by fearsome Furies and give ear to his story, this instead we pray God will see.

Now I took on the mantle of Hepthe. I felt responsible for the deaths of many republicans by my rash descision based on a poor choice of wording.

We kept recieving news of the executions of "spies" throughout the empire that year. I could endure it no longer and resolved to make the journey to Vesulum to find a *selva*.

The account that was once told by pilgrims about the pages of an Illystra *Black Book* loosed from a mule and awash in a torrent of rain only pertains to one volume alone, the thirtieth tome, which must have fallen off one of the pack mules, frighted as he was, and separated from the other animals in the Andolyn mountains after the centaurs had attacked. It is this volume upon which a great mystery hangs.

Now there are many things that must be related concerning

Hepthe and his journeys, for they are not without considerable worth in the telling, and are the stuff it seems of fantastic legend worthy of a poem, had they not been events of historic and prophetic consequence.

My encounter with the centaurs and their work of bloodshed had left me with an appreciation of the brevity of life, and especially a sense that the Christ must govern men not only beyond the grave, but even in this life.

He is a king, and like any king, enemies work to undo his kingdom.

Even more impressed was I that there had been someone who loved his fellow countrymen so much that he died in my steed.

There are other things connected with these events which must not be neglected. Old Budderham helped us to bury the twenty-two corpses of the soldiers and men left to rot in the sun, notice came to me about one soldier who was Rumilian, having not the leonine features of so many Regulians, but rather the Aquiline features of my race. Of course, this was surprising, since the only Rumilians who join up with the Legions enter as officers, hoping eventually to become Vrynth Knights.

Humour me to elaborate this point.

One would not expect a young Rumilian to have the bearing and ferocity to march and fight with Regulian troops, because certainly they excel in other areas, but are in no wise tough. We searched his corpse for identification.

My expectation was that he at least should have some writing materials on him, since Rumilians are taught from childhood to carry scroll cases or other writing equipment with them. They consider codices undignified and urbane. So it was. I found his case opened it and unrolled the scrolls. What I found was most astonishing.

In his scroll he had written several notes on the *Astronomia Prophetica* of Olyphyxus, including some sketches of animals and vegitation which he had observed on our march, as well as some sections of his diary. Now it was the usual stuff in those days.., talk about his love, missing his parents, resentment toward the centurion, an attempt at a letter, even premonitions of dread and death which he had written in the days just past.

It was in a note which he wrote on the *Astronomica Prophetica* that lifted me with great excitement of discovery; simultaneous, in a pitiful way, under present gravity for the fallen.

The note concerned his calculated rising of the planet Saturn that was due in three days. The young man, obviously far beyond his peers in education and general knowledge, asserted that Olophyxus had miscalculated the orbit of Saturn by misreading the pristine Atlantean records.

I thought little of it at first. I kept scroll, unable to return it to the family because no identification had been found on him.

Olophyxus' miscalculation which the Rumilian student detected turned out to be rather a prophetic indication, the quiet speech of the gods. In my opinion, (and as you know I am not one prone to prophecies and superstitions), the divine beings saw fit to warn the righteous of Nystol.

So in this I became a believer: it was a prophecy of the hypostatic rift which would begin with Saturn's rising that very year, in three days, culminating at last to represent the demise of the Nystol at the elyptical arcmouth of the Saturnian orbit in later terrestrial years.

Saturn rose that year on the very day the Centuar Orgo freed Hepthe! What providence! Now further things I discovered in the student's writings; going as far as to propose that although the Arrow of Talus points toward the Scorpion...

(The manuscript ends abruptly).

So passes the mysterious and unfinished History of Epinanaus...

Langstaff

DIALOGUE
WITH A STRANGER

Hieronymous Pike, the illegitimate son of King Graham, was an eccentric would-be adventurer. The action begins not long before his famous disappearance. He and his faithful Langstaff have been hired by corrupt Church officials to locate and terminate the gnome Kruth somewhere in the world's belly. Instead they used the coin to travel to the frontier town of Wyrmhole, from which are coming rumours of a dragon's horde in an abandoned tower. They rent beds for a week in town and purchase restricted weaponry in hopes to go on some sort of dragonhunt. Witnessing some unexpected violence, in fear they remain locked in their upper room. They worry not only that the local authorities consider them suspicious, but that certain other more dangerous parties are hunting them. This dialogue and last letter of Hieronymous have been preserved by Langstaff his companion.

There was a knock on the door, something which we had not been expecting and for which neither of us were prepared. The thought came to mind that whoever had slain the drunkard, now wished to eliminate witnesses. The killer had followed us here. But why would he knock first?

We suspected that some nameless peril lurked and was stalking us. Langstaff went and stood ready, positioned to hurl his spear. He raised it to impale whoever stood behind the door. I was to open the door and move aside, ready to offer my flashing blade and administer extra pain. I took up my shield and held my shortsword ready.

"Who goes there? Announce yourself." I asked to the unknown standing behind the door.

"A stranger." a voice replied. "One who wishes you good faring. —a believer. One who bears tidings precious to you, though I myself am in grave need." It seemed a gentle voice but yet of disciplined word, perhaps of an older man, carrying the well known dialect of a stern but pious people.

"I am not expecting any messenger." I replied, "I am a traveler. But it is really alms you hope for, therefore know that my purse is empty."

"I hope for no alms," he said. "There is a greater good that interests me."

"Then what is your interest, say it."

"In some small way, an increase in the sway of righteousness. Know that I bear a message to that end. It is a greater treasure than mere coin."

"Announce your name, and if you are to relay some message, do so now, or be done with this."

"My name is inconsequential. And of the message? I am a secret messenger, needing privy forum."

"Hear this, if ye will not say thy name, there will be trouble. I warn thee, I am not taking visitors...nor do I have alms left."

"Will you not for kindness sake open the door and speak with me? Among the righteous there is no suspicion, for our life is not of this world."

"I cannot take any such risk. Please, if you are a believer, know that I am a sinner and bother me no more. Look thou to the discipline of prayer instead."

"I am one who highly regards you, and I also am a sinner. I have heard that you are for the quest."

"What was that?. . . quest? I say I do not glean your meaning. But take care, the wise do not spread untaught rumour. Your mind is clouded. Away with you!"

"Your quest: it is known to me." (He answered my rebuke with a statement of provocation, one to be considered even greater impudence. I replied with corresponding indignance).

"Who is it dares speak to us in this way, with intrusive style? Have you no respect for those soon to join the dead? We are soldiers from Aquilar, passing through to fight in the wars."

"You are not." He dared the more, "With the few days left in me I hope to aid you for good cause. Take care not to be inhospitable, though it is true that we live in grim times. Open and I shall tell all."

"Indeed sir, though you are as yet unknown to me, you contradict me as false and your words will soon require satisfaction in combat."

"Satisfaction? ...in combat?....Aye, you are on a quest...but one which you fancy to be of your own contrivance."

"A quest of my own contrivance? What mean you by so daring a riddle?"

"The spirit of the truth works in strange ways." he answered, unafraid.

The call of a local peddler echoed from the street below.

It occurred to me that perhaps I was mistaken to so quickly rebuke the stranger. Indeed, by some unforseen movement of things, this unknown person, (whose tone of voice certainly sounded wise), might be a help, or if captured, he could be interrogated. I questioned him the more. For a moment he said nothing, but then I answered with an utterance of my own.

". . .So do many work in strange ways. But tell, what helpful word can you offer other than what is masked in riddles?"

"Every man about to launch upon an unfamiliar enterprise, however wise, needs the advice of those who have precise knowledge of things."

The strange reply caused me wonder. "You seem to have a ready answer for everything...Are you a churchman? Clergy?" I demanded.

"No, just a believer, as I have said."

"Grim are the times indeed when divine mysteries are so quickly invoked to explain the obvious. Learn this and you may perceive why I am not quick to open: today an unknown hunter, an assassin, hooded and dark, nearly fell me like a stag, though poorly aimed were his poisoned shafts. One poor soul, but a street-fellow who walked by to me, was silenced by those death-bearers hurtling through air."

"I gained intelligence of that...from talk overheard about the town. Yet one eyewitness is better than ten hear-sayers. Let me in, for this killer is known to be a monk, the kind from whom is heard no songs."

"Strangers cannot easily be trusted, as of old, and men everywhere hide daggers for one another. Therefore, pray thee, since I am a man with enemies, say what quest ye do discern of me, for I know naught of any quest, but am a traveler, curious as to the ancient ruins, and shocked to witness violence in the streets." I spoke this in a clever way, testing him.

Birds outside chirped their daily chirp as I awaited answer.

"Ancient ruins indeed." He replied with sarcasm, "You design to enter into lowest dungeons by means of breaking into yon eld tower. You hope to follow the forbidden tunnels deep into the nether-kingdoms, in order to make crusade and war against hell, and thereby win renown and plenty."

"Who told you of this?" I demanded.

"A certain mind, a friend from the hills, whose magical ability is renowned."

"A certain mind? A sorcerer, doubtless, whose company is with demons having many ears. My purpose is something that I do not publish abroad."

"He is no conjurer, but a power, one with whom you yourself have some acquaintance...one whose name is not found in the annals of men: Kruthius Eleusinion."

"You know the one whom men call "The Eleusinion?" Tell me where he is, and perhaps I will let you in."

"No doubt the Prime Interquist has paid you well."

"I know naught of what you speak. How is it that you know The Eleusinion?"

"I have known him for many years. It is my life to do his bidding."

"Then you are vassal to him?"

"He is not one who enters into such contracts. Do you not know what order of being he is...?"

"He is a man like others, but short in stature, like the miners of the Hermit's Hills."

"He is not a man, though he is manlike."

"Then a demon who seems a man?"

"No. He is a gnome, one of the powers."

"I know him not," I replied angrily, "nor do I know of gnomes and the like. I have heard only what others say...they are reckoned trouble. Therefore be ye gone, or this chat might be your last."

"...yet Kruthius knows much of you. The madness which plagues you he considers a desirable rarity. He said that you are one for whom Reason and Common Sense are alien principles, and this fact even now you exemplify...by not opening."

"He has described me without error, indeed my reason is drowned by a will bent on a deluge of slaughter!"

"Idle talk, mere boasts..." he replied with a chuckle.

"You are in grave error," I retorted,"and you make slight of hands which are perilous. You know nothing of what you are saying. In mindless fury I will quell the deep. Has Kruthius sent you on account of me?"

"He has; do hurry and let me in, for the news you publish of the hooded assassin lurking here-bouts worries me, and no doubt his poisoned shaft was meant for me. Open and all these things will be discussed in private."

"Tell me your name and I will consider your request."

"Venerable custom recommends that the name of a suppliant be not required. I will never lie to you...it is impossible for me to confide my name to you or to any others, lest any of us who operate in secret be compromised. Still, though I must remain a stranger, I now require your sanctuary, I am one who is surely being stalked by an assassin of the highest skill. But please, let what is right prevail, for I am come for your benefit. Would thou, a believer, turn thy brother over to lions?"

"You are even now speaking with lions. Listen, stranger, there are many who believe, as ye know, and yet...do they not find themselves doing the Devil's work? I know nothing of what you speak, nor is it my custom to allow strangers in my private quarters. As far as suspicion teaches me you are the very assassin whom we earlier escaped. So consider this: There is good cause for you to dread the onslaught of the banded powers who stand here behind this door with me, irate and ready with iron as they are. You, in truth, are an enemy, or not alone, in either case, our greeting will be one of bloodshed. There are many enemies who know many things..."

"Listen to me, ye herculean mouse," He said almost angrily, "you talk on high but know little of combat...else you would not have just now given away the position of your men. Without examination of the doctrines and writings which I have prepared for you there is little chance that you and your 'banded powers' will not die miserably on the proposed expedition. Submit to the present imprudence lest a greater one befall thee."

"How do you know these things?"

"Because I myself have been to the underworld... Several times, with Kruthius, and I have firsthand knowledge of its perils."

"You have been there? Men say this: where the wind doth not blow one dare not go." With a clever warning I tried to unhorse him.

"Mere talk...but I know otherwise: there are subterraneous winds, contrary to the reports, even down there...but they are rare and slight. In lowest regions air is precious for terrestrial guests. Fire devours air, so means other than torches are best, such as the common glow worm...yet there is another way of finding one's way around down there, a way which only the initiated know... but if even that light goes out, one may be swallowed in darkness, and how great the darkness!"

"I have heard similar accounts. If you truly have been there you should also know how to survive by that knowledge of the gnome...answer a question concerning his discipline....name ye the common food of the secondary regions."

There was a brief silence. How I thought of such a question or how I ever could have verified whether his answer was correct, all was a mystery to me.

"Rats, preferably stuffed with mushrooms, though if the rodents are scarce one may hunt other, more dangerous creatures, such as grey mammoth."

At that moment it seemed like instinctual knowledge. Now I actually thought of opening and letting him in. I glanced for a judgement from Langstaff. He kept his peace and nodded, frowning as warriors do, ready to make a surprise strike if necessary. So I continued.

"I will consent and open the door, stranger, but first let me know that you are at a safe distance: the foot of the stairs. Do this by returning back down. We wish to see you at a distance first, knowing that you are come in peace. One can never be too careful, sorcerers and thieves have been known to disguise their voices as kindly folk."

"It is common news that men of evil-design are abroad. I consent to thy request."

We listened to his steps as he descended down the creaking wooden stairs. I opened the door and saw no others in the hallway. Then we looked down the stairs and saw the man looking back up at us from below. His appearance was amazing. He had a greyish-white mane of hair that fell with wild strands to his shoulders, a length rarely seen. The eyes were crystals of fire, yet kind and filled with what seemed untold experiences of illumination. He had no beard but only whiskers, having been for many days unshaven, and his sun-baked skin had many wrinkles and lines. He was well built for an older man, and had the look of certainty in his stride.

"Put up thy sword into thy scabbard." He said as he made his way back up the stairs to the landing. He arrived at the top of the stairs and reached out to take my forearm in the grasp of greeting, and while doing this spoke.

"Quickly, let us close ourselves in so that I may speak freely." We conducted him back into the room and sat the old man down at the little table with the burning lamp. Langstaff surveyed him, did not take his eyes off of him the whole time, and closely noted everything, (as he is accustomed).

After having bolted tightly the door and drawn the shutters, I poured him the wine of greeting. So after doing that service I began:

"We have some room and blankets, stranger, need you bide here until daylight."

"I will depart early in the morning," he replied. "In dawn's light before the rise of the sun I go. By then, the assassin, wherever he may be, will have succumbed to all-conquering sleep."

"How art thou keen on his sleeping habits?" I asked with concern. "Do ye have reported intelligence or is he an enemy born of friendship turned bitter?"

"Neither of what you guess, but it is known to the wise that the wicked cannot rise early, or at least not before dawn. He is a monk, but not of an Ammouric order. Rather of an infernal order be he, and they do not rise and pray at dawn like the true monks. Nor do they esteem the sun's rays."

"I know nothing of such monks," I confessed. "though I have heard some strange news that devotees of the old gods still walk the green earth. How any lawful folk could warrant them to gather I do not follow."

"These monks are not the kind of which ye have heard, but the assassin is vowed to an order of another and worse kind. They are those who do acknowledge Reason's natural teaching, that there is but one creator, but they are lost in Sin's distortion. They refuse right homage and rather exalt the evil one as creator. Not tolerated on the surface, they dwell below, only coming forth to pursue some wicked purpose which concerns the demonic powers."

"So what purpose do they now pursue?"

"We do not know. Yet I am now certain that the one whom you encountered has been looking for me in here in Wyrmhole."

"And how did you know that we were come hither?"

"I did not, but the Eleusinion sent me, and one does whatever he says without question. He gave me no instructions other than this enigmatic command: 'Go ye to Wyrmhole and find the forgetful, they who have become fools, and teach thou them.' So I did it."

"And how is it that you learned of us here?"

"I heed Kruth's word and arrived in Wyrmhole a few days ago. Since then I have been wandering the town looking for foolish men. I knew by experience that he does not speak thus in generalities, but was referring to specific men whom he did not wish to name. Certainly there are few here who might be called wise. Then I heard that strangers had been detained for "knavish action resulting in the death of a citizen", and immediately I suspected that they might be those for whom I do seek. After your release I followed ye here to these quarters."

"This meeting is therefore founded on some error." I alerted the old man with polite correction. "I had, not long ago, requested that your master accept me as a disciple, by written correspondence. He firmly rejected my request. We must not therefore be the fools thou seekest."

"The gnome does not answer a letter with another letter. If thou intend to raze Hell, than thou art in truth fools enough." He announced with unwavering gaze. "Such a hope devoid of common sense is of the same mind as the master's, so surely thou art the same whom he has reconoitered. In the kingdom entire such profoundly foolish as ye are indeed rarity. Kruth informed me that a certain noble had written to him seeking knowledge, that he had sought to dissuade the fool, but to no avail. You are this fool. So he now offers this to you: if you refuse to follow his advice, then obey his command. Enter the Guild."

"Guild...?"

"Our underground network, organized in an unearthly fashion by the gnome himself."

"A network...? Why did Kruth not come himself?"

"A gnome cannot appear in the towns of men: he fears for his capture. Besides, he is being hunted, hunted by much worse than an underworld monk."

"Hunted? By whom then?"

"Rather 'by what?' We do not know, but the being is powerful."

"How powerful?"

"Some inhuman power, non-natural, perhaps an automaton of some sort."

"A what...?"

"An automaton, a non-living mobile tracker, probably directed by a remote demonic intellect. Its difficult to say for certain, most of the enemy's abominations are made of refined matter and leave almost no traces...a beast of the netherlands."

"I no longer wish to be involved in this."

"You are already involved. This entity may even now have hold of Kruth and have used torture to learn your identity."

"Does this netherbeast also seek me?"

"It seeks someone fitting your description and seems to be on your trail. That may be how it picked up Kruth's position.

"How do you know?"

"Kruth discerned these things through his gnomic power of echo-perception, that is, his ability to discern sub-sensory echoing. The beast is unable to properly mask the noise it makes while navigating the terrestrial sphere. In time it will find you unless you first hunt it down."

"By St. Michael, I'll wait till it finds me and I will proceed in cutting it to pieces."

"When it finds you, it will wait. In short time will ambush you at unawares. It will seize you when you are unarmed or asleep. No, you must hunt and strike first."

"How can I hunt something that leaves no traces?"

"There are methods which the Guild will disclose."

"What does this hellish fiend want of me?"

"Enslavement to its service. Your ability to learn coupled with a foolish mind as well as disinterest in what most men cherish. These are rare and highly valued by the demonic powers. It may also be seeking certain information as well."

"How could it have known about me?"

"That is what I am here to find out." He looked at me and waited, expecting an explanation. No doubt my mouth was agape with perplexity at this point.

"It appears to know many things about you, probably more than we. You are an illuminator of manuscripts?"

"By trade, I have been trained well for illuminating works of the sacred scribes. I am now retired from such labours."

"That makes reason...perhaps the underworld monks desire that skill for some cause. Mayhap they wish to publish some book of devilry. One shouldn't wonder, they have done like things in the past. But how came they to know about you is mysterious."

He continued, realizing that I had no explanation.

"It may also be seeking certain information as well."

"What information?"

"We do not know...possibly something you may have heard or seen once perhaps, usually it's a name, sign, or symbol. We know nothing of its dark intent. Master Kruth needs you. He needs one who is reckless enough to brave the darklands, and one not lacking virtue...but also one who foolishly accepts restrictions on knowledge, so that in torture the enemy will not be able to draw   information from you."

"—Torture? That is not possible. I will die before capture."

"Unfortunately things don't always work out that way. For example, he sent me here knowing that the thing stalking him would most likely capture him, and that since I know certain information which he has forbidden himself to learn, the entity might only obtain partial information. Nor could I do anything to protect him against so powerful a netherbeast, though my training is complete. His decision was an offensive measure, since any defensive move is useless."

"Is this some accursed game of blind man's chess?!"

"I am not certain. Perhaps you might see it as a sort of dragonhunt. You are mistaken if you hope to do an old-fashioned "dragon-slaying." Even down in the underdyrth it is common news that dragons are unsearchable. They cannot be found."

"They go into aeon-rest, a sort of hibernation. Someday soon they might again awake."

"A misunderstood prophecy of popular interest...it is firmly held by all who have experience in the study of the ages that the dragons are forever occulted. However, there are places that no one has gone to in thousands of years...like the Giganth."

"Giganth?"

"The lost prison under earth, confines of the terrible powers from the first world. Listen: rumour has it that the subterraneous monks possess the last of the four keys to its unassailable bronze doors."

"And it is these infernal monks, part-time assassins like our poorly-aiming friend, which I also shall be fighting?"

"No doubt, "the hooded ones," they call themselves, as well as others who hold common league; the monks are both the primary publicists for codices of unholy doctrine as well as the keepers of the cult of the dead. Other foul organizations are known to share agreed cause with them. The strength of such underworld groups is in obedience and conformity of members to a higher will, a stern discipline which many who fight for Truth have forgotten."

"Very well, where do we find them?"

"They operate *in occulto*, similar to the Guild, but unlike us, they are not subject to Truth. Their members are a loose organization, rarely meeting in a known place. Nor can we know for certain if any of our members treacherously work for the enemy, (though it has never been discovered). We have reason to think that there may be infiltration, since we have been losing much ground of late. None of us ever thought that Kruth's operating positions could be discovered. Perhaps the demons have led a soul astray. Much is uncertain, much is unknowable."

"Is there anything certain that you DO know?!"

"The tower yonder will indeed connect thee to the lower world."

"Have you been inside of it?"

"No, but the Eleusinion has; Be there nay anything of worth down in its subterrene corridors, save for a few bronze armlets adorning the skeletons of ancient heathens. Let them rest if it is granted to them. Kruth locked up the tower himself in order to keep out creatures, not keep them in. You were correct however to follow the image of a tower, if by dream or other insight, or how thou knew, I know not."

"Then you will lead us from there into the underworld?"

"I am restricted to the surface. I can only point the way, and give thee certain knowledge. Kruth gave no sign of my next assignment."

"What certain knowledge?"

"I will cause thy mind to bring forth arcane memories which are lost to thy waking thoughts. These are keys to insight, what the Grecian philosophers called *anamnesis*. We in the Guild do not rely on history books, which are usually have grave omissions, or are errant, twisted or even falsified. We rely on memory and Kruth's philosophic tradition. By this power of memory the philosophers see many-"

"Wait, hold on now," Langstaff interrupted "this is of no avail to us. Are you here to talk philosophic drivel? Train us in war if thou art able."

"As I said, I can only do the thing which Kruth has assigned, and I may do no more. You should follow my example."

"Be thou patient, brother. Langstaff studied philosophy and received only the bitings of the horse. What did you intend to say?"

"You must consider the strange doctrines I will utter, clothed in philosophic garb, for these teachings will be of far greater use in battle than your hands. There are three codes which must be acknowledged by those who wish success in this endeavor."

"Codes?"

"The paths of sacred insight have certain codes. The first is that you will be driven, you will never find rest, there will never be a time when your knowledge is complete. Even if your body and mind wear out, the living soul will continue plumbing the depths. The second is that you are not to hope for personal triumph, but only for success of the Guild, and for the revelation of the Truth to the many.

"And the third?"

"That all your judgements reckon thou with divine providence out of deep respect. All things have their origin in the Transcendent Annointed. By this benediction new memories thou shalt realize...and thy true nature, and so may you accomplish what you were sent to do."

"That was vague enough. I was sent to do something? But no one sent me, I came here for my own interest."

"So you did...and in chains of darkness. The Lord of Hosts has prepared a mission for you, which you seem to have forgotten. We must determine what this mission was originally. Kruth's philosophic principles will activate areas of the mind, nay of your being self, which will expose the truth; *Anamnesis* will clarify much that is obscure. Not all things can be recalled. Indeed, you have already much innate knowledge: of underworld lore and of combat, these are curled up in the secret burrows of thy own mind, I am here to smoke them out."

"Strange...but how will you do this?"

"Actually I already am doing it, and soon I will cast burning torches, as it were, into the dead forest of thy wide-branching thoughts, flaming cinders prepared by Kruth. In this way a blaze will alight in thy interior darkness, and soon the entire under-forest will be lit in brilliant flame, and thou shalt remember many things, and understand fully what were only shadowy dens before."

"But this will not avail my skill in combat. It cannot help me to subdue a netherbeast or giant."

"It is time to bring thy belief to a new depth. The greatest warriors have moves which are faster than their minds, and this is a skill which is dangerous, something which only Ammouric Knights may lawfully use, since they subject their bodies to training and prayer, and their minds to contemplation of the Good. As a member of The Guild, you also shall have an ability similar to this, but of a different power than a warrior. Force has no place where there is need of skill."

"How so?"

"You will have the powers of stealth, as certain thieves employ, and you will attack thy enemies with speed and precision rather than crushing might."

"This sounds to me like a Thieving Guild. Is that what you are then, some sort of thieving guild? Bloody redhands be ye, against the lives of innocent sojourners and decent men, ye snatchers of life-earned fortunes from old widows, or ye mauraders upon the high sea, greedy churls for imperial loot?"

"Admittedly, we must claim remnant pedigree descended from such folds. But rush thou not to judgement, it is not measured as you say."

"Offer just one reason that we should not butcher you where you sit."

"Our guild is comprised of men who use no violence against the innocent, nor do they seize what is not lawfully theirs. Rather we are a fellowship of reparation for such sinners. You see, we are the Guild of Saint Dismas."

"Saint Dismas...?"

"The thief crucified at the right hand of Our condemned Lord in his great Passion. Have you no familiarity with the famous account?"

"Only that two thieves were crucified next to the God-man. For it is written: *And with him they crucify two thieves; the one on his right hand, and the other on his left. And the scripture was fulfilled, which saith, And he was numbered with the transgressors.*"

"Aye," said Langstaff. "It was so on the great day of the Lord. One of the malefactors who hung next to Christ impiously railed against his majestic divinity, that the *Deus Omnipotens* ought demonstrate his pedigree and bring them down from those deadly gibbets of woe. *If thou be Christ, save thyself and us.*" What a thing to say.

"And the other?"

"The other responed something wisely," I said. "Some noteworthy rebuke...but I recall it not."

"Do you not harken when at Church, warrior?"

I answered no answer to the mouthy stranger, but turned to Langstaff.

"Langstaff, you possess faith in heeps. Certainly you must know the words."

"I do. Hear what rebuke he answered the blasphemer, aye," acknowledged Langstaff. "Be it something like this; the good thief saying, *"Neither dost thou fear God, seeing thou art in the same condemnation? And we indeed justly; for we receive the due reward of our deeds: but this man hath done no mischeif."* Then turning unto the Lord requested of him: *"Lord, remember me when thou comest into thy kingdom"* The crucified God-man unto him answered, *"Yea verily, this eve shalt thou partake with me in paradise."* In such a startling way with mere words did the thief actually steal for himself the precious salvation which is something without price. So all the upright confess that him a saint, Dismas by name."

"...and he is our patron, the benefactor of our order."

"Heaven will not vouchsafe such a churlish order of cutpurses and redhands, mauraders and horsethieves. Upon what weird plane of existence have you too long tarried, stranger?"

"All men are sinners, friend. All are deserving of condemnation.

Does not the sleek nobleman, popular, kind, and celebrated by all, even so totter on the brink of Hell as he looks askance at the emaciated beggar who cries out for crumbs at the door of the manor? Is he not also in some way guilty of theft? Will not God come for him in the end like a thief in the night and despoil him even of his famous name?

"Some souls do choose and change their ways, but still need the assistance of a beneficial organization. The Church herself once served in this capacity. Now for wolves she is become all ruiniuos in her corruption. We are a remnant flock pure which is loyal to her original mission, attached to her, but must remain secret so as to be preserved.

"When a man has lived his life from youth snatching the livelihood of others who were his prey, aye, he is indeed worthy of hanging. Even so, this may be the only way he has known. We afford him with another way, provided that he repent of his former deeds. In our organization, which is very old, he may live as a penitent, doing right deeds in our martial service as a servant of the Church. He uses all the thieving skills of his many years at the service of those who make war against Hell. With his skills of hiding in shadows, or traversing silently, climbing walls, and picking locks he does whats right and wins salvation like St. Dismas. In such a way he may make reparation, assisting us to rescue souls from the great prison, souls trapped in the Netherworld."

"How possibly could the fallen talents of a thief rescue poor souls trapped in the Netherworld?"

"Why, I have done so myself. We steal poor souls from the jaws of oblivion. Once we extracted the souls of ancient men under a great bronze lock and key. It was an entire army, hoplite warriors from worlds past, Argives and Authapians that had been captured down deep in the Giganth. The lock itself was larger than Langstaff here. Who knows how long they had been down there forgotten and suffering, unable to escape. But the Lord God did not forget them. He used my very mind to undo the Gordian device and free many souls all at once. That was a moment of glory. Such satisfaction can be yours as well, provided that thirst for silver and gold does not hold back your heart."

"I have no thieving skills useful for such ventures, nor does Langstaff here. I tell you, we are merely hot for war and the seizure of booty from the tombs of pagan kings or draconian lairs. You have come to the wrong men. I am a warrior-poet, and Langstaff here is both a feared pikeman and a learned philosopher. We never have been employed as thieves. Let us therefore end this vain discussion with polite regard and send you on your way."

"I am afraid that you have again jumped to conclusions. Our organization is no longer the employer solely of thieves who are in need to doing penance. The Guild has has grown over the years and welcomes the contributions of just about every kind of sinner. We not only have under our employ ex-assassins, cutpurses, and robbers, but also retired taxmen, extortionists, beaurocrats, and politicians, and alien scribes and translators, book-binders and map-makers, masters of espionage, rogue priests and ousted bishops, unorthodox scientists and obscurant mathematicians, alchemists, retired wizards and unlicensed magic-users of all sort, errant knights, outlaw rangers, and wandering monks, barbarians and exiled kings, cooks, bards and jesters, and every manner of fighting armsmen. We are as a crew of a naval ship at sea, being in need of every sort of talent. Our operations are no small sticks. Therefore put aside that vain argument. It is time to mature in your faith. You are a believer, as you have said. So now it is time to be put to the test. God wills it. We shall train you in fighting underground and in narrow places."

"You seek religious-minded men who have turned to God and been restored to good character. Therefore forget about me. I am a man of the worst temperments by nature."

"Go down on your knees and thank God for such a temperament." He said, to my amazement. "For surely it is highly probable that, had you a good temper, being obliging, peaceful, and kind by nature, little supernatural grace could be activated in you. Suppose you were the kind of man who always says yes instead of no, surely your generous acts of risk would not be known as the work of divine grace. Grace now will come in the form of training."

Having no answer to this imposition I simply frowned.

"I know how to defend myself well enough by my own power, without all manner of training."

"You are valued not for your recklessness, though that may avail our cause if well channeled, but for your eagerness to seek trials, as well as your absurd abandonment to the study of ancient poetry. You did not know how to defend yourself when enemies nearly slew you last Thursday on the way here, did you? That was for the better, even had ye prevailed for a time, you would have been defeated anyway."

"You know of that?! How?"

"I heard of it from one of the members of The Guild. He it was who brought you back from the brink of death."

"What was his name, please tell me, that I might pray for him."

"I cannot utter anyone's name, as I said before, not a name of a member in The Guild, and I do not even know their names anyway. Such name-saying is forbidden. It would severely compromise our efforts. A name can be extracted by torture. What is worse, certain enemy sorcerers who discover names may cast their spells from afar."

"Then how is it then that this guild can operate?"

"The Guild is a stealth organization. No one's name is ever spoken, or even known, save that of Dismas the Saint who intercedes for us."

"If no one's name is known, how can the organization be controlled?"

"Only believers are admitted into its ranks. Extensive control is not necessary when men submit to a common cause. Of all men's miseries perhaps the bitterest is this: such things as politic, war, victory, and defeat, life and death, riches or poverty, are out of Man's control. Freed from this bitter desire we perceive many things otherwise obscure. The Guild is operated in a way which conforms to a long standing tradition, first developed by Ammouric Knights. It was they who first employed the thieves of Kasbur during the Wars of the Veil...a little history of the order for you..."

"Ammouri? How could that be? They are nothing but wealthy nobles who look after their own welfare. The days of the paladins have long vanished."

"No, the days are not vanished, but it is true the knights are compromised. Their brilliance, which once illumined the world with the understanding of real things, has set under a darkening sky. Now they are become the flames of torches shining in sempiternal night beneath the brooding earth."

"Torches?"

"The torch is the symbol of the Guild. Our armsmen no longer wear shining armour and ride glorious warhorses, and our deeds are in no way renowned."

"How did the Ammouri lose their glory?"

"The order of Ammouric Knighthood was betrayed. It was not just the power of evil sorcerers or the machinations of the princes of this world that brought the order down. The wicked do not have so much power. It was the shared fault of the individual members. After the knights left their posts as guardians of the sacred shrines, the Ammouric religion itself seemed changed. There were reformers who arose to confront the order, but the grand knights opposed them, unwilling to give up their comfortable lives, comforts provided by the powers that be. Some of the reformers went to the fires and became martyrs for the cause, others went underground, learned the ways of the Thieves of Kasbur, and founded the Guild."

"I have never heard such lore. In my little hometown of Arkt there are almost no learned folk. In fact, I myself cannot really say exactly where Arkt is in relation to other towns and feudatories, other than to say that we are upriver from Wyrmhole and east of the Hermit's hills. Of Nystul and the Antilynk mountains and the other lands you mention, I have but the vaguest idea. I am unable to place them accurately in my vision. Nor are there any charts to examine. We have never seen an Ammouric Knight. Nor does anyone ever speak of things which transpired in the past, wars and such, or of the ages."

"Let me bring you up to date. Learn this: the mercenary warlords of Atalur once waxed mighty in worldly strength and threatened to enslave many lands. They were kept at bay by the magics of Nystul. But another kingdom of the East, Kalar, was slowly rising in wealth and power, but had no knowledge of warfare. Bah Ukah, the Shahi and Master Occultist seized the Imperial throne of Kalar and employed the mercenaries of Atalur to spread by force his false religion: the Cult of the Veiled One. Against that masterful cult of war none could stand. Eventually it engulfed all the Eastern lands. They are the civil lands which are now closed to the West, the lands of Arraf "The Eastern Veil.""

"The Ammouric monarchies in the West banded together in an attempt to free the East, but to no avail. The crusaders were defeated in the end. The Ammouric religion had changed and it had a negative effect on the knights."

"Why did the Ammouri change?"

"It was a great change indeed. After the crusading Wars of the Veil against the Atalur and Kalar, the many knights of these our Nine Feudatories returned home. They sought to forget the woes of war and looked to entertainments of drinking and tournaments."

"Did they not accomplish deeds of martial valour, worthy of song?"

"They did; but every war of men is a world of evil. It is not simple, like hunting and slaying beasts. Many things they regretted. They hoped to ease their minds of the sins which arise in war. As they grew old they forgot the importance of discipline. Less and less were they feared."

"Why did they not pray?"

"Do thirsty men seek wine to drink? In ages long past the Furth High King, the invisible sword, had fought along with them. Then he gave them the commission and the strength of his right hand. The dread of the infidel waxed great, for the sight of just one of Ammouric swordsman could put to flight a hundred warriors.

"After the Wars of the Veil things changed. Too much worldly wealth fell into the hands of the Ammouric King of Ulthuring and his vassals. Knighthood, once a sacred service, more and more was seen as a worldly honour. The grand-knights, who should have corrected their subordinates, also fell, entranced by the beauty of their own glory. The Ammouric orders lost their original religious orientation: to guard the kingdoms and to glorify the Ancientmost by spiritual submission.

"This new generation of knights has devoted themselves to the service of fair maidens. Divine and sacred love yielded to human and profane love. The chivalric path of duty and piety, of chastity and obedience, of holy poverty and prayer are all but forgotten. It has not therefore been difficult for the Red Emperor and his legions to scatter them and crush their remnant power. The Lord has handed them over to the subjugation of unholy rulers. Now that the Knights have shown their weakness and defeat, the people of the lands begin to doubt.

At the same time the Ammouric clergy has grown indifferent, forgetting that the highest charity is to obey their Lord, to subjugate the idolaters, and proclaim the Truth no matter the price. Some clerics even now, claiming that they know genuine Ammouric doctrine, attempt to redefine everything. What traditions have always been regarded as just and right, they now suggest areb unfair and even unholy. What was a celebrated light they now say is cruel darkness. The true doctrines we learned from our fathers are considered in opposition to the divine will."

"How in opposition?"

"Many city dwellers say that there is no divine will, and that the All-law was the work of ancient men, not a divinity. Whatever order of right action that happens to suffice for the day is the best canon of judgement. No one need measure against the All-law. Just do what you suppose is right and don't offend anyone, that is what they say. They justify abortions and the murder of innocents, like Herod of old."

"I have heard men murmur similar unsound doctrines. Why have not the clergy fixed this heresy by righteous preaching?"

"It is because the traditions of the Ammouri have been obscured in them by the smoke of erroneous theologies and creeping laxity. After the fall of Nystul's library, the grand works which had outlined the proper methods of the inquisition were lost, so the censors, after a couple generations, no longer remembered the orthodox mode, the inquisitorial method, or the purpose for the approval of books. What is worse, the censors were unable to provide reasons for their judgements on new writings, rejecting some without proper understanding. Such soon came to be seen as oppressive. The doctrines concerning faith and truth were forgotten. Even the censors themselves are no longer taken seriously, and books are published and glorified which obscure the minds of the clergy. I ask you, is it possible to love at the expense of Truth?"

"Certainly not."

"This is one reason why the Guild operates *in secreto stricto*. The

Truth itself has come to be seen as offensive. It is secret for the good of us members as well, for we also are sinners. Think of it this way: if no name can be attached to heroic acts (which are commonly applauded by mortal men), then no vain glory (which forgets the source of glory) will strangle our work. We have found that in the present age of world-deception this is the best way to survive as an organization."

'So you teach that the world is a deception? I agree, not even my own senses can be trusted."

"No, you have misunderstood. We do not teach that. We teach that the world is about to be deceived, as the prophecies indicate. As far as our own senses go, we put great trust in them."

"Why is that? Every one knows that what appears to be is often not the case. I have often thought that this world is a mere transitory delusion, a sensory deception designed by demons from beyond."

"It is the heart of Man which deceives, not the senses. The Creator can be the author only of truth, never falsehood. A power would not be given to us that would intrinsically deceive. The mind and body are good, not evil. Flesh, the sensitive soul, is undisciplined and dangerous. Is it not written: *the spirit wars against the flesh.?* It is the Holy Ghost that gives us strength to bind such a tyrant."

"But if you do not speak the Truth aloud and proclaim it to the peoples in the light of day, and risk shame and even death, but rather go to dwell in the underground, how can you boast faith?"

"A worthy criticism...There will come a time for bold proclamation. We spend some of our time seeking out the souls of the captives, those not only from the ancient world who got lost before the quickening, the age of faith, but many who dwelt in later ages. We proclaim the Resurrection to them. Elements of the subterrene axis do everything to hinder them from being found and released. Many of these souls, if they were to escape the darkness, could help us against the obscurantists."

"The who?"

"Obscurantists, those scholars who obscure the true wisdom...the movement of the obscurantists throughout the ages has finally reached a new culmination in our own time. By their unified effort the sun of true understanding has been darkened, especially with the dissolution of the Ammouric unity.

"Many Ammouric clerics were consequently deceived by the glittering writings of the heresiarchs. As go the people so too go the priests. Even the obscurantist Ammouric clerics work against us."

"Obscurantists..."

"Yea, we call them that, they themselves go by many other names."

"Who exactly are they and what have they done?"

"Usually they pose as enlighteners of men, and sometimes they even convince themselves that they are such. The Emperor was trained by these kind. Even during your own lifetime, the empty positions in the clerical orders were stacked with the Emperor's henchmen, an unprecedented move of state control. In the military arm he kept the old arrangements but most of the avowal-knights who refused to become his thralls, them he had arrested, put under mock trial, and burned at the stake for "heresy against the Man-god" the Man-god being himself. Those who survived, loyal to the Ammouric Queen, went below or survived under Kruth's protection, though they lost their fiefs. Later, the Red Emperor discovered the survivors through treasonous communication. To counter the Guild he gave the Sorcerers back the city to which they have long sought a return, Nystul. In exchange for this favor they offered their services against us."

"The sorcerers of Nystul?" I asked, somehow recalling a history of which I should know nothing. "We fight them as well? So I have a netherbeast, evil monks, and sorcerers after me...? That's a lot of news for just one day. Sorcerers have not been seen in these parts for over an hundred of years. We were told that they were all passed from the world like the dragons. But you say these still walk the earth and do the biding of the Emperor? And do you wish me to also work against the emperor? His power reaches the stars."

"All the lands from the Vastess Sea to the coasts of the Inner Furth Sea are too small a conquest for his proud soul. Unable to push further East by military conquest he now hopes to conquer all souls with a novel and perverse religion. In the coming Darkness, only those of true faith will be able to see through the deceptions of this Heresiarch."

"So he will replace our faith with his own?"

"He already has done this to some extent, and there are many false doctrines which cloud your mind, and these must be unlearnt in order to pass through to clarity about things. Unlike the other religions, the holy rites of the Ammouri were not designed by men, but by the Ancientmost himself."

"This is too much. I should attend to my original quest, which is dangerous enough. It's not easy for a someone like me to rise up to ideals when he is struggling against poverty. I am more interested in gold, only gold. You know, the problem with seeing too much, like you do, is that it makes one insane. Perhaps some other time. Thank you for your interest. I've made my decision. More wine?"

"That sorrows me...but it is a good thing that you realize the seriousness, danger, and corresponding threat of our cause to the powers that be. But why seek to accomplish what angels are afraid to consider? You have made your decision. I suppose that our hazard is not for everyone. Very well, I will of course concede. I must however leave before dawn, and not before. Let us spend twilight drinking more wine and enjoying the day's end."

"A well enjoined admission."

"An omission for you..." he remarked to my shame. "but we need not talk of such disturbing politics. How about some entertainment? I am the guest, you owe it to me. Kruth says that you enjoy the old sagas. I would like to hear, if you don't mind, some eld verses while I enjoy this cheap wine. Did you bring any poems of war?"

"Take care, the wine was not cheap...the insult requires that you make reparation by drinking more." I took up the skin and began filling his cup, hoping he would forget all that "Guild" nonsense. "I carry my favorite verses everywhere I go, since they provide me inspiration in my quest. It is called *the Bladetongue*, a famous poem Bards sung once in many lands."

The stranger took another sip from his cup.

"How foolish of me, it is excellent vintage. Humour thou me. Read thou the first book of that famous work, verses 53-209 will you?"

"All of it?"

"It is too much for you?"

"No, not at all..."

"And you will not mind if I interrupt to point out certain arcane doctrines to which the poet stealthily alluded. It has often been said that the poet dwelt among the Muses and learnt their ancient wisdom."

"By all means, for I have never heard a good commentary on the poem." I unrolled my pillow and drew forth the *folia*, not the original scroll in the precious whalebone case, but my book, a traveling copy of the poem which I had made myself. I opened to tome of book 1, the part where the heroic crew has just discovered that the king has bade them not return until they have accomplished some worthy deed. I began:

". . .Then did the crew learn the cost of deeds falsely famed, and they knew what was expected by rightful authority, and made they preparations to sail off. "Where should we go forth?" they would ask each other, "To what land sail in quest? Seeking what bright trophy?"*

Taking counsel they searched the annals of foreign lands but found no quest, and many a day passed when they wondered if the Prince would expel them by force. Then one day old Gulathar, the wrinkly face, the oldest of the elf-ears among them, took them all aside saying:

"Our ears have found a new hope, a tale from the land of Ardeheim, an account of a devious wizard who long ago built an immense tower, and lust for power taught him how poisonous council kills a foolish king, and he stole away unimagined loot into underground lairs." Their minds needed no more encouragement. .."

"Surely you are reminded of yourself...one who needs not much encouragement." Added the stranger sarcastically. "Please, do continue..."

"In the forty-fourth year of the Fourth Age they met, there in the dear homeland they knew, Ulthuring rich in sea-haul. So let the tale begin there, at the tavern, bright with the glow of candles, when only a day was left before they were to sail. In a room apart they stood and there were they gathered, the oak doors closed and guarded. Circled were they 'round the famous table of whitewood, the oath-room, there in The Golden Mermaid, the soldiers' mead-hall in Yrbath, city upon the splashing sea. Dedicated brethren and no strangers to hopeless risk, they determined with spoken oaths to go marauding the underworlds and thereby win heaping treasure. Nor did they fail to persuade skillful hands into their venture, individuals no dungeoneer would ever neglect to bring along, for strange and unknown are the deeps below. . .

"Well done in the reading! The poet teaches that one does not go to the deep alone, and that many skills are required. When one becomes a Guild member, like those who took oaths in the story, he has access to the skills of others, the need of which often determines the outcome of a life and death struggle.

"And observe that the poet begins in a mead hall. Why? The mead-hall was where warriors of old recounted their deeds of battle and made alliances. But they are "in a room apart", that is, apart from the common soldiers. This is meant to say that are going to operate in secret, like our organization does. Some have even theorized that our secret order can be directly traced back as the principle successor to *the Bladetongue*, though this has not been proven.

"Consider also The Golden Mermaid. Though seemingly just a graven sign, it is important. She is indeed a sign, but she is a sign of warning. At once woman and fish, she is that magic which lures souls to the realm of the deep. She is the lying promise of carnal or worldly beauty. She will bring to a watery grave any travelers on the deep whose eyes wander from the sign of the spiritual star. They forget the wind, that is, the sacred help of divine breathe, and sail toward her vain song. She is Golden because she will not perish as long as we reside in the natural world. The candles represent the soul of the would-be heroes, burning to enter into the mysteries of life and death.

"Death?"

"To gain immortality one must die many times in this life."

"Peculiar doctrine is that...nor have I ever heard of such an interpretation of poetry. Perhaps you are reading too much into it."

"It is not my own interpretation. It is the commonly accepted *doxa allegorica* of certain scribes who belonged to Hermopolitan school in the ancient world, read on..."

". . .*There was the knowledgeable paladin. Also the geljin (elf-kin, an old deep-born race) who knew the underground, and next to him the one steeped in magian verse, whose mother they say, had been elf kind. He it was who now first spake an oath, binding upon his head the silver-wale diadem of Nystul, embroidered with unspeakable runes. Never did he speak a solemn word without it.<* "Hear ye this, good soldiers, you know me as Thalfin the dark-robe, but let me be called Avenging Onslaught instead, if ever I see my brothers in deadly straights. For by my bones and blood, I vow all fury and death-dealing magic in defense of the man in peril, whosoever he be and whatsoever the circumstance, be it against beast or nightmare, giant or highest sorcery, risking life and limb, everything for the one jeopardized, glory and loot come what may."

"—pause there your recital a moment. . .There were some heathens who used battle magic and did not fret over its use because it did not work by deception or go contrary to nature. That freedom did not at once cease with the rise of the Ammouric sun and the rule of faith.

Notice how, for a magian, Thalfin stands out as unusual, he speaks instead like some warrior. He does not care about the treasures of this world, but rather for his companions. This sort of indifference is required of the deep-tracker. It is this indifference which enables him to devote his whole being, his "bones and blood", that is, his body and soul, to the defense of his companion. If riches are found give thanks, if not then even more give thanks. To which hero does the poet next turn?"

"Urius..." I answered, and continued:

> *"...So made he grave utterance, and then stood forth the reckless savage, a hycman, Urius Crald of the long locks, whose hair was shaved on the sides, leaving a crest like a boar's mane. A fierce look bred of the cruel hills, rugged and bow-legged, but a sure throw with the axe and one who could best unleash the deliberate swordstroke. He set his heirloom bronze sword on the table and spake:*
>
> > *"Life is brief and troubled, but there is much enjoyment for the bold. I honour that pledge and hold myself to the same, no well-woven magic to offer, nor high birth to claim, but rather the hazardous edge of my dooming bronze to send a gift of bloody victory."*
>
> > *So he vowed in turn, and then spake the high-standing lanceman Rohorst. Bald was he, nor hair had he about the face, his dark skin a banner of distant Mahanaxar, his daedal cuirass adorned with leopards rampant and shining.*
>
> > *"I also gravely vow, and let my share of the booty go to the man who finds me hold back my spear, my many-knotted club, or even my fist, unsure of my god-given strength, if ever a mass of enemies overwhelms us, for first shall I go down in heaps of the slain..." So the fearsome-limbed Rohorst spake."*

"Notice that the first warrior, the hycman, one who will carry a crucial role in the unfolding destiny, trusts too much in his own strength, his own mortal bloodline. This is emphasized by his choice of the ancestral bronze sword. Urius is the sort who has developed a grim view of life which he calls "brief and troubled" For him 'might makes right'. Though he is the best among warriors, it is his heart that will redeem him, not his acts of might. To learn this he will pay a great price. The poet contrasts him with the next oath-sayer, Rohorst, the ex-slave born of noble blood, who is ready to go down to Shehor, the land of the dead by tongue of the southern Whitehawk. Rohorst realizes that any strength or ability he has is not his own but is "god-given" that is, divinely granted."

"From whom did you receive all these teachings? These perceptions toward the poet's meaning illumine many things which I had long thought mysterious."

"It is because you only possess the first five books. The rest of the epic was lost in the fires of Nystul. Even so, the Guild has it by credible rumour that a full rendition is somewhere preserved. Nevertheless, the inmost interpretation of the Eldari survived through oral tradition and is still known to certain Guild members. It is necessary that Guild members who are gifted in memory learn these many things. We believe that the poems of the Eldari contain many secrets which illustrate the nature of Reality, true things obvious to angels, but hidden from mortal minds. What is more, it is whispered that the poems, and especially this one, contain keys or guides to the interior chambers of this lost knowledge, which, if restored, will greatly help the cause."

All these things the stranger explained were a revelation to me. It was at this point that I began to actually desire membership in the Guild. I recited more, thirsty to drink of a new yet antiquate interpretation.

> *"Troll-wise Gulathar the gelgin was next, bred of an enchanted kind, his ears pointed, his limbs weirdly shaped, hunched, gangling, an old one. He it was who knew many things needed for rough adventure in brooding places, he who first offered the enterprise and had first known of rumoured gold.*

> *"My vow retreats from no boldness of tongue, nor will you see me leave a man trapped at the bottom of some echoing cave, broken in the dark, abandoned in a sightless pit, groaning under inaccessible gloom. I will never leave his presence until he draws his last breath."*

> *All nodded and thought themselves lucky under the stars, if not divinely favored. The remaining men, reckless soldiers, took oaths of the same calibre, Soren Rulkson of Niruz, a giant who stood a full head higher than normal men, and so unnatural was the threat of his sinews and muscle, that his very presence could not help but cause concern. Handy with the ash spear and warhammer, swore he his simple oath with deep voice.*

> *"By the honor of my grandfathers, this my lance will confound beasts, enemies, and specters until they fear the very shadows in which they dwell..." So frowning swore he, a great*

mass of devastation. Then came the sworn utterance of Norgonce, paladin of the order of Ammouri, ever-mindful of the Father in Heaven, and holding before them all the heavy weapon Mithrohan, the shining holy war-relic, he spake.

"No matter the cost, I shall pray for the companions when the sun rises and when it sets, and may the power of the Allfather work through this sacred mace, a weapon fated to pulverize the fiendish sculls of our enemy. And if they know not enough to bide in the dust, you shall see me speak a holy word that will banish their foul spirits back to Hell." So were the words the beardless paladin spoke, echoing power on high. Next came Parythio the halfling, a nimble scout with hair shorn close, who recently ceased to mourn his wife, for she had passed into the netherworld.

"Even now I must stand on a chair to make my point, but though my size seems no grand asset, judge not too soon, for the helter of war holds many a surprise. You will never see me relinquish from death-dealing, no matter how huge an enemy. I'll go into any hole or crevice, tread lightly on sleeping behemoths, or dissemble any iron lock."

At last came the turn for the other halfling, Harpio, close companion of Parythio, he did not come forth but stood there with his thoughts elsewhere and upon some other concern, Thalfin of the dark robes addressed him.

"Speak, friend, tell us what troubles you, and know that there is no shame in withdrawing from oath-taking." Then Harpio looking up with hard gazes spake directly.

"At first, talk of glory and glittering spoils lured me to this chamber, and concern for my companion's safety; but I cannot abide by such an adventure, good fellows. It is not within my power, for you speak of things dreadful, terrible, of places where men should not go. There are others who dearly wish to see my own life last into future days. Let me breathe in the open air as long as it is given me, and my hope shall be with you."

So speaking he began to leave the room, but the others offered conciliatory words and made his purpose seem the better for him, that he stay behind, live, and seek out good land, for the *life of one who would sack the underlands is short indeed."*

"Do you see? Harpio lived a good life. But the poet remembered him only for slunking away from the great enterprise. That must be his fame, infamy rather, for all time!

Therefore drop these little hopes of yours and attend to larger matters, to a true quest, as did the old heroes. After all, unlike the ancients, you have the advantage of the soul's quickening. Nor is there a family for you to look after. At least Harpio had an excuse, lame though it be. This is an object of stupendous magnitude which presents itself to you. The Wormlords take at will the innocent and offer them as bloody sacrifices, the Sorcerers rise anew with no one to counter their conjurations, while the subterranean monks write books spreading lies and heresies throughout every kingdom. Darkness visible looms on the horizon of the civil lands and demons weave a shroud to cover the earth.

"The sorcerers...only an element in a movement of iniquity which stretches back like an obscuring smoke into the oldest questions of reality."

"What mean you?" I asked.

"I mean that Nystul is only a link to that treasure which you seek, which you vainly imagine to be gold and jewels, or precious writings and knowledge, but indeed is worth an inestimable value."

"What then is that treasure?"

"We only know what it is not. If we knew, or if even just Kruth knew, the War of Iniquity would perhaps be over. We have ideas, we have traces of something important, fragments, whispers, and riddles in the dark, that's all. It is for you to discover this, or at least recover some portion of the puzzle. It is said that no human can solve the dark design of this war, but there are certain ones, such as Kruth, who have lived long upon the earth, who can see its pattern vaguely, as through a dark glass, and know of where or how it might surface next. He is able to take measures to guard men and their families against its evil. If you wish to work for him and uncover fragments for him, you must journey to the south of the Whitehawk continent, through the desert wilderness of Kedemoth, to the ancient towers of Nystul."

"We have not the means to travel that far."

"You will not be traveling overland."

"Absurd!" I exclaimed in a confounded tone. "There is no sea, nor any grand river in these parts that flow through the impassible Antelynk mountains."

"Again you err. There are such waters, and they flow beneath our feet. But we need not discuss these things now. We must first open Kruth's instruction book and learn of Nystul, for ignorance will not serve you well there, and you must also soon come to full knowledge of your mission." He took out a battered little book with a rawhide cover from within his tunica.

"I am going to give you this precious tome, but not yet, since ye are foolish. First give ear to what I must divulge concerning the intention of the words, for I am to bring you through the process of *anamnesis*."

"Of what? You said that word before."

"*Anamnesis*...a word which Plato the philosopher used to denote a technique of recalling the mystical realities which he proposed the intellect could see. Kruth also uses the term, for similar but different reasons."

"What sorts of things will I remember?"

"You will recall the missing years which Kruth says you often wonder about. It may cause you to go into a state of shock."

"I wonder how he knew that?"

"The Eleusinion knows many things which are cut off from mortal view. I dare say it had to do with his analysis of the wording in your letter."

"I did forget some amount of time, many have suggested this to me. How did I forget those years?"

"If I knew, then we would not need this process. I myself will also be experiencing new memories, according to what the Eleusinion told me, and it has something to do with the towers of Nystul"

"Why then did not Kruth say how the memories were lost?"

"I don't know. How does a fly so easily escape the speedy grasp of one's hands? Could the perception of Time be different in different creatures? A second for us may be ten seconds for a fly, and hour for an angel. The gnome walks according to a different mode than we, he sees things, he is a sooth."

"Have you been to that place Nystul yourself? Tell me more."

"No. I have told ye too much...if you wish to know more you must become a member of The Guild. Consider this: withdrawal from The Guild ends in swift death."

"So if we accept and join, say you, but later turn back and wish to withdraw, then we shall forfeit our lives at your hands?"

"Not at our hands...we are not in the business of murder, no, we seek to please God. Membership causes certain powerful but non-sensory protections sent from above to become active. The oath is not to be broken, and it is sin to do so. Those who break oath lose this protection and are easily identified by the enemy, who see many things via the *crystali*. It is the enemy, not us, who hunt down oath-breakers and liquify them...usually in their sleep." He paused, and seemed to think of something else, and there was a trace of sadness in his face.

"Have you known someone that was taken by one of their assassins?" I asked.

"Yes, a friend...but those things do not concern us. We must remember that *the crystali*..."

"Crystals? You mean like magic crystal balls?"

"Yes, as in the old fables, but they are magical only in the sense that they employ a kind of ancient technology lost to our understanding. Our members however utilize a contrary virtue, a *crystallinum* of salt to wear around the neck, blessed by an Ammouric priest, and this shall wrap thee in an obscuring power, which the eyes of crystal balls cannot penetrate."

"Salt? That does not sound very powerful."

"Again ye err. It is an affirmation that you are the very fools whom I have sought. Do not mistake the commonality of a substance for its real value as a spiritual vessel. The value that men place on things means little. Water, for example, being the most common substance, has immense power.,.whereas gold, for example, is worthless with respect to spirit."

"We are fools, that much you have proven. Therefore do with us as you wish."

"Answer this: Have you ever signed contracts with suspect persons or spirits, in blood or other strange ink?"

"No. I am not constrained."

"Do you renounce the evil powers and their unholy works?"

"Perhaps. It seems the devil is a bad influence."

"I must have a definite answer, "Yea" or "Nay", from both ye."

"Yea, we renounce all that is evil."

"Understand, of his minions, some are humans. It is our policy that they be granted the good of just punishment. We must fight them in order to drive them back and bring them to repentance, but we try not to deprive them of life, avoiding anything of vengeance. If they happen to be accidentily slain, because our corrective blows may sometimes be done a little too roughly, we will pray for their souls, as the law recommends. Of other fell creatures, beside human, you may destroy them if they war against you, or if special necessity demands."

"Agreed."

"Swear an oath to do never any evil deed, no matter how seeming minor. This be strictly forbidden, even were some major good resulting be forfeit of it. This is absolute. And do you agree to do all that the master says, except somehow, impossibly, that he bid ye do evil?

"What if....what he bids folly?"

"That is not to be determined by you. The soldier does not correct his commander and teach him the points of strategy. Nothing hard there, after all, how can a fool judge his own folly? But what means this? There is a worthy kind of folly however that we like, the kind that corresponds to brave action, to be unwary of many perils. For our purpose that kind of folly is praiseworthy. The enemy considers us ignorant because we cling to outdated modes of understanding, and in the same way many upworlders say that we are fools. In this we can agree however, we are fools in the same way that lovers are fools, we shall risk our own good for the sake of something much higher, by means of an unseen and obsolete knowledge. It is this quality in you which the guild seeks."

"And of wisdom...?"

"Members of the Guild generally do not question Kruth's judgement. We men have but two eyes, near and narrow be our vision...but there is added an unseen eye of illuminating Spiritual Reason in the soul."

"Is that the very power of seeing in the dark which you had mentioned before, the way which only the initiated know?"

"Your insight has not failed you, for you learn the *arcana* quickly and have paid reasonably close attention to my every word. Indeed it is true...but the power of insight is not from the reasoning, but from the Faith which restores the soul's faculties. By faith a man may see through the darkness of the ages. It is a miraculous power not well known, only granted through the proper formula and intensity of prayers."

"Why then are so many, who claim faith, led astray?"

"Many spiritual sons who would be faithful are tempted by the flesh and they fall. If the spirit is subject under the flesh it sleeps a deathly sleep, and the spiritual eye remains shut. Many have forgotten, and they have ceased to understand. In its place another spiritual eye is fashioned within the intellect by the demon: Where once faith should infuse the eye with knowledge, now the demon manipulates with scepticism...all that leads to a most uundesirable folly. It becomes the great eye of Nimrod, proud and vain human Reason, divinized and self-ratifying. Such is the mark of the beastial intellect.

"Mark of the Beast?"

"Of course. The mark is not a visible mark. Just like the mark of babtism, which is the indelible mark of God, there also is the spiritual mark of the diabolically deformed soul. It is said to be of the beast because a human becomes a beast when he no longer has the spirit of a man, that is, when that which distinguishes a human, right Reason and divine likeness, dies in the soul. If a member becomes suspect of this condition, or of contracting with the Devil, he must role the dice."

"Role the dice? What manner of test is that?"

"I speak of dice that are sacred lots. Certain bone dice fashioned by Romans many centuries ago. There were once four dice. One die is lost. Of the set we now possess three six-sided dice."

"How came they to be called sacred?"

"They were utilized 'neath the Lord Messiah on the grim day of the Crucifixion. They legionaries cast them for the sorting out of his seamless garment, to divy it up among them. Along with the Holy Lance and the True Cross, the Nails and the Crown of Thorns, bone dice are included. Other relics are famous, but men have forgotten about the legionaries' dice. They are titled the Dice of Golgotha, Supreme Relic of the Guild. Only Kruth knows which member possesses them."

"By All the Saints, I have never heard of such. What are their powers?'

"Too great to speak of or dare mention... But learn this: if a member is suspected of having turned, or of returning to the former vices, or of mutiny, or double-cross like Judas, or being a wolf in sheep's clothing, be he even priest or bishop, he must roll the three dice. He must do it under constraint, in the presence of the sacred conclave. This ritual has occurred on several occassions. The Guild is not immune to infiltration, for although they are all penitents, suerly all sinners are tempted again, and not all are steadfast."

"But what then is indicated by the tossing of such ancient cubes?"

"The accounted dots that he roles, the number added and rightly interpreted with a Pythagorean index tells if he be false or true."

"And what would then happen to him, be he untrue?"

"For those guilty of lesser offenses, public penance is demanded."

"And for those of greater offense...?"

The stranger answered with but a deadly silence.

After this I could not help but think of the madly glittering eyes of the one who had led the pack of wolves that had once waylaid me on the road.

"And what of Kruth...? Being not so much a man, he must not be subject to the same operations as men.

"Kruth is a gnome, and a man in as much as a gnome is also a man, but in sooth more akin to angels. He is one whom we say sees with seven eyes. You and I may reckon only two of them in their sockets, the two eyes for seeing physical things. With the other eyes he can see much that we cannot, metaphysics and paraphysics, he sees broadly and beyond. But even he must throw the Dice of Golgotha if called upon."

"One more question concerning that ancient relic: tell me, stranger—"

"Call me stranger no more. Now you should call me friend."

"Very well, friend. Answer this truthfully as a friend, eventhough it will be a dreadful question. It is this: whatever would be said or done if the dice-toss of the individual in suspicion tumbled out three sixes?"

"The very next logical question...which I expected you would duly propose. So duly will I answer. There is a prophecy that someday the Guild must be infiltrated by the Son of Perdition. We pray that this time is afar off, but we fear that it is not. The imposter will be detected by a certain member. It is unknown who will gain that intelligence. The Judas will then be arrested. The prophecy says that the suspect will be conducted to the conclave to toss the dice. Upon his rolling of three sixes, he will be revealed to be the Antichrist, for so it is set down in the sacred writ of John, thus is it *his number, being the number of a man*. However for the Guild it will be too late. He will already have made too many allies and loyalists within our ranks. We will not be able to hinder him. The end of the story is unknown. That is why we pray often."

"Your accounts and superstitions thus far are too strange, but not religiously impossible."

"And now that you know what it all means, what is your answer to the question of absolute obedience to Kruth?"

"It is too difficult to say. Your words have disrupted me. The Prime Interquist warned me of this."

"Of course he warned you, since he himself once was a member of the Guild. Didn't he tell you?"

"I thought you said that the only way out of the Guild was death....? Why does he remain alive?"

"We guildsmen may be righteous, but we are not strict legalists. No one has ever been executed for leaving. It is the enemy who easily executes those who break rank. Eventhough we consider The Prime

Interquist a rival, he is still an Ammouric cleric, so we respect his wishes...Even so, I see that my words have disrupted you and made you uncomfortable. The philosopher Plato, though a mere pagan, spoke of this disruption to the *oculi mentis*. Being painful, it is the bright reality of true things for those who have long dwelt in the cave of unknowing. Now you know. Can you not distinguish the path of true light breaking through the dim dungeons of the false wisdom?"

"I can neither fully see nor grasp what my faith nevertheless presses me to accept in confirmation. Its true that soldiers must obey their superiors, for this is how victory in war is obtained. We are to be soldiers of faith, if I understand correctly. Therefore I vote "yea" again." (Langstaff also agreed). Langstaff then suddenly spoke up and observed;

"But what if some power presents itself to us in agreeable form, and having no knowledge of names we are deceived, and so deceived execute orders given by an enemy claiming Guild membership?"

"Certain gestures and signs attend our coming and going, these are the *disciplina arcana*, and this is learnt at once upon receiving membership."

"We understand."

"Let us then return to the initiation. Another question: will ye go so far as to surrender all treasures, gold, property, titles, etc. if asked, if commanded, in order to please the one true Ancientmost?"

"Hmm. Yea, but only if asked." We both agreed.

"There is another matter of protocol which may jeopardize thy admittance to The Guild if ye cannot bear it."

"What is that?"

"We do not raid tombs; either of mortal kings or other wealthy mortals.

"No heaping treasure?"

"To take from the dead: it is impiety. This ye must agree to, for we often enter tombs in order to read inscriptions or other writings, but we do not disturb the ancients in their rest."

"What if he had been an evil doer, a tyrant on his golden bed, or dark warrior and rapine."

"Only a knave purchases the world's blessings with cursed gold. The wise man stores up for himself the spiritual gold of true insight, treasures heavenly, that moth or thief cannot despoil. Therefore mind you, the life of an extinct lord is not for men to judge. Removal may be done in the cases where whatever is sought is of grave import, such as a relic hidden away in a tomb so to hinder the Truth from being known.

The rule is this: let it never be done for personal gain. Thou mayest however raid the tombs of other non-human creatures, save dwarves."

"What about elves?"

"Where is thy mind!? There are no elf-tombs, for those who were slain in the Auroran wars were burned on pyres according to ancient custom. Any others have passed to the stellar-regions or elsewhere. Now, what say you of the restriction?"

"Though it is contrary to my way of thinking, since the dead have no use for their wealth, I nevertheless consider it not an unworthy restriction."

"And most importantly, doth thou foreswear magics, being a mortal man, since these are forbidden by sacred custom?"

"I have heard that many magic-users seem good, but they turn to evil life on account of the allure of such power. The Ammouric Knights and Clerics of old were great, yet they used no magic. It is better to die alone and obscure in the belly of some dragon than trust in lawless power."

"We exchange the vain allure of magical power for the power that Faith gives, and the thaumaturgy of the Spirit."

"I also adhere, though my common sense urges otherwise," said Langstaff "for though I enjoy magic and would prefer to use it, it is likely that I must now abandon the practice on account of the love of my companion, whom I shall not let go into the depths alone. My sword-hand is a divine gift. Yea."

"By thy build and bearing it seems to me that ye would be best at strength and feats of war-craft anyway, not magic. Now I address ye both in solemn: Become thou members of The Guild, foolish ones, and kneel in fealty to St. Dismas and Christ."

He told us to kneel with hands joined as in prayer. He tied about our fingers a little chain with the salt crystal and bound us saying:

"I exhort thee to virtue and quest. I call upon ye to utter this vow of the guild: 'By the unutterable, I who am uttering sacred things willingly vow this my mind and body to the ancientmost war, in full knowledge of the triumph of Him who made me with unspeakable hand, and in hope of the rescue of souls imprisoned in the dark, the recovery of the Church's sacred relics, and for love of the imperishable Truth. Hear that I now bind myself to His service and claim recognition among the unnamed members. May the Lord of hosts fight for me, and the angels of the dawn light my way, and the discipline keep me vigilant' ...Say it."

As we were uttering this vow together, there seemed not a single phrase with which I was unfamiliar, but somehow I sensed that I knew it already. Of course, this was perhaps near to what he called *anamnesis*.

"I will now teach the *disciplina arcana*." He straightway showed us many secret signs and techniques by which to identify other members, as well as certain formulaic devotions of the thaumaturgic order. These I am not permitted to describe to the uninitiated.

"Your first assignment is to capture the monk-assassin that stalks us and interrogate him. Feign that you are merely enjoying your hunt and get him to follow you. You may use wholesome encouragements in order to obtain the intelligence we require. Remember, the Guild forbids torture. Instead by keen wit find out who he is and for whom he is working, and why you have become his target. Also be careful to inquire about the entity that also pursues us and how it may be hindered. I cannot be involved in the interrogation lest I be recognized and the monk escapes. Now I must quickly remove myself from your presence. You will not have knowledge of where I am staying. When you are done with the monk you need not leave him for the town jailers, for his own kind will quickly seize upon him. We shall meet again in three days, or sooner. Proceed with great caution. Here are some monies...and these as well, I have here in my pack, I obtained these for you, grey monkish robes, blessed by a cleric of the Guild. Wear them over your armour while in town. Going about all armoured up attracts too much attention."

"We are ready."

"Not really, but you must begin at once."

The next morning we arose and immediately visited the tavern for pancakes and bacon. We sat on the porch of the inn and enjoyed a great deal of hearty pancakes on account of our new coin. As I was drinking the morning wine and watching the various townsfolk busying themselves along the streets, I caught sight of the monk making his way through the crowed in quasi-pious stride.

We had surprised him.

"There he is, Langstaff. Don't look. Sit and feign to suspect nothing, catching sight of him not."

"He must have been expecting us to be cowering in our quarters." remarked Langstaff softly, stuffing a pancake.

"He has immediately realized his mistake..." I observed. The monk turned about slowly hoping we would not notice him. Then he quickly moved back to go the opposite direction.

"Or he is going to get his bow? He will disappear into that crowd gathering about the market." He was moving toward on the other side of the narrow dung-filled street that leads to the King's castle.

"We must follow him now, come!"

"Fie! But I am still hungry."

"I know it, and you don't wish to die on an empty belly. So stuff the rest of the pancake in your mouth, and arm thyself."

We strapped on our baldrics and scabbards at once, but the monk had been to quick. He had disappeared into the alley where swine were grazing for litter from the market. We sped toward where we had last spotted him, confident that we could catch him by surprise. We halted at the stone corner of an apartment and I bended to peak. The monk was far down to the near terminus of the not-so-straight street. He did not turn back to check. There were enough pedestrians about for us to follow him casually. He turned a corner and we went hurriedly down the street, but not so fast as to arose the suspicions of lawful folk.

We came to the next turn, and again I saw him. He happened to look our way, but these streets were busy and it was not likely that with all the bustle of wagons and many townsmen that he noticed us. We were gaining on him.

We came to an area of town that featured an old Regulian bath house turned into bazaars, high walls of immense proportion. Here it was known that less savory types from Arraf were accustomed to set up shop against the walls of the bath house, where inside only accomplished sellers waited. We bolted down a narrow alley as a short cut and got even closer to him, but this caused him to note us. He now knew that he was being followed.

He did not run or in any way give away his surprise, since to appear as a thief in this town could itself be deadly enough. He picked up his pace and now kept glancing behind, watching us. We no longer needed to pretend. We were closing in quite well and soon would be able to seize him. He did just what I had hoped. He slipped into one of those dirty alleys just opposite the old bath house. It was a dead end, now we had him. Langstaff and I turned into the same alley, but lo, the monk was gone.

There were a few doors of various apartments, but all were closed. He had covered his trail well by not leaving the clue of an open door. I tried one door, the closest and most probable, but it was locked. Langstaff tried another. A dweller looked askance out of a draped window and angrily shewed us off.

I had just turned about to speak to Langstaff when I saw a flash and a slight movement of some sort from the corner of my eye.

"The roof at the end of the alley..." I said, but did not finish my words. Was it our assassin, or just a lady putting out rugs to dry? If it was him, he was on a roof at a much further distance than I had expected. How could he have moved so fast?   My thoughts were not on this, but rather on the possibility of it, and the association of a roof as a place to launch a ranged attack. In a spit camel hair of a moment I realized that a missile might be headed our way. I slammed into Langstaff knocking him to the ground.

"What in the name of all madness did ye do that for?"

"I thought I spotted a well-aimed shaft hurtling towards your head." I explained.

"Well thank you for the generosity, but you might just simply say "duck" next time, and spare the rough-housing. After all, the monk was not carrying a bow, that was obvious."

"He does now..." I exclaimed. A shaft passed right over Langstaff's head and struck the dung in road. "Now come and lets get him." As we arose yet another shaft whizzed by, this one so close I felt death brush me.

We bolted for the door which we found closed and locked. Langstaff did not hesitate to smash apart the flimsy lock with a thrust of his mighty leg. We entered and rushed up two flights of stairs. We could hear his footsteps as he went   back and forth on the roof. It seemed he was trapped on the top of a four story apartment.

We climbed to the roof and peered out. He was only a few steps away and his bow was not loaded. We rushed at him and he jumped on the ledge of roof that drops of into the moat of the King's castle. He would have had enough time to shoot one of us, but would not be able to load for a second shot to take out the other. He was not great of build and would easily be captured in a wrestle. So the monk dropped from the ledge and went into the drink. He was swimming in the moat of the King's castle, and foolishly he did not let go the bow. The splash had already alerted the guards in the towers of the castle. Armed men were sent down to retrieve the intruder at once. Obviously he feared us even more than he feared the local authorities. The grand question is why. What were the motives of this assassin and why did he fear if his very intended prey capture him? What did he know? What did he fear? He was drawn out of the mud and arrested by the gundermen. He looked back at us but Langstaff and I were well hidden. The portcullis was lifted and the monk was taken into the castle under armed watch. We slipped away immediately.

That night there was indeed a sense of failure and confusion. We did not know anything of the local prince here, a petty king but probably fairly despotic as they usually will be in this part of the world. We took roast beef for our supper and drank gladsome wine. We awoke late the next day.

Over our morning bread we discussed possibilities on the porch of the inn, but we could come up with nothing.

"I hope you do not fail your first trial." A familiar voice said. I turned and saw the stranger, our Guildsmaster, standing there, being our new manager. "Do not be alarmed. We can talk here for a brief moment. Have you been on the streets this day?"

"We have only just finished our morning bread." I responded.

"It is advisable, that ye not sleep late, but do the dangerous work of the Guild, gathering information about the town. Already I know much more of the condition of your assignment than you, and I am not the one charged with its completion."

"So you have heard that our monk has been arrested."

"I have indeed. This is a grave concern. I have heard much talk from my sources here and I know the intentions of the local authorities. If you had been out looking about the town this morning you would have seen the notices of his arrest. As it was there were more witnesses than we imagined, the shaft-hurtling monk has been identified as the very same who slew the poor drunkard. It was this drunkard who, to the general dismay of all, turned out to be the dissipated and pitiful nephew of the King who had for years rejected the help offered by his uncle and preferred a life of abandonment to wine on the streets. All the townsfolk knew him well, so it was immediately suspected that some stranger had done the deed. Nevertheless, the king was enraged at this slight upon his family and word went around about a killer monk. Then he is told that a monk armed with a long bow and arrows has been captured trying to enter into the castle in broad daylight like a mad fool crossing the moat. It was concluded that the monk hoped to finish off the king. No trial has been announced as it is deemed unnecessary. The monk has been tortured and found insane, and it is thought that he had some special grievance against the king. He is to be hung at noon."

"What do we do now?"

"The authorities have no knowledge of our Guild operations in this realm. Whatever you do, make sure it remains that way."

"Perhaps there is some forgotten sapper's tunnel to the dungeons beneath the castle?"

'The castle has never been assaulted."

"Langstaff here is brilliant. He will surely contrive a plan."

"Someone had better. Whatever means you employ to obtain the required intelligence we do not scrutinze. The Guild sent me for this: to remind you of the mission and of your responsibilities, and of the final consequences that must be visited upon the earth if you fail."

"And what, pray tell, would those be....?"

"An Age of Darkness Universal; lasting for all subsequent days of men, even to the end of Time. But if you need to rationalize the taking of risk by operating from a selfish purpose, consider this. Your own very lives are at stake. The monk is not alone. He is an assassin. Others will be sent. We must take the axe to the root. For whom or what does he work? If you do not learn this before the monk hangs, other assassins will come, perhaps those with greater skill. In that case you will no doubt forfeit your lives."

"So what must we do?'

"just remember above all what I have said about the Guild operations here."

"Aye, and that was...again..?"

The Guildsmaster responded only with an intense stare. Then he spoke.

"You do understand, don't you, my great ones, that this mission does not exist, nor will it ever exist..."

No verbal response did he expect, he wanted only actions. He turned away, and he left in silence without word of farewell.

We were left to quickly fashion some vast and impossible plan to trick the authorities and retrieve the prisoner, freeing him from his deserved punishment.

"To do such a thing is absurd. We would need to raise an army and storm that castle. We must enter by stealth."

"But even were we to scale the castle walls in shadow, something neither of us has ever done before, we would then be confronted by seasoned guardsman and prison wards, and we are only two against many. Nor is it right that men should die by the sword, no matter how grand our cause."

"Then it must be trickery."

"It is no easy thing to trick knowledgeable men of state."

"Aye, but it has been done."

"It has been done by other knowledgeable men, but not by our kind. You are a man of force, strong but undisciplined in mind, and I am a dreamer and bard. Neither of us has any studied knowledge of lawful reasoning."

"That is a fair judgement. Even were we to be admitted as guests, our words would give us away in the King's court. That is why only high dignitaries, emissaries, and prelates are admitted into the King's presence."

"It would take years of study to appear at law with their manner of eloquence, even were we to seek a breif audience with the prisoner. Prelates? Did you just say prelates?"

"Aye, prelates too have appeared before kings. But it is not custom. Instead a king must go to the prelate, especially if the prelate be a great shepherd or some other visionary, as is right according to the order of things."

"I say, your words cause me now to consider a plan of high consequence. Come, there is little time, we must prepare."

"Gracious king, I am Brother Hieronymous sent by the Prime Interquist of Arkt, the Limitur of all Ormwood. We have news that one of the monks from our monastery has been taken into your custody.

"We are here to obtain his extradition from you so that he may be interrogated by the Prime Interquist and burned at the stake for his heresy, if he is found unrepentant."

"A monk? What monk? You mean that assassin who slew my nephew? He is not really a monk is he? Surely you do not imagine that he will escape my grasp. He will hang in the morning or else the sun best not rise."

"We have indeed learned of his murder, and the injury against your family is most grievous, as is the attempt upon your person. Surely he must pay dearly for his crimes.

"However his execution must be delayed so that he can be questioned by the Prime Interquist and found guilty of his treasonous heresy. In this way you shall gain the satisfaction of Heaven."

"Satisfaction of Heaven? What do I care about that? Nor does the character of his heresy interest me. The Ammouric faith is of little consequence here. Your ancient superstitions have all but been erased from the world. Now be gone with you and leave me peace, that I may finish my evening repast."

"As you command, your majesty." said Langstaff, turning to leave.

"Your wish alone must be heard, your majesty. May your soul have its peace...at least for now." (Bowing from the waist I said it in a loud whisper, as a monk would when uttering a prayer).

"What was that you say, Monk!" roared the king.

There was an uncomfortable silence.

"Forgive me Lord, I said "May your soul have its peace."

"Yes, and what was the last part?!"

"I said 'at least for now'"

"And what, pray tell, is the meaning of such a saying?"

"Again, my Lord, forgive me, I only offered a prayer for your soul, that Heaven be pleased with you, and that you have peace in this life."

"But you dare left out the added words 'and peace in the next life, you insulting knave. You know nothing of the burdens a king must carry. I need no back talk from such as your kind. It is enough that we tolerate you as we do. Do you not think I will enjoy the favor of Heaven for my efforts?"

"I am truly sorry, but were you to execute one of God's servants without the divine mandate, I fear greatly a doom may come upon you, not only grief in this life, but judgement and fire in the next. I will pray for you."

"I know what your kind preaches, that men will burn for their sins, not only the soul, but the body as well. That there is the punishment of fire for the wicked. I yield not to that folly of imagination."

"Indeed, righteous Lord, it may be folly. True, the body must suffer fire because it has cooperated in sin. Those who commit sacrilege also must burn.

"And what man, I wonder, would be daring enough to wager that there is no God, no divine judgement, when there is evidence all about us of a divine creator, and still more, when we see that even in this life, men suffer dearly on account of their sins.

"Perhaps then you will gamble that nothing will touch your majesty after death, and that no deity will summon you to judgement. Perhaps you dare to hope that there would be no deity, but only an empty sleep awaits you. However, if you are wrong..."

"Get out of my sight!" The king roared.

We left without another peep, hastening away as quickly as possible. We made our ways through the corridor of the castle truly fearing for our lives, lest the king's men arrest us as well for some trumped up charge.

"Now we have done it." said Langstaff."

We were almost to the portcullis, and our hope for an easy passage was about to be realized. I motioned to the gate keeper raise the iron gate for our passage.

"Grand plan, aye, that one was..." Langstaff added.

There was some shout from another part of the castle. Men were rushing through the parapets. Something was said to the gate keeper.

"Alas..." I said.

"I say, we are to leave by the king's order, raise it up, man!" Hortense commanded. Just then four guards came marching from the gate towers up to us. One announced to us this:

"In the name of the king, you monks are not leaving. You monks will appear before his Lordship to answer suspicions."

Right away both of us imagined ourselves swinging from a rope. The guards conducted us into the throne room. Now the king was no longer seated and eating and drinking, but his stood there in his ermine raiment and scanned us intently.

The guards let go of our elbows and pushed us toward him. We both bowed low and waited for the king to speak. All that was left now was complete abeyance.

"What is the name of your order, monk?" Now this was the worst question that could have been put to me, for I knew nothing of such things. I would have to make something up. This was very alarming.

"Glorious King, we do not generally speak of our order to others, since its name is sacred, and only to be heard by ears that are sacred."

"Are not a king's ears sacred? Am I not an anointed Ammouric king from the ancient lines of Maceonid pedigree? No, you will tell me what order of monk you be, else risk a treasonous charge for yourselves."

My mind raced through various kinds of monk's that I had seen, but I could not think of any order's name I had learned, neither from my conversations with the Prime Interquist nor with the stranger, the Guildsman. I thought of a monk's robes I had seen in town. Our robes were grey.

"We are similar to monks, but do not adhere to that rule of life. We are instead a guild of like-minded confessors, the Grey Robes..." I said.

"Grey robes...well that's obvious, monks all the same, it seems to me, going about in pairs, and meddlesome, like monks. You are Grey Monks, then, of where?"

"We are the Grey Robes of St. Dismas." I said, and that sounded right.

"Very well, you Grey Monks of some obscure Saint. Now I wish to tell you something more, and this must be kept secret. I bind you, as an anointed King, to religious secrecy. Here it is: although you have been overbold fools to anger a king, it is nevertheless true that I fear the fire that awaits the wicked.

"Nor I can I fathom that a monk of God would become so deeply involved in heresy that he would assassinate my kin.

"Personally I find this man quite creepy. He has pale skin and a bald head, and his eyes...his eyes have a certain emptiness, and the pupils are shaped weirdly, just as a serpent's or some other grim creature. He is doubtless involved in an evil that is beyond our understanding, and this causes me grave concern.

"Therefore I will hand the monk-assassin over to you, afterall he has withstood our tortures like a man of iron. I wish to know who sent him and why. You may inform the Prime Interquist that when the interrogation is finished, he must extradite to me for execution, as is my regal right."

"A wise decision, your majesty." I remarked.

"I know it is."

ɣ̂ɪRɣẽã

I will not describe my "discussion" with the imposter monk to you in detail, so as to spare you any unchristian imaginations of violence. Indeed, I broke the rule of the Guild, the prohibition against torture. This is what more than anything the Guild wishes to avoid, since it distinguishes them from that rival organization, the Holy Inquest, which is led by the Prime Interquist, who accuses the Guild of Heresy.

It was the Prime Interquist who first called Langstaff and I and requested that I undertake this campaign into the underworld. My primary allegiance was to him, not to the Guild.

It was foolish to have put myself under two masters, the Prime Interquist, who served me up a glittering helping of Mammon, and the other, whom in truth I imagine, or at least I do sincerely hope, serves God...but no man can serve both.

To my utter dismay, the assassin-monk admitted under torture that he himself was a former member of The Guild! He had been discontented with things in the Guild and had gone to the Prime Interquist, and as a loyalty test was hired by the Prime Interquest to assassinate both Langstaff and I!

How could such a high-ranking member of the Church have ordered this grim deed? Why had the Prime Interqist betrayed me?

I had not betrayed him, or did he somehow sense in my character that I might soon encounter and throw in with the Guild? Perhaps I was right not to preserve my fealty to him, but instead to trust in a being whom I had never even seen, Kruthusel Eleusinion, Grand Master of The Guild of Saint Dismas.

And now to the Guild it has been reported, by whom I know not, that I used torture to interrogate the monk. This of course would be a serious breech of Guild protocol.

I have sent away Langstaff on an errand so that he will not risk his life to defend me, as I am to be arrested tonight and brought to the underground conclave. There beneath the torches of Ghom I must toss the Dice of Golgotha!

That is why I have written this last testament for you, my friends and long lost brother, so that I might not be forgotten, and that you might pray for my soul, for though I have the spirit of a poet, I am in earnest a violent man. Like a beast that must be restrained, I fight with reckless abandon upon the slightest dishonor even if vastly outnumbered.

So am I put to the test. Nor will I go down without a fight against them, be they Christian men or nay, save for one unthinkable circumstance: that I roll the count which holy writ designates as accursed, which is the number of a man: six, six, six.

THE GREAT BURNING AND BANISHMENT

Sun, Moon, and Stars, the secrets of fire and wind; all these and many other mysteries they investigated. They searched out the enigmas of mountains and seas, from the sightless caverns of earth to heaven's remote galaxies. The visible and invisible they described in every detail. Few things escaped their gaze. They were the wizards of old, and never did the salt of earth reach their lips.

Terrible were the magics they knew, and lawless were they. And from their experiments monsters were born. It was not long before a superstitious fear took hold of entire nations.

Five kings of ancient time swore oaths and vowed to put an end to the chaos. Oaths they swore in blood, and they silenced the wizards. With their own hands they cut out each spell-wise tongue.

Then they sent the wizards to dwell apart, banished to a desert place, a mesa surrounded by sandy wastes, high upon sheer cliffs, a lofty island of stone upon a sea of shifting dunes.

But the wizards were not humbled and did not cease from their works. Great towers they built. From within the cavernous rises they set deep tower-roots, and even to the clouds the pinacles reached. Keepers they appointed and set a watch upon the horizon.

And on bzebus leaf they set down their arcane knowledge. They recorded every spell which they no longer had the tongue to speak. And within those towers they stored secret and deep researches, scrolls and tomes by dry airs preserved; the strange writ of centuries.

Wherefore great power was had, and they gloried in their many scrolls, sending out notice to every realm: "Who can compare or stand against us, for behold, are we not as gods, reaching to the very edge of knowledge?"

The kings renewed their vows against the wizards, martialing their armies. But it was too late. If haunting rumour did not keep away the strong, sand-laden winds sent even the bravest into retreat. Entire legions were lost in the waterless wastes, and the soldiers heard of certain doom by dooming magic hurled.

Even so, the rivaling princes of the world wanted harness the power of the scrolls; and sought they commerce with the arcane schools. They soon found a way, a safe passage by secret route obtained, for beneath the sands a meandering system of tunnels and caves connects that oasis to other lands.

Who can avoid the turning of ages? The day of grace dawned and the powers of heaven and earth were shaken. Remembrance of many things was lost, and men would say: "A great voice has been heard and a new light has appeared, let us renounce those towers by name. No longer shall we speak of that place, Nystol of the Ancient Rises."

An age past and the rolling deserts grew, making vast the reach of the sands, but the towers remained. Even now, when a clear night reveals galaxies above, the nomads catch glimpses of her ghostly ruins; the strange glimmer of her spires on the horizon.

"Take heed," the nomads warn. "Even the outlaws have abandoned that place, driven away by her lingering Furies. The earth herself expels the wizards from her vaults, even from their own tombs, for ancient are the stones beneath."

But there were some who did not forget those towers...

It was in the third age, as the yore-writ annals say, that great minds conceived new towers. Nine tall towers they planned, and under favorable omen they erected the first stones. Dwarf-masons they summoned to work the rock with wondrous skill.

So commenced the laws of the Arcanes, and after twelve orbits of Saturn, the magian college waxed mighty, and gladsome gardens adorned her terraces. A benign magic spread throughout all the realms.

How brief the time, for soon, through overweaning pride, did they begin to lose favor. Evil, undetected, made a silent claim. Rebellious men were elevated to high places, Sorcerers were tolerated. Strange utterances were heard, and soon the lawless could no longer be restrained. They twisted the arcane inheritance.

It was the oldest of their orders, the Eldari, who first learned of the wickedness. They rebuked the Sorcerers, and prophesied against them saying,

"You summoners of spirits, do you not see how the infernal wisdom of your art will bring ruin to us all? You call down the scorn of Heaven, and the world cannot escape the doom you have earned."

Unable to endure such words, the lawless took hold of the Eldari and banished the old men to the waterless wastes. Therefore bright Nemesis bade her time, awaiting a day of retribution…

The nations of the earth, the allies of Nystol, every one of them who had commerce with her, learned of the impiety. They soon abandoned her; one after another. In the end, she was unable to convince even a single mercenary to her cause.

Far to the North, a savage race learned tidings of broken laws and devilish rites, of many towers where lived men untrained in war and without wives, hoarding many treasures.

The raiders of the North painted their torsos with marks of fury, restless for plunder and spoil. Even so, they waited for a propitious day. Ready

horsemen though they be, they would not go without strong surety and dare
The Great Southern Desert, only to arrive at Nystol's sheer rises.

But a viper lay in the bosom of Nystol herself, a treacherous one and
conspirator, who had sent a secret invitation to the axe-bearing chieftains.

So did the horde at last ride forth from the pine forests out of their barbaric
camps. Only the colossal Gates of Hermius stood in their way. The massive
portal was locked inextricably, a bronze giant bestride the great pass of
Dariel in the mountains.

A cave-elf it was, so they say, whom the treacherous one duped into
unlocking the massive portal. This must be so, for only such a deep-delving
creature could recover the lost key from the abysses beneath the world. The
gates were opened and a thousand raiders passed into the civil lands, four
times ten thousand horse's hooves thundering a new time to come. The
savage riders entered the torrid wastes and endured the sands.

So it was that on a day of solemn observance the watchers of Nystol spotted a
line of painted marauders upon the horizon. The Arcanes bickered. The beast
leaned close and waited.

Suddenly, by the one whose high treachery was long prepared, a narrow
passage within the rocky rises was revealed. Brandishing sword and torch,
the barbarous scourgers entered the tunnels, and their sandaled feet climbed
the steps to the towers above.

In a single day and night the order of the world was changed. No more would
the nations groan under the fearful spell of Nystol, no more would men hear
the cold drone of her unearthly chants on the wind. For three days the smoke
of her burning blackened all the sky...

In our times Heaven has renewed the hope of men, and our eyes turn away
from the failed wonders of doomed ages. Fame has long departed her
windswept terraces, and such glories have all but passed into the skein of the
World's memory. To her a well-known prophecy let be applied: She shall
never again be inhabited, nor dwelt in from age to age. Desert beasts shall
howl in her corridors, and jackals in her luxurious palaces.

So preserve what I now set down, my brethren, and let it not come to dust, for herein alone is recounted how the towers of Nystol fell, that day the Magi were deceived. Only here is told how, under the waiting shadow of the wicked, the wise were confounded, and how their libraries of forbidden knowledge burned withall, and how, after a darkened age of unknowing, I, a monk, came to learn of it, and of other things: of wisdom and prophecy whispered from out the caves of the fourth world.

THE TOWER- WYRDD

Once there was a strange and wizardic tower, magnificent and terrifying, outdoing any of Nystol's great spires both in reputation and design. It was known as the Tower Wyrdd, and those who lived to see it spoke of it in the tones of dread, describing a most ingenious and disturbing construction of seeming impossible magnitude. A certain "Zenops the wizard" designed it, employing the many-handed *anthrai* to build it. Long did he haunt its chambers, living far beyond mortal span. Even more disturbing was the fact that he never once bothered to explain its purpose.

At some point in the reports of men he acquired the appellation of a creature, the *grith-wyrdiung*, or "The Tower-weird." This is not disputed, for it was widely known that only a wizard of his renown and ability could have contrived such architecture. Not only is it of gargantuan proportion, but it is intricately buttressed and spiraled. The most amazing thing about this tower is that its greater part lay in a narrow gorge whose steep cliffs encircle it, and whose profound depth reaches even down to the mystically flowing intermundane waterways.

How the feat was accomplished is part of the mystery that this account investigates, but let it be done through an eyewitness's words.

I, Orbian, record for you here the adventure reported of one sadly mistaken youth, Wassel, who told of his journey with the dwarf-lord Nergalf, and how misadventure brought them into that place, and into many ordeals, the claws of many horrors, even to the maw of the wizardic monsters which lurk below.

Over the centuries, many over-confident adventurers had broken into the colossal tower hoping to seize the loot rumoured deep within.

Only a few have ever returned. I, a mere wandering monk, traveled as far as the remote eastern town of Khnum to obtain a hearing of this account.

I located Wassel, the once irrepressible youth, who by then had become an old man. He would sit every day on the porch of his little shack in the woods "awaiting the consummation of ages."

As I recorded the continuous account he gave, sitting on his cabin poarch, I became more and more convinced that Wassel had truly been inside Zenops' tower. I have captured most of his own words and phrases.

So hear you then this entire journey of Wassel and learn of the deep worlds...

yrĕûyộ

"Know that I am Wassel, a man of enough years who now but keeps to his garden. I have not always been this way. I was an energetic and strapping lad like you once, in the days when there were no realms safe from the terrible Nergalf, a masterful dwarf-champion and the conqueror of many kingdoms. Stay for a time and let me teach you about the world of those days.

Hermius the Great, first lord of all the Aideen empire, did not keep his admiral Nergalf from the inheritance of the golden oak leaves, thusly by default bestowing upon him also the empire in its entirety.

Nergalf came to rule all the Archonate with strict justice, satisfying himself on all wealth and power, tyrannizing over the many provinces of the Aideen. To his clever rule he joined not frivolity or entertainments, but jaded pranks and cruel combats.

At the arena he took part in the games himself, changing the rules to suite his mood. It was not long before the people correctly perceived him to be beyond help.

I will describe for you, friend, my encounter with this unsavory being, who, for a time, not only led us into grand folly, but by some strange twist of destiny revealed to me the nature of realities about which I cannot easily speak.

In those days there were few who had not already heard many songs of his exploits. Nergalf had been a famous general. In fact that is why he became the principle successor of the Aideen hegemony and Archonate, as if so favored by the great founder himself. You see, Hermius the Conqueror had no child of his own and needed a successor. Suspecting his last martial expedition might soon be undertaken, he trusted the diadem and Orb of Dominion into clever Nergalf's keeping before he marched out. Some of the lesser generals secretly protested.

The generous Hermius at last came to the end of his days and parted from the world, dying in that famous combat on the mysterious Island of Harpies.

At once it seemed the entire creation became silent, not only with foreboding, but with worried anticipation. The bloody work of Nergalf's *malchus*, his short-sword, (not a dwarven axe, mind you, as many paintings depict), was already infamous. It was not long before his reputation, of the dwarven blade in one hand and the Orb in the other, had the effect of keeping the Empire Aideen in fearful obedience for a nearly decade.

The new ruler did not assume the title *hegemax*, for he cleverly announced that only godly Hermius could be worthy of an imperial title. Instead he titled himself god-hero of Aideen and the "divine son" of Hermius, by adoption, and thus, also ignoring the Great Patriarch, virtually bestowed upon himself both the miter and the diadem.

In subsequent years when the world hoped to rid herself of this baneful tyrant, I myself and a few companions had joined the war-parties assembling against Nergalf. We were hoping for glory, and the prince of Ulthuring had allowed me to enter the conscription, eventhough I had only seen seventeen winters and did not yet fit properly into my ancestral hauberk of chainmail.

Our forces had met the loyalists on the plain of Gederon in Arahom, ancientmost field of war, to decide the matter. The battle was a terrific one, and it seemed the earth shook while the sun was obscured by swelling dark clouds. Amidst the gore and screams of fatal demise, our arrows hissed down upon the enemy, blackening the sky and reddening the plain. Twenty thousand fell that day.

Nergalf could be seen in the distance riding on a war-elephant, its tower-saddle bobbing to and fro as he kept shouting instructions to his captains. Finally, realizing that the battle was dead-locked, the man-dwarf dismounted, letting down from the tower a rope and descending. He leapt forth in order to cut his way to the thick. He brandished his sword in bloodlust and disappeared into the fray himself.

Overcome with folly at that moment was he; the folly of supposing that all his loyals were convinced of his invincibility and immortality. He thought that they would never doubt of victory, be he visible to his troops or not. It was an unexpected turn, and no longer could his war-captains look back to see him standing on the elephant with exalted horn or pointing with his sword. The imperial ranks began to weaken, and very quickly most of the spear took flight, supposing their champion lord fallen.

In the end, we routed and scattered Nergalf's entire imperial host, tracking the enemy into the swamps. His great and loyal champions lay in purple heaps upon the cruel plain of war. Eventhough the grim dukes of Kargiwall had backed him and remained loyal, their heart was not in the fight. They had been no match for the divinely ordained kings of Whitehawk the Ammouric confederacy. Nergalf was nowhere to be found.

Tidings of Nergalf's defeat and an end to his iron misrule would spread quickly throughout the lands. I myself was celebrating with my companions in our pavilion upon the dusty plains, not far from the scene of victory.

Nergalf, it was reported, had fled East, but this was a deception or a mistaken intelligence. In reality the dwarf somehow had been separated from his small band of survivors, and had been traveling South, to reach the backroads of Kargiwall, perhaps in an attempt to bypass the allied forces and make the Ebberhar. There, reaching his ancestral stone halls within the Lessarlik Mountains, he would escape justice, disappearing into the volumes of rock, the Northernmost end of the Antelynk chain.

None of us soldiers perceived any of the things which were transpiring that evening after the battle. Instead we were drinking our victory wine and contriving exaggerations of martial exploit.

To my dismay, looking up from the couch, I thought I saw the felonius dwarf himself standing at the entrance of our lieges' own tent. Impossible, I thought. The cold rain outside mixed with wine and excitement was causing me to be mistaking what I saw.

I looked again. It was surely a dwarf.

Was the shadowy figure enticed by the savor of the smoke from the fat of the boar we had been roasting? Watching closely I recognized his profile immediately, since he was larger than most dwarves and his eyes were distinctive. My companions, playfully filling their drinking horns and singing lowly songs, did not heed anything else but their own joviality. At first I could not say anything. Perhaps I had been stunned speechless at the mere suspicion of so infamous a figure so near, or perhaps I did not believe my eyes.

The grim dwarf stood in shadow watching us, and only I noticed him and could not or would not act. A moment passed and then he spoke in loud voice to all.

"What? Some noble company filling victory horns! Here, here, righteous crew, to celebrate the high news, greet a gladsome ally arriving, a friend with tired limbs."

Our field captain, Sir Dunstaark, the company-commander, was also an Ammouric Ranger. Now someone was interrupting him and keeping him from gulping his victory wine. Being turned away, he did not look back to see. He spoke, irritated.

"Who is it? Not another stray, another renegade without?"

"A stranger, a soldier," I answered. "Perhaps some dwarf lord, wounded."

"Who goes there?" the captain barked. "Declare your liege and rank, if you cannot salute."

The dwarf made no answer.

"You dare refuse? Has he a mouth left? If he does not salute at once, we shall seize him. Are you an escaped cur of the old hegemony...fated to join many others who are hanging from ropes today?"

"Now now, keep in good cheer, friends," The dwarf said. 'How proven in war you all must now surely be...(he was ignoring the command!) "but please...help a miserable soldier of noble company, invite me in, a poor dwarf. I was struck on the head in the havoc of war and have lost me-companions...I think mine memory has quit me...but let me out of the wind and rain...if only for a spell. See, it is pouring something fierce and I am near starved, faint from the long ordeal of the day."

"Your kind is not welcome here...dwarf!" warned one of our men.

"Is it possible that you are not wise to what I just required of you?" warned Dunnstark, turning around with dismay. "By my life you will not stand a moment longer. Declare your liege and rank!"

"I am Alfir, a dwarf who has no place to hide from the cruel elements. Please, do not mistake me, good soldiers. I know that your crew saw part of the battle. I am not so fortunate. I was separated from my dwarf-lord Vorta when Kargiwall came about and surprised us, scattering our lines. We were all separated when we took to pursuing the enemy in the swampy forest, Maboloth, aye; it is some dark in there. But now I come across this company of heroes! Were it not for this reckless crew, our confederacy would have lost the day."

"Something is not sincere in that account," replied Sir Dunnstark. "I recall nothing heard of there being any dwarf lord "Vorta" upon the field. You seem to me, by the trim and hue of your beard, to be the kind allied with the Red Dwarves or with the house of Eberrhark. You are Nergalf's kin no doubt, trying to make it back to your mountain. Arrest him!"

We, five of us ready yeomen, sprung to our feet and darted across the tent. At once we grabbed the uninvited guest. The tired dwarf was easily overcome. He was armed with a dagger and short sword, which he did motion upon both to unsheathe. Those we quickly snatched away. We held him fast.

"I wonder..." Dunnstark asked. "Has this soldier given a true report? What say you, lieutenant? He is too weary to resist and take action to counter my men."

Our lieutenant, Perigraunce, answered. "He must be interrogated."

"Why, I'll be!" I exclaimed. "Lieutenant, look, it's no dwarf soldier. I say it is the Emperor. –Emperor Nergalf himself in flesh and blood!" We were enclosed around him, each having held fast of one of his limbs. Holding him up, we carried him into the middle of the tent. He did not struggle.

"What? Can that be?" replied Dunstaark. "Out of the way, let me take a look!" The Ranger peered down at the dwarf who lay now feigning helplessness on his back upon the floor of our pavilion. "Be-gads! It is in sooth the Emperor! We should have recognized him!" Immediately Dunstaark darted over to his long sword resting in the corner and, taking aggressive posture, he readied his arm for combat.

"We have good hold of him," I said, "he will not escape us."

"You do not know about him like I do...Nergalf has been in stronger bonds before and escaped having many heads tied to his belt. Are you wise to the strength and speed those little limbs hide? They don't call him "Hermius' Vengeance" for nothing."

"Unhand me, I say...ye foolish. I am not Nergalf, no. I am a cousin of his, of passing semblance. I will not hurt any of you. It is true, I did fight for him once, in the old days when Hermius was great, but not here today at Gederon. I would never fight for that wreck Nergalf. Everyone knows the old bastard's fate was fixed. He is all done in for. All announce that Nergalf is slain. 'Twas an arrow I heard...his body stolen away by pit-borne devils for punishment, no doubt. None of us care anything at all about the Archonate. It will fall apart. It's all over. All be done with all. Let us celebrate an end to wicked killing and fearful days."

"The dwarf deceives us." said Haroun, another of our company. This soldier was a lancer from Gohha, a determined fighter, swart-skinned, gangly, and tall, perhaps even descended from the legendary Egyptians themselves. The Gohhans, it was said, had long known about tyranny before ever Nergalf touched the world: they had known centuries of oppression by the Kalar Empire and its Cult of the Veiled One. Nevertheless, eventhough Nergalf had freed them from one tyranny, they were not satisfied to exchange it for the new yoke of the Archonate. Many Gohhans had come to join in the alliance against Nergalf, making the long dangerous trek through regions patrolled by the Atalur and Kutaal. Haroun had deep suspicion.

"We must bring him to the field-marshal for interrogation."

"Did you not hear?" asked Dunstaark, "The field-marshal lay dead upon the plain. We must hang him ourselves."

"It may be the Emperor as you say, but it is perhaps not, and we may end snatching the life of an innocent man." said Perigraunce.

"Many innocent died today, it is the way of war." said Dunstaark darkly. "Can anyone identify him with certitude?"

"Is not Nergalf's profile imprinted on silver coins mint from Hermius' second triarchate?" I asked.

"It is so. Does anyone have a quotid?"

"I do...here..." said Haroun. He passed over a coin. "See, it is the same man...-dwarf rather: Nergalf when he was commander of Hermius' fourth legion, before he became heir to the Eastern Empire, the last lips who ever spoke to Hermius. It is him, who would later become the Butcher of Namaliel, city of Ymmin's laughing shores."

"No, no...(the dwarf chuckled)...I should have just come out and said it, it's a common mistake...I said: I am one of his several half-brothers, being a rather harmless dwarf."

"We shall see." said Dunstaark in a foreboding tone. "It is known that Nergalf, before Hermius purchased the work of his butchering hands, operated with the sand pirates of the Dry Blood Sea. Like all the others, his shoulder was painted with the triple mark of the snake patterned *ophis*. So if this dwarf has the mark, we will know certainly that it is Nergalf. Strip him off the shoulders!"

We began to roughly handle and unstrap the dwarf's shoulder piece. He began resisting by twisting out of our grasp. Indeed he was mighty.

"Now there is no need to strip me of my leather!" he shouted, almost free of us. "Very well then, I do have the mark and I am Nergalf, Master of all the Archonate!"

"Master no longer...!" said Dunstaark standing ready with lifted blade. At this, in trepidation for our lives, we all took our hands off him and instead drew our weapons. By this time, with all the ruckus in the tent, some of the drinking cups and horns had spilled over. Now we watched like frightened dogs as Nergalf bent down and lazily picked up a wine skin. Ignoring us entirely, the bloodthirsty warlord did not pour into a horn, but putting the pigskin to his lips sucked down red wine unafraid of us, letting the blood-red liquid run down his lips into his beard.

We were surrounding him, too uncertain to move against him, but ready for combat.

"Those weapons will supply ye scant defense against me, humans." he said. "I could snatch all yer lives right quick, together in a heap, if I so wished it. Were I really a churlish spirit, like so many claim, I should put down each one of you in a few moves, with my bare hands. But what would that avail anyone? Now the fates have doused my burning pride. My empire is broken and I am without an army. My Will is spent. I have no mundane struggle left in me, no more thirst for blood. –wine rather, to drown my sorrows. Aye, a dark cloud has for many years hung over my soul."

"And yet you must still pay for your crimes." I said. "These soldiers will make sure of that."

At that he drank even more, as if to deeply soak his soul. After he finished swallowing the wine he spoke more.

"Do you really think it so important to relieve the fears of a few fattened kings by the killing of a forsaken dwarf?" he asked. "Mark ye instead this revelation: what they and the many "distorters" have called crimes, I know to be right justice. Take for example the title I have been burdened with these past years, "Butcher of Namaliel." It is true that a better leader would have found a more peaceful solution, but with The Cult of the Veiled One so entrenched in that city, I was forced to employ torture in order to find the whereabouts of their evil clerics. When the people revolted against me, it quickly became apparent to myself, and to all the army, that the entire populus had been secretly initiated into the wicked rites, and that they were planning to offer us up as blood sacrifices to their evil version of God. We tried our best to spare a few women and children. Perhaps a few innocent men died, but that is war, as your captain remarked. So I have already payed for what they claim are my crimes, at least in part. I paid not only by the woes and scandal that false religion harvests, necessitating us to blood, but also by the immense shame of this defeat."

"We have heard that story before, Nergalf," replied Dunstaark. "But your record shows a grievous history of war crimes even before you took the diadem. Hermius himself had to rein you in many times. After he was dead, any restraint flew away with the birds."

"So do my accusers claim. But they themselves are deceivers druelling for power. You may not realize that many of those so-called "righteous" and "divinely ordained kings" to whom you have vowed loyalty are actually scions of the underworld conspiracies which have plagued men since of old. They are experts in making the just seem wicked and the wicked just. The subterrene orders and their evil confreres the Sorcerers, and that wicked city, Nystol, are to blame."

"Nystol...that old city lost in the desert? How so? It is a forgotten place."

"It is not forgotten. The Nystoli Arcanes, those liars among others betrayed me at Gederon, never sent the wizard Anherm and his crew, as promised, to my aid. They assured me that they would remain loyal. So they lied. I know why. My own allies, the dukes of Atalur, had become too much a threat to them... Had the wizards come and used their magic, the battle would have been mine. If only I had spent my troops trying to conquer Nystol instead, that harlot of a city. Fool that I was, I trusted Nystol, foolishly overlooking how they treated my ancestors. That city must pay for its evils, I intend to see it come to ruin."

"Can you never cease to think of war, Nergalf? Nystol is impregnable." said Dunstaark. "No one can enter it by force of arms. Not even Duke Ikonn of old, maurader of worlds, could have led an army through that merciless desert to the Sardu mesa. The thought itself is a vain imagining. Nor even Hermius, popular as he was, would have been able to raise an army for that purpose. So unforgiving is the way there, and so dreaded are its unholy towers, that no man would so risk the loss of his own soul.

"But come now, offer your neck. Your days of conquests are over anyway, bloody-handed dwarf. At best you will spend the remainder of your span shamefully in the Othgog prison, a fate worse than death. The place is, if you have'nt heard, like a strange reverse-brother to Nystol, a massive prison-city on the isle of Cranit from which no one can escape."

"That is what you imagine shall be my end..." The dwarf replied with wry confidence. "It is true that no one has ever made it through the merciless desert to Nystol, but many have made it there by a secret route, an underground passage." Again he drank down more wine. "How else do you suppose the cunning wizards and worldly princes exchanged potions for power? No females are allowed up there, so be assured that no one born of woman suckled at the breasts of that city."

"An underground route?"

"Aye, and hear this: I have found a map drawn by the gnome Kruthendel himself. This rarity is highly valued. It is nothing less than a subterrene chart of the tunnels and underworld waterways 'neath the desert which, twisting in silence, lead to Nystol. This is a high prize indeed, from the original gnome-horde, Kruthendel's *de itinere caverneo ad nystulum*. If I could enlist a band of reckless warriors to accompany me into the deeps, we could find the shadowy trade-route and acquire magics and wealth untold."

This word caused great stir among the soldiers. Several indicated that such a booty would make up for our lack of glory upon the field, nor were the captains adverse.

"It is a fool's legend..." I said, "the whispers about "Gulconda," an underground route. Besides, even if such tunnels exist, it is unlawful to awaken the dwellers-beneath. Even if it were lawful, and we did pass through the lower world, no commoners have entered Nystol for decades. Now be done with such talk, for you only seek to delay the just punishment that awaits you." So I spake. If only those placed above me had the common sense to heed it, but Dunstaark bade otherwise.

"No, let the captive finish his proposal, Wassel. You men put aside your weapons."

"Surely you do not entertain this folly?" remarked Perigraunce. "Although it is a curious tale, I admit."

"Aye, my liege." I dared to interrupt again. "May I first warn you of deception, for I too am lore-wise."

"You are indeed lore-wise, Wassel, but young and stupid. This dwarf is clever indeed. But I give you leave to speak a little...quickly say what counter-lore you have in mind, boy."

"The dwarf thinks we can pass through Astodan, the complex of tombs beneath Nystol where the wicked Arcanes of old are buried. There they stir, restless, for it is right law that the ashes of the wicked generation would not be placed at the top of Nystol's towers, in funeral urns, not like the others, righteous of old. So think on this: the legends say that dwelling in the necropolis Astodan are many a terrifying lich, not asleep, but awake, the undead of Sorcerers jealous to guard their lairs.

"Say a group did get past them, and into the upper city somehow, and even were to capture some magical things from Nystol, they could not use them without right knowledge. Nor could magics avail the waning world in any way, for everyone knows that magic is no longer touched in all the civil lands. It is against the old laws as well as the new."

"Is that a fact?" Nergalf interjected. "Then teach us how the princes of Hyrcanth and Kargiwall acquired their strange spells. For many years, against the universal decrees, they have taken viziers secretly trained in Nystol, and have even been smuggling potions and arcane scrolls. All these years it was a mystery to your confederacy: they have been using the same deeply delving route since the times of their grandfathers!

"I myself shall lead a fearsome troop through Gulconda and up into Astodan. We shall sack Nystol, putting and end to the wickedness that is brewing there. They shall drink the foaming cup of my wrath!"

Nergalf seemed to foam at the mouth, his veins turning the colour of the wine. "You enrage a dwarf, anything can happen." I thought to myself. "That sort of avenging hate can only end sour. It is a dangerous state of mind you are in, dwarf. Where shall that consuming wrath lead you? It will never end well, only in more death...I did not much like him and I was determined to expose him as false.

"Can't you reckon how things are out your hands now? " I said to him. "Better to let old hatreds rest, sparing yourself the miseries of a godless labour. To loose your soul is much worse than to loose your empire. The ambition of someone like you, who has nothing to lose, is doomed. Accept your fate and let those old Arcanes be...the waning world does not harken to them much anymore these days."

"Not so...rather I am one partial to the idea." remarked the fellow soldier, Shu Kurgoman, a Kath. He was one highly respected for his skill even among the knights. "Why do the civil lands not band against the unclean city? Should righteous kingdoms let a nameless fear of weird invocations and curses rule over them, and over us all? Must every land continue to send them sacrifices, many hecatombs, the fattest cattle? What will the Arcanes demand next, your virgin daughters, your first born? We should take up cause with the dwarf. Nor can the Nystoli be thought innocent by repute of distant forefathers: many slaves did those early mages once burden, working them to death. It is time for retribution."

"The old magic is useless and does nothing now." I said. "Nystol is powerless, as I heard it, and she is just going on her reputation. That is the real reason why Anherm the wizard never came to aid the Emperor yesterday. He had no war-magic to offer. We should spend our effort convincing the kings of this. The demon-gods have been expelled from the temples. A new hope is upon the earth, the voice of the Man-god crucified. We should be done with wars and hatreds now. Time for penance and bitter tears worshipping God, lest avenging angels harass our tormented minds."

"You foolish humans never cease to talk of angels as of late." Nergalf said mockingly. "I don't ever remember an angel following my orders for battle, or cooking up a fat dinner for me. But who is this soft-skinned hand, this Waffle, farting so much talk here, an overgrown sprout?"

"I am the son of Barnas, Wassel of Ulthorc, war-vassal to Dunstaark who has arrested you. I am ready to do his bidding come hell or highwater."

"This lad is nothing but a lowly lugger, no warrior, certainly not of a chivalrous stalk. Can he even grow a full beard? Wherefore does he dare censure my wit? What lands has he conquered?"

There was a silence.

"Conquer thyself." I replied, frowning.

"Ha..ha... *conquer thyself*, what profound wisdom. Save your wisdom to the monks, Waffle, for unless you consider the wealth that I offer, you will end up locked away in some monastery on your knees with them."

It was at this time that I began to secretly desire a like share of the cleverness and advantage of matching words that this oversized dwarf displayed. Nergalf, the kind of being who did not dwell completely within mountains or underground, was really only half dwarf, a demi-dwarf in whose ancestry there was some human blood intermixed. He had the desirable qualities of both races. The keen and stamina of dwarven kind, and the ingenuity and gracefulness of men.

I resented the way he mocked me and scoffed at my youth and inexperience. He had made me seem the fool. But yet I craved to be as great a warlord as he, to inspire others like he did, change minds, and be an accomplished adventurer.

I had been trained by my brothers in sword-craft and had exceled in fencing and the joust. In my home town I had achieved notoriety and even been enrolled in the feudal militia. At some point, I had resolved to make fighting and skillful military accomplishment my career, so I left for greater kingdoms.

For years I had tried to distinguish myself and had finally been noticed by the grand knight of the Ammouric order. He promised that in time, if I survived the war and distinguished myself in battle, that although certainly by birth not eligible for knighthood, I might be eligible for captaincy in the yeoman's brigade and someday have a hope for fiefdom and feudal title.

In the engagement I marched at the *trope* of the lines, and everyone saw how I routed many of the foe, recklessly leading the charge. They had remembered my effort and declared me worthy of commendation. However, the grand knight, who had watched me, and from whom I received those hints of hopeful elevation, now lay dead upon the gory field.

Now was that dwarf come.

Only someone with the skill of this Nergalf could simply walk into an enemy tent and persuade them to his cause. It was then that I realized how clever diplomacy and planning could advance a man even more than the sword, but neither did I have that skill. So I prided myself in supposing that I must be at least be equal to Nergalf in fencing. I soon came to a resolve of proving this and causing the arrogant dwarf some dismay, for certainly, if we followed him, we would be confronted by the underworld army of darkness, as all the old sagas describe.

Nergalf turned to Dunstaark and continued.

"It is your brutal squadron, knight, that now is given the opportunity, the first offer of sharing in the work, and therefore in its bounty. Help me reach Nystol and we shall put to the stake those wicked necromancers and seize their most valued treasures!"

"The dangers of such a diversion are too great." warned my brother who also was with us, having come to fight in the wars, (at last meeting up with me on the plain of Gederon after so many years). "...Nergalf is a defeated world-tyrant, a high criminal. You," he added turning to the dwarf, "should be swinging at the end of a chain! Your capture is worth coin enough."

"Is it? What are a few bags of copper and silver compared to priceless magic scrolls, potions, precious stones, gold, perhaps even the Nagamaud Amulet itself? What is more, I hear that the Spear of Destiny, a priceless holy relic, the lance that pierced the side of the crucified God, lay in a king's tomb, somewhere in the intermundane caverns."

"It is unlawful to steal from the dead." Perigraunce warned. "What is it that you want with such a relic anyway?"

Nergalf did not answer, so I, knowing the legend, explained it: "The army of he who holds the Spear and lifts it, for the conquest, that army cannot be defeated in battle."

"It is the vain and useless legend of a shattered god." Dunstaark remarked.

"Vain, perhaps for some," said Nergalf, "but not useless. Armies can be persuaded by legends. The legend of Nystol's power herself has been enough to keep would-be conquerors from raising armies against her. We must present an equally potent counter-legend."

Let me treat on those years a bit more for you. When he ruled, Nergalf had sought to increase imperial sway in far places of the furthreaches. When some of Hermius' eastern governors, generals in the Arahom princedoms and the eastern lands of Arraf, heard that Hermius was dead, that the legend himself turned out to be mortal, they boldly endeavored to cut out hegemonies for themselves. They even began neglecting tribute and raising their own militias. Even some of the Ammouric kings allied with them.

Nergalf, having long before perceived their lying flatteries and hidden arrogance in the years when he had stood next to Hermius receiving the submission of kings to the empire, had cleverly anticipated their moves. He would act with a severity that would put a decisive end to their plans and secure his megalomaniacal threat over all.

After the return of the *necrophylactoi*, the burial wardens of Hermius, a month after the secretive interment, the ruthless dwarf immediately held an enthronement ceremony. He invited several of the suspect generals and captains.

Having the doors locked behind them, Nergalf hinted little by little at his grim intentions. They feasted unsuspectingly, and he gave a speech, likening them to the very game upon which they were dining. Now his reign of terror began. One by one he himself brutally with his own hands decapitated each suspect in the feast-hall of Hermius, while in their very seats, in sight of all the guests.

Unleashed with violence, he struck fear into all legionaries and caused them to swear oaths of loyalty to him alone. He lifted his sword and went forth with his legions across every land. He quashed rebellion and mutiny in northern frontiers and made devastating war with the Durgoth barbarians in the northern Arahom, for they alone among men first dared defy his new rule. He punished them severely and their kind has never recovered. From there he pushed into mountainous Thasos and established permanent garrisons, even demanding tribute from the gigantic races. Then, with the assistance of the feudal Barons of Kargiwall, he gathered an even greater army.

He marched all the way down to Kutaal and put an end to uprisings among the nomads. A year later he marched East and seized the twelve mountain-forts of Atalur. He conscripted their warriors and invaded Kalar, (a vengeance in honor of Hermius who had died at their hands) and he put to the sword the Emperor Bamusk I and all the arrogant princes of the Succon and Gohha, sparing only the eldest province Sarnas out of superstition of the accursed land. He re-established the fortress of Ptur and the ring of strongholds in the Valaghir mountains, at last forcing the entire Eastern isthmus into submission. His loyal army next penetrated as far as Xasbur cutting out that same dark region beyond the Eastern Mountains, the same into which Hermius, years before, dared not venture. He had become the new legend, celebrated even by opposing armies, and so percieve how this living legend could even now persuade any soldier, like Mahegal of the *Lay of Illystra*.

His ambitious conquests however exhausted the treasuries of the Aideen Archonate. Soon the long-humiliated princes in the Western feudatories began to imagine themselves strong again while Nergalf spent years occupied in the east quelling all the Arraf-tongue.

So the Western princes and senators came out of hiding and revolted against Nergalf's reckless and overbearing dictatorship. The Maceonid kings, who had saved themselves by becoming his client kings, "obedient friends of the divine hero," being too long relegated to a mere honorary role, now banded together in a fearsome alliance against him.

Now the war was over. Gederon had decided the issue, the storm was abating. The rain outside had died down.

My brother's warning (and my cautious words too) rung hollow as thoughts of glory and untold riches filled the minds of the other soldiers. They had only seen scant action and nothing of glory while fighting for Ulthork, and now an enterprise of merit touched their ears.

The right thing for us to do would have been to conduct that criminal warlord to the general council. Just trial could rightly gauge his guilt, and so off to execution or the inescapable Othgog.

However, as is common among men, the worse counsel guided vain hearts and untrained minds. Most of our crew spoke up in favor of such an expedition, fearful of returning home with no booty from the war.

"It is not a disagreeable ambition to me," said Dunstaark, "and in truth, I think it a grand strategy. I too am quite curious as to what places brood beneath our feet. You, dwarf, will be our ungracious guide, though in your *mania* you still speak of conquering the world by lifting a magic spear. Perhaps it is an entertaining last hope for such as you. As for me, I am certain that a diety who could not hinder the Romani from nailing him up, surely would not offer much in the way of world-conquering relics."

"You underestimate the new deity," said Perigraunce, interrupting. "His spirit waxes more powerful since his passing from this world. Even Hermius fell under his influence, though you are right in this: the king of kings has no need of magical spears."

"The gods are mysterious." replied Dunstaark "and I am satisfied enough with that saying, but now let us look to the mysterious things that are at hand: you men have sworn oaths to me and are obliged to follow my adventure. Therefore strike we upon waters of the deep at once with this dwarf, or return home in poverty. And there is a further reason to do it. You all know this: that I am envied and hated by the other captains because, unlike they, I did not inherit this. I am not a Maceonid. On that account, the noble houses would not even give our banner an honorable position in the lines.

"Now that the uprising is over and Dunstaark no longer needed, the princes will try to eliminate me in a bid for power among themselves, for they will accept only one leader. Nor will the kings protect me. If we turn over this dwarf to law, I have no doubt that they will accuse us of harboring him, and since they will wish to erase every witness of wrong-doing, the entire platoon will be put to death, charged for having made conversation with the enemy. It happened to my cousin Urlash and his red-star shields after the Battle of Longhairs. That is how much they want our kind out of their way.

"Nergalf speaks the truth when he says that some of the Maceonid dynasties have become embroiled in power struggles, scions of deeper conspiracies. They accepted the white-robes of the Ammouri and raised the banner of the lamb, but it is now become a lie. Inwardly they are ravenous wolves."

"Even so, as you say captain, but let us not dare go into the deepearth." my brother said, urging caution, "It is unlawful to awaken the dwellers-beneath!. . .The doom-writ must not be transgressed. It would be better to die at the hands of men than in the jaws of whatever lay down there."

I knew that they would not heed my brother. However I myself actually began to desire this journey, since I had not really proved myself in either war or adventure. I cleverly protested in order that I might not be able to blame myself if things went wrong.

"Aye, the law forbids it," said another soldier, huge Hakkarl the fearless, sounding even more gravely, "the dwellers-beneath must not be awoken!"

"Then you will not mind being executed with me tomorrow for treason?" said Dunstaark. "Very well, it is an honorable end in the eyes of the gods. However your families will only hear that you went to a shameful end. So I shall go and inform the next tent, and have them come bring away the captive, this dwarf, to appear in chains before the kings."

At this there was a great outcry by all the soldiers standing there. The commander was clever and effectively silenced the warnings of the cautious. (They might have saved their breath, for they seemed not to have even spoken).

"So then, yield your minds to it. . .let us no longer waver. Hark ye all," continued Dunstaark, "We will do this...as you have all consented by cheers, not for mere loot alone...nor only to save our own necks from the rope. . .rather unto a higher cause: the dwarf, though he is doomed, convinces. Does any of us not foresee that the evil of Nystol will soon prosper? Everyone confesses that its dark influence has grown these past years. No cunning general or even ambitious foreign prince would dare lead an army against Nystol."

"'Tis true...time increases their knowledge, their power." Nergalf said, adding fuel to his flames, "...and her Mages laugh about it loudly in their ivory towers."

"It is not right that such an indolent city should yet stand." Dunstaark continued. "This dread work is for a select few. Now may be the only chance that the civil lands will be given to put an end to the vain magics of their ill-omened towers. The prophecies say that Nystol shall someday wax mighty in her sorceries and take dominion of all the furth. I, for one, must stand against the witchery."

(Who can judge what hidden desire for glory or wealth my captain's heart had secretly coveted. It were true that the princes were plotting against him, but this path too would go ill for him, as for the rest of us under his command).

"First, mind ye...all ye," announced the bloody dwarf, "the key to our success lay close. It is the chart drawn by Kruthendel Eloniah, that prudish gnome who seems to get involved in every manner of mysterious dealings. We must first acquire the copy of his subterraneous chart. Zenops, vizier of the King of Kargiwall, had several copies of it drawn three quarters of a century ago, in the years when I was still with the sand-pirates of the Dry Blood Sea. One copy was sold to a prince of Ayrs, another to that devilish queen of Hyrcanth, yet another to unknown buyers, and the last to the Ammouric Divines, the clerics of Vesulum, the holy city, adversaries of

Nystol.

"After I was elevated to Admiral in Hermius' army," the dwarf continued, "I came across the copy that is kept in Vesulum. As a conqueror beside Hermius, when I visited the holy cliff-city of the deeply-carved canyon, I had easily required the lesser clerics to admit me into their library, forbidden to all others. I came upon it almost by seeming chance, for none of the monk-librarians could right sure identify what regions the map-scroll represented.

"The linework of the chart was an amazing piece of artistry, drawn on the featherless wing of the Acquavarian bat of Setet. But was it dependable or at all accurate? To gain the edge, I thereupon sent a letter to Kruthendel himself in Whigg, for the gnome never lies. He replied, as he usually does, with annoying enigmatic phrases, assuring that he could not remember how accurately drawn was the chart. Only its copyist, Zenops, could right say. The gnome explained that the map identifies the proper route of those traveling through the labyrinths of many passages. It is the only chart able to navigate one through Gulconda. However the magic does not last for indefinite years, but persists in accord with the experiential power of the preparer. Only Zenops, whom the Nystoli trained, could reckon its duration and activate its magic. The gnome then added that, at any rate, me-self and everyone else should keep clear of those nether regions.

"I requisitioned the chart in the name of the Emperor and sent it north to Zenops for verification, not being able to make the journey myself. I had to stay there in Vesulum with Emperor Hermius and continually console him, for my master Hermius was in a dreadful state of lover's perplexity over that demon-queen in Hyrcanth, sometimes acting maniacal, even suicidal. It was not so bad for me, At least the acolytes of that holy city treat their guests rather well. Hermius however was not even able to enjoy the benefits of the imperial quarters in which they housed us, for he was all a-fluster about that fair queen and could think of nothing else.

"It was a foolish risk to let the magic map part from my hands, but who would ever imagine that some low magician might dare meddle in the affairs of Hermius the Conqueror and me his Field Admiral?

"The day that my messenger arrived in Ironport carrying the letter and chart for the wizard was a fateful day. It happened to be the very same day that the king's vizier Zenops, a wizard, had been implicated in his famous plot against the throne.

"In order to preserve his own life from the mad throng of townsmen who expected to burn him at the stake, Zenops, always an opportunist, at dagger-point, seized my messenger Alember, bearer of the chart. Retreating into the milltower just outside Ironport, the nasty wizard held Alember and the map hostage. He was claiming that if the people tried to smoke him out of the milltower, then his new hostage the very ambassador of Hermius would perish as well. It would be an act of war that would call down the fury of the greatest commander the world had ever known.

"The old king, Valherc, was too delirious from Zenop's spell craft to take the matter into his own hands. So the people of Kargiwall and of the town Ironport, remembering the strength and authority of my master Hermius, Conqueror of Worlds, feared to smoke him out. They let the tower be.

"It was only after several months that we got news of these occurrences. By then Zenops had finished his excavations and disappeared, escaping through the basements of the milltower into the vast connections of intermundane caverns below, taking with him the precious chart."

"Did he then go to Nystol?" I asked.

"No, silly...word is that Zenops did not like to travel, and besides, not only did he have enemies in Nystol, but he was unable to gain blade-mastering allies to protect him on any proposed expedition. Not even his personal guards would agree to such perilous work with an accursed traitor. So for a time he lay low, having it published abroad that he had perished at the hands of those famous raiders of saga, The Bladetongue. It is said that he himself is the author of that famous saga, a hexameter poem whose description of horrors he hoped would deter nobles from leading expeditions into his new tower, and it has. He also arranged for spreading rumour that his tormented spirit wanders about the lower tower. Meanwhile he garrisoned the lower roots of his tower with mercenary centaurs and drow-elves, waiting until King Valherc above passed away.

"Afterwards, iron and other material became available to him again, and he resumed construction on the cyclopean walls of his deep-rooted tower. These walls are extended many fathoms downward until they come to rest on floor of the intermundane caverns, by the Rathsurge. It is the only tower known to pass through two worlds!"

"And so what of it? Must we descend below Zenops' tower and look for the map down there?"

"That is our prize. Once we have the map we shall take the river Rathsurge to where it re-emerges and joins into the river Alph that flows at the very bottom of Hermius' Canyon, far to the south of Vesulum. From there by foot it is only eight leagues South and East through the wilderness of Kedemoth to the Sardu plateau and the cavernous entrance of the lost Gulconda route."

"That is a harsh land." I said. "Even though our journey overland might be short, I fear the bands of a brutal hyena tribe known to be in that area, they might easily track us down."

"What worry if you have the feared sword of Nergalf with you? I know that on your own you all would die, but I myself know well their tactics, having slain many of them when I was with the sand-pirates. They are the least of our concerns."

Nergalf confidently dismissed my concerns. How unnecessary was the boasting of the dwarf.

"And what of the Mages and Wizards of Nystol?" I asked. "How can we hope to sack their city, the few of us, if they can cast their enchantments upon us and bring to ruin our spell-bound souls?! The wands and rings still work!"

"Gird your loins for the daring! We will not be making an overt attack, since all such attempts have failed anyway. Instead my plan is a clever one: but heed now closely and know that when ye hear this ye may not repeat it or pull out of the pact. My words must now enter oathbound confidence. Agreed? Swear ye."

We all swore an oath, like heathens, not to betray his plan.

"We shall go up past the tombs of Astodan, make our way through the corridors of the city and find the famous tower of Hennsooth, a library where the most powerful of magical scrolls and tomes are kept. Advancing by stealth into the tower we shall alight embers and bring forth flame, burning the scrolls in their cases and the books in their bindings, though saving anything precious for ourselves. With flames arisen from each of us placed in different areas, the inferno will shortly consume the great tower withall. The unholy power of mortal magics shall be forever crippled. Nystol will never recover. If that is my last act, I shall end a happy dwarf, both avenging myself on them for the betrayal of my army today at Gederon, and for betraying my ancestors in days of old, righteous dwarves who engineered the city itself."

"Betraying your ancestors?" Someone asked.

"Do you think that old wizards raised those monuments of stone in Nystol by their own primitive magics?" Nergalf asked. "Let me refresh your history. It were dwarves, no other race, that aided in the designing and raising up of those colossal towers, in an age forever past. But our dwarf-fathers also built many secret passages and chambers in the mesa beneath, wherein to hide their own treasures and forbidden tomes.

"But suspicion and jealousy for power subjects even the wise. In fear that the dwarves themselves might use their secret knowledge against them, some of the Arcanes, wary of our race, plotted against my ancestors, who only sought to obtain a labourer's wage from them. When the great Elkomenon, first Archmage of Nystol, was dying, the Arcanes conspired and made a plan. They hired the dwarves to engineer a huge tower-tomb for him.

"When my ancestors had at last finished the construction and the old mage had died, the Arcanes held the burial ceremony of Elkomenon there in the new "Mausoleum of Elkomenon," the Tomb of High Rest. Even before the ancient rites were completed, they cruelly tricked my forefathers, eagerly locking the engineers within, permanently sealing them in their own artistry. So did they pay the dwarves for their labours with treachery, and keep the vast monies for themselves. It was an abomination that has cursed the city ever since."

"Wizards and such are of clever mind." said one soldier, "But what about us, we do not wish to die in the corridors of Nystol, cut down by furious guards. Accursed be he who dies in an accursed land."

"Oh ye who know so little! Have you not heard how overconfident that accursed city has become?"

"Overconfident?"

"Even now they tolerate the likes of Sorcerers in their midst, Arcanes who have resorted to the practice of summoning of demons. The Arcanes are call down wrath upon themselves. Their overconfidence is there undoing. For over an hundred years now there has not been armed guards in Nystol, so seclusive has been the protection of the impenetrable desert. These fools (who claim to be sages), fancy themselves to have designed a city of peace and tolerance, yet they will not even tolerate the Soothfold or the embassadors of Argunizial. What is more, a very ancient and venerable order of sooths, the Eldark, not long ago, prophesied against the new tolerance-laws of Nystol, and against permitting Sorcery. So the Arcanes, indignant, expelled the old men into the desert! Those old men cannot strike back, so let it be us who are the tool of divine judgement upon them!"

Such a speech went over rather well among the crew of eager warriors with whom I had become involved. With the war over, and having barely even gotten taste of battle, they were now most willing adventurers.

First there was our chivalric commander, a man of heroical seed, Dunstaark, a strong earl recently girded with the sword, and a man of honour, worldly, but not averse to risk. It was he who made the final decision that we join with Nergalf, though he regretted it ever after.

And there was another captain, Sir Perigraunce. It seemed that many years had left him too slight of build to become battle-hardened, but he was faithful in all things. His grizzle hair was long and uncombed, his armour old, like mine, and he wielded a footman's mace rather than a sword. I never heard him speak well of Nystol.

Hakkarl was next, the sergeant at arms, a huge man of Ulthork, a reliable spear in a close fight.

Also came Raffing of Kithom who enjoyed many pranks, quick with the dagger.

Then Haroun the Gohhan, a dreamer and a hothead, but who knew many things about reconnaissance and infiltration. Such men were well-trained and ready for anything.

Shu Kurgoman, descendent of the famous Urius of the sagas, a hycman from distant Vath. He was swiftest among us men when delivering doom by deliberate swordstroke, and though filled with curiosity and lively interest, he rarely ever spoke. It was he who was the first to support Nergalf, for their race also bore a great grudge against Nystol.

My brother Hercil, a man of hidden talents and mind, had some years of training by the physicians of Vesulum, and was greatly valued by the company.

As for me, my only skill was to fight, and since that skill was unproven, I was usually consigned to any considerable gruntwork, but I had my iron swords and yew-hewn bow always at hand.

II

That very day we readied ourselves to follow the reckless dwarf into the netherworld, equiping ourselves with ropes, hooks, and many other unusual supplies that the dwarf brought forth out of his packs. We fitted all our rations as well in the rucksacks and grip-bags, being well outfitted with various leather paddings and straps, breathing tubes and sacks, special hides, and various torches and lanterns. For all that, there was no doubt in all our thoughts that we were undertaking the expedition blind, consulting with no one other than that devilish dwarf.

There was a cavern-entrance not but a day's march, which Nergalf claimed somehow connected with the river Rathsurge and would take us beneath Ironport and, running further down, land us at the gloomy base of Zenops' tower.

We left at the crack of dawn, armed to the teeth, slipping out of the perimeter before the rest of the army awakened (heads pulsating on account of the festivity of victory wine). No authority would count us as absent, for many had fallen the day before and chaos had won the fields even more than had the alliance. It was an easy cheat. No one could learn for certain which battalions had survived or which had perished, nor had any authority gathered a count of soldiers and knights from every different land.

We carried one of the long wooden skiffs which Ulthork had supplied to our platoon (for crossing the swamps of Aramthe to meet the enemy on the plain of Gederon). Now it had a new, more questionable purpose. As a joke, we named it Hell-breaker. It was a long boat with iron bracers and reinforcements, fitting just eight men prow to stern, (with an eighth and perhaps a ninth man to be squeezed in) rather heavy for its size, especially for the grunts like me who had to break backs for portage, but her girth was sufficient.

Although Kargiwall is an infamously desolate land of rusty dirt, rocky crags, crevices, and awful storms, we encountered no problems from weather or even Kargiwall's militia. Some took this to be a sign of divine favour of our mission. I was not so foolish as to think Allfather approved, only foolish enough to submit to the enterprise in the first place.

At last, weary from carrying that heavy boat, we arrived at the cave entrance. We set "Hell-breaker" down and sat upon the stones of the massive entrance. Saying one last prayer we begged forgiveness and prepared to enter, sealing our doom. How knavish are those who pray to avoid evil while purposely stepping into its very den! I should have fled right then, slipping away after they had all went ahead.

It seemed to have at one time been some sort of mine, perhaps quarried in ancient times by the giants, its threshold reaching some forty feet high.

"It is a mighty heavy boat for only three men to bear," I commented, rubbing my shoulders.

"Rest up a while then." said Dunnstark.

"The day has not yet even reached midward and we have a ways to go before we reach the river." observed Nergalf, standing on a boulder. "We must hurry. Order your men to work. I would never let my soldiers rest."

"Perhaps that is why you are in your present unseemly position." Added Perigraunce, with a chuckle.

"Ye dare address Nergalf so!' the dwarf said angrily, "Had I my sword I might teach you what respect is owed the empire!"

"That is why you must remain unarmed, at least until we return from Nystol." snapped Dunstaark.

"That will not do." argued Nergalf. "There are horrors down there, the winding passages of Gulconda, from which only I can protect you."

"We shall see." replied Dunstaark "As of yet there is no reason to trust you, and every reason to put you in chains. How even do you know of what's in there?"

We all peered into the huge mouth of the cavern which was lit up in the still morning by a diffuse light of overcast brilliance, a rare thing in stormy Kargiwall. We could hear the drip of water and faint echoes of hollow places far below. Massy slabs of broken stone, many cast down by earthquake, lay in hazardous barrier which faded into the diminishing blue illumination.

"You had best not have any knowledge withheld." Haroun

added. "If you are leading us into some deadly trap in the dark, dwarf lord, or some weird enchanting, ye will see much spillage of blood."

After the resting of our sore shoulders from the load of that Hell breaker, we began again. The two knights, Dunnstark and Applegorn, marched us further, navigating us around the huge slabs blocking the entrance cavern. We followed a path of high vaulted shafts into the hill and the morning light began to fade away behind us. We at last came to a place where a grand shaft descended sharply and the refracted light was cut off.

"Now, ye man kin," said Nergalf in an eerie tone "take one last look at the light from above. I cannot safeguard you in the dark below, some of you may not return. It is your choice!"

The descending shafts were comfortably wide and unrestricted, and fortunately no wild beasts inhabited its cozy dens as we hurriedly passed through. The huge corridor slanted downward at a sharp angle and on several occasions we were forced to use ropes to lower ourselves. The most difficult moments occurred when the boat had to be lowered by ropes and near rolled over upon us several times.

We knew that we had reached the appropriate depth when we heard the tumult of rushing water near. Soon the dwarf led us through several rocky and dim chambers as the noise of splashing increased. As we approached the shores of the great and turbulent river and spotted its vast ceiling, it soon became apparent that we would not be needing bright lanterns. An eerie green and brownish glow of the subterraneous lichen on the walls and on stalactites gave off ample light, but not enough for the eye to penetrate the depth of the swirling black water. A dank odor of mud and limestone permeated the subterraneous air.

There on that sandy narrow shore we embarked upon the cold waters of the Rathsurge. I sat in the front, just behind Hakkarl at the prow seat whose keen eyes could spot rocks. There was barely enough room in that narrow little vessel for all of us.

Soon entering a vast waterway we let the swift current take us into places unknown, undreamt of.

Perhaps an hour passed in this alien environ, Eastward flowing, massive halls of stone, water, and shadows. As we drifted I had much time to contemplate my possibly obscure death. The only satisfaction I could take was that my own townsfolk would imagine I had perished fighting in the war against Nergalf. They would never learn the weird truth of my fate. I imagined my bleeding head adorning the end of some hobgoblin's pike.

Here I was, still a wiry beardless youth in oversized chainmail tunic, cutting my life short to satisfy the dreams of a mad dwarf and curious captain. I could not imagine how a few warriors could possibly penetrate the notorious tower of Zenops, filled, they say, as it is with

heavily armoured Wyrmlords and bolgs, trolls and goblin, or worse. Who knows but that Zenops himself might still be alive with his unholy magic to hurl at us.

Then, even more insanely, we imagined that we were going to raid Nystol, a city of Arcane masters.

While lost in my dreadful and melancholy thoughts, I stared into the hypnotic whirlpools that slipped by just beneath my arm resting on the boat's rim. I noticed that presently no rower was causing this churning by a paddle, for only Nergalf steering at the rear had his rudder in the wake. What then was causing the swirls passing by? I leaned over slightly to examine more closely.

"Gaze not into the waters." warned Nergalf, gravely. Surprised and alarmed at this admonition I tried to look back at him cast down by earthquake, lay in hazardous barrier which faded into the diminishing blue illumination.

"You had best not have any knowledge withheld." Haroun added. "If you are leading us into some deadly trap in the dark, dwarf-lord, or some weird enchanting, ye will witness much spillage of blood.

After the resting of our sore shoulders from the load of that Hell-breaker, we began again. The two feudal lords, Dunnstark and Perigraunce, marched us further, navigating us around the huge slabs blocking the entrance cavern. We followed a path of high-vaulted shafts into the hill and the morning light began to fade away behind us. We at last came to a place where a grand shaft descended sharply and the refracted light was cut off.

"Now, ye man-kin," said Nergalf in an eerie tone, "take one last look at the light from above. I cannot safeguard you in the dark below, some of you will not return. It is your choice!"

The descending shafts were comfortably wide and unrestricted, and fortunately no wild beasts were inhabiting its cozy dens as we hurriedly passed through. The huge corridor slanted downward at a sharp angle and on several occasions we were forced to use ropes to lower ourselves. The most difficult moments occurred when the boat had to be steadied by ropes but near rolled over upon us several times.seeking an explanation, but I could not turn round fully in the cramped space.

Now a strange mist at once arose over us and covered us about. The sound of crashing waters came up swiftly, and soon we found ourselves in tumultuous rapids.

"Hold fast, yeomen!" cried Nergalf. "This torrent is the final descent into the intermundane level!" The current rushed the vessel onwards, at times nearly tipping us. The greatest terror was when the craft was propelled swiftly into swaths of complete blackness and several times smashed against rocks unseen. How is it possible that this boat, even with the reinforced metal, did not shatter?

It seemed our skiff was hurled into the air several times over a series of cataracts. There was no doubt in anyone's mind, save perhaps Nergalf, that the final moments had come.

We finally came to the terminus of raging and swift flowing waters, and slowing down the boat no longer drifted. I began to perceive, by the many echoes and distant glow of underlichen, that we had entered a vast subterraneous lake of some sort. A misty cold rain released from some unseeable ceiling high above constantly showered us. Nergalf began to chant in some strange but familiar rhythm in his native dwarf-tongue, by which the rowers could pull sequenced oarage.

I soon noticed that the soldier who was positioned in front of me, in the prow, Hakkarl of Ulthork, a huge man and good soldier, had somehow fallen asleep. I shook his shoulder with my hand and his head fell back. It was split apart horribly. Somehow in the raging chaos and darkness the strap of his metal cap must have popped. Hakkarl of Ulthork was dead. I had known him only four weeks.

"First sign of ill omen!" cried Haroun, his fellow,"We will all perish down here. Sunk down so deep into the earth, too far to climb out, where no sunlight can ever penetrate, and where unspeakable volumes of rock hang over our heads to crush us at any moment! It is a fool's bargain!'

"Restrain your dreading and any more like-haver, get hold of yourself." demanded Kurgoman, the hycman from Vath, a sturdy man-at-arms. These hyc are close to the human, perhaps even human. Bad-spirited folk with impunity name them half-orcs, as if they be the whelps of vile orcans. It is a slight against a wholesome old race, an insult born of cruel pusillanimity, a sinful ignorance. Such a be-mixture of the corporeal spindle with troll-kin is an impossibility, as it is written, there is one flesh of baalites and fey, but another of men.

"No," cried Raffing, "we should cry out for help, we are lost, in hopeless darknesses upon darknesses! -faint and airless under threat of crushing rock!"

"Havering knave! Who now will come save you? Any more of that kind of talk," Nergalf warned, "and I will crush you with my own dreadful hands before ever the rocks come falling through the dark. Now keep silent. We shall lay out the good soldier and prayers over him when we attain an undershore."

Now much time passed in this dark underworld lake, the good part of a day, if there be such things as days down there. It were impossible to measure distance or direction, therefore we were entirely at the mercy of Nergalf's dwarf-keen.

After a while Dunnstark spoke.

"Perigraunce, you have not said much, and you are long silent. Say what thoughts you are secretly thinking, for though you are of insufficient bloodlust, there is no one who can match your perceptions and wise council."

After some pause he gave reply.

"Unwise were we to tumble down here into this gloom, to heed such impulsive suggestion and rashly hurl ourselves into the bowels of earth. It might well be our undoing. Every hand among us should fold for the saying of suppliant prayers."

"It is true." I added "We did not even think to bring an Ammouric priest with the proper rites for the dead and for prayers against spirits."

"Who needs prayers of a priest?" Dunstaark commented, "Men should accept their fate."

"A priest would never have followed the likes of Nergalf into this anyway." observed Raffing.

"True, and we should have reached the roots of Zenops' tower by now, Nergalf." said Dunstaark. "We should be all the way to the waters beneath Ulthork by my reckoning. You cannot fool an Ammouric Ranger. One soldier is already dead. So cherish thou well that we also are a grim company with whom you must reckon, lest you risk our necks unnecessarily. Answer then or be wary of our wrath: whither are you steering us?!"

Nergalf did not answer right away. There were several moments of silence as we listened to the water droplets hitting the black surface of the waters. Then at last he spoke in a loud whisper.

"Be silent and listen close to what sounds may drift to your ears on the ripples of this vast pond. We are not wise to travel these waters, and we are not given leave, not without a tablet of passage from the elf queen. Therefore first we go to her castle, since if her elf-sailors should ever come upon us, they will send their shafts without polite introduction. If her navy does intercept us before we get there, they must attack, not expecting the likes of armed men down this far. I have heard from my cousins that she is at war."

"At war? With whom?"

Many long moments passed by. Again Nergalf did not answer, but only softly intoned a long "Shhhhhh. We will guess it if we spot them. We don't want to attract any attention."

Another unmeasured span of time in silences and shadows passed.

III

How it was that Nergalf had been able to steer the boat through such sightless tunnels I could not fathom. I whispered a question to my brother.

"How did that mad dwarf have the keen to steer us through? It is incredible that only one man was knocked dead in that torrent."

"Dwarves and other *elphim*" he replied, "they have a racial power of what we physicians call the infravision, and which the elves call darksight, the faculty of perception at lowest levels of light."

"I fear we have already attracted attention." said Nergalf suddenly. Cover your heads down, some enemy ship hither approaches. We can still conceal, mayhap at a distance they should mistake us for some log or rock!"

"Who should?"

Nergalf pointed to a vague shape barely discernable at a distance in the darkness and mist. It was a ship of most alien design, a sort of grizzly-shaped galley decorated with horns and threatening jawlike shapes.

"Curses...it be the Wyrmlords already," Nergalf whispered loudly. "They must be patrolling. Their ears must have heard us. But their eyesight is not the best, at least not anymore, its not even as powerful as your own. I think we can fool them."

"Wyrmlords?"

"Warriors of Chaos: berserks, possessed by the *drakodemon*, their humanity consumed. They are instead like men soulwise being of dragon's seed, and of unmatched fury!"

"How many?" asked Dunstaark.

"Can we escape these demoniacs?" asked Raffing.

"Not a fair chance."

"If we make the ship look like a log, if we crouch down, might they pass us by?"

"That's what I was hoping. But no, not likely, too late for that now. See, they come about toward us. We cannot out-manuever them."

"Carry arms!" ordered Dunstaark. "Give no quarter!"

Within moments the horrendous dragonship was bearing down upon us.

"Our vessel is too small for them to board and offer their bladework." said Nergalf, as the grisly dragon ship closed in on us. "So our boat's size might yet be advantageous, but we must keep clear of their flaming darts!"

Soon we lost any hope to escape the onslaught of those berserking "knights of Chaos." As they neared I could see more clearly perhaps twenty of them, most of whom were occupied rowing. Their helmets were of dreadful horn and their armour scaley red-dragon fins, while their shining red eyes betrayed how possessed they were with unholy power. Their weird galley of bristling spikes and grimacing shields bore down upon us like a hawk upon a duck.

The first thing they hurled at us, when they came in range, was a grappling hook, and this was lobbed through the volumes of air. This great claw, a many-pronged grappling hook, struck the corpse of Hakkarl, still bent over in front of me, and lodged its iron talons deep in the dead flesh of his back. The corpse's weight, since he was a well armoured man and was wedged into the narrow prow and his legs under the thwart, enabled them to begin pulling us in quite easily. The hook-claw was right in front of me, in arm's reach.

"Sever that line!" cried Nergalf.

I lunged forward and began to work at the taut line with my knife. Next a volley of flaming arrows rained down upon us, most of which passed into the black water. A burning shaft passed by my head, of terrifying speed and fury, and struck inside of the skiff, catching its fire to the canvas that covered our supplies.

The dagger was of no avail, for the line was especially strong.

"Try this tool!" said Raffing behind me, handing me a small hand axe. Still, the axe did not accomplish it, and I could not swing at a sidewards stroke properly without tipping the boat, since the corpses' weight and tug of the enemy had unbalanced us enough.

"Dump that soldier's body!" yelled Nergalf.

'That is sacrilege!" I cried.

"Not if it spares our lives!" retorted Nergalf. "Go ahead, do it."

There was no other choice in this engagement. I do not regret the decision to obey, heeding even that dwarf, and I do pray every day that the man's spirit learns not to hold it against me. Hakkarl's corpse sunk down swiftly, vanishing into watery darkness under the weight of his armour.

The fire from the arrow was not easily extinguished, for they had used some sort of burning jelly to spread the flames. The battlehand Brodain of Yahoros was struck and much effort was made to put out the burning of his leg. It did not spread easily however, since everything was still rather drenched from the cataracts.

Once free of the grappling hook we hoped to evade them, escaping into the mist, but they still further pursued us even though they were slowed by the line dragging the corpse through the water. The body weighed their ship down. Such iron instruments as those sizable hooks, I later learned, are expensive and highly valued in the underworld. The dragon-men would not sever the line and part with it, but found it necessary to slowly dredge up Hakkarl's heavy body and armour. Nevertheless they were soon in close pursuit again.

"They have terrifying speed on land, in hand to hand combat, and at sea their ships are swift, though they have some disadvantage when lacking of fighting space." said Nergalf.

We paddled sternly and were running out of breath. Surely if they caught us we would be all been slain either in combat or, having surrendered, summarily executed. Though we ourselves had some training in battle, it was quite obvious that these warriors were of a skill quite beyond our understanding.

"My limbs will soon weary of this race," said Duunstaark, "it is most met that we resolve the issue. Come about...and attack these demoniacs...head on." In broken phrases this was ordered, for he was out of breath from rowing with hard push. (There was heard no assent of "aye" from any of us).

"Did no oathbound hand hear me? There will be no more of this cowardly straining. Let us not live without honour! You all know how to meet edge with steely edge and hazard defiant force against them. Will you yield your own ground?"

"What ground? There are but pools. Respect and honour mean little in this deep world." warned Nergalf. "All your men would wastefully perish in a frontal assault. No pitched battle be necessary. Even one Wyrmlord is a miserable fight for an experienced swordsman like you. Besides, ye are bound by word to destroy Nystol."

"I'll not lose honour doing so! Not by my ancestors!"

"Yes you will." retorted Nergalf. "One thing all my years of striving in vain warfare has taught me: honour among men is no safely kept thing. It fades away as quickly as it is won. Look at all my victories. Did it hinder the loathsome gossips and lying scibes from spoiling my name? Did it even teach lesser kings not to band against me in betrayal?"

"I have the charge of these men, Nergalf, but you are my hostage and have no say."

"Men," said Perigraunce, "we must obey the commanding lord,

paddle hard on the port to come about and make ready to match aggression."

The black dragon-ship was breathing down upon us, just barely in range for them to use the grappling hook again. The splash of the paddling was quickly drowned out by the increasing noise of the enemy's beaked prow cutting the water close behind.

Before we could come about, all of a sudden the horror ship turned away, rushing from our port side in a direction quarterwise of our bearing. It vanished moments later into the mists.

"Tartar-ship is gone off." someone said.

We let the boat drift for a few moments and recovered ourselves.

"You are, in my esteem, a dullard and haughty crown, sir..." said Nergalf with admonishing gravity, "to make such a claim of authority in these deep waters. It seems you barked those orders out of a sorely hurt pride. It is best to divest yourself of that honourable title here, for in the vast jaws of these enchanted places, your sword and buckle are no more than a child's rattle."

"As my prisoner and my guide you should overlook the fault, Dunstaark retorted, "lest you soon learn the chastisement of my dullard's fist."

"...you hope for treasure? Then you must hark to my word."

"The great emperor, in royal robe of borrel, ragged, speaks!"

(Dunstaark was mocking Nergalf's cloak, which he had taken from the armed-peasantry and covered over his fancy armour for disguise).

"Your jest will savor of shallow wit when all your warriors lay in purple heaps by the hands of devil-men, for selfish purpose of chivalric display."

"Both ye: still your tongues!" Perigraunce interrupted, (he was the kind of man in whose voice was wisdom, and whom everyone, even those ranked above, carefully heeded). "Take care not to gainsay each other or exchange contentious words in dark places, or else, like condemned souls, we be overwhelmed by it, lost in this watery abyss."

Suddenly we heard a great uproar of voices, a great clashing of weapons at some distance, where the Wyrmlord's ship should have gone. There were deathly screams echoing and the sound of victory pipes and drum, sword and buckler, the hurtling thud of darts hitting their targets. Some merciless sea-battle was unfolding. Nergalf steered the ship about. After the clangor began to pass we slowly made our way toward where the sounds had been made.

It took some pass of many moments to find it, since there were many echoes down there. The mist revealed a drifting ship on our starboard. First noticing the bright burning and smoke of flames, it soon became apparent that this was the same tartar-ship of the Wyrmlords. The bodies of the Wyrmlords were strewn about, their dragon-armour now fraught with arrows. There were no survivors left on that inferno-boat.

"Nergalf, who did this?" Dunstaark asked.

"The fighters of the Elf-queen, mayhap, or the karythar devoted to her. They can strike with just as much ferocity, obviously even more so. They may have been stealthily following the Wyrmlords for some time, biding for the right moment, and thanks to how we diverted the pace of the horror-ship, the right moment they had needed came. The Elf-queen does not bother to take hostages, especially not the fanatical dragon-men."

"What now, mad dwarf?" asked Dunstaark

"Now we row to the queen herself, and if we too encounter her navy, take care, and on no account vaunt or act with foolish aggression."

"The ship is sizable." I said. "Let us check her for their supply, before the minor fires become major."

"That is right wise," said Nergalf. "Come, let us do so quickly."

Upon entering the strange horny boat we examined the corpses of the Wyrmlords that lay about here and there on the boards, or doubled over the side. They had most unusual flesh, which seemed ashen and drained of blood, and yet some how also reptilian in texture. It was obvious that they had once been fully humans. Their armour was a most amazing craft of what might be horny dragon-scales, but on closer inspection it became obvious that the scaley armour was actually bodily, a sort of chiton attaches to their very flesh, as one might see on insects or other animals such as a turtle.

"What strange metamorphosis these men have undergone!" I exclaimed. What shall we do with their mortal shells?"

"We must bury them at sea." replied Dunstaark, "We cannot row the extra weight, since this ship is too large for three rowers as it is. We must put them over."

"Shall we say funeral rites?"

"Not even elves know funeral rites for such as these." said Nergalf.

"Let them go to the grim halls of their fathers as they are." commented Dunstaark.

As we began to take up the corpses, I spotted one of the bodies still breathing. There was an arrow in his side, but it looked as if he had been feigning death. I turned him over.

"This one is still quick, lungs still breathing." I said.

"Then cut his throat." snapped Nergalf.

"No. It is not right that we take no prisoners."

"We are at sea, we need not take prisoners." Nergalf retorted.

The Wyrmlord opened his bulbous eyes and looked at me. His eyes were hideous to behold, for it were a far less then a human stare he offered. The pupils were not round like our eyes, but rather creaturely slits, vertical such as a serpent's. It were a dreadful sight that caused me to jerk backwards recoiling in horror.

He was too overwhelmed by wounds to re-attempt combat. The others left what they were doing and stepped over to see the half-man draconian creature alive.

"Had we brought along an Ammouric Priest we might have performed an exorcism on him." Said Haroun. "Now however, in the name of the Most High, I will end the life of this abomination. Stand away!"

Haroun unsheathed his Gohan scimitar and positioned it to make a clean cut of the Wyrmlord's throat. His face was red with rage, ready to exact his own retribution for their attack.

"Wait, Haroun." said Perigraunce, who was standing just behind watching. "Stay your hand, lower your blade. Do not strike. There may be a way to free him of the evil spirit."

"How so?" I asked, as all were wondering.

"I have not been entirely forthright with this company."

"Not forthright, not true?" asked Sir Dunstaark. "What mean you, lord."

"I tell you this, and fail not to believe it: I am a priest, a man of the cloth, and I have the power to work an exorcism."

"You jest at an awkward moment, Perigraunce. You are clearly not a priest, though you might dream of it. There is not any way..." Dunstaark wondered, astounded and baffled.

"It is so. When I was a youth I spent many years training for the knighthood, but hear this: I am not a knight. In the year that I grew my first beard I realized that I did not wish to live a knight's world-weary life, of ring-taking and the keeping of fiefs. I began to sense that Allfather was calling me to make sacrifices, so I went to live with the monks. After a year they considered me too undisciplined and dismissed me. I wandered, but was soon taken in by Proclus, an aged priest who trained me in sacerdotal wisdom and practice."

"That is preposterous." said Dunstaark. "And how did you come to enlist among us?"

"Listen and you will learn. After the passage of seven years the patriarchs found me acceptable as a *selva* and prayed over me in Vesulum, beseeching that I be changed into a priest. The deepmost altercation was accomplished and the interior beast was deadened by divine intervention. I was elevated to the selvad. I took the sacred name Athanaric, cleric of the Ammouric faith.

I took years traveling from town to town and castle to castle as a selva in Ulthork, Chyldishire, and Kithom, preaching and shriving the flock for sins. Later I was given the care of the people of Arkt.

It was not long before I became very aware of how much the empire was causing the people to suffer, even in Arkt: they were exacting burdensome tribute, and enslaving the sons to Nergalf's ceaseless wars.

When the Maceonid nobility united against Nergalf and the civil war began, I decided that I must also fight for justice. I convinced the Thane of Aitherl, my liege, to join with Ulthork in the alliance. He agreed and I prepared to accompany our cavaliers. But my religious superiors, whom I had not seen or even heard from in over a decade, forbad this. Nor would the baron side with me against them. Nevertheless, I could no longer constrain my sense of indignation. With the help of some friends I feigned to withdraw to a monastery, and so escaped from the arm of the hierarchy.

I took up the arms of war and posed as a feudal lord. Soon I realized what kind of terrible mistake I had made, especially at the sight of Nergalf's host. I prayed that, were I to survive, I would return to my post as *selva* and beg forgiveness from the great shepherds. At a distance I saw my liege the Thane fall at Gederon.

Then afterwards Nergalf appeared at our tent. Perhaps I should have left there and then!"

"That is suspicious news indeed," said Dunstaark "and I should arrest you for impersonating a knight. So now do something right and demonstrate that you speak true, and so assure us that your mind has not been confused by these weird underworld airs. Perform the Ammouric exorcism on this pitiful soul, and restore him."

"A priest must keep the proper texts with him." I said. "He cannot perform his rites with out reading the thaumaturgical incantation."

"In cases of pressing need I may say an abbreviated form of the ritual, which I myself and all other priests memorize. So, please hold him steady with all your strength. The dragon-spirit will be fierce, for it has strong hold in these kind of demoniacs. You others, pray for him while this is accomplished."

I, Wassel, am not knowledgeable enough, my friend, to repeat the strange phrases for you in Latin and Akratic which Perigraunce used. To do so risks profaning what is sacred, and such prayers are jealously guarded by the Ammouric hierarchy. Nor have I learning enough to determine if it were proper to even repeat them.

Perigraunce made several mysterious gestures and placed his hand on the throat of the Wyrmlord, calling the demon forth in the unmentionable name of our deity the Lord of Hosts. The beast-demon struggled fiercely, and the Wyrmlord even bit Raffing, who did not complain, and kept hold of him. Now all this wrestling and convulsing put a great strain on the creature's body, which was already wounded badly and bleeding.

Soon it became apparent that the demon was stronger and would not leave the body, so Perigraunce tried a new prayer. He called upon the Archangel Michael, vanquisher of the great rebel, petitioning for his strength to force out the evil spirit. With this action the frame of the Wyrmlord started trembling and reeling wildly, and a most horrid guttural groan, which at the same time was accompanied by hissing sounds, resounding through the caverns. It seemed as if the creature were in its death-throes.

"What do you want of us," said the many-voiced demon, as I later learned, for it was in Latin, "Athanaric, renegade priest? Why disturb you the many heads of the great hydra?"

Perigraunce did not address the demon, nor in any way respond to it, knowing already the execrable name of the many-headed *drakodemon*. It is a knowledge prescribed for exorcists, who should only speak with such spirits in order to require their name, by which banishment is more completely accomplished. He continued to announce his authority in the indescribable name of the Son and therewith bore down the dint of divine power upon the beast-demon.

Then of a sudden, the eyes seemed to glow red, and there was a flash of white light that lit up the mist around us.

(The hycman later claimed that he did glimpse the wings of that demon).

The body fell backwards and slumped on the boat's deck.

"Has it been successful?" asked Nergalf.

"We shall see..." replied the priest. He bent down and opened the eyelids with his thumb, looking for a change in their condition. It seemed that scales fell from the eyelids and vanished. The eyes were rolled up, as one sleeping, not dead, but they were human now, even though the skin had not yet changed appearance. My brother next felt the body for pulses, as they are signs of life.

"He will be dead within minutes." My brother said.

"It has worked." Perigraunce continued. "Allfather has released the man's spirit and begun to restore him. But I cannot determine if the human spirit shall return to the shell of the body. I shall hear his sins."

"He is no Ammouric child." said Dunstaark. "Let him die in peace."

"He will die in peace as he utters grievance for sin," said Perigraunce, "his faith or lack thereof is not my concern."

Perigraunce bent down and spoke to the wounded man in whispers. The wounded man softly something back to him, and then his eyes shut.

"What did he say?" Nergalf asked.

"I am not permitted to convey it," the priest replied, "suffice it to know that he is in the hands of Allfather, not the claws of some accursed demon like the others."

"But how is it," asked Nergalf "that you, being a renegade, a disobedient priest, could have worked such a work? Does not that god of yours withhold his power from bad ministers?"

"The power is not consequent upon the sanctity of the cleric. It was not I who cast out the demon, rather it was the deity himself ...but I trusted that my God not withhold the mercy on account of my wrongs," Perigraunce further explained, "and the Soothfold does not provide for such straying sheep as myself to lawfully employ the exorcism. However the Lord is mercy, and uses even me especially when a good work must be accomplished in a dangerous place. The law was given for men, not men made for the law."

"But it were the Archangel that cast out the dragon spirit?" said Nergalf.

"He he uses angelic powers too, an invisible warrior whose spear is wielded with a divinely ordained strength."

"But why would your God save a man who worshipped the demon?"

"Who knows...it is His to decide. Perhaps the poor soul through but minor fault of his own fell in with the band of devils."

"Now then..." said Dunstaark wryly, "is there anything else that anyone needs to tell us about themselves? I suppose it be a relief for some, for the superstitious yeomen, that a cleric is come. Lo the fires. All aboard Hell-breaker then, and bring the wounded prisoner, if he still lives."

"He does live, but his wound is mortal, his mind is lost. He will die within the hour." my brother noted.

Suddenly the ship tilted and it became apparent that it had been rammed and was quickly taking on water. Several rats appeared from below deck and began a panicked search for safety.

"...we must haste to disbark..." I said.

"Leave him then, it is no use to take him." ordered Dunstaark.

So we returned to our boat and watched the great dragonship submerge, and a yet living man with it.

"This life is only a passage to the next." said Perigraunce. "No one will escape death. It is best that he died well, and was kept from dying in sin, what remains is out of our hands."

Onwards in that vast pool we rowed out boat, until the water merged into a far-flowing waterway. The mist had greatly distressed Nergalf's navigation, and it soon became apparent that we were lost. Perhaps a day had already passed, though it were impossible to calculate on account of the absence of sky or any timing device. Our only sky was the huge slanting ceiling above us, whose faint luminosity of under-lichen was only enough to make out strange reflections of ripples dancing upon the stalactites, and massy rocks overhanging the alien shore or tumbled down like great fallen giants. Other areas that the twisting waters took us through featured strange hollows of rock sculpted by perhaps untold ages of running waters, older than anything on earth's surface.

We were terribly cramped in that little boat, for one man, Brodain, had been wounded in the leg with a firey arrow and had to be stretched for his leg, which eventually would need to be cut off. We all rowed in turn but soon our cramped knees were very weary of sitting.

"-How many sandglass have we kept on this waterway, Raffing?"

I have lost count." (Raffing, a rather nervous soldier, was not always alert. I was not surprised at this failure).

"Lost count!?" exclaimed our commander, indignant. "What boon will you give as a member of this company, Raffing?"

"It is useless to keep track of time down here." explained Nergalf still standing at the stern steering with oar. (It seemed that the dwarf never tired). "The Underdark has many distorted spaces, and timewise reckoning there is not. Some I know have lived down here for centuries, yet ask them and they say only a short time has passed. Others return to the world above, believing they have lived a few days underground, shocked to find that their families are long dead and their home towns populated by strangers. At any rate, one can find much time for thinking, for meditation, in the hollows. This time, I sense, or perhaps I have a fear in my dreams, that some new evil has worked its way into these hollowed halls."

"Why say you that?" Haroun asked. "You have visited these regions yourself in the past?"

"I lost much of my youth exploring these regions, but that was so long ago that I barely remember it. Now, however, I am beginning to remember. I am beginning to realize some things. I have spent too many years among the sons of men, serving in their feudal armies, leading their battalions, governing their assemblies, keeping track of the treasuries. I have lost my dwarven way in the lands under the sun. Now down in this place something both old and new has re-awakened in me."

"What, some sort of knowledge, old memories of dwarf-life?" Some one asked.

"It is some deeper than that. My years dwelling in these lands left long-buried insight. These strange environs, the silences and stillness, once fused into me a sort of joy and interior power, a union with someone greater, greater than angels, even greater than all the universe. In these places I once meditated upon the rarified doctrines of unknowing, the contemplations of the highest reality.

"And I find that I have long forgotten that sense of being tied to the deep serenity of dwarf-home that these stones halls bestowed. I became too busied with the affairs of men and the building of their empires upon the ever-changing surface of the world. I never returned to my depths, never remembered."

"Perhaps you should lay down the sword a while." said Perigraunce.

"Not in this hour, and such counsel does not recall how new things taught me otherwise in the shining world above. So it was, and I wager that some demon lured my mind or compelled me to become a creature of blood-letting. In the breech I sold my soul to the quest for the Spear of Destiny, without any thought why, other than I happened to hear about it once when I was in Atalur."

"Tell what you mean." I said.

"I will tell. Near the end of my service to my lord Hermius, he sought to convince me of his strange faith, that fulfilment of prophesies which the Ammouric Kings now embrace.

"I openly refused to follow his faith, the doctrines of his "golden pages," Hermius was scandalized. But the Ammouric Patriarch himself forbade Hermius to imprison me, and the great conqueror could not even dismiss me! Still, it was an illness of mind he was suffering, a melancholy disdain for the world: the great hegemax no longer wanted me around. That was when he assigned me as governor to the remote mountains of Xasbur. He claimed not to need me then, and scorned me for a long time, until the day came when the Kalar Maurob rose up against him.

"So fetch that spear I will, to brandish that relic for reeking vengeance before I pass to twilight. After this last debacle at Gederon, I have realized that I cannot acheive it myself. I may have to make offerings to the strange God of the spear and convince him to help me. Perhaps someday I will bother to learn his doctrines, if ever I weary of war. What is the final point of blood but to secure peace? But peace is a thing I would not know if it slapped me."

Nergalf was almost certain of his own creed, and living by the sword, what could I do but offer contradiction to him with some doctrine of peace heard from preachers, though I did not really believe it myself.

"War offers peace." I said, "the peace of men who lay still on the frosty field in the dawn after the din of battle fades. The God whose spear you seek is titled the Prince of Peace, but not that kind of peace."

"Your prince's Spear will bring peace to Aideen. I would smite down any opposer to possess the sacred relic. It is the only magic weapon, I warrant, that can tumble down impregnable Nystol. We may very likely not recover it in these vast networks and subterranous waterways. In such case we shall attempt the madness of tearing down Nystol's towers with our own bare hands. The Spear however should guarantee our success. What delightful madness of victory it would as harbinger. I doubt such an experience could be replaced by anything else."

"Were you to kill to obtain it, I think its power would fail you," said Perigraunce. "It is against divine law to kill with such intent."

"There are certain treasures" said Nergalf defensively "that belong to the archonate: The Spear, The Amulet, and the Black Books. The God himself will not interfere. It is our right to require them."

"Is that why you have so brutally suppressed all Arraf?" I said.

"It is part of it...before I heard of the Spear, we tortured many in our attempts to find the beautiful Amulet, the Nagamaud, known to be hidden somewhere in the East, a thing of bliss coveted by sorcerers. Also, there are many important things in the compilation known as the *Black Books*. Therein, says the Gnome, is writ an exorcism for the Amulet. Also in the *Black Books* are recorded the exact verse-line of eld runes that should also be found on the Spear. Why is this important you wonder?

Public verification that the spear is genuine is a must, if any warlord would convince his army to follow the wielder into dubious battle, for he who leads an army with the spear is invincible."

"You should cease from impious endeavoring for power." Perigraunce said. "Your own soul will cry out. Change your ways while there is time left you."

"My soul is my own. Do not attempt to counsel *elphim* on their destiny. We are not like ye humans. But now be silent and observe, look around you, how thick the mist has become on these waters. Keep stern watch for underwater rocks."

"I can see nothing." I said. "I can barely even discern the prow in front of me."

"I cannot determine our drift in this turning flow, in this dense air, or if we have passed the Crags of Agarond or not. The palace of the Elf Queen-"

Suddenly my frame convulsed as the boat crashed against a rock jutting out of the mists. Nergalf falling forward lunged back, and the others equally were jolted. The boat swung round, pushed by the drifting flow as Nergalf tried to strike a bottom rock somewhere below with his rudder oarage. There was a small shore of boulders and sands, forthwith into which we slammed broadwise, nearly tipping almost to capsize. The shallow keel buried itself in the loose sand.

I looked around and saw that the warm water-fog no longer hung upon the rocky strand, of what seemed to be a minor island of fair size, but not to be generally disregarded by cartographers. The sharply curving shore featured huge pillars of stone lodged in a narrow deposit of sands, colossal slabs piled one on top another around which passed swags of that strange underworld mist, which now appeared to be limited in altitude to the warmer air hanging perhaps twenty feet above. The mist obscured the view allowing only a faint profile of the entire shorescape. But when I gazed directly above there were visible other huge pillars of rock looming over darkly, being steeply piled up as on a precipitous seaward hill, and there loomed even further beyond upwards, what seemed at once both a massive stalagmite, tapering toward the abysmal ceiling far above, and an elaborate dwelling of carved palisades and towers.

"The Elf-Queen has found us instead," whispered Nergalf. "The cherished isle of Agarond, where be the palace of my fair elven queen. Now take care about what I warn: her elven paladins, the karythar, may be patrolling these rocky shores. Let there be nothing spoken aloud, but only whispered, for we are not safe until we enter her hall, when she may remember me."

"May remember?!" said Dunstaark in an indignant whisper.

Nergalf ignored him. "Such hoplites as they tend to send a greeting of elf-shot first, hurtling through air, after which time they might be found ready for polite discussions..."

"That's just grand. But we observe this shore awhile before we disembark," said Dunstaark "lest there be need to hazard a fast escape back to the main."

Hard tack and apples were passed out by Shu Kurgoman for a quick meal. All of us sat in the ship in silence and listened, but we heard nothing. At length, when sufficient time had elapsed, Nergalf spake in a whisper.

"We must not yet go up. Let us picth a camp here, captain."

"I do not know, I am not sure." said Dunstaark. "Let us wait a while and see if anything stirs."

But at once we saw Nergalf still himself and gaze, just as he was setting down his rudder. His gaze was directed up toward the huge rocks looming over us. I followed his gaze and soon spotted what he was watching. At first it seemed a white goat, or perhaps a pony, looking down at us from the edge of rock.

"Quiet." whispered Nergalf. "Be still, all, and look to the rocks above where you may spy the rarest of beasts."

I strained to look more through the mist. I could see its graceful main that fell about its neck and a singular horn which sprouted in spiral groove from the creature's head, a head which was neither goat nor entirely horse-like.

"It is the unicorn, a creature of priceless worth." said Haroun.

At that moment, although the creature had already learned that we were aware of his presence, it right away vanished behind the forests of stalactites and huge slabs.

"Had you heeded my bidding and been silent," Nergalf chided, "we might have yielded some knowledge or other gift from the beast."

"It is a strange omen." Perigraunce commented. "And what it might presage, whether benediction or warning, I cannot right say. I fear that we should walk into some trap. Such creatures, as is taught by the Ammouric Soothfold, the Most High doth send."

"So why are they never seen upon the surface of the world?" I asked.

"They were once seen, in the forests, but now no more are seen. Some say the sins of men that drove them away."

"If it is accurate that we are on Agarond," explained Nergalf "then I warrant that the beast perhaps has taken refuge under the aegis of the Elf Queen. Its seems to me that war may have here driven the creature."

"There will be no way to carry the wounded Brodain up through those crags and rocks." said Dunstaark. "Wassel, you hold up here and watch until we return."

"On these alien waters alone...?"

"That is the plan, aye."

"Now pray maintain silence as we navigate the boulders and crevices upward." Nergalf said as the others waded onto the shore and readied packs and gear. "There will be some strenuous climb and footwork fraught with peril. For you there has been no training, so take care and go slowly."

After Perigraunce and Haroun tied Hell-breaker tightly to a stalagmite they set out, leaving me there in the boat. I cannot say that I was too upset at missing a visit with the mysterious and possibly dangerous Elven Queen. I watched as the mad dwarf went off leading the way over and around many giant rocks.

The climb up those jagged inclines was a mighty struggle for them, since this hill, in places, was very precipitous indeed, more so than what seemed from the shore. The walls and entrance of the castle also seemed much further away than appeared from below. When they looked down they could still see me on the dark undersea far below. Twice they had to use ropes. One slip and they would be hurled to a miserable death.

Into the dark they vanished. I waited many dragging hours and they did not return. Eventually I began to glance into the waters out of boredom. Casting little stones into it or just gazing at the miniature waves I made with my sword tip. It soon occurred to me that I was unable to turn my eyes away from the transparent waters of darkness. As I sat there, bent over the gleaming black surface that reflected my face, I began to hear faint voices echoing from the depths of those pools. It seemed that I was upon the verge of the lowest world. Then, peering as much into the depths as I could, I saw from whom those voices came. Within the reflections of water I dreamed many images of human beings floating past, but they had no awareness, and rather seemed as souls that journeyed through lower worlds, perhaps the spirits of men who had lived during the hopeless ages, and who had refused to leave the darkness. I sensed somehow, and it is difficult to explain it, that they were inviting me to join the endless sleep with them.

It was then that I saw a familiar visage among the numberless dead, Hakkarl floating past under the waters. This seemed not to be just an image, but his very body. The head of Hakkarl was still freshly broken with a gaping wound. His head turned and he saw me, and reached he out to me from under the water as if he wanted to be saved. At once I reached out to pull my companion back into the boat, regardless of whether he was dead.

At last I was able to stretch my hand into the water so far down as to grasp Hakkarl's arm. I began to pull him upwards but instead, I myself, as if in a nightmare, began to be pulled downwards.

I was yanked out of the boat into the shallows, which now submerged me. I tried to struggle free, but some numinous power seemed to weary my limbs and overtake me.

This was no ghost, I realize now, but a creature, which is called the fetch, and it was able to perceive the images of my mind and manipulate its appearance to mimic a certain being, in this way attempting to feed from my living strength. Now it took on my exact appearance and walked about.

Indeed, I now recalled my sins and foolish actions, for the imposter-entity would have had no power over me had I not sinned, had not greed for loot overridden our reason. I spoke prayer with my lips asking Allfather for lenience in the judgement being made, how wasting our lives on many vanities had cost us. May God overlook all the asinine activities that had led to these extremities. May the companions not end up as some sacrifice to unholy demon-gods of the restless dead, but rather that each man continue to be living and whole, acceptable to the one true father of all, able to discern the imposter going off to drain them.

Opening my eyes again I saw the vile creature darting away, taking my armor, appearing as me, gone upwards through the forest of rocks and stalagmites.

Then a huge flash of white crossed before my gaze like a thunder.

It was the unicorn.

Somehow this noble animal had seen, or perhaps even foreseen, what had transpired.

The miserable entity had sensed the holy terror of the unicorn's presence closing-in and was thwarted, driven off.

The unicorn, an awesome beast to behold up close, eyed me with his head turned sideways. As I lay there, still terribly weak and unable to move, I tried to thank the animal in turn with my eyes. The unicorn somehow understood, for, if we can say that certain higher animals have some sensitive soul that falls shy of intellectual power, then we can be certain that a unicorn, a beast that many hold to be enchanted, is doubtless even more endowed with a higher capacity of animal mind.

The animal, if you will, was even more impressive than

illustrations you have seen. Alhough he didn't even have any former acquaintance with me, he tarried on the shore there with me and guarded me as I lay incapacitated.

The creature communicated comfort to my soul, and had such a charming manner of courteousness, that I could not but be revived, if not in body fully, than at least in spirit. It so happened that, after all the sinister images and spiritual scars which the hideous fetch had left me with, these all now vanished completely. What is more, soon I began to experience within my mind what seemed an infusion of knowledge. It was as if this beast were communicating to me its assemblage of wisdom. Oh how envious I am of the saints who enjoy perpetually the company of this beast in fields of Elysium!

Soon I was on my feet again, and the unicorn abided there observing my actions. I took care not to present myself too close to the beast, for though I should never be able to finish discoursing on its rarified charm and gentle manner, there was neither any doubt in my mind that it were capable of a noble ferocity and wildness of spirit that is associated with the most fiery of horses. Such animals, if startled or somehow provoked, can enter into the most deadly of kicking and biting attacks. Yet such a thing seemed far from this serene creature as he reclined on the narrow beach of sand. Nevertheless, I could tell that not only was it a being never touched, but also that there was something quite detached and holy with regard to it in spirit, and indeed it was not an animal to be touched by profane hands.

I returned to the boat and began to forage through the supplies, requisitioning what I needed. Brobain slept. In order to do my mission guarding the boat, I needed to take dry cloths. That was my explanation for any soldier offended, higher or lower in rank. I found an extra tunic, dry, owned by Dunstaark, and certainly I was not slow to use it, at least not anymore. I found leggings that Haroun had brought along, and an extra pair of boots, just right, that Perigraunce had stored in the luggage. However there was no suit of chainmail. The fetch had slipped off with mine.

Who knows, perhaps it had gone up and in disguise receiving welcome from Nergalf and the Elf Queen. That would be terrible indeed. It would make sense that such a creature would do that, gaining strength from its victims just has the legends say: the shades that must drain the living. If this were so, depending on how clever be the creature, it could infiltrate the crew, even claim that he were the genuine Wassel. Perhaps Perigraunce might see through the guise, perhaps not. I had to act hastily, but it would be too risky to climb the precipitous rocks alone. As I stood there in the boat wondering what course to take, I occasionally glanced up at the unicorn.

IV

I heard voices coming our way. Into the wreckage of rocks piled up far above I peered and spotted my brother and Nergalf frantically navigating a way of descent around the fallen boulders. Dunstaark and Perigraunce also appeared, and they had carried shields and swords, and by their frequent pause and turn of head it seemed they were retreating from some pursuant enemy.

Others followed. Shu had taken a hostage, a female of slight build, whose skin was slightly another color, perhaps a bluish hue. This must be some elf they had captured, or perhaps it were the Elf Queen herself. Shu Kurgoman the hyc was conducting her along quickly. Haroun had the rear of the line, crouching down and ready.

"There's trouble," I said to myself.

The unicorn uprose and departed my company, for such creatures are shy of men, and rising I bowed to it. I took this to be a sign of foulness coming.

Nergalf was first to the boat. I noticed that he was now carrying a rather well fashioned broadsword.

"Grab the oars, hurry, make ready to cast off the lines!"

"What is afoot?" I asked. "Is there something after us?"

"No time to explain! The Elf Quee-" Nergalf did not finish his sentence. Instead he stared at me with a startled look of both rage and perplexity.

"You! What were you thinking to do? Seize the Elf Queen's treasure? Take on the whole- -but how did you get back here before us?"

"You saw a creature, a creature who can take on appearances. You have been deceived by a specter in my likeness. He follows us."

"What? Is that possible? Perigraunce, tell, is it possible for a specter to take on human likeness?"

Perigraunce had just arrived at the boat and was astounded as everyone else was.

"Yes...but there's no time to discern now, although it must be so, there are many kinds of magical ghosts."

For a moment they all stood there eyeing me, wary to board the vessel.

"I know my brother," added Hercil. "He would not have hazarded those insane acts we witnessed, nor would he abandon his assigned post. This must be the real Wassel."

"Or he might have well foreseen our return." said Haroun. "Perigraunce is certain he saw him?"

"I saw the treachery." said Perigraunce, "and what is more, even if what he says is true, we must yet determine that this one is not a doppleganger. Haroun, Wassel is under your watch until we might have time for court marshal."

I was utterly dismayed at this.

"This is absurd, do you not trust even the word of my brother?"

Haroun stepped into the boat and took me by the arm, his sword hand on pommel. He kept watch on me closely.

"Sit on the forward thwart where I can keep observation of you." Haroun said, no longer speaking as friend or companion.

"Quick, let us all away!" the elf-maiden urged, "The archers of the Elf-Queen are hard on your heels." Just then an arrow with a swoosh lodged the sand near Nergalf's feet.

"We should get our own gifts ourselves." Nergalf said climbing into Hell-breaker with the others. "It's not like the old legends where guests are given fairy magic from angelic elves...not at all...we should not expect any help from them. Save for this one elf-maiden who claims she can fight, (how possibly I do not know), but perhaps she can make up for our loss."

Dunstaark gave the boat a push from the shore and grabbing Perigraunce's arm was pulled in as another two arrows just barely missed him.

Now we had rowed a visible distance from shore when the company elven archers was discernable barely through the mist up on the beach. Now they had a clear shot at us, for we were still in range. We used the knight's shields for cover as the missiles came raining down. Several hurtling arrows struck against Hell-breaker, some bouncing off her iron casings, others sticking into her wood.

Nergalf, enraged, climbed over the thwarts to get to the stern of the ship. There he stood up and made profane jestures, vaunting aloud to the elven archers. He yelled out to the enemy.

"Inform your Elf Queen that it was Nergalf, Master of all Aideen, one of the *naugrim*, who has urinated on her sacred rocks!"

At that moment an arrow, seeming to hurtle out of the expanse of obscuring mist, struck Nergalf on the collarbone, where the gold clamps of his double-pieced corset meet, breaking through the leather beneath which guards his skin. The tip, intending to inscribe an epitaph on his very skin, punctured these layers, and right away cloudy dark blood swagged, just as when the red snakes of Garmsir slip out of cracked tombs long ago emptied by thieves, a thin stream of blood now snaked down his armour. He cried out, and fell backwards into me, and I caught him. Had he not been standing there, I myself would have been hit.

Dunstaark, incensed that one of his most valued assests had been put down, passing forth the bow and quiver, spake:

"Elf-girl, now make good on your claim and display your worth and new loyalty among oath-sworn mortals, if you would make our cause your own, use your elven eye to reek vengeance for us, send an arrow home through obscuring mist to one of your forsaken kin."

The elf-maiden took the bow and paused as the rowers halted. Her hands were not unfamiliar with the taught gut as she loaded the shaft in place and pulled back. She peered into the hovering gloom of cave mist, but I think that it were her elf-ears that knew the target's position. The arrow flew disappearing into the mist and, by the sound of it, struck a body echoing through the caves. Nor was there any doubt that she had hit her target. One of the foe in speaking elvish words to direct another did not finish his sentence. Nor did the elven frame, though light and unearthly, fail to make a sound as it collapsed to the dull earth's sandy shore.

We rowed even faster away. Nergalf we pulled into the mid-hull of the boat and laid him there.

"I am quite without remorse to put an end to one of those," she said, "...for they are no longer my kin as you might imagine. Nor are they even worthy to be called elves. I say they are more like gallant goblins of some sort, and though they appear to be elves, the poison of the spider's leaf twisted them, so that their elf flesh is become grey, the first outward sign of corruption in an elf, and among the elf-clans their banner has lost its once worthy name."

What exactly these words meant and who she was or what we were to make of her words I could not possibly ascertain at that moment. Obviously the Elf Queen's reception of our men had not been as kind as we had hoped, but we had recruited an elf, no queen herself but she was elegant, though there was a alien coldness in her flashing eyes that would dissuade even the most senseless suitor.

The elfshot would not end the mad dwarf's life, but it did vex Nergalf badly, and he would not be able to fight.

"Look alive, Asclepiad." someone (I cannot recall who), urged my brother. (Asclepiad is the old name for physicians which yet was in common use in my time).

"It is a hurtless thing that has touched me." Nergalf denied pain as we transferred him with much effort to the middle-hull of the boat, and lay him next to Brobain, who was nearly dead from gangrene.

Someone else, perhaps Shu, provided a flask of brandy for the dwarf to swallow down in order to deaden the smart of pain.

My brother Hercil passed his oar to Haroun and foraged through the shoulder-sacks for supplies. Trained as a *medicus proeliorum*, he it was whom the commander appointed to care for our battle wounds.

After extracting the tip with much ordeal, he bandaged up Nergalf.

"I know only scant lore on the dwarf-flesh." said my brother, "but I have ointments, wine, and herbs here from Nathycanthe, as well as some jellies from other lands. By the consistency of the blood I would say that his is indeed dwarf blood, though he ages just like humans, more slowly, so these might have a sympathetic draw."

"Ah, what does it matter..." said Nergalf who was in semi-shock, "There are other elven queens, such as are rumoured to dwell in Nathycanthe."

"What did he mean...?" I asked. No answer was heard.

Obviously Nergalf, weary and tired from all the dreadful pain that extracting the arrow had caused, had his thoughts somewhere else.

"It is an interesting side effect of Nathycanthine lymph-weed oil," my brother explained, "that it forces most intellectives to speak only the true words. Perhaps this is now effecting the anesthetized Nergalf."

"The truth? From him that would be high time to garner. Pose him a question, Hercil." said Dunstaark. "Ask something such as 'where are you really leading us?' "

"I said it before," replied drowsy Nergalf, half grumbling, "We go together to sack the city Nystol, place of wicked masters..."

Now that question almost seemed finally to be beyond suspicion.

"Did you order the butchery in Namaliel?" I asked.

"I ordered the butchery."

"What did you mean," Hercil asked the dwarf, "when you said that there are other elven queens?"

"Well, what do you think? The intermundane elves are not the only ones who have a queen. There is a queen of the...brown elves in....sunny Childishyre. There is also Avannarse of Ayrs, the grand ...kingdom of northern white elves, so the legends...say."

"But you said before that you knew the elf queen, the intermundane queen, Morvilindart."

"I did have some acquaintance with her..."

"How so?"

"I loved her. I wished to devote my life to her."

"Devote your life...?"

"Do you think I made imperial commander because I had nothing else to do? Ale is a better past-time. Morvilindart only had eyes for great warriors, gallants..."

"Gallants?"

"You know the kind...tall...like Dunstaark."

"You desired this lady?"

"Her beauty is sublime."

"And...did you seek her hand?"

"Her whim was unfavorable, she looked...with scorn upon me. She despised my shortness. I offered her countless gold and the....jewels of the dwarf lords, beyond her finest imaginings if she would marry. I prayed to the Father of All that I might win her...heart."

"He did not answer?"

"He does not induce a heart in such a way, it seems."

"What did you do?"

"Confident....confident and suspecting that she was bluffing, I, a half-breed and mortal, proposed to her before all the grand...lords, some...some were human guests, and all the elven assembly. She did not answer, but broke out...laughing. Everyone else at court, standing there, including my own dwarven companions, began a round of hysterical laughter. I was made a laughing stock, as if one without honour. It stung deep into my soul. I vowed to show the entire world that I meant business. Frowning, I waited....till the laughter subsided and said, "You will rue this day, all of you, when you see the earth entire under my sway." Then all fell silent, uncertain of what rage I was capable, so I marched out of that grand hall...alone. I stood alone and looked upon the grim horizon. I knew my destiny. I could not have what I craved, I probably could never have it. But one thing that my will would seize: mastery of the earth. I knew that I could achieve my new ambition. Not even the Father of All would stand in my way, and if he would not grant my prayer, he would be forced to listen to my answer."

Nergalf quieted with a frown as he lay in the bottom of the boat, looking off into the distances above him.

"That is all past now...." he continued.

"It is the pain of youthful years..." said Hercil.

"You know, with all my waging of war," said Nergalf reflectively,

"I do not recall ever being struck by a weapon."

"Now sleep, mad dwarf."   said my brother, "you will need much rest." Nergalf closed his eyes and drifted off to sleep.

Hmmm...I began to ponder these things. Now I began to understand the little dwarf more deeply. Ever since we had entered into these dark waters, I had not esteemed him well: his demands, his mockeries, his fighting with Dunstaark, and now this last misadventure: no radiant Elf Queen. It was then that I began to wrestle with my own soul, for now I had heard of something good in the little dwarf, which, though twisted by long frustration, was somehow noble.

But this made me resent him the more, for whereas before I could attribute his evil and stupidity to a mindless distortion of personality, a contempt and disregard for others and for what's right that had brought him successes, now I could not. I had seen what was noble in him and could not write him off as depraved. He was not unlike me, but he had succeeded in the things that I had failed in, for he was brilliant and a master, and he was willing to be ruthless, a quality that I admired at the time. I had some limited success as a man of the world, and hoped someday to be a commander, and to know honours, but I knew that I could never achieve the fame that he had acheived, however stained it might appear by his recent defeat, for he would make the histories.

So now I began to desire his failure and undoing. I gave thanks to Allfather for Gederon's humiliation, and for the elfshot, but it was not enough. The clever dwarf had already made new schemes to regain even greater renown. I secretly hoped to see him weeping on the ground for his own folly, punished for his brutal successes in war, repenting his mockeries. This would make things right, this would demonstrate Allfather's justice. Therefore I began to turn these things over in my heart, and to consider in what ways they might be accomplished.

"...Morvilindart...but that's not the name of the Elf Queen which the great songs recall." said Hercil. "They speak of one Ariandol, a beautiful maiden of gracious wisdom and enchantment for travelers."

"Perhaps there is a new queen?"

"I think not. Everyone knows that Elf-Queens do not leave the world, at least not until a lapse of a thousand years."

"What you say is right." said Perigraunce. "An observation I had not considered."

I noticed that one was missing in our group.

"Where is Raffing?" I asked. There was a silence, and need I say, a guilty silence.

"Where is he! Did you leave him back there?"

"He is dead." Perigraunce answered. "A merciful arrow in the back. It were a miracle that not all of us are wasting to death there."

"We must return," I said, "we must retrieve and bury our companion's body, we are sworn."

"We are already under the ground, burial is not needed." Someone said.

"His body must be covered over. Does anyone here have respect for sacred law?"

"We cannot go back." Said Dunstaark "The current is strong. Continue your oarage. The waters take us away and the men are weak. Besides, he has earned the burial rites of a treasonist."

"What mean you by such an insult on my oath-brother? What exactly happened up there? Did you not meet the Elf Queen? Who is this elven girl"

Dunstaark remained silent.

"I am the daughter of Morvilindart the elven queen, feudal monarch of all this realm. I am Hydarta and I will fight to be free. My mother herself is no longer among the quick, but lay in a weird sleep, overwhelmed by the soulless dream of the spider's poison. I could do nothing to restore my mother from doom but only this: resolve to live and return someday with the elves of Avim to take back our ancestral castle."

"You said you would not return, elf-maiden." Said Dunstaark. "Now do you make yourself false?"

"No, you are right, I have said it, and so truly I myself will never return there. I will someday send my son, who yet walks in the upper world."

"Are you not too early to have a son?" I asked

"Among the elves we speak of sons and daughters, fathers and mothers, brothers and sisters, and so we take on such a disposition, but we are not given to generation, to birth and death like mortal men, but we are begotten like angels from the beginning."

"And that is why I shall never go to another elf-castle. These places are not for mortal men like me" Said Dunstaark.

"Then what is it that you found there on that isle," Dunstaark?" I asked, "Clearly not loot. Tell me now while I still live."

Perigraunce will tell it." he answered, "his way with words is better."

"I will say, Wassel," said Perigraunce, "I will tell you all, but perhaps you will not believe it."

"Then begin," I said.

"How many hours, Wassel, would you say that you awaited us?"

"I did not count, perhaps three hours."

"Try more like three hundred of hours."

"How is that possible?"

"They say the presence of certain enchanted airs may warp the sensation of time." explained Dunstaark.

"When we attained the top of the cliff," Perigraunce began, "we saw the grand and grim castle with a mote whose spires kept rising like a titan before us, rising up to the shadowy ceiling of the great cave. Immediately the drawbridge came down with huge clanking reverberations and we crossed over to stand before the immense doors made of an alien wood. We knocked with the great grimacing knocker of silver which echoed throughout.

The massy doors opened and there stood several grim looking elves well armoured with lance and bow, bearing shield devices of a decorous but rather ominous looking white spider. They signaled for us to enter but did not speak. They put their grey hands out to receive our weapons, like fools we followed the custom.

"We seek audience with the elven lady, the Queen, Morvilindart." says Nergalf, and he says "Pray, convey us to her."

We followed them through the portcullis and entrance-tunnel into the courtyard. The lavishly stone-carved courtyard was a sight to behold, and it displayed a beautiful but disturbing architecture. Nergalf commented that it looked exactly the same as he remembered.

We were brought to a line of men and other humanoids standing and waiting to appear before a table where sat a fat elven clerk of some sort, not ugly, but perhaps a soldier of long standing. He had a rather large ears, and a great stack of papers.

We tried to inquire as to the meaning of the long line but received answers neither from the elven warriors nor from the unarmed humanoids standing there. Workers kept bringing in bags filled with leaves which were given to those who reached the desk. Certain records were being kept and numbers being written down. After perhaps an hour it was finally my turn to appear at the desk.

The fat elf demands of us saying   "Name...?" .

"I am Perigraunce." I reply "I am come to meet the Elf Queen."

He ignores my reason and shifts through his papers.

"We have no record of you. Is this your first time?" he says.

"First time? To visit her? Yes," I answer, "I should say so."

"Then we will give you a share," he says, "but you must work several long shifts. After that you can come back for more."

I was given a sack of leaves and led off by a guard, separated from the others. As I was conducted down strange castle passageways and I could hear Nergalf behind me making an uproar and demanding to see the Elf Queen. There was what sounded like a scuffle. I tried to turn round to get back to the others but the file of workers, as if they were zombies, blocked the way. I struggled against them and fell down stone steps, but they kept on, pushing for their destination, actually trampling over me, as if I were not there. I barely escaped being trampled to death.

"We tried to get them to heed us," Dunstaark added, "but they treated us as the rest, paying no attention to our request. Nergalf, not having a weapon, rashly attacked the fat elf with his fists demanding to see the Queen. Those elves have some sort of powerful magic that put him right to sleep. Like Perigraunce, we also were brought into little cells within the castle basements and locked within."

"They were small cells," said Perigraunce "very confining, and we tried to contact one another but failed. There were many cells and many workers. Someone came around with bags of leaves and they all cried out. Each was given a small grey bag. The workers in my cell started eating their white leaves at once.

"Not long afterwards the work began. We were taken deep into a mine and worked many long hours digging for diamonds. It was a terrible labour and a harrowing experience. I fancied that I alone had come to woe, a fitting punishment for having been an irresponsible priest. My purgatorial job was to carry rocks up and down a narrow airless shaft. It was grueling and seemingly unending work in which I lost all sense of time and situation. But when I once paused while the trollish-overseers were away, suddenly I noticed, in the grim shadows of another shaft, another human profile, holding a pick and standing in a familiar posture. It was our Haroun. At once I called out and we spoke for a few moments. It had been like a thousand years since I had seen him, doubtless there were unseemly tears.

Finally, after many hours of secret watching, and slipping about unnoticed by others, we found the rest of the crew on a separate mining team in another shaft. We looked to contrive some plan of escape but could not, for it had come to our attention that no one is released from the castle unless he has finished his twelve bags of leaves, and each bag was numbered.

Those who were our over-seers in the grim mines were cruel trolls of some sort, heavily armoured with spiked plates, armed with cudgels and whips. Every hour we were beaten and abused in some way if we did not labour with the greatest of effort. After it was all over they sent us back to our cells where we tried to sleep on the cold stone floor next to zombie-like strangers, elves, men, hyc, fey and others, who would not talk or even acknowledge us. Terribly hungry and exhausted, I ate some of the white leaves. They tasted excellent and very nourishing.

Soon, however, I did not have thoughts like myself. My belly began to ache terribly. Trembling and shaking, it were as if I were holding on to dear life. This physical terror lasted for what seemed an eternity, but perhaps was only an hour. At last it seemed as if the devastating pain were transforming into a lightness, first in my stomach, and then in my head. This sensation began to grow, even entering into my thoughts. An easy but numbing warmth and weird light began to glow within me, causing me to want to laugh, but I could not. Yet this was not the end, for the sensation shortly increased in magnitude to the extent that I could say I had never lived better, a glee of unthinkable proportion. Yet my thoughts were sluggish and torpid, nor was I in full control of myself.

This mania soon lifted me into such an altitude of ecstasy, that I forgot in my mind all cares and concerns, all desire for higher thought and discipline, and at last I surrendered myself entirely to the alien power, thinking it a vain sin to vie against such a good sensation. I had many splendid visions and airy notions as well to delight both my mind and flesh, yet I would not do aught but gape into the empty air.

When the effects, after many hours, showed signs of slightly wearing off, I immediately reached for my bag and devoured a little more lest I lose the ecstasy.

Though I did not express joy or any other emotion, and knew no desire to interact with anyone, the power of the magic plant was so great that I forgot time itself. My body was partly numb, and though I could experience pain, it meant nothing to me but an irritation distracting me from the euphoric sensation of being emptied.

I realized now how the other workers had easily persevered through many weeks or months of such dreadful labour, if just for a few daily moments of the magic leaves. The next time that I met Haroun, Dunstaark, Shu, and the others in the mines to experience more horror of slavery, I realized they also had taken it, and we all agreed to make the under-castle our new home, the mines our new work, and the magical plant our salvation and purpose for living. We also agreed how ridiculous all our previous life of striving had been, and admitted to one another that it no longer meant anything if any of us were to die, or lose our companions. This was agreed, mind you, by men not still under the blissful mind-alteration of that magic, but who had regained full control of their intellect and reason, and hoped to return to ecstasy.

The trollish sentinels cruelly punished all of us for talking on that shift, assigning even more grueling labours, but the mere thought of what we would experience at the end of each shift drove us on.

So this continued, and we arose and worked the dark mines yet another shift. During resting hours our sweet ecstatic sleep was tainted by visions of a white spider.

Among all who had ventured into that castle, only Nergalf had wit enough not to try the accursed magical plant, since he had long before seen its effects on his sand-pirate crew in the Dry Blood Dunes. This was fortuitous, for the little dwarf with his herculean strength and relentless will pulled apart the metal bars of the special solitary cell, an iron chamber where the elves had confined him for his outburst, and escaping undaunted he climbed out.

He snapped the necks of sleeping bolg-guards and smashing about broke open every door. He went forth unrestrained, and grabbing a common pike, he quite deliberately skewered as many as eight opposing trollish guards that confronted him as he searched the corridors for us. He was too quick and too uncertain a target for the laboured swings of their massy clubs.

I was the first Nergalf found, laying in the cell listless, pleasuring a vacuous ecstasy. When I did not respond to him he grabbed me and yanked me out, putting a rope around my neck. Finding no further opposition from guards, he found the others, one by one, and those of us who resisted he beat with fists. After tying our necks about with a rope, forming a line he dragged us through many corridors, through secret passages, up into the upper reaches of the castle.

Nergalf locked us in a remote storage room, in some far part of the castle, for what seemed an entire day until the effects of the magical plant wore off. If any of us tried to escape, Nergalf would beat him with a broom. Haroun got a few good wacks that woke him up out of his obsession, and he was first to recover. It was Raffing, however, that had the greatest difficulty. When he did not get those moments of bliss for which we all had been longing, he went into a fit of screaming, convulsion, tremor, and hallucination, crying out to the white spider as if to a superior master. I prayed to Ambrosius, guardian of intermundane travelers, on his behalf, (it does not matter to me if a faithful soul or not, they still need prayer). It seemed at times that he was nigh death, and having no knowledge of the magic's side-effects, I determined to reconcile him with Allfather. He agreed and spoke what misdeeds he could remember. I uttered the priestly shriving formula.

Nergalf returned at one point with our supplies and armour, for he had taken along Haroun, who knows everything a soldier can about locks and other such mechanisms, he had dissembled the lock opening the armoury and retrieved what iron had been taken from us.

Thereafter Nergalf spent many hours lecturing us, treating on the destructive effects of the stupefying plant. Who knows how long this dreadful vomiting lasted?

Then I, having at last, with great pain, recovered my will. I was recovered only next after Haroun, and I sermonized against the wicked ecstasy with great admonition, warning the remaining whiners about oath-breaking and eternal damnation in the hell-fire that rages not far below us, where they would receive no wondrous pharmacea to ease the unthinkable pain.

At length we roused ourselves and took oaths to make for the boat, though Raffing seemed yet often delirious, he at other times looked quite aware and ready, but watching him, one could see that his mind was elsewhere.

Moving quickly through the various chambers and corridors of the under-castle, a place devoid of any real life or festivity, we barged into a meeting hall of several grim white-haired elves, including a female. We acted without restraint and before they could seize their weapons, Shu Kurgoman, in his usual barbaric fashion, had seized the young half-elf daughter of Queen Morvilindart by the locks of her hair, and planting his shortsword by her throat, threatened to finish her if they attacked. I protested this as being unchivalric, but my words fell on deafness, for in the havoc of war civil ways lose all meaning.

As we paused in that chamber calculating the best moment to make our next move, with the Queen's daughter locked against Shu in perpetual threat, Nergalf, who can speak the elven language, interrogated the elves.

It seems that the magical plant was imported from Nystol, which, having been illegal for a thousand years, had recently been traded about throughout the intermundane regions. Apparently, since the rise of the Archimage Adeuces, restrictions on the use of the pharmaceutic, which only grows in the remote lower forests of the Sardu, have been lifted. News was heard that the Queen herself now uses the plant. Nergalf demanded to see her. The elves at first refused to conduct us into her chambers, but soon realized that Nergalf's newly found blade had no real concern for their scruples.

They brought us through another hall and we entered her chamber. There she was, a female of a dark hair and ruby lips, of glamourous beauty, laying in stillness on a perfectly prepared bed. She seemed dead, but they assured us that she was alive, yet remaining in that state of recluse for several days at a time, and must not be awoken. Indeed, the Queen herself had become an avid eater of the weird plant.

Nergalf reached out his hand to touch her cheek, but quickly pulled back and withdrawing marched out of the bed-chamber angrily. Now that we have learned of his history, how he desired her, I understand his mind.

Shu dragged the Queen's daughter and with us went all the way down through many narrow winding spirals of stairs down to the court yard. There Nergalf demanded that the elven guards open the side gates and portcullis, that we were to depart, and that they should dare not thwart us if they valued their limbs.

Now once we were clear of the mote we could see them observing us from the battlements, we saw Wassel up on the battlements as well, quite clearly pointing to the location of our boat to inform our pursuers, so we rushed into an area where they could not see, and taking the elf girl as hostage went through a good bit of steep trail and climbed down.

When we were far out of sight below immense boulders and grand stalactites, we began to talk on whether to release our hostage and make a dash for it. But then the hostage spoke, saying,

"Do not send me back there, if you do they will not fear to hunt you with great skill."

"What is our fate to you?" I asked.

"I am the Queen's daughter" she says, "but I have long sought a way to escape from the iniquity of that place. Spare me and keep me your hostage, lest I become myself hostage to their spider-god. I will aid you in your journey through these great caverns."

"If you throw-in with us, Dunstaark said, "You must never return there. You must renounce that place forever. We should not risk taking someone who has no battle-hardened strength, and an elf like you, there could be trouble. You are pretty indeed, not unlike some of the maidens of Rumil, and my warriors might find you a consolation to look upon, a reminder of home, or they might fight over you. So it is a risk."

"Even were they to claim me and fighting think to have won me, they would soon find me no angel, but a terrible elf to bring distress upon mortal men," she says, "and if you doubt my prowess in combat, lend me your bow and you shall witness how swift are these soft hands to convey hurtling death to an enemy."

"You make a fine warrior's boast for an elf-maiden, but I am slow to believe," says Dunstaark. "There is a little further to go, and I shall make my decision before we make shore."

Then we hastened the climb downwards even more.

It was at this point that someone noticed that Raffing had ceased climbing down. He was paused above, on a rock, holding himself in a curled position. Many of us shouted exhortations to him, using every manner of overbold war cry, foul language, or memory of friendship, or description of home to goad him. He answered crying out:

"Days in the world above is of scant value to me, and what is best in life I shall never see, save this fair dream. Therefore tell all my relatives and family that I chose to stay as a shade in the land of the dead, where I could find more reason in my existence than fruitless war."

As he spoke elfshot came raining down upon us, and nigh struck Haroun and Dunstaark. Raffing turns to climb back upwards to recover his dark destiny. It was in these moments that Nergalf rouses the ire of Dunstaark.

I see a foreboding voice and dark look from the dwarf, and then he says "Knight, as a soldier you know what must needs be done."

"The wars are over, Nergalf." the knight replies and sternly.

"The wars are never over." the dwarf says "Deserters are men of treason and must be dealt with harshly," he says "lest the entire company loose heart."

"Do not lecture to me, dwarf, on martial discipline. Haroun," he cries "pass me your yewing bow."

I saw that Haroun was hesitating.

And next Dunstaark yelled out to Raffing warning him to return, lest he be called treasonous and die. Raffing either took no note of it or purposely ignored it.

Then adds the dwarf,

"Do you not have pity, captain? He will experience living death, within those mines he will be another soul upon which the white spider feeds, is that what you would let him embrace? Oneirogenic spiders are never satiated," he says, "his body will be kept alive...but his soul...He doesn't know it, but within a few weeks his soul will be empty: he will not die, he will not live. That's much worse fate than the way iron cuts a life short in many mortal wars. At least a warrior dies with honour." Nergalf then says to us that he did not wish to lose another sword hand, "but I warn you, he says "even greater foes await us. To execute the martial law with strict justice, as an execution for a victim of magical bewitchment, and certainly no draker, would yield him up a worthy clemency."

Dunstaark I heard cry out "Haroun! Pass me the bow."

Haroun passed his bow and quiver to Dunstaark.

"What is more," added Dunstaark as he loaded the bow, "if the enemy pains him to talk...and they have ships to pursue us."

"And the grim elves have a collusion with Nystol," Nergalf added, "from whence they import the accursed plant."

The wooden arrow shaft clicked against the bow. The taut gut moaned as it was stretched back. The death-twang resounded and the missle hissed as it flew. We watched Raffing fall upon the jagged rocks, tumble, and stir no more. I spake the Ammouric prayers, though I was some distance from him, and his spirit went off to the judgement. I give thanks that he had done his admission of sins with me not long before.

It was moments after this grievous scene that we hurried in frantic rush to the shore below, fearing for our lives, since everyone knows that elves are much faster than men."

So goes the incredible account of the Elf-Queen's castle. This account which Perigraunce told gave me great cause for bitter thoughts. Not only did the little dwarf demonstrate outrageous heroism and exceptional luck, as if blessed by the divine, but now it seemed as if Allfather were laughing at me, being currently under arrest and suspected for treason! In my heart I thought as if some cosmic joke were being played out in this weird journey.

I wondered if the dwarf used his new status among us to put to death one of my own companions. Nor was this a thing that I could argue against in an assembly of warriors, for it is well known code, and under such code all reasoning was cast aside. It was a code that I myself lived by and had many times before demanded should be strictly kept.

That dwarf was becoming a high cause of frustration for me. His every success was like a thorn in my side: to see the work of little dwarf gain renown worthy of sagas, while I sat in the boat on shore. My jealousy was sinful, and with such sins there are no rewards. There was however some blessing, which at the time my selfishness would not let me see. Afterall, I did spend hours with the unicorn, but surely that would never be sung of in song.

I could not help but reflect inwardly how often Dunstaark had rebuked Raffing for being useless, a charge that had not slowed the executor's final decision. In the mind of such practiced warriors, a man's worth is a measurable thing.

We rowed onwards through the dim halls of high-vaulted cave

and abysmal sea.

Nergalf lay on his back in the boat and Shu steered the ship. How very amazing it was that the dwarf could give directions to Shu on his steering, treating on how exactly to shift the rudder and by what degree he should correct bearing.

"How can you tell, dwarf," I asked,"how do you know whither the boat needs to cut on these vast waters. You cannot mark the shore."

"By a certain dwarf-sense I navigate, and by the arrangement of crystals and semi-precious stones, lodestars lodged on the ceiling of the intermundane cavern far above. If you look hard enough, you will see their glint, as if they were lodged in Heaven."

Onwards we rowed even more. After some ridiculous interrogation, my own companions finally determined that I were not myself some wretched fey-creature out to drain their life away. I was no longer under arrest. Nergalf fell asleep again, weary from his wounds.

After a time Nergalf awoke from stupor and began to look about.

Dunstaark noticing this alert spake.

"If you die from that miserable wound, dwarf, by gangreen or whatever, just hang on a bit to be of use to us."

"How nice to be needed," he replied. "I am in great pain. But dwarves do not contract gangrene."

"Just keep talking," said Hercil. "Do not fall asleep again."

V

We floated into view of what from a distance seemed a mountainous stalagmite piled to the ceiling, but on closer inspection it was no cavernous structure, but a mighty tower.

The base of the tower was colossal in extent. As we floated by the shore and looked up to how it tapered to the ceiling of the grand Intermundane Cavern, even into an opening of bright sky. I could not imagine any other creatures besides giants who would have been able to lift and set the huge stones in place. The stones themselves were the size of elephants, or larger. The foundation stones were of even greater size. Nor did this fail to immediately bring us trepidation and fear, because the thought now impressed upon our mind was that the masonry showed few signs of wear, and there was little doubt that whatever gigantic beings constructed the tower would likely still be around.

As we disembarked upon the shore and dragged the boat

Hell-breaker upon the sandy beach, concealing behind a huge boulder, I wondered if this would be the last of our luck.

"A great foreboding comes upon me." I murmured to Shu Kurgoman who was helping as we dragged the boat.

"Then you are wise." he said, ". . .fools do not have any sense of dangers. But if that does not encourage you, then take heart, we all must die the death someday, somehow."

Perigraunce had heard us, so after we had dragged the boat a safe distance from the great waterway, he spoke his thoughts to us all.

"Hear me, companions, and consider my words well. It seems that we have again come to a place of great mystery, and I can see by the pale look upon your faces that ye wish it were not so. We men, who are small, however, have nothing to fear from huge giants or their kin, neither from the hand of death itself, if we are believers. And of those among you who do not discern the sacred truth, it is sufficient at this time for you to fight with honour if the chance comes, remembering the righteous teachings of your fore-fathers. On this account Allfather will extend his blessing in battle, provided that you are not against his holy will. So now let us take a moment and prepare, and let those of us who can pray for divine protection."

At this Shu Kurgoman, Haroun, and I knelt down, and Perigraunce began to pray aloud in the ancient tongue. I did not turn around and look to see if Dunstaark or Nergalf kneeled, but commended their souls to the angels. Perigraunce next gave the blessings for war.

We approached the base of the tower not far from the rocky shore. The foundation-stones loomed above us. Up close it did not even seem a tower, but rather the bottom of some huge sea-cliff, slightly curved, for so huge was the tower's circumference, that one would barely discern the curvature of its roundness when standing close.

"Whatever army cut these stones was certainly not of normal sinew." said Dunstaark.

"Whoever they were," added Haroun, "their mothers fed them too much goat's milk as children, as it seems."

We began to search for an entrance, but soon realized that the foundation stones would have no entrance. These stones were unclimbable. We thought that there might be some entrance or way upwards in one of the many cracks between the foundation stones. We found nothing with out mortal eyes, but it was the daughter of Queen Morvalindart who found the secret entrance, invisible except to an elf, and so we entered a dark porch with torches held high.

Many perils we faced in those corridors. I myself slipped and fell from a winding stair, only to be swallowed by a massive slithering beast in the dark. Had I not the companions been there I would still now be wasting in its belly, digested slowly over a thousand years. Of these things and other incidents which befell you will soon hear from the mouth of those who were there. First let me tell you of Zenops himself, and the weird circumstance of our encounter with him after we had climbed up through dangerous stairs and passed through deadly traps to reach his grand chamber of rest.

So we passed up through the spiraling corridors of the tower of Wyrdd, armed to the teeth with famous bronze and life-wrenching steel. Already I could not wait to leave those dim stairs. We ascended the spiraling stairs and entered several abandoned chambers of broken furniture and crumbling masonry. It was obvious that some remnant of an army was still wandering these halls, perhaps goblin or bolg.

We found the wizard's chamber, after much labyrinthine searching, the oaken door locked tightly by one thick adamantine lock. I spoke to my companions in whispers lest we lose some element of surprise:

"Legend says that Zenops resides alone, beyond this famous door, that he reads slowly one of the *Black Books*. So now it comes down to this. No one is strong enough to break apart such a well-nailed door, but there is one among us, whom we all know, who can dissemble so terrible a lock with silent skill."

"Do not look at me, my friends." said Haroun, "I warrant it is booby-trapped. Even if I possessed the nimble fingers to unlock such a devastation, like Godiun Fout thief-master of old, then who among us could stand against the magics of the Wizard Zenops who doubtless waits within, reading, as you say, one of the *Black Books* over the period of a hundred years, prepared with every manner of bone-blasted magic. Aye, after so long he might not bother to lift his head at an interruption of abysmal meditations, but if he does, I would not want to be the first person he notices, not even the seventh. So let us depart and live, being wise soldiers, seeking easy loot in chambers above, and we shall ascend with shoulders burdened by handsome treasure. It's wizard's tribute for those adventurers who will leave him in peace, just as the stories say. We will be glad to find a quick stair out of the intermundane expanse to the world's teeming surface."

"Not so..." said Nergalf sternly, "...we pass all the way to Nystol, accursed be her name, and we traverse under the earth, on this shall your captain and I will not yield, not after having navigated so far as we have. Do not suppose that the chambers above are easy to pass through. There are doubtless bottomless pits to cross, horrible traps, and monstrous creatures the wizard has designed for the intruder, not to mention many patrols of goblins. Nor is he generous with gold as the children's stories say, but they who dare venture through find nothing but bones and rusty swords. So let us make new resolve, and be assured, the wizard will not have the time to cast a spell once I see him, for surely he will be too busy begging for his life."

"You speak well, but your plans will come to nothing, Nergalf, replied Haroun, "for I assure you, and mean no guile, I only need to look once at it and know, such a massy lock cannot be mastered. There are no others among us who come close to my skill."

"Are you so certain, Haroun? We need more than skill, we need experience. Let the wrinkley creature come forward and try, being more of use to me than yourself, for though he is a frail cave-dweller, he has spent hundreds of years in these subterraneous lands and is trollwise and tombwise more than any other."

The wrinkly old cave-dweller was Gulathar, an elfic creature whom we had discovered, rescued, and recruited just hours before. We pulled him out of a vermt belly. Now he was pushed forward up from the back of the line by the soldiers in formation up the stone steps to the landing. He spoke in that whimsical but yet foreboding fey-voice of the ancient race. He had not been listening to the conversation as he stood there in the back of the line, so he asked,

"What have ye to do with me now? Have I not given ye thanks and much lore-wisdom already?

"Do you recognize this enclave, Old one?"

'That be Zenops' Chamber." he said, confused. "Why halted we here? Should we not already be fleeing away? Certainly a band of goblins or patrolling centaurs will come and be glad to imprison me again."

"Not as long as Nergalf is with you." The dwarf boasted. "Now, ye old gelf, inform us how to unlock these massy bolts and enter here, for in such a way you will earn a place on our boat in the river below."

Gulathar peered at the lock with his large night-vision eyes.

"The lock is a fiction. It hath been artfully made by Zenops to fool the dense creatures doing his bidding. That it hath fooled all of ye does not bode well for this party. Wizards of this sort cherish deception, trusting it a much more trustworthy defense than hiring brutal henchmen. It is meant to convince his subordinates of the importance of his privacy, with the added benefit that no one needed to be keeping its key, and yet if there were some urgency even a weakling could break it. In this way he provides for himself that no one attempt to bother him or interrupt him as he reads the *Black Book*. And so his mercenaries never bother to come down this far anymore, just as he prefers, but stay above to carry on their wickedness and hinder raiders from getting down this far. The lock is made of a frail tin worked in such a way as to appear to be the sturdiest of irons. You may open it with minimal force. However beware of the trap which lay beyond the door."

"Trap?"

"A trap consisting of less than tin, mere paper, *The Black Book* itself. . .hungry for knowledge the foolish Zenops has been trapped for life reading it. May such a vanity for the power knowledge bestows never seize you."

'A book...?" asked Nergalf, nearly laughing. "What gladsome news!" Nergalf was delighted and his eyes lit up with glee. "An easy time now we will have of it after all. You soldiers ready yourselves and carry arms."

Nergalf reached out with his arms and tore down the fake tin lock, as if it were paper, and it seemed that, eventhough it were not truly a lock, it nevertheless was well-fashioned art.

And so Nergalf, though still sore from his wound, went first, kicking open the door and barging in with short-sword ready in hand. We followed and found the chamber not dark but well lit, and not by candles, but rather by luminous liquids, potions in glass bottles on many shelves. These were comprised of glowing and unstable "radiant matter" placed here and there about the Wizard's cell. Before us we immediately spotted the white-haired wizard, sitting in his ivory wizard-chair at a huge desk sporting an ornate griffon-leg design in a windowless chamber. His head was still, tilted downward as if gazing into the rather large tome opened before him. Various inks and paints, pens and gums, vellums, convex glass, scales, gems and precious stones, arcane diagrams, sealing rings, a dagger, and a variety of unknowns were left on the desk in front of him. In the corners of the room were scattered about all manner of devices and instruments that one might find in an alchemical den, clamps and rods of many different uses, rubber tubes and wires, nodules and valves, several furnaces and ovens, a well with buckets, iron barrels and bronze urns, boxes of various minerals and metals, vast collections of natural substances and ores not easy to identify, coals and chalks and sands, crystals and translucent rocks, liquids of a strange yellow color that seemed alive in glass jars, liquids with a bluish glow, (some still bubbling), tubes and vials, organs and shells of various creatures, a dragon skull, horns from a various deer, elephant tusks, worms of various kinds preserved, various woods and roots here and there, a few plants but no herbs nor any animal skins, and only a few other books.

There were also crates of common foods for grains, cheeses, dried meats and beans and the like which were broken open and empty. Obviously he had run out of supplies and had not the will to leave his quarters or summon his henchmen in order to obtain more food. There were plates and boxes strewn about. All that was left for him to greet us with was a lifeless and withered visage.

"I would say he has been dead many years already." remarked my brother. "By the look of it, the chamber was well sealed, nor were any rodents or other pests able to enter."

Nergalf approached the desk where sat the wizard frozen in time. Cautiously the dwarf approached, with his infamous sword raised.

"Who can glean what trickery this might be...?"

Nergalf went round the desk and stood near the wizard's head of greyish flesh, examining it. Suddenly the partially decayed wizard raised his head and what were thought lifeless eyes suddenly opened, and he moaned a great moan. Nergalf's response to this was swift and immediate. (He seemed to be one who was very spooked by the dead, and one whose actions were always over-reactions). The dwarf immediately and without hesitation used his blade and with an easy but panicked swing deprived the wizard of his head. All were dismayed and appalled at the sight. The head fell to the floor with a thud.

Nergalf looked up, his mouth agape. "The deep airs must have caused my nerves to go haywire," he explained. "Right badly it spooks me. I didn't mean to mutilate a corpse. I have seen this kind of thing before on the plains of war, after a battle the dead do not always stay still. Some even sit up again, after having been dead several days."

"It is all the better anyway," said Gulathar as he stepped over and retrieved the Wizard's head from the wood floor. "I would have cut off the head of this one myself, to bury it in the tombs of Astodan where it belongs, and where the souls of wicked Sorcerers and their confreres like Zenops must be finally imprisoned. Otherwise the spirit of a Nystoli Arcane will haunt the living even until the Day of Judgement."

Gulathar wrapped the head up in some cloth he found laying about and put it in his nap sack. It was a most displeasing sight to see a wrinkly old elf handling a wrinkly human head.

"It will not smell too bad. But this must be done."

"And the body?" asked Perigraunce. "We must see to it that it is burned, as is custom among men upon the earth's surface. Suffer not a witch to live. Let them be consumed in fire."

"It is not wise. Fire will not burn well down here unless it be dragon-fire." explained Gulathar. "But take the ore which he has collected here, lay out the corpse and pile the ore-rocks upon him. Use holy water, priest, pouring it over the body. It is your Christian duty."

This was done right away by Perigraunce, for none of us wanted to be in the presence of that unholy corpse, and I secretly feared that the

Wizard would somehow return from the dead to protect his goods.

We all began to search through his quarters.

Nergalf reached for the precious tome the wizard had been reading and moved it over to himself athwart the table, knocking over candle-sticks and various inconsequential objects. He began paging through it.

"It is indeed one of the *Black Books*, but which one I know not." grumbled Nergalf, "Nor would I know how to read its ancient script, and even if I did, there are well over a thousand pages. Somehow we must learn which page, and read it, in order to verify The Spear or else I will never be able to raise an army against Nystol. Do you know this language, priest?"

"I know only what it is not." said Perigraunce, looking over Nergalf's low shoulder. "It's not Greek or Gohhan, and certainly not Acaratic, although there are notes written in subterraneous Latin in the margins, but neither am I able to comprehend that without some help."

"If not even the priest knows...what hope is there?" Nergalf sounded very lost in mind. "But what do you say about it, old Gulathar, surely you know the eld tongues."

"I do have some keen on the eld tongues, and much lore. However I never learned to read letters, spending most of my days in unlit caves."

The old elf approached, and looking over the pages with Nergalf, continued.

"Show thou me the book's cover." Gulathar requested of Nergalf.

It took both of Nergalf's dwarf hands to pull back the leather cover, which was not so much leathery as scaley, like a lizard skin. What seemed darkly colored blackish-red scale-hide made a strange but not displeasing pattern of oval or convex shape on the cover, from the top right corner to the left bottom.

"I think it is one of the long sought-after elylinth volumes, which are accursed, according to some lore-masters.   Close it. It should be left here."

"We cannot leave such a rare work, protested Perigraunce, precious to the destinies of men, simply on account of rumour, or of some vain curse...See, it lists many grand but lost works, including a translation in Gohhan of the rare philosophic tract by the sage Averroes, *The Incoherence of The Incoherence*, condemned by both the Kalar and the Cult of The Veil, which being weird and albiet erroneous, is a precious reference for demonstations that the world has no beginning and no end!"

"There is no room to carry such a huge tome on the boat." replied Nergalf. "Besides, such a proposition about the world is preposterous. If there were no beginning and no end of things, beings like us would have always existed, and therefore there would be an infinite number of dwarves and gnomes, humans and elves. Certainly that's not the case. So instead lets not concern ourselves with the ramblings of mad philosophers, but we can tear out some of the pages, the ones with illustrations, or special designs, glyphs and the like."

"That is outrageous!" cried Perigraunce.

"To guess fair on such high matters be not wisdom." warned old Gulathar. "You know not what you do when it comes to such matters. None of us do, not even the priest can determine to destroy such a mystery, be it accursed or nay. Look around, I say to ye all, let us scan through these rooms for a sign. Yea, ware be thou, touch nothing, neither strange devices nor anything seeming to be gladsome loot. Especially quaff not of yon glowing potions or any other liquids. They be not labeled, or even if they be, they most certainly display fictional lore meaning to usher in speedy death instead, for the wizard prepared for unwary raiders that would someday enter."

All ventured further into the eight alcoves of this wizard's den, slowly and carefully, for there were many things placed here and there. Nor were there any of us who stepped into those areas without weapons drawn.

"Here is a potion, and it has a label," announced Shu Kurgoman from some enclave at the other side of the room, "...bearing written these words in familiar script: *Potus Isde Vitae Aeternalis.* This potion is special. It was hidden away under a slab of stone. I am certain that it translates 'The drink of eternal life!' Perhaps, Gulathar, I wager you are wrong, perhaps this is the elixir that made the wizard live so long, hundreds of years, as well as many other wizards. What human would not drink this? No, you are right that these others are deadly, but if this is a poison meant to kill me, why would the label be written in Latin, a tongue so few know? Someone even tried to paint a skull on it as if to scare us away. The opposite is true. At any rate. I'll take a sip...I have no family awaiting my return..."

Straight way did Shu rashly pull the cork and sip.

"Why it tastes better than any liquor I've ever had..."

He then drank down the entire potion. I watched in horror and dismay. We waited a few moments. Nothing happened.

"Aye, all honey to the lips the taste," proclaimed Nergalf, "but bitter to the stomach, like bad women. It's not real, you fool. The wizard himself is dead. Would he not have used it on himself to save his own dear life? Nor did potion save him from my blade. Or if that's not the case, maybe he was alive up until the moment I deprived him of his head, and it is afterall the potion of life everlasting, for who can be sure if what you have greedily drunk down is truly the famous elixir? ...but how foolish the one who drinks it, for the label should read "draught of eternal life." The fool who takes it forgets that he also needs a potion for endless youth as well, like the knavish singers in the stories of the Greeks whom the gods finally transformed into cicadas. You will grow old, like they, and never die, but you will just watch yourself grow older and older, to slowly wither away, not decaying, but not getting any better, weaker and weaker, unable to do much or obtain help. It is no doubt what happened to the Wizard, who, they say, lived near three hundred years. The worlds will pass away into nothing and doubtless you will still be around, unable to hold your bowels, toothless, hairless and frail, withered and wondering why you can never rest your thoughts in death's gift of quietude like all else of the beings. Pity...may the gods not hold it against you. You have no one to blame but yourself."

Nergalf smirked. At these words Shu's face betrayed a horror. He stood there transfixed for his own stupidity.

It was in this moment when a certain realization of possibility came to me, possibility of what secret the wizard's past might hold. With great excitement at this new question in my mind, I acted at once.

"Come, Gulathar," I said, "lift back out Zenop's head from your sack! Place it on this shelf up here, upright suspended between those two stacks so it is eye to eye with us."

"What? What meaneth thou, boy?"

"Just do as I request, you will learn my thought soon enough."

Gulathar unraveled the wrinkly head and placed it on the shelf beside some glowing liquids that lit its hoary visage nicely. The withered eyes and mouth of grey-skinned Zenops were shut tight. The others came near and gathered about, curious as to what I might be up to.

"Zenops!" I yelled in a loud voice, "Zenops! Grand Wizard! Awaken!"

Immediately the eyelids in the head opened in their sockets. Eyeballs jerked and rolled and looked about, and peered at us.

"What? Who are you? . . . Where's the book I had?"

"You are then he. . . -Zenops, Grand Wizard?" I asked.

"What is it to you? How dare you intrude. These are my chambers. Where is that book? Inform me at once or I will cast torment upon you and thrash you within an inch of your life!"

"Which book mean you?" I asked.

"Thou knowest which book, intruder. The book I was reading."

"Not so. . . but I did notice a book, yet I have no certitude of which volume among these you mean. Would you tell me? And I also have something else to ask of you...

"-Alright that be enough! Now I am going to rend thee to pieces, all of ye. Wait, wait...where be mine hands, what has been done to me? Untie me I say."

"We cannot do that."

"Either untie me or else I utter a painful spell on each of ye, a spell which will usher in pain undreamt."

"Do not heed the threat, he cannot accomplish that." announced Perigraunce, "Of course he can speak words of magic, anyone can, but the spell will fail. You need not fear his threat."

"And who says so? " asked the head, looking fiercely at Perigraunce. "What knave dares insinuation and estimation on my wizardry with such impudence. Soon thou shalt learn the gravity of thy errors."

"I am Perigraunce, Ammouric priest."

"No wonder, priest. You must feel intimidated by the power of a grand wizard."

"I am not. . ." replied Perigraunce stoicly, "...for everyone has heard how that power wanes. Let me convey some tidings to you, wizard. Something has happened in your mother city Nystol, something that has forever altered the metaphysic structure of the arcane systems, something called the Hypostatic Rift. There are few able to explain how it happened, but to tell of it briefly, heed this news concerning the arcane cosmologies: the preternatural source-fonts are closed off."

"What? That's impossible! They cannot be closed off, unless...well it would be so very unlikely...unless the psychical vortex were to seal off against the valent imagination."

"I have no wit at your weird jargon, wizard, but as far as I know that sounds just like what must have happened."

"It cannot have happened. The Archimages have long secured against every comprehensile, permutation, and variable from all possible systems!" the head said sternly.

"Here it and mark my words, wizard, I am a priest. Your spells are useless, they could not do much against a mouse even if you tried. What motive would I have to supply you fictional news? If any motive, fear of your power be not one. The vortex is sealed, and once sealed,

sealed forever."

"So thou imagine it, but fail to understand that such a thing is impossible. Do I not know my profession? You harken to misreport. The entire *paraphysik* of superstantial reality would be turned awry were that the case."

"It is not mere rumor. I say it knowing that you have enough mind left in you to cogitate the facts of what has come to be."

"Thou pass on such strange and dread news, unaware of how such a thing is impossible. Any new system of thought-projection that pretends detachment from the preternatural sources and from their capacity to flow directly into sense-objects is impossible. It was a fallacious position that a young student of mine, one Scardetes, a rebellious rascal, tried to push. He based it on certain innate mathematic fusions found in the microcosmoid which could be extracted into irreconcilable limits. This apprentice proposed that once the preternatural valencies were disembodied the fonts would close off completely. Why anyone would even entertain his vain idea, I cannot fathom."

"And did you examine his proposal? I hear that his name was famous in Nystol, or rather, 'infamous. . .' "

"Laughable, it could never happen, priest. If such a situation developed, superstantial reality could no longer be accessed to inform the imagination. Neither could the sub-lunar modalities nor the celestial spheres be apprehended. Ethical derivatives could not conform according to established ground. He was a poor student, incapable of rational demonstration. I had to send him back to Nystol to be re-educated. The last I heard was that he was going about claiming that I was in breech of the ethic...daring upstart he. Surely the Soothfold never granted him the indulgence...let alone would the Archimagi or adepts of Nystol have graduated him...or did they...? Could they have not seen through his folly? No...No, in any scenario it is impossible. If his theory were put into demonstration, proven and accepted, it would no longer be possible. . .a balance of between the two Arcane ideomantic positions..."

Zenop's voice slowed as he came to the realization of what had transpired. "But...but the Archimagi are cleverer than that...they know that such a theory, if accepted and if...put into practice, it..."

There was an uncomfortable and dreadful moment of silence. The wizard continued.

"...would cause an actual schism...between the two potentialities...a schism that would be projected into the externals, redounding disturbance onto the volitional series of word-formation...and that it would surely cause...a thought-rift...a chasm in axial inherencies would develop out of control...incrementally, resulting in irreconcilable positions, and actuality would over-compensate to principles grounding potentiality, a split in the...hyperstatic union. Please let it not be! Bring me a grimore!"

"You will not attempt to harm us?" asked Dunstaark.

"Just bring me a grimore, there are several there on the shelf. There, that one over there on the ledge, the one with the crocodile-skin binding. It features a number of Gohhan verbal spells. Open it! I promise no harm to anyone."

"Go ahead, Wassel." said Perigraunce "Take up the book up for him and let him try, nothing will come of it, and then he will know for a certitude."

I took hold of the book and opened to a random page. There were diagrams and strange glyphs. Gohhan is a kind of Egyptian cursive, difficult to read, but no problem for an experienced wizard.

"Just turn the page. . .turn one page more. . . good, there. Halt and hold."

Zenops then opened his mouth to voice a spell in that strange sounding language. He must have spoken only one sentence when he checked his words.

"These words have no power. I can feel it. There is nothing to them. They are useless...alas, a great change has come!"

Zenops stared off into what seemed the spaces of his own mind, and it was obvious that he was thoroughly disturbed.

"So this report of thine telling is worthy, without deception. I should have known this would come. I foresaw it all along, if only in the back of my mind, not consciously, but in dreams, as a possibility. Somehow I understood that this catastrophe could and would happen someday...no, thou art no deceiver. This news has changed everything. All our magic scrolls and grimores are now become useless curiosities."

"But potions...do potions still work?" asked Shu with great urgency.

"Who is it asks me there? What hast thou done? Hast thou drunk down one of the potions in my keep? Thou art the fool to enter a wizard's den and drink potions as if having a drinking bout in some tavern. But come, do not worry, the side-effects are nothing and some harmless fun will be had. Yes, the potions must always retain their magical nature until they are consumed or destroyed. The rift I have just now learned of, it was forseen...but it cannot effect *composita,* no verbal components are used to administer potentiality to potions. Their hyperstatic unions and superstantial causalities remain fixed in radiant matter as on the day they were brewed. They are all knavish little trickster-potions. Do not worry, untie me and I will show further wonders. The only potion that remains dangerous is the one marked as a 'potion of aeternal life'. I wanted to make sure no one would ever drink that. There even is a skull painted on it as if it be some poison, a sign to dissuade the illiterate. Of course no person would be so daft as to wish never to die, to have endless life, at least not the kind which that bottle offers...Now release my head as well! Why can I not move or sense mine body?"

(Is there any need to describe the look on Shu's face at hearing the wizard's answer? He was speechless).

"But was it not you yourself," I asked, "you, Zenops, that once drank of the same weird potion, or one like it, and so you too will never die, or rather, you have forfeited death's gift of eternal rest?"

"And how is it, boy, that thou hast learned such things about me?" asked Zenops "Hast thou read some rare history? Do ye know other wizards who told that secret about me? Aye, indeed it be right lore. When I was just an overbold youth I did it, during my apprenticeship, loose like a mischievous fox in the dens of Nystol. How such a potion came into existence, by the agency what god or demon, I know not."

"What happened to you?" asked Shu.

"As I realized my mistake, I was overcome by an unnatural melancholy. A sense of meaninglessness began to pervade my very being. It seemed as if every undertaking was all for naught, given the potentiality of every human experience being repeatable *ad nauseum*. I spent my unending years searching for an antidote. Fear alone, and an innate sense of right law, as well as respect for my dear mother, kept me from annihilating myself. Self-destruction would not have worked anyway, but only yielded greater misery sooner. When I realized that no antidote could ever be found, I began to make other preparations, such as building this immense tower for myself, so that I could spend the passage of time in solitude and comfort, for the years weighed heavily on me and I grew weary of company who did not comprehend my pain. I tried to create an imitation of death, working to make my elderly years as death-like and as restful as possible, undisturbed."

"So these chambers were also meant to be your final place of rest?"

"It is a silent place, but although sleep comes and goes, true rest eludes me, and my soul is ever in turmoil. Enough said of self-pity however. I also did wish to bequeath the race of men some benefit of my vast knowledge. To this end I have writ books and designed a number of magical items, all of which can be found here, but, take ye care, ye seigers and thieves. Ye will not have wit enough to use them unless I am released from this stockade."

"You cannot be released," I explained. "You are neither fixed in stockade nor tied up. You are in a much more difficult situation, on account of that potion you quaffed long ago. Zenops, one of our warriors has severed your head from your body. You, I am sorry to inform, or, all that is left of you, that is, well, all that you are, is but a head. But thank God the capital somehow speaks even without heart and lungs, spine and shoulders. Your throat is intact and you converse. Now do not take it too sore hard, wizard, after all, your body was mere skin and bones anyway, seeming to have not eaten a slice of bread for years. We found you asleep, but by an accident you spooked one of our swordsman, jerking your head up in sleep. Shocked by what he took as some undead horror, he has hewn your gaunt head clean off. He did this and even then you did not awaken, therefore your body must have already been useless. After the dwarf did that, and I heard of the weird potion found here, I gathered that you yourself must have ever taken a draught of it long past, and now only seemed dead. You really were sleeping.

"It is true what the great poet Heraclitus says," added Perigraunce, "*death is brother to sleep*."

"Ye hath beheaded me?" the wizard cried, "Alas, a mind without a body, a head without a heart! What hath I to deserve so foul a destiny? My quick hands, my fast feet, they are gone? Whither hath ye taken mine body?"

"It is buried here, under yon stones."

"Then I am to continue without limbs?"

"As it seems, wizard." I replied, with pity.

"A fitting penalty for the crime of wizardry," announced Perigraunce. "You worker of delusions."

"It was never a crime in my day. Have you any pity? The wizard-head retorted, "In days of yore works of wizardry were necessary to stave off major chaos. It is an art that must be done! But am I doomed to continue through endless ages as a mere bodiless head for it? No, please, have mercy. Many were the Arcanes and Divines who pointed their fingers at me and called me the reason for the magic-troubles throughout the Furth. They exiled me for it, but they did not examine how it were their own hands that worked the much devilry of recent ages. I was expelled from Nystol for my researches, and so the king took me in. Even he betrayed me. I escaped into this tower which I had long prepared, foreseeing evils, for many enemies there were. It is true that I am guilty of creating abominations, monsters, and weird potions here, in order to learn things. I am also guilty of endeavoring to tease out the secrets of the universe, secret knowledge, if only to save the lives of others. I did not care if the laws were transgressed, if animals suffered in my experiments, or sentient creatures were imprisoned. Life was no longer important, only knowledge. But they had judged me guilty of these things even before I set about the work. So I reasoned, why not forsake ethical requirements in the name of advancing wizardry? If I am already guilty, what harm will come to me? I see now the folly of my ways. What was sacred became defiled. Once long ago I was given the indulgence by thine own Ammouric Soothfold, priest. They revoked it when my ill-repute spread.

"I hear your defense, and perhaps we shall not seek to convict you of transgressing, but learn this: Nystol still has a stranglehold over the earth. No longer do the righteous wizards of old dwell there, but Sorcerers possess the hegemony, men who hold consort with demons."

"No righteous wizards there? Can that be? Sorcerers have obtained the Archimagistrate?"

"It is so. . ." added Dunstaark, "but not for long. We raiders do journey underground to Nystol, avoiding the dooming desert, and we will slay its pernicious inhabitants and sack the collegium, and to lay hold upon its magic treasures,.. To this end we seek the map of Gulconda drawn by the gnome Krithusel Eloniah, *de itinere*. . .uh. . .the rest of the Latin I do not have..."

"*de itinere caverneo ad nystulum*," said Nergalf, "on which is drawn the way through the many tunnels of Gulconda, a map with magical enhancements too."

"That old chart?" The wizard said with surprise, "It is lost to oblivion, burnt in flame. Too bad, it were a finery I once looked over closely, enjoying the gnome's many artfully drawn details. When the ambassador of Hermius escaped from here, he stole it back and took it away with him. . .a fine man he, one "Alember", committed doubtless to return the chart to its owner."

"Alember was a good messenger." said Nergalf, "He was loyal and true to me. I heard he never made it back to the surface however, slain in some trap of yours or devoured by a beast. As for you, Zenops, our alliance still stands, even though you have broken trust and heaped lie upon lie."

"You are not forgotten, Nergalf, admiral of Hermius' army! You are one proven trustworthy in leaving corpse upon corpse heaped up over the bloody plains of many ruthless wars!"

"My military prowess has been the cause of a few fallen, heroic foes mostly, but your endless lies have slain many more innocent men than ever could the god Ares."

"I knew you would someday dare to come, Nergalf. The ferocity of your sword and the endless slaughter of which you are capable was well known, so I prepared myself to be your rival. I placed many traps and weird creatures here to hinder your onslaught. It seems my preparations failed. As for Alember, I treated him well, and he lived like a king here, but he was not content to stay. He escaped and made for the surface, but returned from the chambers above burned awfully by some horrid monster. I knew great regret for having built and prepared this awful place when I saw him thus. My Greek physician endeavored to revive him, but to no avail. We did bury him with solemn rites. It was after that tragedy that I began to change my mind, I started to fear the gods again."

"Then he was blasted by a dragon's exhalation?"

"So it seems, there must a dragon that has taken up residence up there on the chasm-cliffs surrounding. It would make sense. The spaces between the tower walls and the cliffs of the great gap are enough space for a dragon to fly about with ease and seek prey. There are numerous other creatures to feed on, and they have easy access into the tower itself. Why do you think that I myself never escaped after all these years? I was trapped in my own trap. I apologize for having taken your map, but I had no choice, the king was meaning to. . ."

"You claim innocence, wizard." I said, "You say you were forced to flee into this tower. Yet we all know that you stole away plenty of the king's gold. It was an infamous deed famed throughout the lands."

"I have kept a great deal of gold, but no gold stolen from the king. He published far and wide that rumour so that he could hide away monies for himself and pay less tribute to Hermius, while exacting more from merchants and burghers. He assuaged his conscience by considering his lying rumour a half-truth: it was potential gold that was stolen. Afterall, the alchemic key of effecting the transmutation of lead into gold, which I had discovered, was his property, myself being his vizier, and therefore in fleeing to this tower I had, in his view, stolen what was his own, since in owning me he also owned my knowledge! Even before I escaped here, I could percieve how greatly he feared lest my power be released to others. He first had planned to imprison me in his castle to bring about transmutations at his will. To this end he feigned a dreadful sickness and demanded that his Greek physician treat him to health, who of course could not because the entire thing was a set-up. Then he sent for me, demanding that I heal him with my wizardry. I responded that I am a wizard, not a physician, whereby at once he arrested me and sent both his physician and I into the dungeon. Even the physician had to suffer for mere pretext! Alas, what greed! We escaped together, but only after much trial."

Zenops paused, being very disturbed, but continued.

"I have nothing left, so let me explain how all these other things came to pass as well, and in so doing refute many other fictions. Everyone knows that there are two ways to finish a wizard. The most common is burning, as the Ammouri recommend, especially for Sorcery and Summoning. Now I was long ago given the indulgence, as all official court-wizards must, and it was revoked, but not because I was found sorcerous, no, rather it were a minor oversight in my usage of resonances, which was quite an astonishingly insincere reason.

"What really transpired was that when the king secretly turned on me, the petty tyrant, he paid off some vain clerics to influence the Soothfold. He spread falsehoods in his court about me, that I might be traitorous and had been eyeing his gold, things I could not disprove because men trust a king's word more than a wizard's. No strong noble therefore stepped in on my behalf when we were sent to the dungeon.

"Add to that the fact that the thankless pupil Scardetes was going about Nystol giving me a bad name there, well, my reputation as wizard turned quite sour. (Only many years later, after my detractors were all dead, did the publication of my epic *the Bladetongue* earn me some redeeming graces in the eyes of the world).

"As I say, there are two ways. To cut off the head is the other way to execute a wizard, and this way was favored by the Maceonid kings. After the escape, a good bounty was on my head and I knew that if any mercenary-raider came down this far and broke into this chamber, he would cut off my head for proof of the bounty. Such a raider would surely come... I thought about how to respond when the time of attack was near, and of all the powerful combat-spells that might be used, but I came to the realization that there is nothing, even in the most dreaded tomes and grimores, that can safeguard much against the onslaught of a savage swordsman.

"My head was destined to be struck off. They always go for the head first, as warriors are trained, and this dwarf here has now done it. Raiders of their kind know that it is the quickest way to silence an arcane voice. Added to this is the simple fact that this has long been an admitted problem for Arcanes, the speed of a swordsman always overtakes the twisted tongue of the spell-caster. Even a mage-missile, that fastest of battle-magic, requires too many counts at close range to use efficiently when swiftly advanced upon by experienced fighters.

"Anyone who adventured down this far after having overcome every monster and adversity which I could provide, would have no problem taking on an old, old, man like me.

"Now knowing that I can fain death after having been decapitated, and that the raider would take this head of mine away to the king in order to receive his bounty, I made plans. First, I could offer the raider a higher price if he restored me. This however a mercenary would not trust, thinking that after he put my head back that I might raise a deadly spell against him.

"Deception therefore was my only option. After a bounty hunter would give the king my head as proof, I foresaw that the king would order it placed outside on a pike or spear on the castle wall as a display for all to see, in order to show the wage of treason. To avoid further damage to my head thus impaled, I knew that the soldier instructed with the task of displaying my head would need to be bribed so as to use some excuse, for if he failed to impale the head, he would loose his own head as well. So I prepared to-"

"Enough of your talk!" barked Nergalf, "That is what I always regretted the most about adventuring with you, wizard, your endless talk. Forget it. . .we shall find our own way. The book you were reading however, one of the *Black Books of Melancholy*. ...we prize its lore, as well as any other wizardic wit you brain holds about Nystol."

"Aye, *the Black Book*. . .it is a worthy tome."

"There it lay on your desk over there, though none of us can read it." I added.

"Why have you been reading it, wizard?" asked Dunstaark. "It is no spell book."

"It was in that famous volume that I hoped to capture sleep. I could never sleep for years and years, as it was one of the side-effects of the potion. As I got older, I slept less and less. It seemed like a living hell after I had passed the natural years allotted to men. At last it seemed that I could sleep for ten counts once every few years. What manner of horror was that? Then I heard from my Greek physician that somewhere in *the Black Books* was to be found a recipe for a very potent sleeping medicine. It took years to get a hold of the right volume, but when finally I did, I realized that I might have the solution to all my ills in my very hands. The only problem was that I had to read through its thousands of pages to find the recipe, for there is no table in the book, nor any index. I never found the recipe. When I finally finished the book my eyes were so profoundly weary I did fall asleep! Now I realize that what I heard was true, the medicine was the book itself, to read the entire book would cause a grand sleep! But you knaves have awoken me!"

"And what of Nystol," said Nergalf. "What have you learned of that foul garden in the world's wide waste?"

"All the more, in taking that medicine I discovered a vast amount of eld and forgotten histories. Ye seek the city of many towers?" said Zenops with incredulity, "Fools, ye cannot destroy Nystol. Its cliffs and walls are impregnable, and besides, it is the jewel of the earth. If it is as ye say, and Sorcerers now rule there, then demon-gods do their bidding. The Sorcerers will be too powerful to submit to the hands of mortal men."

"Not if our hands carry the Spear."

"The Spear? Meanest thou the Spear of Destiny, sacred relic of the Nazarene?"

"We mean the same relic," replied Nergalf, "and we seek it because by some ancient power it renders an army capable to conquer any city."

"You are then faithful to the Nazarean, and claimed for salvation, thy name being written his book? How weird a cult. Has not that wretched superstition perished from the earth yet?"

"Not even, but our kind have increased," said Perigraunce "for we are bound to a sacred destiny, a mission, and now our faith holds sway in many lands. The Ammouri have announced it the only true faith and all others false. The Maceonid kings in every kingdom of the West have received the white robes and renounced the old gods. So now you have a chance to redeem yourself, wizard, and show yourself worthy of standing before the new god. May God give you peace if you accept it: help us find the Spear by your knowledge of what is writ in *the Black Book*, and as a priest I assure you that in so doing you shall escape the hellfire, and not be terrified at the Judgement."

"Join with you, to destroy my beloved Nystol?"

"Not so beloved any more," said Nergalf, "they have long titled you an ignominious traitor."

"Such words are cold steel. Even if that Nazarene god is the judge and master of all gods, what does that mean to me? I know something of his teachings, and they do not apply in my case. I will not be judged thusly as they say, since, according to such belief, a man is judged only after he dies. The potion has caused me to continue in the world for unending time, doomed never to die, doomed to never taste death. Unfortunately, even if all other things pass away, I will remain, and so never dying, then never to be judged either."

"Your wizardry has misinstructed you, old feeble-mind." said Perigraunce, "The scriptures announce that the Christ is 'Judge both of the living and of the dead.' One does not need to be dead in order to warrant the judgement. Therefore even if you endure uncounted passage of years, a day will come that the Lord will judge you even so, even though you still dwell upon these intermundane shores."

"He shall render judgement even upon those souls who did not worship him? What gives him such authority? Is he the god who authored all things?"

"He is, and he is the one true god...it is written, every knee shall bend, on the earth, and in heaven above, and even under the earth. So you cannot escape, therefore why continue to flee from the all-seeing and all-knowing God? But come, take heart, if you do good, you need not fear losing death's eternal rest, but it is common knowledge that only the wicked do never rest. Also learn you these words, as holy writ instructs, *"it is appointed for all men to die once, then comes the judgement"*. So you must die, regardless of what prolongation of life that potion attempts to persuade is yours. It is merely a potion of longevity, that's all, but to get a better price the mischeivous alchemist titled it "of aeternal life" and in bad Latin I must say. Still, it must have had some weird alchemic power that causes the soul and brain of man to continue even after the vital body has been severed. It were the contrivance or trickery of some evil demigod inspiring that ancient fool of a chemist, who now is ashes himself in some urn. His demon hoped to excite in buyers like you fear, horror, and despair. So be glad, you will assuredly in the end die, but how far into future years you will persist because of that chemical, who can say? Aye, death must needs come, as is testified by the master of both life and death. You are already dead in your soul, as you have always been, and that is much worse. God will quicken your soul to new life. Therefore repent and believe in the gospel."

"I do say, your explanation of things is beyond what I have ever heard. And much of what thou said seems not bad council, Christian. Thy words give me some consolation and dispels fear. The Eldark long spoke of a singular deity, a cosmic mentality ordering all things, an all-being power which gave rise to all the gods. They arrived at this truth through their powerful reasoning, and they even composed hymns and prescribed ritual meditations. Then came the Ammouri, claiming to be sent by the One True God, a living Allfather who created everything. All of us students in Nystol thought them to be religious fanatics in suggesting that the divine spirit was a person like you or I. Nevertheless, the educated among them were able to hold their own in debate and disputation, and though peaceful, many strange powers like unto spells they seemed to know. So arose the Divines, and they dwelt in Nystol, but were set apart. Out of fear, many of the Arcanes sought them for approval, *logos* conformity and an ethical ground. I myself rejected them as novel, but entertained a worried suspicion they might not be just another mysterious cult. Then one day messengers arrived carrying sacred scrolls, and they began to speak of an "anointed messiah" who had come into the world. The Ammouric Sooths announced that "the great time" had come. Their words and prophecies sounded sublime, but made no rational sense to most of us wizards.

"Now, after long passage of time, even the kings have turned to the unknown god, a god that was executed like a criminal by a conspiracy of men, but was even himself a man. Now I have awoken upon a crucial day, a nadir on which my soul is suspended, a putrifaction, as the alchemists call it. No other gods have helped me or offer me hope of rest, but I have never betook the unknown god. But lo, has sent his priest to me. So I think I will turn to this Perigraunce here and seek his counsel. Perhaps then by believing the deity will look with favor upon me, or what's left of me. They claim he is merciful, forgiving wrong doing and saving wretches like me. Therefore let this good news be accepted, and promise of new life, and to vouchsafe my turning I will give my knowledgeable counsel to thee and thy crew."

"The Ammouric Soothfold will review your request to be officially admitted into the assembly of faith." said Perigraunce. "However, since we cannot soon obtain their writ, I dispense you from such a formality, as is lawful in places of danger, and I will administer the sacred rite of baptizing in three day's time, after you have shown sufficient resolve. You no longer are Zenops named. You are a believer. The new name I give you is Zenopio. It is God's will."

"Thank you, I do enjoy the sound of that name even more than what I have known as my own for centuries."

"Ware be thou, gird yourself to endure the torture of the Devil."

"Many devils already have tortured me for years. But something new I sense already. A little peace in me I detect, albeit from the scattering of despair. I do not have knowledge about thy sacred rituals, but I hope I can be there to watch. So I ask this favor in return for my every assistance: do not abandon me here placed on this shelf to wait endless years alone in the dark, left at the mercy of whatever rat comes by. Instead, take me with you. I will treat on all things about which I am wise, every lore found in that famous book...but I also require something else."

"Require something else? Not so fast, wizard, you arrogant swell-head..." growled Nergalf. "it is ill luck to have a wizard come along on a raiding party, there will be no oath-saying for you. We don't need your lore so much. I can hire other wizards who can tell many things."

"I hear that it be also ill luck to bring a dwark, as far as I remember." the wizard snapped back.

" 'Dwark' you call me? Why...I'll make dainties of your head right now." bellowed Nergalf, "You will not have to worry that you are still alive, you spook, no. My blade will just make mince-meat of that skull of yours, like I should have years ago. Then I'll feed your cheeks, nose, and lips to the rats, the worthier denizens of this tower."

Nergalf lifted his sword, ready to put an end to weirdness. Dunstaark was alert however and with speedy arm caught Nergalf by the shoulder before he could take a step past me to swing at the head.

"Hold back, Nergalf," Dunstaark warned, "you may be strongest and deadliest among us, but take leave and instead let your wounds heal. Don't doubt my command. It is my word that the men heed, and my decision on who takes an oath to join this raid. They will all disband if I perish, and follow they no other, being a discontented and reckless crew, so take care to govern your wrath, if you hope to teach Nystol vengeance, and remember that you do not yet stand justified."

Nergalf looked askance at Dunstaark with increased irritation, the ashamed but defiant look of one who knows that he cannot deny the facts obvious to all.

"Do not suppose, valiant raiders," Zenopio said, "that I did not myself foresee that something of this sort would transpire. Adventurers hoping for gold were coming to this tower all the time to fight the many deep-born monsters which I collected over the years, some of which I myself bred or manufactured. They hear the story published about my stealing the king's loot and hiding beneath the earth in this tower, and so they come all battle-hardened, hoping to make it down to my chamber, past goblins and troll-guards, past the horrific tentacles of the hydras, past all the giant beasts and deadly traps. I thought we had done an ingenious job of setting up trials for any would-be hero. In fact, I came to consider it my duty to call them hither by spreading rumour about this place. Usually only rash battle-mad fools harken and come, like this dwarf here, the kind of soldier ready to use his blade at the drop of a wizard's hat."

"Were it not for a human's pity, Zenops, those others who lie strewn about this ruinous tower would be already be avenged by now." remarked Nergalf.

"No longer call me Zenops! No longer, you... I am called Zenopio, the believer."

"How can a wizard be changed to a Christian so quickly?" snarled Nergalf, "It must be a deceit to delude us, just like what happened to the heroes whose funeral monument is their common grave, this tower."

"Had they survived the trials I prepared, they doubtless would thank me. I merely supplied that for which they dearly hoped, a chance at glory and loot. Come try your ready swords in my dreadful tower, and learn that you too will surely die. Of those violent and greedy ones who accepted the challenge, who broke open the surface-doors and entered the spiraling passages, armed to the teeth, did any ever return above carrying shining booty? -none to my knowledge. The end result was that the world above no longer was plagued by such arrogant types, unemployed men-at-arms who raid small towns, nobles who impose burdensome taxes on peasants, or mercenaries who delight in bloodshed. The way I saw it, I was doing the world a favor. That is my confession, and if it be sin I ask forgiveness. They chose their own fate, they knew the risk. If a burglar breaks into a house, is the owner guilty that his pet mastiff mauls the intruder? The world however is none the worse for it. It were the Bladetongue only who adventured all the way to these bottom levels, breaking into my antechambers, and I met them with magical bolts of fire and clouds of debilitating smoke, with deafening noise, paralysis and fear, mind-bending confusion. All for naught, they captured me and interrogated me, and then told me their story, and they were virtuous indeed. I bargained for my life by offering my service to glorify their deeds, composing for them the famous epic. But I would not let any of their sworn fighters enter this chamber as you have done. It was their Urius who found the ancestral sword and slew the great dragon which tyrannized the kingdom in those days. Many supposed my poetry fiction, so fantastic were the deeds described. Ah, but those bold souls be gone now to far off Elysium."

"Not all be gone away so far. . ." said Gulathar. A silence followed the old one's utterance.

VI

"Hark! It is a familiar voice that speaks," the Zenopio-head wondered, "the voice which just now spoke... is that voice not an enchanted one of old, one I knew? Is it not Gulathar? It must be, for no other is like him. Old gelf, come forward and let me see you."

"In sooth I speak and stand here," said Gulathar, stepping forward, "The very one who 'first learned the lore and told of rumoured gold', sworn of *the Bladetongue*. All those heroes now reside in the afterworld, having passed into immortal renown, save myself. Like you I also am long-living, my wrinkles not caused by foolish magic, but rather weird elven blood preserves me countless years. These others here don't know it like you do, wizard, that   I be a ginder elf, that is, "gelf," an old deep born race of elf-kin, and like the elves above, formed not from dust like men, nor doomed to die. I am the reason for their entry into your inner chamber. It was during those ages of solitude, trapped at the bottom of the tower, that the realization came to me about your lock, the massy lock of the door there which long ago I had noticed you preparing. Aye, I remembered that it be fiction to the eye."

"Gulathar! Welcome, old friend. I foresaw that one day new adventurers might come, and if any could get down this far, that would be rare indeed."

"Aye, they have come and broken through, and I am to blame, only because I wished to learn how you fared."

"Surely none would have the wit to perceive that the lock was fiction." said Zenopio, smiling. "But these yeomen were wise enough to employ you. How is it that you came to take up cause with this crew? They are no Bladetongue, but seem reckless nonetheless."

"These new seigers came here not from stairs above, but through the deeps, the intermundane waterways, and like myself found your back door at the bottom. They disembarked and came up from the nethershore, and first entered by the tower's secret door. The young female there who stands with them found it out, herself elven daughter of the Queen of Nethershores."

"An elven daughter is with you?"

"Did you not recognize me, wizard?" Hydarta asked stepping forward. "daughter of the Netherqueen herself, queen Morvilindart the lost."

"Forgive me, I predicted that thou too, like thy mother, had been lost in the dream-spider's spell. May the father of gods and men help thee, poor child. I learned the plight of thy clan, as did all who hear any tidings in these intermundane shores, how the malevolent drug had crept into thine home, the plant whose leaves are marked by an onierogenic spider. I sent my Centaurs up river to rescue thee many years ago. They never returned and I lost the loyalty of the many centaurs. Did any news come of their exploration?"

"We heard of their journey, Zenopio, but they were lost in the treacherous caves. May you be rewarded for your concerns. The few centaurs who made it to our Nethershores came to the same end as any other of our guests, they became slaves to the lotus of the white spider. No one has ever visited there and returned, save only this crew. By what power I know not, but they themselves have said their escape and rescuing of me was worked by the hands of this dwarf-kin Nergalf."

"Well done, I say, well done. I commend you all, even the dwark."

(Nergalf's face turned bright red, but yet he retained surprising control, given his history, which, had the wizard known all of it, might have curbed his tongue).

"Tell me, please," Zenopio urged, "how made ye up the way through dangerous floors to this chamber, for there are many things between here and the shore of the intermundane sea."

"We navigated to the tower, and I located the secret entrance," Hydarta explained. "It was not hard. On the shore I saw hoof prints, since in this world of caverns such vestiges do not fade away even after many years. Following them around the great circumference of the tower, the tracks revealed how centaurs had been accustomed to seemingly emerge from out of solid stone itself, the tower's massive foundation. We passed through the illusion and proceeded forth into the dark corridors with torches held high. It was not long before we found the great circular halls where slithered a huge Vermilion Worm at the very bottom of this tower's roots."

"Aye, Zenopio, and that worm has grown much larger." remarked Gulathar, "Even in the time of the Bladetongue the thing was perilous. More than ten-times the size it fattened since those days. A vast bulk of hideous flesh it's become indeed, corpulent from dining on many a torn limb and countless carcasses dumped down the shafts from far above."

"And you Gulathar, you returned here some time ago?"

"Aye, but I never reached you. I returned and lived in a cave near the surface for many years," Gulathar explained, "and there came a day when I realized that a hundred of years had passed since the exploits of the Bladetongue. Upon the green earth men had nigh but forgot about their adventure. So I went down and set upon the deep waters again, returning here to your tower in order to obtain a copy of the famous epic, for publishing in the world above. It was right well needed. Few examples of heroism were left to give the humans hope, and I also had my own reasons, after all, this business had grown slow and hardy yeomen no longer sought me for deep adventure. Even a gelf needs to make a living."

"And my worm, did you avoid it by your trollwise ways?"

"Nay...I too had not kept mindful of the worm, and my memories had faded. I had no thought of it, nor did I even imagine that it might have grown. Nevertheless, this is a wizard's tower, so I entered cautiously, hoping to avoid any encounter. I went along like a thief, trusting I would find my way back up the many labyrinthine stairs to your chambers. Confident, I took the spiraling stone stairs along the great pit, keeping in darkness without torch or lantern. I heard something below and moved to ascend quickly, but slipping on the sightless slime deposited by the worm, I fell headlong into its lair, nay, into its very jaws. Aye, it swallowed me right down the gullet."

"How horrible that moment must have been for you. I should have more control over my pets..."

"The juices of its belly were unable to digest me on account of my elf-flesh, but instead numbed me and put me into a weird soporific state. There I stayed trapped for many decades, unable to live, unable to die, or as the elves say, enter the halls of twilight. So I remained in misery, hoping to be vomited up, but it never came to pass. Much like yourself, I was caught in a kind of suspension in time. It was this crew who found me yesterday, when this young upstart here, Wassel his name, also fell into its gaping mouth under the same slippery circumstances."

"He is a lean boy, and perhaps the worm did not care for such a morsel?"

"It would have digested his mortal flesh easily in a few hours, but he was rescued by force. These marauders cut open the belly of the beast, and found us both. To look upon I was much more wretched than their own comrade, and they knew not what to make of me or determine even what I was. Out of curiosity more than anything else they cleansed my body with water and helped me recover my mind."

"An amazing account you tell, Gulathar." said Zenopio. "If only I myself had gone down to that worm to harvest the purple ink for which I had long been wishing, but on account of my illusions about eternal life, procrastination turned into complete inaction, and my pets were neglected. So was the beast slain?"

"The great worms do not die at once when cut open," explained Gulathar "but quickly grow new flesh to close their cuts. However pain they do feel, as do all sensitive animals. Nor is the beastly worm itself accustomed to any resistance when taking prey, and so became frightened. It slithered away in fear of this deadly crew, even abandoning its ancient lair for unknown caves."

"And it was I who accomplished it." announced Nergalf, "I it was who cut the worm's belly with an ancestral blade, and I who pulled them out, so let it be writ in the annals. I alone it was who durst approach the terrible beast. After my exploit, in the glory of triumph, let it also be known that I did not fail to accomplish a long-hoped-for revenge on the Mahark barbarians. Like the Nystoli, they betrayed me at Gederon, never showing up. Let it be written therefore, that I, Nergalf, cast the Key of Hermius into the worm's belly!"

"Wizard, this dwarf, as you have heard, is none other than Hermius' infamous General." I said. "He has done many things, mostly not charitable, but now we need his dread hands. We must tolerate his vaunting aloud, how the gates of Hermius will remain locked forever."

"I have known him for many years, yeoman," replied Zenopio, "and kept my distance, allowing him to continue only because I am bound by a weird secret that can never be told. We shall soon see if he can also threaten Nystol."

"You are wise to keep distance," I added. "As if he had long awaited the time, charisma and a loyal army allowed him to seize the Archonate after the Hermius the Conqueror died, and he carried on the legacy of dominion, not with gestures of peace like his former master, but rather with oppression and issuance of blood. His deeds excited rebellion against the Aideen Archonate and now he is deposed."

"Whatever grave matters have transpired in the world above I heard not of them these past decades," said Zenopio. "I ask this: is it because you, Nergalf, wish that no barbaric army ever pass through the bronze gates again? As you know, they were built by the great Hermius, to keep out the savage invader. The colossal gates in the pass of Dariel protect all the civil lands, and they are not meant to be kept at the whim of a single being. Speak out if that be not true, for all know it to be right, what say you then, dwark?"

"Insult my race again and no one will be able to check me from cutting out your tongue, wizard."

"So you not only would deprive me of my body, but my tongue as well? Have you no restraint? Indeed you may do me violence, but then you will never learn the secrets my tongue guards. Nor will I confide them in someone whose motives are unknown to me. If you would have me provide wizard-lore for you, then say your intention, be it for evil or for good I care not, only let it be truth. Why have you defied the common will of all the civil lands and profaned the good works of Hermius?"

"I will not fail your request and announce my motive, wizard, for it is righteous. In my need to win by advantage of numbers at Gederon, I availed us the ferocious arm of the Maharim, enlisting that barbaric horde, promising a vast trove. But they chose deceit, and heeded the lies of the rebels. How could I not answer such low treason? I had never seen a famous Vermilion Worm, but I had hoped that one might even happen by in my underworld journey. So seeing my chance yesterday, without hesitation I cast the Key of Hermius, (mind you how unique a relic it is, impossible to replicate), into the worm's gaping mouth as it passed away to escape us. Truly I am a clever dwarf, and my name shall be sung by courtly bards in ages come."

"Perhaps not always to a cheerful rhythm. Do you not injure the memory of Hermius? And what of others beside the Maharim?"

"In forging those massy bronze gates, he meant to keep such hith-trekking raiders out of the civil lands, and I should have heeded his distrust, for the narrow pass through which the gates now bar passage is the only known access by land from out the hithwood and northern wastes."

"So you were clever indeed. If revenge were your purpose then, should you not have wished the key permanently destroyed?"

"Even I have pity. Why should the descendants of the barbaric horde pay for the crimes of their parents? By casting the key into the mouth of the Worm I am assured that, as long as the Worm lives, (perhaps another four decades remains for that one), the key will remain in its belly, in the netherlands, out of reach. When those worms reach the age to die, they come to the surface of the earth and migrate to the frozen wastes, why they do so in such cold whether, not even the sages can say for certain. The barbarians find the beasts stranded and harvest the dying worms for purple ink, and they fetch a high price in the bazaars of Kalar for the liquid. So doubtless some barbarian, many years from now, will come across the Worm and, cutting asunder its flesh, find the sizable key. That is why I did it, so you can see, I am not as mad as they say."

"But you do have madness or something close to it," remarked Gulathar "else you would not have acted so rashly."

"Why say you that, old elf?" asked Nergalf, indignant.

"Did you seek the advice of any others before doing so daunting and risky a thing?'

"Were I to seek other's advice at all times, nothing much would get done. I needed no advice to rescue Wassel and you from the hell-belly of the worm. But this line of talk wearies me."

"There is set on a table over yon a small birdcage that I had been saving for the day I was to explore deeper into the caves," said Zenopio, "being curious as to whether the races rumoured to dwell so deeply might have some magic antidote for me. In fact, that is where I suspect the several vials of that accursed potion to have originally come from. To go deeper than the intermundane complex is perilous indeed, many deadly fumes float about and are trapped down there, so one must take an indicator sensitive enough to warn, or else no companions will dare accompany. A canary proved difficult to obtain, and I thought I might go it alone. Too risky, I could be trapped down there till the end of time. Now however, it seems that I will accompany this crew into dangerous places. So place my head in the cage instead. It will fit in the cage with a small pillow in back. In this way, if I am dropped or abandoned, I will at least be protected from wandering rats and the like. There are many perils that could cause me to be suddenly dropped, such as many turning to flee in terror of the shadows, or if the crew meets calamity, be it by tumbling rock, or drowning, or trapped at the bottom of some pit, or set upon by cave lions, or an orcan arrow, or any number of ways...may the gods preserve us...rather, may that God of the Ammouri watch over us.

"Wassel, go fetch it." said Dunstaark." We shall bring along the wizardic head."

I returned with the birdcage and one of the several pillows that were laying about the arcane den. Taking hold of the head I opened the cage's top, placed pillow and the poor head in the cage and positioned them within comfortably.

"Who will it be then," asked Dunstaark," who will risk carrying the living head of this wizard?"

There was no answer for all were dumbfounded.

"...and to him who would volunteer, remember the warnings of old about traveling beneath the earth accompanied by a wizard. Ill luck may check you."

"I do not lean my creed on luck." I said, "Let me carry the head, and if ill luck comes, fie upon it."

VII

The boat Hell-breaker arrived at the shores of the fungus forest. We drifted for someways along the black shore gazing at the towering bulbous canopies just above and listening to the alien calls of unknown creatures dwelling within.

"We are very near to where the path begins that leads through the fungus trees." said Zenopio.

"Keep your eyes looking about the threshold of the forest..."

"I espy the opening in the shroomwood there," said Shu.

"Aye, there it is, the same one." said Zenopio," But know that I never dared enter it, even as a powerful wizard accompanied by an army."

It is said that once an entire army of elves was lost to that forest, but I think it just a fable contrived to keep others out.

"The fable is no fiction." said Hydarta. "It happened in the third age."

"It still could be just a fable." said Nergalf, "Being so long ago. Eerie creatures do dwell there, and mayhap even spirits."

"It is no use speculate on dangers not even known, nor does it fuel courage" said Perigraunce. "Instead let us disembark now and arm ourselves."

"All must now go ashore."

So we entered the fungus forest, uncertain as to what we creatures we might encounter there, though certain that creatures would indeed be encountered. We marched in pairs. Dunstaark and Nergalf took the point together and we slowly passed through the great trunks of orange fungus-trees and looked up to the weird filiated canopy far above. The place was indeed rather eerie, for between moments of silence there could be heard strange owl-like sounds echoing, though certainly not owls, then something like a cicada ringing, but not a cicada. Then far off a wolf like groaning howl, but certainly not a wolf.

After a half sand-pour we came to a fork in the path.

"I was never this deep in these forests as a boy." said Nergalf. "I cannot say which way to go."

"Bring forward the wizard head, he claimed to have been this way before." Said Dunstaark.

I carried Zenopio forward and lifted the cage high so that he could see the trail.

"The last time I took this route there was only one trail," said Zenopio "I think it went to the left, and the other that leads to the right is new, but I cannot say for certain." So we came to a fork in the way—"

The old man Wassel cut short his wondrous tale. Some thought or disturbing recollection struck him, as often happens in war veterans. It seemed he could utter no further words. He began to weep inconsolably. He moaned that he could not relate any further. I asked him if there were any survivors who might. He fell silent and left the poarch. Later he piled up tinder for a cozy fire in his lonely cabin and shared some wine from a skin, and spoke about a lost love. Then he went off to bed without dinner in his little room. He did not come back out. I went to check on him after an entire day and found him to have given up the ghost...just how so I could not glean, did he expire from a broken heart? It did not make sense. One must suspect foul play surely, for he coveted crucial information. As I was leaving that afternoon, I espied unidentifiable hoofprints on the path which certainly had not been there the day I arrived on foot, yet he had received no other guests.

Wassel left no descendents. He related his story to no one but myself and perhaps the local blacksmith, the only neighbor who had attended the burial, who was a hycman and would not speak with me or any townsmen.

Therefore we will never learn the contest of arms that ensued over which path to take, and how Wassel challenged Nergalf, how Nergalf thereupon humiliated Wassel by force, and what weirdlings of the fungus forest crept forth and took advantage of the strife, nor of the details of how the gelf Gulathar took advantage of the same things amiss. How he slipped away with the boat and returned to the upper world, having concealed the Key of Hermius fetched from the innards of Vermillion Worm, to convey it above unto the Cheiftan Yuthmahar, whose massive barbaric host waited nigh two seasons at the Gates of Dariel, anxious to raze Nystol.

Nor will we hear how Nergalf went forth and tracked down Cartaphilus the Wandering Jew in the maze of streets in Vesulum, and had him conduct the crew to the tomb of Longinus the Centurion in the canyon below. So did they recover the Spear of Destiny. And once again descending Nergalf carried the holy relic through Gulconda and then at last up the steps to the opening just athwart Nystol's Rises, and climbing up on a great rock was about to show it before all the host of Maharim and Tungoth assembled upon rim of Sardu, to initiate the assault on the doomed towers, and how unforeseen was he struck down, and dying told Wassel to take up the Spear instead, and how Wassel took up the holy relic and brandished it before all the host, giving them confidence of divine favor, beguiling the mind of the treacherous Wizard Arizel.

And we shall never know what became of those valiant companions; of Shu Kurgoman, Haroun, Hydarta, Perigraunce, Dunstaark, and the others.

THE LAST DAYS
OF THE MAGI

The History of the Corruption of Wizardry, by the gnome *Krithusel Eloniah: writ in the ninth year after The Great Burning, his testimony to the members of the Guild of St. Dismas. It includes testimony of an eyewitness, and treats on the many dire occurrences that have come to pass in the world.*

Some years past, I, Kruthendel the gnome, sojourned in the desert city of Vesulum with its pristene cliff-side libraries. One day, to my utter amazement I came across certain writings long thought lost forever. Centuries before everyone had deemed the original scrolls extinct. All witnessed how the only known copies were consumed in flames at the hands of a man in panic. But lo, there they were before my eyes. Somehow they had been preserved in *The Black Book*.

How this befell now will be investigated. Here is what I heard from the authorities in the sacred city. One of the excavation-team members, a particular servant-archeologue, one who had famously escaped a most horrid death, had lived out the remainder of his days praying unceasingly in Vesulum and was on his deathbed. This was twelve passings after the demise of that particular monk who had originally discovered the site. To the priest who administered last rites the man revealed burdensome knowledge: the locations of the monk's archeologic documents and charts in question. Apparently this workman could actually write a little, and his ill-starred employer the monk had long before instructed him to make copies. Returning after his employer's death he had enclosed them in an urn, tucking it away in a cliff cave, supposing them accursed but fearful of destroying them. So for sixty-five years the member had kept their existence a secret, until at last he admitted to the Ammouric priest   everything he saw. It seems that in the heights of ecstatic prayer the man had almost entirely forgotten about his terrestrial concerns. Some angel, I wager, duly reminded him.

The location thus disclosed, retrieval of these texts was too bothersome for the priest, who had many other duties, or perhaps did not care for such a strange and, in his esteem, profane history. Although the scribes of Vesulum recorded the location of the cave in the records as reported by the priest, the scrolls were never fetched. They remain to this day in the desert cave not more than eleven furlongs up-canyon overlooking the Alph River. No one dares go to that place and step foot on that accursed ground.

Some four-hundred and five years after this prayerful servant's death it was I who had identified and cooborated these writings with *The Black Book of Melancholia*, during my relentless questioning of some scribes of Nystol concerning the rumoured existence of fragments of *The Black Book* in Vesulum itself, hitherto untranslated.

I had journeyed to Vesulum and took my first glance at its mysterious pages, for somehow during the centuries some Vathic nomad had found the scrolls and brought them to Vesulum, recognizing them as similar to the sacred writings of the Ammouri. Scribes rightly copied them into a new and unique version of the seventy-seven-volumed *Black Books of Melancholia*, assuming though not certain of their importance. The nomad then received an incredible sum of coin for his effort and retrurned the scrolls hastily to the place he had found them. He then died in a most horrible way.

During the time that I was sojourning there in Vesulum I was unable to procure proper copyists, for that city at the time was engaged in a civil war with the nomadic tribes of Kutaal. (the remnant Kutaal was under King Hsarghoh, so excellent a king, one who claimed divine right over Vesulum. In those days Bah Ukah was not a threat, only an obscure name written with poetic verses on a sailor's bath wall in Kalar). It was dangerous for the only copy of the volumen to remain in unstable Vesulum. Graciously I petitioned the scribes if they would allow me to store the precious work in the quiet Library of Nystol.

Of course they angrily denied my "foolish request" and locked the book away in a rusty iron chest in some aumbry behind a shrine.

Unfortunately, in the very same vault where rested the iron chest there worked some young acolytes, (three of them, for a turning of the first wheel), and they keep constant and sleepless eye-glued vigil on the sacred well of dreams, blessed by the impious cult leader Shahi-Nuzzib "the cleansed one." His heretic faith had nearly taken over Vesulum at this time, and most of the Ammouric priests had been exiled and replaced by clerics who spouted doctrines of Hell from their lips. The Nuzzib was the only political rival to King Hsarhgoh the righteous.

The acolytes of this heretical sect vouchsafe by their vigil that no unclean flys or such alite upon the well, no spider or insect or mouse crawl in for a drink, and no unclean hand touch it. For if this happens they will need to invest an unknown length of time and expenditure finding a new well and pure water, devoid of disease, unseen creatures, dust and waste, and upon which the "divine" Shahi Nuzzib, a heresiarch, "the most cleansed," will be able to wash, "tasting his own soul in the dream-waters." So I did not care to disturb their constant vigil, but secretely did crave to do so. The iron chest was in a far niche of the prayer chamber, a simple mud brick shrine once used by the Ammouric Divines for ritual cleansing.

The heresy focused on that particular aspect of Ammouric rites, taking it to absurd extremes by claiming that the human body was unclean, a dirty prison for the soul, and needed to be continually and ritually washed. It held that in fact all material substance was held of evil origin, the work of a mischeivous power and false deity. Only freedom from physical reality through some sort of spiritual "enlightenment" through dreaming could reveal to men as to their true destiny. Yet not all were capable of this enlightenment, but only a select few, the population of which could not number more than 144,000, the number recorded in St. John's *Book of Apocalypse*.

In contrast the Ammouri confess that both the spiritual and physical are proven good, and are suitably wrought by the father of all, and that all men who believe and do lawful good, regardless of how much enlightened knowledge they have, may share in the rewards of the afterlife.

I was unable to slip into the guarded chamber where Nuzzib's *Oneirocriticon* and other tomes were stored. That was not the worst of my troubles, for the "divine" Shahi Nuzzib, the high priest, had the key to the iron box in his pocket! It was to my great rejoicing that I found a most simple solution for my plan. The white-robed acolytes of the "divine" Shahi Nuzzib take an oath not to move their gaze from the well under any circumstance, under pain of expulsion from the chosen fold, which in the end, they believe, leads to the enslavement of the subjected person to worldly forces.

Using a little gnome trickery, I caused the guard who stood by the entrance to become aware of the hundred spiritual serpents writhing about his unchurched feet. Ah but if you could have seen the look upon his face! Crept I into the well room and glided past them. They yelled out for help however, but they would not avert their gaze.

After two attempts with my hand-axe upon the iron lock the heavy chest lid yet held firm. Then in anger did I curse the name of that

Shahi Nuzzib, ever to the horror of the devoted. My rationalization was this: It was he who had opened up the great pit, the abysmal gap in the Pyramid of the Scull, all those years ago, releasing the locusts of Anath, he who thus revived Synostochs, dread-master of the wyrmlords, who even today wanders the intermundane lands.

A flash of fire suddenly ripped through my body, just punishment for my verbal sin. I thought of the donkey Atlas whom I had left at the entrances. What would become of the poor beast if my badly planned escape betrayed me? I was not ready to take on the pains of an untimely death.

"You cannot deny the supremacy of the Shahi, lost one," echoed a strong voice. I turned about and saw a large man invested with garments from some infernal rite of power. His voice had a dry tone that was strangely mesmerizing and caused me to become suddenly drowsy. His eyes were grey and shallow, hung by flaccid bags in shape like his paunch, but he was not without muscle.

With what words can I explain my attracted repulsion at the awful sound? Indeed, it was the High Priest Nuzzib himself, who had been strolling lazily the corridors and had heard a less than serene commotion. At once he instructed his body guards, scale-armoured mercenaries from Urguard, to arrest me. They did so without difficulty, like the brutes they were.

"Seize him! The little one! Do not let him escape. . .I'm sorry for you, little gnome, that you do not see. It is not by sorceries that I have been led here to see with my eyes this your dirty crime against clean righteousness, but it is the power of fate that has built your abomination of physical sight but neglected to train your mind with foresight. As for that book you seek, I know little of its useless contents, only that one so foolish should waste his time in superstitious drivel and not consider what I can do for his soul. Consider your offences against me and repent, or you shall be offered as sacrifice after a Saturnian orbit confined in misery..."

I was lifted up by the brutal guards, stripped of my mail, weapons, and tunica, and coerced down the passages of what once were the sacred porticos and cryptoporticos of the Ammouric selvad.

Straightway they cast me headlong into a cold underground chamber.

Scant light, a broken chair, some hay, and an occasional mouse, these were now my companions. It did not matter, I still managed to mumble thanksgiving to the Allfather, for I had not been forthright slain. One must give thanks in all circumstances. The Lord sent a sparrow from the light shaft above to comfort me, and I knew there was still a fight in me.

What is most dangerous about being in prison, for me, a gnome, is the fact of how things go for our kind when we slip into one of our "grand sleeps." The extremely subtle physic which comprises our corporeal state may become fixed in a weird and fabulous pattern, and will eventually assume a mode undetected by unaided eye. It is part of a hibernation tactic built into a woodland gnome's physical attributes. After that happens...there is no one, not even an elf, I assure you, who can detect a sleeping gnome and awaken him. My own personal suspicion is that most of our kind have fallen asleep and will not awaken even until the end of the world. Only animals that employ superior olfactory sense, like my dog Finbar and some other sniffing breeds, can, inadvertently, awaken a dormant gnome.

Even so, no dogs or wolves haunt those jails, and with no one to awaken me, I might doze for a hundred years or more, during which time anything might transpire! Kingdoms might fall, races vanish, *The Black Book* go missing again. On the other hand, were I awoken prematurely from a grand sleep, it were likely that I should suffer a twelve year massive headache, (in this case to be put to an end probably by the stranglehold of some chanting sacrificer). There must be something, I was pondering, that could occupy my thoughts and keep me awake.

"I will stay awake for several days," I said to the sparrow far above, "at least as long as I can, but I am in danger without my planet-clock alarm. If I do happen to nap, will you awaken me? It will be a short snooze no doubt."

My eyelids were already becoming heavy and I was tired. I nodded a couple of times, catching myself...just in the nick of time. (We gnomes really do not need much sleep, and it's really a luxury for us in times of complete boredom). However I had no alarm device, and perhaps the sparrow had other pressing business besides monitoring my sleep. Usually I depend on higher animals, a hawk or fox-friend, to perk me in the Torgrith tower after spending days reading an ancient text.

Suddenly I was startled by the sounds of remote voices in the hollows below me. I looked about and remembered that I was in some sort of dark cell, and only a highly placed and very narrow wall-slit allowed in a shifting ray of daylight to pour down.

I now heard the screams of those whom the hideous servants of darkness tortured, down in some distant place and far below me. Horribly did the poor souls cry out in the other grim places of that terrible dungeon, as if by twisted tunnels it were connected to the dreadful chambers of Hell itself. I could not help but silently pray for them, (taking care not to close my dreary eyes), and I prayed even more so for their distorted tormentors. Finally my prayers were answered and the screaming ceased. My mind could rest from troubled imaginings, and perhaps their pitiful bodies could rest from pain.

I had been asleep, but was it for very long? Certainly not long, since I had closed my eyes for just a moment, feigning sleep for the sake of my weary eyelids.

Something moved about in the opposite corner of the shadowy cell, in the hay. Was it a human? It was not, but it was man-like, though not man, rather elf, an elven figure veiled in shadow. I soon discerned that this figure's flesh was terribly torn with many scars.

I was relieved that I was at least awake and did not fall deeply into napping until world's end. Even so, the light nap had left me steeped in dizziness. Resolved to somehow uphold my discipline, and at least to avoid any despairing sloth, I thought it wise to at least address the unknown prisoner sitting before me in my cell.

"My eyes do catch the image of one who breathes there, who sits opposite me, in shadow. Tell me, whosoever thou art, what is this catacomb of screams and horrors? What kind of place is this where cries of pain echo thus?"

An extended silence followed. After some time, a low voice returned answer with resounding melancholy.

"It is a place where the guilty rule the innocent."

After a moment considering the meaning of his answer I responded accordingly.

"And yourself? Who are you? And answer honestly if you are innocent; tell whether, if being righteous you are here imprisoned by false accusal, or on account some other reason, as one unjustly constrained for a minor offense against major evil, like myself. But if not, then speak what manner of evil was it that you once accomplished, some mischeif which now you must rue in pain."

There came no answer, but another silence which I found rude. Then I spoke with a demanding tone.

"Declare yourself, for there is still strength in me, and though small of frame, I am trained in combat unearthly."

"And wherefore, or what manner of *elphim* art thou," He replied in a tone of indignant admonition. "... who suddenly appears in my cell after so many years, being so bold as to address a prince of the Avim thusly?"

Startled by such a reply, I declared myself to be Kruthendel, disciple of Duggan of old, and besought him move into the light, so that I could get a good look at his face.

Now did I recognize him as one of the nobility of Ayrs, one of the Valraphim, for his features were not unlike many that issue from that remote realm. His skin was slightly of veridian shade, but yet seemed not fully elven. I gave him conciliatory word.

"My apology and condolence I offer unto thee, high one, for the awful treatment of having been cast into such a loathsome dungeon as this. It is unworthy treatment for a noble of so high an issue, and to now discover that you are cell-mate with the likes of me, so unworthy a servant. I am a gnome, just as I appear, *nogoth* in your elven tongue, and my years are advanced into ages, though my heart is young. Allow me therefore in recompense to dress thy wounds."

Discerning his consent, I crossed the cell and passed under the singular ray of light to examine him, and I began to prepare certain powerful ointments. I was not lacking a bag of medicines, my personal *narthecium*, a thing which, by secretive gnome power, the violent guards did not find when they stripped me.

The valraph had recently been beaten, quite severely, and whipped within a camel's hair of his life. His entire body, save for the face and feet displayed various injuries, especially bruises. I questioned him as to the cause of his punishments and he replied.

"I was arrested for teaching moral doctrines contrary to those popularly held. . .and I was even accused of aspiring to seize the state, as if that were the interest of elf kind."

"Merely for teaching, high one?" I wondered.

"They persuaded many that my teachings are designed to inspire impiety in the youth, and that I secretly conspired to seize the Imperial throne upon which a madman now sits. These ones, who gave false testimony, some of them having been my own students. They plainly knew how all my teachings were offered openly, in the presence of all, and nothing was left hidden. The punishers have been scourging me more and more often, and I foresee that very soon they shall execute me, and I shall no longer dwell in this age."

He thus explained, and I did not need to weigh in my mind this valraph's character, for indeed his manner was noble, but also gentle and kind by pattern of speech. He did not seem like other elf-kind that I have known, for there was much in him that was of men, so I asked. When I had finished tending to his injuries he spoke again with weary tone.

"Please, I have not much strength in me. Will you not retrieve my leaves and pipe there in the corner? Please light it with the dragon hair. I have long hoped for more fire, but my torturers denied all but my last tinder-match, which is left for the end, eventhough there are as yet many hours of leaf."

I did this without delay and resting the pipe on his lips he lit the bowl. The leaf was a goodly elven mix, probably from Childeshire.

"Why did ye then relinquish thy native kingdom?" I asked "Were ye not happy in the glorious half-elf strongholds of the North, Ayrs of deep forests?"

He gazed up to the rising swirls of smoke, which to me seemed to portray the most unusual trans-liquidic warps and seraphic arcs. So watching the twisting coils float away he replied.

"As you have already doubtless detected, I am only partly elf, but my elven inclination is great indeed. The higher nature encourages me to remain unseen and solitary, in remote contemplation, at peace in the forest's of my father's kingdom. ..but I am also born of woman, a valraph. I saw fit to go forth into the broad world and be among men, for the princedoms of mortal men have declined greatly and are in need, and long have the many been going astray from righteousness and instead accomplish evils. Little hospitality and scant charity abides in their hearts, my friend, and all think it a wondrous thing if they merely do not sin. With high teachings imparted to me by my elven ancestors I hoped to steer all men of good will from woe."

I gave him encouragement and right away told him the recent events of my journey, which you have afore heard, emphasizing unto him that I had almost recovered a long missing volume of *The Black Book*. I asked him how he had come to this desert and cliff city, and he then told his own story.

"How did I end up here? I too quested for a section of the seventy-seven volumned *Black Books*, one that had much detail concerning the lost relics of my kind, as well as the ancientmost teachings of men dating back to the world's dawn. Indeed, I have heard of ye in the songs, whom men call the famous Kruth the long-living, known for bold exploits across many lands in the company of Duke Ikonn, the adventurer whom all confess seemed more than a man...and I know of thy ever-hungry quest for knowledge. Aye, but such things do not so impress we valraphs of Ayrs."

Now mortals might take exception with such a statement, as if he meant to boast of elven wisdom against all other races, and it seems a challenge to the honour of gnome-knowledge, but understand that all the *elphim* are otherwise by their intention. In accord with long accepted custom, it is necessary for high elves and their pedigree to gently tease other kindreds. This valraph was so highly ranked a being that there was a danger lest he not consent to humour, and the conversation would remain laborious. A good chastisement it was, for in truth how arrogant my own kind had sometimes been, zealous for knowledge, and I did have such a flaw of curiosity just like many other gnomes.

"Fear not," he said. "We are both men of good will, that is clear, eventhough you are a gnome and I am a valraph. The kindred races, along with the dwarves, are no longer well loved in the civil lands of this age. So we share a common pain."

Yea, his words comforted me. Even so, I could not fathom that he was born of mortal woman, for it is known by the learned and common alike that elves do not take a human spouse. Nor has it ever been reason that an elf's union with a human would give rise to a child, for this is thought impossible. Perhaps therefore such word is a contrived myth to hinder racial mixing. Many have claimed the existence of remnant elves, and some manuals insist on it. Centuries ago it is known that all the High Elves left the Furth and migrated across the Vastess Ocean, but their blood remained in the clans of men: the valraphs.

The existence of a half-elf also poses a labyrinthine dilemma for philosophic inquiry. What sort of soul would such a being possess? Would it be spiritual or material?...indestructible or dissoluble? Indebted or exempt? Certainly it is rational, but if rational, was it also to be regarded as supernatural? Like the Minotaur who is neither bull nor man, could this being be neither elf nor man, but some *tertium quid* which is at once both and neither, and which the world is accustomed to name the race of Valraph? There are some minds who propose that Valraphs are greater than both elves and men, since they combine the virtue of both and certainly lack the vice of men. Yet even so, others insist that the elves and their kin are just other races of men.

As I was working through this dilemma in my mind, which is a true mystery, I found my reasoning power to be rotating somewhat like a rusty mill. I was still rather dazed, having come out of that nap. This lead me to suspect that the doze had lasted longer than an hourglass, so I questioned the man-elf about his memory of years, especially to say what year he had been imprisoned, since elves do not hibernate invisibly like us gnomes. He had been certainly absent when they first cast me into that dingy place.

His answer was not surprising, for after we had calculated the number of solar years reckoned according to his counting, as well in lunar eclipses of Calduin, it came out that my minor nap had cost me some one hundred seventy-five years! The time lapse lasted what seemed but a blink of an eye to me.

"What has come to pass during those many passings of Calduin?" There was a prolonged silence, unnerving.

"Doth thou truly desire knowledge of such great changes wrought upon the waning world?" he replied in ominous tone. "Honest reckoning of these tidings shall confound thy mind."

I nodded and so consented to learn the fearsome news.

"Thou must then listen whilst I treat on the history of what has come to pass whilst ye slept, little friend."

I agreed readily.

"Then I will say it, and mean no pretense or guile, but rather the hard truth entire give: Thy beloved and wondrous city of scrolls, Nystol, is no more. Its towers have fallen and burned in holocaust. The hands of untaught men accomplished the deed."

He paused briefly and I sat there in silence, under the blanket of shadows, unable to digest his words or imagine the Whitehawk continent and all the Furth kingdoms without the magic of Nystol. He passed me his smoking long-pipe.

"I keep this pipe hidden from the guards." He added, seeming to be one who talks trivia even while worlds collide. "The leaf is brought to me by the friendly sparrows, and they have been attentive to my recipe. Here, friend, thy nerve may need this mellow mix, smoke it slowly."

I took the pipe, a patient receiving medicine from one, just a moment previous, was his physician. Placing on my lips I inhaled and recognized the herbage.

"Thou must surely be dismayed beyond words," He continued, "that so great a cataclysm unforeseen has unfolded, a ruin which has pulled the furthworld to slip into this present darkness, to the extent that even the elect are deceived, and demon-gods of old are worshiped anew!"

There was another silence, an abyss of wordless dismay, this arisen from my own profound confusion of mind. I did not know whether to laugh or cry, on the one hand, to be glad that so great a corrupt power had been abolished, or on the other, to weep for the condition of men, who must forever hence forth live bereft of the great good that those collections of knowledge preserved.

"It is not possible," I said with stunned words, "nor can my mind conceive of so dire an event as thou describe, and I would denounce it as cruel fiction had the news been sent from the lips of any other save an elf-lord."

"Trust my word then, for a soul about to learn the tortures of the bloody stake does not speak untruth. In the eyes of most mortals these events are long past, and how they transpired and what they meant is a mystery which they shall never contemplate. I myself experienced the grave events which have been lost to thy dreams. Long before anyone had ever imagined that the high-towered plateau might be in danger, I went to see the famous place myself."

"I can barely speak at this news. Help me, for I grow faint."

"Sit back and rest yourself. Ease thy mind. For your work on my wounds I offer great gratitude. May Allfather reward you."

"And so you journeyed there? But the way is impossible."

"Overland, yes, but don't play ignorant. I must start, of course with thy own influence. I had acquired a copy of thine own famous work, Kruth's *Handy World Map*, and though it is in places inaccurate, it served me well as guide to those wondrous pavilions. The invisible ink palimpsest was beyond exquisite, and all with mere lemon juice."

"It does need some correction, but overall it has not been a disappointment to any buyer, and perhaps is my singular boast. Why did you seek those arcane towers?"

"There was certain knowledge I sought in Nystol, and I did make my way there journeying for two passings of Calduin. I traveled Hermius' canyon and the Eager Dog Trail disguised as a Kutaal herdsman until I reached the Sardu mesa. Finally leaving the dry lands, I at last approached lower Nystol, the lofty walls and many towers. It was a place more beauteous and strange than I could have imagined.

The scribes there welcomed me and questioned me on the conditions of my native land. They proposed I stay and work for them, and so I undertook the long task and wrote them an exhaustive history of the valraphic dynasties, especially of the Avim in the lands of Ayrs.

Now I stayed there for many years and received great kindness as a guest, but declined to enter into an order. And, as may be of interest, I befriended the great Nicodemus Blackrobe who had just been appointed High Magus and was in the middle of a tribunal proceeding against a certain Simon Invernalius. He spent much time with me describing the delicate matters of high philosophy and sage-craft, and pointing out certain historical matters which Voethius' famous history, *Decline of the Eldark*, had neglected."

I passed back the glowing pipe to the noble prisoner and he in turn smoked. After an extended period of silence he continued.

"The account of the history of Nystol I wish to treat on for thee, my friend, contains an array of highly technical terms, not meant to impress thee but rather give a sense of the actual wizardic cogitations, thoughts of most subtle varieties, barely able to be grasped by terrestrial minds. It seems to me that ye are no knave and have no small training in philosophy, and if this is so, then I shall continue without delay to describe in full the customs and orders of Nystol's Ancient Rises."

Looking at him and somewhat dumbfounded, or perhaps

intimidated by his superior elven intellect, I nevertheless held myself honored that he would impart to me such deep learning. With nothing but time on our hands in that dark durance, I nodded and replied in earnest.

"Please, speak without hesitation, friend. Surely there will be concepts and words which I will not fully comprehend, so strange is that lofty land of Nystol, and I pray that ye vouchsafe me not to end in confusion."

Indeed, rein me back when thy mind by labyrinthine verbiage is wearied," he replied smiling, ". . .for a complete description of that ancient wisdom I cannot impart, but only a sketch, if ye will." He took another long hit of his burning leaves and then breathing out he began:

"In the second era of the world, when men first took to the sea in ships, when they first began to encircle their cities with walls and fight with bronze, the race of men gave rise to heroes. These great ones found it not enough to overthrow kings and their armies, but wished even to vanquish death itself. Accordingly, they devised expeditions into the underworld to achieve this end.

Many tombs they found obscuring silver and gold, precious gems, and treasures beyond imagining, the remnant craft of the antediluvian kings. It was not long before the heroes of those days forgot about vanquishing death. Instead, they began to loot the tombs of the wealthy. Then, greedy for more, they would return again into the dark of the underworld and seize the treasures of sleeping kings.

But the greatest hordes were hidden away in tombs guarded with many ingenious traps, traps not even a highly accomplished thief could disable. Thus did the heroes employ magic, not only to detect and destroy the traps, but even more to dispel the forbidden glyphs and curses which were placed to protect those gleaming piles of metal, the bane of men.

It is sacrilige to steal from the dead. In so doing the magics opened many spirit-holes that had best been left closed. Most terrible to come through were the *nephelids*, bestial demons which are the Netherbeasts, and they crept up out of the pits of deepest Hell.

Although the light of the Ammouric faith was not yet well known among men, some good-willed chiefs saw that the race of men was in peril. These were great warlords like Ikonn Duke of Gorre, and they installed fortresses and massive iron gates in subterraneous areas, at the hell-holes, that is, the upward passes into the intermundian caverns. In this way they meant to hinder the comings of these Netherbeasts, huge creatures unleashed from Hell to harrass the world. It did avail us but little, for mere dint of iron can render scant damage against such demonic beasts.

Soon some of these titans escaped, and the eyes of these creatures adjusted to the sun. It was not only Netherbeasts who brought trouble. In those days many other terrible creatures also became numerous, monsters and lawless races who had no fear of the light and who did not stay in their caves. Some were sent against men as divine chastisement for sins, others had been designed by mischievous wizards conducting unwise experiments. How perilous had become the forests and the lakes, the hills and every pathway through the wilderness!

Aware of a growing threat, a league of foreseeing wizards sent notification throughout all the kingdoms for a great assembly in order to decide how to confront the problem. The assembly met, and it was decided that no more wizardry be permitted in the civil lands, lest worse creatures arise from foolish manipulations of cosmic energies. Only in one place would the knowledge of the arcane arts be preserved and survive, a place secluded in the remoteness of the desert wilderness. A special order of wizards, the Eldari, was commissioned to found the new city and act as a advisory council for its colleges. These men journeyed into The Great Desert and founded the city Nystol upon the cliffs of the Sardu plateau.

Wizardry in all the Furthreaches was outlawed and the clerics of Allfather throughout the kingdoms enforced the decrees of the high priest Iraltus.

As the years passed however, the monsters increased in number, evil armies grew, especially the goblins and trolls. There were no wizards remaining in the civil lands to oppose them or at least keep them at bay, and the might of the sword was far from adequate. Two entire cities were sacked by the bolg and hobgoblin tribes. Ambassadors went to Mt. Argunizial with great tributes, and beseeched the prophetess for answers. The only answer was this: "The crimes of men reek to heaven. What they suffer is the fruit of it: they have angered earth too, and so brought twofold wrath upon themselves. But lest all men perish for the wickedness of a few, let the Eldari appear before the gate of the sacred groves of Argunizial, do penance, and beg for help, but let them not set foot upon the holy threshold."

So the Eldari were called forth out of Nystol and appeared in sackcloth before the sacred assembly of priests at the gate of the holy mountain. There they beat their chests and, renouncing their pride, petitioned the priests, that their arcane powers be permitted, and be used to combat the horrors that tread the earth, in order that all men might not perish at their claws. Indeed, this was granted to them, and was known as *The Indulgence unto the Mages.*

In order that all things may proceed in righteousness, the sacred assembly appointed a soothfold to be established in Nystol, to oversee any new developments in arcane knowledge. Many restrictions they placed upon the mages, the most important ones being that only battle magic may be employed, and that it never be used against another human soul or on a day sacred to Allfather.

Often, throughout centuries were these rules broken, but the Indulgence was never suspended universally. At the dawn of the subsequent age, wizards many different lands began to ignore the restrictions on their researches. It was then that the five kings of the ancient world joined cause, arrested, and exiled all wizards to remote Nystol, but not before cutting out their tongues to put an end to their spell-casting. They preserved their knowledge however and wrote down the arcane power in many scrolls.

With the revelations of the third age, a council of clerical wardens was appointed to oversee the indulgence at Nystol and it became known as The Ammouric Soothfold. It came to pass that they built their own spires in Nystol."

II

The Ancient Thought-Vortices

The noble one continued.

"Let the story of Nystol be described first by explaining the intentions of those who developed the primitive system. Then ye shall imagine centuries passing, innovators and wise men arising who develop alternative and more advanced systems. Knowledge doth increase and a golden age dawns early. Seven wondrous towers are built to house many a scroll and numberless thaumaturgical books. Learning from all over the Illystran continent and beyond are collected. The libraries come to boast a collection of works in hundreds of different languages and literary wonders from thirty-three cultures. The sages and other schools work together to build an eighth massive and towering library in the center of the Ancient Rises, the Library of Hennsooth in the Tower of Manihord, a labyrinth of corridors and winding staircases.

You will hear of how a time of universal wisdom and order lasts and men come to understand many mysteries of the world. Then, later, as in many things, you will learn how prideful and disobedient children arise. These are the Sorcerers, the *Gulthangir* in our elven tongue.

Due to a subtle imperfection of philosophic integrity, the balance of things changes and soon a great spiritual Rift occurs. You will be scandalized to hear how good men fail to confront falsehood, while the wicked are filled with zeal for their cause. Their consequent sins bring about divine wrath upon the towers of Nystol.

Recently, vulgar and sophistic speculations of how exactly magical powers are "tapped into" have been even recorded as historical accounts. Entire libraries of garbage and sensationalism about Wizards and Sorcerers have begun to dominate the popular imagination, from certain truisms, such as consort with spirits (which is sought only by the lawless orders), to such nebulous notions of "tapping into the astral energies" or "using innate powers." These vagaries must only confuse posterity, and add nothing to genuine knowledge. May those works be *commissa in voraginem*!

The culture of lofty Nystol has mostly perished and whatever remains almost no mortal knows how to translate or employ. I here commit to thee what may possibly be all that is left of those once vast halls of learning. The Archsage Voethius wrote an incomplete history entitled *The Decline of the Eldark*, which I have read, but this also has been lost with all others, and now I commit this story, the true version, to thee. It includes everything from the beginnings to the last day, and the maze of turning ages in between, and do thou rememberest it, for ye may be the last with whom I speak."

So did the half-elf explain his need, and I assented, vowing to affix his teachings in my mind. Every detail of his spoken account and conversation is here recorded, and thanks to a gnomic soul my memory on this conversation is without error. Voethius' terminology is complex and arcane, but I have omitted nothing and have followed it with a glossary to aid the discerning.

The noble valraph continued. . .

"The ancient orders of Nystol had no established cults whereby to win divine aid. The closest they ever came to religious observance were the hymns of Ammouri and some proto-avestic chants derived from the Antediluvians. Although they were free to make pious offerings and thanksgiving to the traditional gods, there were no accepted formulas of religious observance. This may be attributed to the prohibitions against ritual magic which are found in the Ammouric Decrees as well as almost every traditional cult of the natural gods, the penalty for which in earliest times was death.

Some historians have typically confused elphic or natural magic (*dos Valaris*) with the kind that has always been prohibited to mortals. It was this prohibition, some say,that drove the early magicians to the remote rises of Nystol, which is surrounded by deserts to the north and inaccessible jungles to the south. I do not agree with this version of the history, but I assert that they were driven there to find refuge in the time of the dragon terror of the second world, or perhaps they had been there from the time of Anathron.

The requisites for entrance into the orders of Nystol were as follows: One must have passed the Gordian Exam of the Urguard Scribolium and successfully resolved an official ethical dilemma of the Rumilian Nomotorium. Initiates must also be willing not to bring women anywhere on the Sardu Mesa upon which the Ancient Rises sat. Certainly it was not forbidden to marry, although fatherhood, with all the children's needs and playful ruckus, is a rather serious and constant obligation keeping the mind from the depth's of concentration. It is said that no Mage was ever known to have married and continued in the fold, probably since few wives would consent to their husbands living in a remote restricted fortress. . .men who would also very likely outlive their wives for many years."

At this point I cut in and asked:

"Friend, tell me, I have heard it said that the place up on those distant Rises is filled with a gentle solitude, is this possible for such curious folk?" The man-elf nodded and continued. "For a thousand years, everyday life in Nystol did not consist of fire-shows, magical ceremonies, or contests, or the fashioning of monstrosities (contrary to popular notions). Instead daily life was involved in meditations, the gathering of sustenance from the Lower Red Forests, the copying of manuscripts, and the collecting of data from the natural world. This involved everything, all the way from galactic modal measurements to developing superstantial formulae out of snail secretions. "We dwell in thought-pools of relative tranquility," wrote the Sage Ptoleus,"detatched from the hapless waves in the sea of human passions." In fact, "spells" were originally used as inducements for overcoming the demands of various human weaknesses, distractions for the soul whose eye is fixed on the beyond. They had passed far beyond the materialistic experiments and paraphysic crafts which got them into such trouble in the past. Seldom did an Arcane wish to expend his synergies on impressing others or gaining power, or trying to escape the inevitable flow of the $\lambda o\gamma o s$."

It was an amazing description. Again I spoke my own thoughts,

"Surely some men wish that magic should be used for personal gain, but that seems wrong. There must be some mental starting point at which the ancient mages, those who were of a wholesome ethic, had kept in their hearts the one true good."

"Yes indeed, my noble gnome." (the compliment "noble gnome" was also a disguised jest) "The basic principle of the magian art which Arcanes learn is something known as the Παραφυσικος (*Paraphysik*). This involves the realization that all things which exist carry certain potentialities which may be activated. For example, mud has the potential to become a tower, a frog has the potential to be a giant beast (but certainly not a prince), and certain qualities of air have the potential to become a thundering electro-bolt or a retainer for moisture. The mage discerns the formal vibration of the potentiality and activates it by stripping it of its limitors. Radiant matter is released when the limitors are stripped."

"Radiant matter?"

"A most important state of matter which may be manipulated by subtle percepts projected from the imagination. Any object, such as salt cube, is both the form of something, (in this case crystaline structure), and the matter, the atomic parts all together. Thereby one can perceive a substantial reality, the essential what that something is, the substance. There is also the superstantial reality, a cosmic mirroring which anchors the salt cube or any substance in time and place. Although the superstantial reality shares the formal cause of the substance, radiant matter subsists as the energetic cause."

"I am confused already. Your technical words perplex me."

"Ignore the discomfort of your mind and pretend that you understand. After much pretending you will realize that you are comprehending. Now listen: the radiant matter of the four elements permeates the entire Terrestrial Sphere and can be likened to a rarified gas that exhibits extraordinary properties. This state comprises the energetic causes necessary to activate battle-magic, such as a fireball or magic missile. (Note however, that in the case of such spells as lightening strike, one of the five incandescent elements of the Celestial Sphere must be magnetized into radiant matter)."

"But how possibly can this accomplished, the astral plane being so remote?"

"As am I trying to impart, this is done by knowing how to project the proper phantasms or percepts which the mind constructs. That which is invisible is superior to whatever is visible, thought is superior to matter, and therefore thought has authority over matter. Although one is superior to another they are nevertheless equal in importance, just as a human mind is equal in importance to the body, though one serves the other.

Any change in matter can be brought about by causing the potential to become actual. Most elements have many potentialities, and since they are often mixed, as in the case of primordial mud, there may be even more. Yet a mage could never fashion a complex being like a toad out of lifeless mud, since the complex form resides in the Νοῦς (cosmic Mind) and the power over life is thereby reserved. Nevertheless, he could well fashion, for example, an instantaneous brick wall out of mud.

Such folk tales describing a frog turning into a prince or vice versa are vain imaginings and have nothing to do with the actual powers of a mage. A man can never potentially be a frog or vice versa, since their flesh, though revealing similarities, eyes, nose mouth, digits, sensation, digestion, etc., these are not related in derivative or in any other manner besides having a common designer, creator, and sustainer. Humans are vastly different because they require housing for spiritual faculties.

The element of air however is indeed potentially electrified or humidified, and so "lightning-strike" or "ice-summoning" are possible, and these as well as similar paraphysiks were used often in magical warfare.

Two interdependent trains of thought would develop and exchange information, dominating the sciences of Nystol: the mathematic contemplative school (initiated by Ptoleus), and the vibrational naturalism (initiated by Rhistogorst). And now good friend, listen close while I explain in detail."

He continued in depth...

"Those who in days of old did accept any doctrines about the supernatural usually posited a single, impersonal, self-generated and omnipotent ground of being; an all-seeing, crystalyn, thought-reflect, manifesting as a detached demiurge, a "Prime Mover" that happened to be dangerously close to the description which the ancient elves left concerning the pseudo-deification of "Thendil the Archdeceiver," who had tried to assume such a title.

Some others were pantheistic and worshiped the "Titanic forces of Nature" as impersonal "δυναμεις" (powers), or they developed a dyadic system called Zhet, derived from the meditations of the distant Khitai.

For a long time it had been thought that to impute to the Prime Mover personality not unlike human personhood was superstitious and even impious. It was not until the later times, the first years of Nicodemus Blackrobe, that belief in a personal divinity was accepted as tolerable, but even then the belief was looked upon with contempt. The faithful of the Ammouri for whom this was a foremost doctrine were always relegated to servile positions on this account, and they could never gain influence on the mesa, save for only the brilliant Nicodemus. He wrote about the dystrophic spiritual condition of the Arcanes in a letter to his faithful brethren, let me think now, how does that paragraph go...

...they are ever learning, these comfortable, world-conscious men, and never attaining to the true path, and so, just as they resisted the warnings of Maceon of old, their descendants now also have resisted the true doctrines I unveiled to them, and those men thus reveal that they are corrupt of mind and heart."

"A mysterious and righteous prophet he must have been." I

remarked.

"Indeed he was, and it is a bazaar twist, or providence, that Nicodemus Blackrobe presided over the Nystoli as Archmage in the hours of greatest turbulence."

When the illustrious narrator paused to enjoy his pipe again I took the opportunity to speak.

"Whoa, that's alot, but what was this great spiritual rift you spoke of and how did it rend apart all things?"

He answered through the hypnotic haze of swirling smoke.

"It was called The Hypostatic Rift, after the disagreement over how matter and form combine to become a given substantial (and corresponding superstantial) reality. As the centuries passed, the two schools, the contemplative and the naturalist, together thrived, and a congenial pattern of science and learning was developed by various sub-schools, which kept one another in check. But centuries later, nigh the time of Nystol's fall, there came wide spread acceptance of certain novel meditations, the *implacibales* or "Irreconcilables" (the work of one Scardetes writing sometime in the century of the Nystol-destruction). These showed that the golden era of Rhistogorst's system had begun to falter. The arcane schools experienced extensive thought-disruptions."

"Irreconcilables?" I wondered.

"Indeed, good gnome, and I shall jump ahead to a more recent time first to explain this before going on to describe the ancient Arcanes. *Irreconcilables* are logical paradoxes that cannot be reconciled, what have been called *insolubia*. These paradoxes were weirdly exalted by Scardetes rather than cast out, as tradition insists.

His work starts with a meditation on one of Valaghost's songs against the Old Ones, the old demons whom men blindly worshiped (many hundreds of years before Scardetes).

Valaghost, the ancient Hyrcanthine King and hero, had written diatribes against the fictional gods and their unholy priests of the Dark Shepherd.

In their turn, the unholy clerics composed insane songs to counter Valaghost. The song in question was sung when the king discovered that the devotees of the outlawed cult had been so bold as to declare The Furth High King to be dead. Within a short time underworld monks published and circulated many *volumina* in Hyrcanth. A short recollection of what the annals record shall help. A collection of these infernal compositions were being widely read, having been entitled "*The Hearers of The Dead.*" Another work "*Utterances of The Dead*" was an hexameter poem describing certain monk-initiates who had traveled into the dark crypts below Ashkehon. There they claimed to have found the mummified body of their deity. They repaired the head of the mummy upon the body and harkened to it, for as if living, it did prophesy. It called itself "the All-thought from beyond" and prophesied unto them many false doctrines. Later, these same hooded-monks, "the hearers of the dead," erected a tomb upon the surface in their cultic gardens as a memorial. They claimed that the mummy was the Allfather who had died and no longer governed the upper world, but could only be visited by dream-journey into the garden tomb.

Outraged by this insolence, Valaghost the king, who had fought hard to overcome the seductions of The Dark Shepherd, composed his own satyric verses against the heresy. This included a very famous and absurd verse which seemed to make the great Valaghost guilty of the very heresy he had condemned.

That is how it began, how *irreconcilables* were made famous. So it is that the wise should never involve themselves in the conundrums of unreality and that which is born of falsehood.

So Scardetes and his new doctrines were the turning point. Before Scardetes, most of the Arcanes would have claimed that such enigmas were merely proof of the Non-void: in other words, that there is no Void, but only being and truth.

Scardetes however asserted that since beings come into existence and change, and then go out of existence, therefore there must be not just Being, but there is also Non-being. He proposed that it must be a sort of conjoined state of *coming-into-being*: "becoming." However *Becoming* admits the possibility of void, since it implies that there was a time before Being "became." If this is the case, then nothing in the category of Being can be trusted, since it is all resting upon the surface of Non-being. Like the paradox of the □□□□-marked,[1] once the Void is said to exist it ceases

---

1 *Ophis-marked and Irreconcilables*: Originally a series of songs and enigmatic sayings published by the infernal monks. The most famous is Valaghost's song against the monks themselves in which he used their own absurd jargon against them. It was published along with decrees condemning any who would dare read or copy the opposition's volumina. The great lord recited his work in court and bade his scribes publish it far and wide, lest the heresy of The Dark Shepherd again arise to predominance. The song was put to music by the bards and sung in court daily. The first stanza Valaghost addressed to Allfather and reads as follows:*They have erected a tomb for thee, Oh holy and high One, The ophis-marked, always liars, evil beasts, workers of woe! But thou art not dead: thou livest and abidest forever, For in thee we live and move and have our being.* The paradox in question is found within the phrase "the ophis-marked, always liars" Scardetes pointed out the following logical

to be the Void!

This inverted philosophic ground gained popularity in those days. Corruptive intellectual vices, such as projecting absolutely irreconcilable dichotomies (without the limit of sense-ground) and hyper-abstracting the *logos*, took hold of the attentions of many learned Arcanes.

Scardetes' collimating system was no easy trick. It was at base a series of clever mechanics, divorcing the perceptual immediacy of the reflexive *Nous* from physical objects and their elementals (the sense-ground), thereby diminishing (in mental judgment) all non-intellectons to subtle but desacralized $\alpha\upsilon\tau o\mu\alpha\tau\alpha$). Whereas all former traditional systems were concerned with delineating the mysterious conjunctions of the superstantial with the flux of the preternatural gifts, now they were unable to work without desacralizing the life-sources. All this prepared the way for Sorcery."

Running out of breath he paused and I thought myself obliged to speak. "My word, how on earth will I ever remember so many arcane and mysterious words. Most folk will have no idea of what thou refer to. I tell thee, if ever I write down in a book all that ye do treat on, I'll need to put a

---

conundrum: The verse is understood to mean, literally, that all those who bear the bestial mark of the *ophis* on their bodies, (that infamous painted tattoo of the *snake* Ladon), are unable to make true statements, since they are "always liars." According to the verse, therefore, they cannot but lie, being never known *to not lie* and unable to speak anything true…but then the statement itself could not be true. This is because Valaghost had upon his own flesh the sign of the $O\phi\iota\varsigma$, the serpent, which he received as a youth while under the spell of the Dark Shepherd. The great Valaghost certainly understood the implications of what he had composed.

It is said that many times the barbarian king had tried unsuccessfully even to burn off the mark in great pain, until one night he heard the voice of the All-spirit in a dream. He heard the woodland drums of his barbaric ancestors and the All-spirit said to him, 'Think the serpent-mark to be nothing more than artful, and be at peace, anointed child of the Maceonids, for in thy spirit, not thy flesh, did I set my mark indestructible long ago by the waters of Ephre.'

Now Scardetes claimed that the assertion in this song of Valaghost is to be taken literally. Further he points out that if there ever existed a tattooed initiate who even once spoke the truth, then the categorical statement "All *ophis*-marked are liars," would be false, and Valaghost might simply regarded as having made a false statement. Yet if Valaghost so intended that statement it then must be understood as asserting its own falsehood, and the statement cannot be consistently false either, because its falsehood would imply the truth of its self-asserted falsehood! The situation is irreconcilable.

sizable glossary in the back for readers. Tell more, my magister, and I shall commit all to memory, for although it is vexing, my memory is of a special ventricle so that whatever thou speaketh it is permanently recorded and I can go over it again later, as one might do with a scroll, to find out what seemeth to be hidden meanings. So do thou continue, and do so boldly..."

He answered me without hesitation.

"Great patience will be required of those few whom this Muse selects. It may sound non-sensical, but it is of utmost import for all the future. Therefore you must not fail in listening. Focus closely and try to work through the philosophic terms."

Now relaxed again, he continued more slowly.

"By the time of Nystol's Great Hypostatic Rift, most of the Sages had gone Sorcerous, (except for Morpheus Memnos and a few others), and many Arcanes rendered homage to demons for the sake of obtaining occult powers rather than conforming to the *logos* where to increase righteousness. When someone asked Simon Invernalius, for example, why his new orders do not accept the adoration of the gods, he replied with a statement which pains the ears of the pious:

"But we do accept the adoration of gods . . .for we are the gods."

My jaw dropped of its own accord. He then began in earnest:

"Now, my friend, let me describe to thee in detail the system of the Order of Magi...

The word Mage once loosely referred to any Arcane who had mastered the arts, adopted in the early time when only the Mage school existed. Later the word came to identify a particular order, being the eldest and most mysterious. The Mages were the developers of the original arcane system and lend their name to all users of the arcane arts.

At this time, before discoursing on the Mage-system, it would be good to first briefly review the various Spheres and Vortices of Thought common to all schools.

There are three known kinds of combining systems: The Dyadic, consisting of the Terrestrial and Celestial spheres, the Tryadic, consisting of the Terrestrial, Celestial and Etheric spheres, and finally the forbidden and diabolic Hex system, which includes the Abysmal sphere among others.

There are also three Vortices and a group of sub-Vortices. Learn thou the name of the First: The Astral Vortex. It is the pivot for the spheres of the dyad, and then secondly another is called The Pneumatic Vortex (not discovered until the ascendancy of Sorcerers) and this is the one which pivots the Etheric sphere on the *logos* ecliptic. Thirdly, consider the one called The Psychical Vortex. This vortex gyrates the Valent Imagination. Now keep in mind that none of these things are directly observable by the human eye, but they are invisible structures that relate all elements together. If you must make imaginary constructs in your mind in order to learn about them, that is fine.

Finally there are the various thought-vortices that mirror the great vortices and which generate pure mental forms and modalities in the pools of the reflective *nous*. It was not until the time of the order of Sages that most of these realities were perceived, although even at so early a time the Order of Magi also had some knowledge of them, as is proven in the translations and researches of one of the greatest wizards, Rhistogorst."

Then was I again perplexed and unable to penetrate his verbiage, let alone consider yet another wizard, so I asked,

"Before you continue...what mean ye by the phrase: "thought-vortices which mirror great vortices?"

He held his thought but for a moment and then answered.

"We now know, (and it is become a doctrine common to all since the time of The Expulsion of The Demon-gods, the Old Ones), that one Omnipotent Allfather holds all beings in being. Without this divine sustaining activity all things into nothingness would quickly disintegrate. Just as a man might look in a mirror and see his reflection, the universe is the mirrored reflection of the far greater reality, and this reality all sane men confess and name "Allfather." If a man looking upon a reflection mirrored to himself were to move away from the mirror, the image would move off and disappear. The same holds for all created reality.

This simple but impossibly remote insight had not yet been revealed by the Ammouri to the earliest inhabitants of Nystol, for in the time of the demon-gods, the learned class still considered the Ammouri to be a bizarre and cultic offshoot of Eldark teaching. But were they?

One must first examine the actual philosophic underpinnings ancient religions of highest merit, the Eldari and Ammouri. What were the doctrines of the Eldari? The Eldari were called of old the Elthildor, a name given by the High Elves, and the Elthildor had great influence over the years upon these teachings. When applied to magian texts, they introduced the synthesis that became thaumaturgy. The Eldari were ontologicians and did not deal in dogmas or revelations, but in what could be understood of the prime deity and the sublunar gods through reason, and they held that the highest principle of reality was also the base cause of all, the self-generative One, the Prime Mover. I will give a ridiculously brief account of their doctrine.

It was a doctrine formed in ages forgotten, hinted by Plato and even suggested by certain axioms found in the records of his wayward student Aristotle. Although the philosophers were the last to receive the doctrine, they were not the only ones. It was adopted and modified by Gnotus the bronze dragon. Later it was ingeniously utilized by Rhistogorst for wizardry, especially to explain superstantials.

According to the precepts, first cause overflows into pools of Cosmic *Nous* (Mind). In this system, the world was not created *ex nihilo* by a creator, but simply emerged out of the overflowing expansion of Mind into void, or else always existed and will never cease to exist. Our particular minds, by adhering to *logos*, reflect the emergent Mind by ordered and transcendental reasoning (logic). The more closely the intellect adheres to the *logos*-ecliptic, the more closely can it influence the orbiting vortices. The ultimate goal is to merge into the transcendent Mind, and become lost in the One. We must struggle against the sub-reality of this material world by accepting with resolve our place in the universe.

According to the Elthildor, the only evil was the outer darkness of the Void, into which unreflective souls wander and perish without reaching their purpose; the purpose of all beings: union with the One. Too much clinging to the transient physical world and its enjoyments causes a forgetfulness of one's purpose. Only by training the natural body in ascetical excellence can one restore the pneumatic life unto conformity and begin to merge. Hence the personality must also surrender into a universal sublimation. It is a system very close to the Neoplatonic, but it actually requires ritual and is governed by a hierarchy, and can only be accepted by a sort of quasi-religious training, which is exactly how the Eldark have passed it down for all these centuries.

You asked about vortices, what exactly are they? The answer is also is mysterious, but suffice it to say this: vortices are spontaneous duplications of the One, the emerging thoughts of the cosmic mind whose spinning contemplations of the ultimate cause result in the experience of time. Does this clarify somewhat for thee?"

Refreshed only a little by his explanation, I returned an dubious answer with greatest difficulty.

"Yes, my friend, and no...but ye keep mentioning "the *Nous*", which thou imply is some word for Mind, tell me please of this strange concept."

Answering he divulged more.

"This is truly what they taught, and those things are but half-truths, yet the thoughts themselves have power, and what I will explain is the Ammouric understanding, which is correct, for it is not from mere human reason like the Eldark but from Revelation. Therefore listen well. The "greater *Nous*" (Utmost Mind) they understand as the outpouring of the Archthought. Archthought is the first thought from before Time, the divine λογος, or, as we now know, Allfather's perfect contemplation of himself. It is the active intellect-principle (mind) that permeates immaterial potentials of time and Non-void, and know that there is no existing Void, in truth there is only Non-void, which is All-Being, for nothing is not. Ammouric teaching holds that the Eldark sages greatly erred, for they received the doctrine of Void that taints Revelation and is not proper to Eldark holy texts. They were correct however in some things: the lesser "*νους*" (small case n) is the refection of the archetypal Νους (capital N) in the thought-pools of individual minds. Minds are the microcosmodic-mirror of λογος

Micro-cosmoid is the reality that all things in the Cosmoid, including disturbances or wonders, are reflected in the sensible unity and noetic threshold of each sentient being, and so each sentient being is, in turn, a miniature Cosmoid, a micro (smaller) cosmoid. Thus, each *micro-cosmoid* must have not only a physical mirror in which the Terrestrial fluctuations are reflected and integrated into the whole, but must in turn have a common mirror that reflects the governing vibrations of the Celestial bodies. This mirror is known as the logos."

Then I pondered the more.

"I am convinced, but there be another word that vexes me, *logos*, Greek no doubt, but what mean ye by it?"

"The *logos* is the governing order and organizing principle of the macro and micro-*Cosmos*. Later the Ammouric Divines adopted the term to identify the thought which the Allfather thinks of His own blessed divinity, the Incarnate Word, and this divine person dwells with the perfect Truth. He once was born into the world to save men from spiritual death and to expel the demon-gods. The older meaning of the word, derived from the Eldark and formed without benefit of Revelation, is different but similar in a few ways. The Eldark spoke of the logos as if it were an impersonal spiritual reality, a sort of clear pool. If the pool is muddied by works of evil, thoughts and works contrary to the purity of the divine ordering or integrity of the mirror, the reflection of the Goodness inherent in the *Cosmoid* becomes warped. Every sentient being that participates in *Nous* is called an intellecton, thus we speak of little kobolds and even bolgoth as intellectons, since they are a diabolic dysflection of the Archthought-image configured in the *nous* of humans.

"The Eldark also have their sacred texts, but they would be hard pressed to admit the pristine origin of such works, filled though they are with what seem myth or superstition, of which they seem embarrassed. They do not even call them sacred, but have managed to cover themselves on this point by explaining that their ancientmost fathers spoke in mythic terms when determining ontologic principles. In this way they demand that their pristine texts be interpreted strictly as allegorical, a thing which the Ammouri refuse.

The texts affirm that at some point after the creation, the powers, principalities, and angelics made titanic war against the Primacy of the Arch-thought (the prime cause of all things whom the Ammouri interprete to be the Allfather, The Ancient of Days). Many related traditions assert this and some record seems to have been set to song in the lost *Xilmurian Epic*.

After the rebellion, certain apostate angels and rebel *nephilim* were not stripped of their appointed powers, powers of fashioning intellective beings to inhabit the Cosmoid. Thus it was allowed that these spirits manufacture races of fallen creatures, kobolds, for example, among many other races. As the Ammouric interpretation of the Eldark text has revealed, the Archthought considered it necessary that all natural consequences of the Cosmodic rebellion unfold, (and some supernatural consequences as well). The fallen angels were left free to fashion intellective beings with complex (destructible) rather than the simple (indestructible) souls. Men, in contrast, have simple spiritual souls, for only an utterly simplex unity, like the supernatural spirit Archthought himself, can be the formal and agent cause of utter immaterial simplicities, such as immortal souls."

"Magister..." (I almost sounded as a school-boy complaining and on the verge of tears), " Please explain something else to me, in simple words...if what the Ammouri declare is so, if men have souls that are becoming immortal, why then does the human race not demonstrate fully godlike natures, filled with every good blessing that a divinely infused soul might bestow? Instead, behold, the opposite is true: everyone can plainly see that most are not looking forward to the divine life, rather some are too weak to keep from doing what they know is forbidden, while others are quick to become the authors of many wicked deeds?"

Wrinkling his elven brow, as a *magister* who is pleased at how his pupils suffer for the sake of higher learning, he answered.

"Good gnome, know that because the race of men have fell from the state of primordial blessedness, their microcosmodic mirror is now warped and their original pureness forfeit. The result is that the simplex reflection of Goodness needed to be re-established through a life-long series of choices toward the Good, founded on obedience to the All-law.

Nevertheless, the human body is subject to destruction, eventhough the human body was originally informed with a deathless unitive simplicity: namely, the refection of the Good in the Terrestrial mirror, (according to the Eldark interpretation). You see, the text reveals that the preternatural state which solidified the will and infused the intellect with integrity were lost in the chasm of the Archsin. The previous state in the realm of Akra had once been a gift unto the unborn man "the son of Dust" who dwelt in the isles of the blessed athwart the sea of Aral.

The Ammouri asserted that this state of human life had been real, a thing recorded in the sacred texts, and the Elthildor had not denied this doctrine. This state included what are called the preternatural gifts, such as the ability to judge truths without error and apprehend substances, as well as superstances, in an immediate, almost angelic, fashion. The human mind was not shackled to the clumsy discursive step by step way as we are now.

The humans alone still have a functioning Will that arises from their possession of an immortal intellectual soul. No other sentient being has this gift. Other intellectons, like bolgoth, although they seem to make free choices, are bound by the coercion of the *logos* to be a vexation for men. This is so in order that men be chastised for their sins. In this sense we must confess that such creatures cannot commit an intrinsically evil act, for that is something only a free-willing intellective can choose, and such creatures as bolgoth are not free. Even though non-simplex intellectons like trolls have language and demonstrate cogitation, they nevertheless are closer to the sensible thought activities of animals, with the difference that they are under the sway of the demonic, (but to a lesser extent than say, a vice-ridden man). A man can be yoked to evil influence, as in the case of the Sorcerers who unlawfully inherited the work of the Elthildor and turned the brilliant towers of Nystol into haunts infested with every foul kind, and those fallen Arcanes accomplished many a deed, the kind of deed without a name.

It was not always so, there were the days when the Sages held sway with the Elthildor and their wizards spent wholesome and worshipful lives collecting all manner of wonders."

Then I again forced in a word.

"Ye have illuminated me, my blessed friend, but ye promised me before that thou wouldst discourse on the Order of Magi, yet of that order I have heard almost nothing."

He curtly replied. "Be patient, ye salivating one, for soon thou shalt have thy spicy meal. The discipline of the Magus is no light matter and it was necessary to preface it with essential information on the influences of the Eldark. Now listen and learn, for this will begin the arcane history of the schools and orders, and I will end with their dissolution under the infamous Sorcerers. The Magus was to be an adept in the proto-Avestic system initiated during the Antideluvian Era, which combines an archaic glyph system of Astral tuning with thought-manipulations that generate in degrees radiant matter from the preternatural fonts. Volitional patterns were originally concreted into the sub-lunar modals and vibrational permutations specific to Cosmodic essences in terrestrial objects, as far as is known."

Then, after he produced that load, I tried an interpretation of his words.

"So they were using sound vibrations, the pronunciation of certain words or tones, to activate matter?"

He responded.

"No, not matter, but what is called the superstantial, which is the polarity of the substantial. If the substantial is what a thing is at this moment, the superstantial is what a thing is at all moments, with all its potentialities discerned. Now do ye see?"

"Somewhat, but continue, for I will later return to it in mind."

"The sacred and primordial Avestic hymns were also recited for the harmonization of *logos*-sequential rhythms whose vibrations will morph and confuse distinct orders of spheres and spirits, but whose overlap and distortion release energies that can be re-channeled to amplify the versatility of radiant matter. Although the ancient Mages had little understanding of this process and its causes, they found it highly potent. Perhaps all they knew was "behold, it doth work.""

In such a way the object was apprehended and the *logos* conformed to in a static displacement, in as much as historians know.

The Magi also were the first to render astronomic sympathies for the four elements and track their inter-elemental rhythms. They even developed ways in which to graph the inter-elemental exchange."

Then, perhaps looking stupidly, I spoke again.

"I confess that I understand about as much as a mouse would of what ye have just disclosed to me, and it seems almost meaningless. ...but pray, continue"

He replied without concern.

"I assure thee that all of what I say has meaning which is thoroughly worked out, though it makes little sense to the uninitiated. Perhaps someday someone will hear of these teachings and have a powerful enough mind to realize its implications. Take comfort, I will try to use words that do not confuse.

The Mages had always lived under the danger of demonic infiltration in the volitional source (the Will) since they must confuse the distinctions of spheres and spirits for a lapse of a camel hair. They never left behind a rift in either the *nous* or the spheres, however, because they could not knowingly transgress natural law."

Then I quickly added:

"Yes, it seems that they were good, and I suppose ye mean by natural law those truths of behavior which are set by the Creator in every man's heart. So how then did the Mages decline?"

He answered in a slightly sad tone.

"The Mage system is very old, unearthly almost. It was mostly obsolete by the time of the great Sage discoveries beginning with Hyrclistos at the close of the second age. The Mages' overly complex and clumsy glyphology was written in characters that dated to extremely primitive times. It could only be accessed by the few who were very, very old. Their astronomic calculations were so ancient as to have lapsed an entire Phoenix Day, and their planetary models only described the orbit of the Moon and Saturn.

Finally it is important that thou note how the Mages had no philosophic ground, even though theirs was a Tryadic system. They were concerned only with statics.

One notable Mage that should not be left unmentioned was Elkomenon. That Archmage built a vast laboratory and even an observatory on Nystol. These were destroyed by an Earthquake around, well, it is not known, but perhaps nigh 690 years before the fall. The Order of Mage did indeed continue until the end, but they were very few indeed. The "wise" Archmage Elkomenon lived the longest, but was stunned by the beauty and songs of a fair lady that he came across as he accompanied Duke Ikonn, to the extent that he traded his life to hear her songs. From that point thence the old man searched the earth seeking the "Orb of Mastery" in hopes to win her admiration. He died miserably alone on a desert island in the...well, let me not too much digress."

"He is truly famous. I once studied under him, before he fell, and learned a few of their systematics." I replied, "It was the most mysterious. And now, if it pleases, continue thou must. . ."

He consented though even his mind seemed already wearied.

"Of the Mages there is no more needing to be told, for all now is lost. Now take courage and let me then describe the next school. It is less magical but very important: the Sages.

These adepts are to be understood as an outgrowth of the Mage order. The name originally given to them was "The Wisened," since they surpassed the Mages in wisdom. They were the first to develop a philosophic ground. These Sages would eventually become the governing order of all the Arcanes. Although not a material essence-morphizer of the archaic order, the Sage would come to excel in conforming his volitional patterns to the concussions of planetary-radials. And now my friend, if ye have learned patience and thy mind is able, I will unfold the teachings of this fold."

He paused, smoked, and continued.

"Rife with modal residue in the sub-lunar vortex, those concussions I just mentioned displace non-astral kinetic surges from their anchors in the Non-void. The concussions translate them into causal vectors in the *Nous*. In this way hybrid philosophic principles may be organized into a helix-shaped causality receptor for radiant matter."

"In other words," I said, "they use their Wills to bring about sound warps that interfere with the basic energy that corresponds to cause and effect."

My bold interpretation aroused a brief fantasy of vain intellectual showmanship. It swept over me and no doubt was reflected in my sinner's face.

"Yes," he said, (I was somewhat relieved), "yes, something along those lines. This may sound impossibly complex but its rather simple. To explain it in different terms, words are infused with diverse inter-glossal universalities that synthetically project the preternatural reverberations of the unborn man into the remnant *logos*. Through the acceptance of Ammouric wisdom utterances in glyphic representations of the telestic derivatives, they discern the deep mysteries of the celestial spheres. By means of apprehending percepts represented to the intellect by the vibrations aroused in the disciplined recital of certain wisdom lore, and other such vibratory acts, they concrete the Will to be receptive for spirations of prime sodality.

Mathematic axioms are then deduced and judged according to the agreed canons. The mental object is delineated and luminous perfections apprehended. The result is that the telekinetic and morphic action is properly aligned according to the *logos*-eclyptic.

This was the governing order of Nystol until the Great Hypostatic Rift. It suffices to say that they could not operate after that time, after the great rift in which space, time and cause were idealized beyond the metaphysical predeterminates of the known. Of course how could they? The objective order was no longer canonically regarding as the sense-ground for transformative activity."

"That is indeed much to ruminate on," I said, "but how did they know that they were doing the right thing and not letting their imaginations interfere?" He answered.

"It is important thou understand that the Sages up to the time of Anherm (a much later disciple) had no understanding of the Valent Imagination or the preternatural synthesis. No office of glyph-censor had been established to evaluate the ethic of various systems and magical processes. But that is not anything that should presently distract us from our main discourse on the history. So let me explain the developments by describing some of the most influential persons involved.

The first of the grand Sages was Thulez. He demonstrated, quite early on, that the sub-lunar warp caused by Oceanic tides influence even sentient beings and may be apprehended by entering the first quietude represented in the Eldark worship."

"He is famous," I added, "...his name is well known".

He nodded and continued.

"There was also Hyrclistos, a very influential Sage, who studied the residual fluctuations remaining from the nexus of the sub-lunar axes with radiant matter in the proto-vortex. He discovered the modal residues of the planetary spheres, which he found constantly shifted valence when represented as glyphs to the intellect. However, he erroneously concluded that glossal universalities are diffuse and not versatile enough for infused words (aspirations). Thus, all dyadic sodalities must actually be in flux. His short work, *Elemental Rapidities*, is famous and represents the epitomy of prezorcadian paraphysik. At this time, not even the concepts of superstantial identity and spherical integrity were much developed beyond the hypothetical."

"That be very nice...Please, treat more on Zorcades," I begged, "...was he not the greatest Sage ever...?"

"Ah yes, I was about to come to him. It was Zorcades who revolutionized Sagian knowledge with his explorations of intellect-bombardment, thought-vortices, and logos-conformity. His work is the foundation for demonstrating the necessity of a philosophic ground. Zorcades established that some mode of ethical examination must be a prerequisite to any paraphysik. This is an absolute if the dynamic of *logos* is to be the causal determinate of morphing materials and radicalizing inter-elementals. Through his examination of the pure formalities trapped in sub-lunar frequencies, he was able to propose an ethic of *logos* conformity based on the rate that thought-vortices shed contradictories.

His humorous and comprehensive *Goat Meditations* became the cornerstone of Sagian philosophic inquiry. He also expounded on humanity, love, and various madnesses which plague the world. His version of the Sage was a man of insight and healing graces who was not power-hungry or bowed down by superstitions, weak-mindedness, or a lack of passion. The Sage would search out the truths of life and mysteries of the divine even if he needed to drink an entire urn of wine all night to do so (which he himself did).

Unlike most other Arcanists, Zorcades served in the Urguard

warrior ranks for several years. Before the battle of Blackbird River someone asked him "why don't you cast a spell and confuse the enemy? Do you not see how vast their numbers and their confidence so great?" Zorcades replied:

"Not so, but I thank the gods, for a close battle will be more enjoyable. My good man, truly think, the gods did not wish to see one army overcome another by overwhelming power, but by deeds of valour and comradeship."

The warriors of Urguard, including Zorcades, were defeated miserably in this battle, which was also called "The Battle For Enjoyment" (because of Zorcades' comment). Zorcades himself was taken prisoner by the Pirate Army of the Gorre-coasts and spent two years in a walled canyon confine enduring the most inhumane conditions. Yet it is said that when he was asked if he repented of his pre-battle vaunting, he said, "What? Do you not know that death is preferable to the cowardly victory? No difficulty in Life is so great or battle so crucial that men should resort to tricks without honor Besides, an honorable imprisonment is more enjoyable than an unfair victory." His ethics were later known as the First Sagian Ethic and became the philosophic ground for the mathematico-contemplative mode."

"Yet it has been said that he almost never wrote anything down," I added, secretly ashamed of my penchant for gnome-tricks. "but his intellect and wisdom must have changed many minds, but how, who could remember it all?"

"That's where Ptoleus, the pupil of Zorcades, enters. Ptoleus expounded on the paraphysiks of the Sagian Tryadic system and perfected Zorcades' ethic, unveiling a certain mystical substratum in Zorcades' pure formalities. Inspired by the strange mathematic and mystical meditations of Thypagorlash, a Gohhan cult leader and wise man, Ptoleus wrote *The Cosmology of the Preternatural Intellect*, a mystic commentary on pure formalities which reside outside the intellect, independent but derived from the expansion of the *logos*-ecliptic. The Sage was now required to apply the *logos* ethic in a series of self-examinations in order to establish integrates capable of root-generative application.

Ptoleus also designed a series of Zorcadic-inspired glyphs revealing how they conform to the *logos*, which became the basis of all Sage education. Thus he was given the honorific title "The Sage" and is considered the founder of this order by chronographers and everyone else. The sign of the Sage order is the golden Ουροβουρος (a snake biting its own tale)."

My thoughts, now weary, began to wander a little and I added.

"I have seen this golden *Ourobourus* embroidered on a wizard's book, but wizards are not the same as Sages."

"Indeed," replied the elven magister, "they are of an entirely different line of philosophic reasoning, but the schools would all read each others work in order to come to deeper truths. So let me inform thee now of how that other line of reasoning arose. Wisdom concerning reality is not necessarily confined to and only to be divulged by the Ammouric Soothfold, but as they themselves confess, there are many ways by which human reason might obtain a certain metaphysic wisdom, (though halting at the door of divine mystery).

The school I shall now describe dates back from before the Atlantean Invasions and are named after the very title, wise-men, the most famous being those astrologians who were the first men to adore the divine infant in the manger (later confused with magians). The Illystran Order of Wizards, the *istari* in elven tongue, arose in the vast wilderness beyond Chyldishire. When they first came to Nystol in the second age, they were entirely of a different disposition than the other orders.

Non-philosophic and folk-oriented, as well as generally robust, spirited, and hard-headed, they had developed a positive outsourcing of the transformative activity via rifts in the fabric of what the Eldark lore called the world-soul, caused by the sub-physical radiation of the celestial spheres, or so it is credenced. Since their lore and glyphic representations were emotive and non-intellective, they could join their entic passivity onto reflections of an innate tribal-vortex and derive vibrational modalities of primordial measure for radiant matter.

"In other words", I ventured, "They use their instincts to tap into their own inward powers" He looked at me askance. Disappointed with my ineptitude, he said:

"Thou slow wit, that is not at all the meaning, in fact such frivolous notions are exactly opposite of what truths we intend to examine." Now appearing somewhat foolish, I had to swallow some humble apples, but he smiled and continued.

"It meant that they could bypass the typical deference to the remnant logos and pass directly to the object, apprehending a super-reality immediately through the mediations of physical components in the sense-ground of morphic substances, an act of paramorphic cancelling, no judged axioms or canonical conformity."

"But who began this novel system and why?" I insolently butted in.

"Rhistogorst..." he answered. "Rhistogorst was the first of the systematic delineators of Wizardry and he broke with his tradition by explaining the process in categoric terms, thereby establishing a new arcano-philosophic ground. Although he broke with Ptoleus' mystical cosmologies he nevertheless had been schooled in the Zorcadian ethic and would never fully diverge from the Zorcadean method. He first sought to reconcile opposed patterns of approach which he found in the innate formalities of the mathematical and metaphysic that threatened to negate the tribal vortices. By systematically recording his findings and delineating proper tones to accord with sense illumination, he discovered a chromatic veil of perception which allowed the superstantial realities to be apprehended in their respective causes. He called this the sense-ground.

In his *Paraphysiks* he countered the Zorcadian approach. Where Ptoleus began by bombarding intellect with pure formalities transfixed in the celestial sphere, Rhistogorst demanded that one must first begin with the sense-ground and detect the mode proper to volition. With vast writings and methodical records that categorized both modes and superstantials, Rhistogorst introduced the key to accessing the vibrational mode (as opposed to the pure formalities). He was also the first to understand the vocative use of material components for spells, realized as a nexus for the vortices. He classified elements for their vibrational impact on the chromatic veil of perception and the corresponding components that might explode potentialities never before activated. He thereby revealed the vast sympathies hidden within radiant matter."

"Well, I suppose I get it. Somehow Rhistogorst designed a categorical system that was more grounded in sensation rather than contemplation."

"Yes, that approaches true understanding" he said. . .(I was relieved that I had succeeded at making some observation to redeem me from my last erroneous interpretation). "Now you are beginning to see, my friend."

"But what difference did his novel system make for the mystic contemplatives who don't care much for such things?"

"It had a great impact." he continued, "From all over the world specimens of every kind and sort were collected and expeditions were even sent into the Underdyrth. Insect secretions, various rare mammal glands, snake, lizard and even dragon-eyes, animal liquids such as mythyn deer milk or cavecat urine, sponges, grasses and fungi of all sorts, birds, shells, jelly fish, horns, bones and teeth, poisons, skins and furs, aetheric dusts, primordial relics, varieties of woods and metals, plasmas, the list goes on...they were all collected and categorized into terrestrial tonalities, potion-activate derivatives, semiotic incanting groups, and morphic ink types, and their elemental proportions were graphed.

The entire furthworld seemed to have become a sort of library at their disposal. Many things that were once mysterious were no considered longer so, and Nystol would become a sort of microcosm of the Whitehawk continent, attracting not only speakers of Oruscan and Mizraic, but many other languages as well, including many works from the other continents.

The eighth tower, the Tower of Manihord, was the tallest tower ever built, seeming almost to reach heaven. Thus its new library could easily be described as an Illystran wonder. Its Library of Hennsooth had 44 labyrinth-levels, housing scrolls and artifacts from the 22 princedoms of Whitehawk. It was the grandest collection of books and scrolls ever assembled before the notorious Requisitioning of Adeuces.

To this end a great expedition to circumnavigate the coasts of the Furth was funded under the maritime explorer Aetholus, whose journeys rival that of Rumil and Bamusk II. Although most of his vast array of collected specimens have vanished, his travel record is the greatest and a most necessary source for component gathering."

"So," I said, "his work really did change the way the adepts thought about the cosmoid."

"To some extent yes, the rival contemplative schools had to make certain concessions of logic and admit weaknesses in their system, but in turn they loudly proclaimed that Rhistogorst's naturalist system seemed more like a science. The dyadic sphere system of Rhistogorst finally became the dominant system for arcane divulsion in Nystol and in the entire corpus of magic manuals and tomes. Nevertheless, the contemplative Sages still retained the prominent place of governance in the magian hierarchy of Nystol and their scholasts were never definitively dislodged in the demonstrative disputations held during the Hyperlyptic Alignment."

"No doubt they must have become foremost," I wondered out loud, "but didn't they ever decline like other schools?" He seemed to ignore my question and continued.

"Rhistogorst's whole arcano-scientific system often ran contrary to the Ptolean ethic, although it always kept within the limitations of the *logos*. According to the later anti-Scardesian Archisage, Anherm of Whigg, in the area of numerologics and glyphs, Wizards (unknowingly) directed their valent imagination to celestial objects and apprehended their essential materiality by the sense-ground of sympathetic forms, (for example, the eclipsing of Saturn was vibrationally represented to the intellectual numen by the fusion of octagonal tonality with spherical).

The Wizard's undoing however lay in the somewhat haphazard technique of underestimating the dominance of mystic representations and relying on the accessibility of physical components. Furthermore, since the dyadic system relies so heavily on the sense ground, the etheriality of radiant matter was not easily discerned... are you getting weary my friend, for there is so much to take in, perhaps thou shouldst take rest."

"It is true that I am weary, good friend, for your words are so obscure to me and vex my mind considerably, but let us break for a while into a different subject, easier for the mind to grasp."

"Yes, brother, I too tire, for the spiritual energy expended in divulging such knowledge is great indeed. Let us instead speak of thee. How then, Kruthendel, did ye end up in this wretchedness, for it is well known that thou won glory when ye adventured with Duke Ikonn of Gorrencia in the bronze days of legend."

"Indeed it is true," I said, "I am much older than I appear, like thyself being subject to no physical decay. Yea, but by some paradox beyond comprehension we are able to be destroyed physically by the common cold."

"Tell me then what things you saw in those days when dragons still winged it upon sky and bronze was the only known edge, for I myself had not yet been sent to into the world."

"There are many things I could relate concerning our adventures, but I should select a small tale that pertains slightly to the subject at hand."

"Yes," he replied, "I myself have examined the journal known as *the Oceanicon* which was writ by the famous Duke himself, but I have always wondered about what events took place before he set sail into those frozen seas. Did he not war with pitiful evil-doers that threatened the order of things in that age?"

"Indeed" I answered, "he did make cunning war against them, and if you will permit I shall unfold in song a story of some interest to our subject, although the Xilmurian epic predates it."

(The original song Kruth did not translate and is unrecoverable, but this extract of a translation survives: a sample was inserted into a world history in the language of Albion that survived the inferno of 1666, possibly from an anonymous collector of ancient manuscripts, and this seems to have been derived from the common source, as the other manuscripts indicate, the original song probably being first sung at a victory feast to commemorate the fallen heroes):

"Harken ye then to this account of those fearsome wars in the lands of the wide world, those conflicts which unfolded upon the departing of the High Dragons, in the ages before the ascendancy of Nystol, which also measured to the epoch of Heroes in kingdoms under the sun, having commenced with the Sinkage of Atlantys and closed with the Usurpation of the Roman kyngs.

In days of old when Duke Ikonne of Gorre sailed the Vastess Sea there were many great conflicts and wars uprisen from the unholy work of certain kinds who dwelt in the Underdyrth. Most grievous for the upper realm were the quest armies of Synostochs, Prince of Urguard, Lord of the Underdyrth. Many slaves worked endless mazes of tunnel neath cavernous mountains in order that the shadows myght gain ascendancy. The sciencia of aire venticle and bronze smithy was highest lore.

What is more, Hessar Echenblad, most infamous, commanded many an expedition deep into the hollows of the world which no Man has seen since. It is said that even though the Neoplatonian Dragons, once dwellers of the Atlantean hill-peakes, have now long departed the world, yet still deep in the Illystran Earth sleep huge winged vermes with bellies of smoldering fyre. The eye of living mortal hath not marked any such scaley wyrm now for six hundreds of orbits o' Calduin; that is, since the day of Saint Arsacius, last of the dragon slayers. For it is writ in Oruscan Histories that such beasts may in thedeepest hollows take aeon-slumber.

So it was when the first arrows came whizzing down in the miserable battle of Ghorwcod, place of infinite pain. On that day there did pervade in the aer, amid the horrid din from throngs of bolgoth, an odor loathsome. It was of sulphurous omen, and swiftly a grave darkness came upon them. No man knew what demonry was afoot. Then, with the two vaste opposing armies locked, sudden parted they in twain upon a shock of thunder, and each looking up beheld doom, for there in the winter sky hung the draco Scourg, an abomination of ochre color on featherless wing flapping.

The foremost host of goodly knyghts, vassals to Duke Ikonn of Gorre, were the first to be burned yet living where they stood, spear in hand. With great tumult then did the bolgoth, renewed with an animal vigor, brandish their axes and so doubled they the assault to bree the hastily constructed battlements of old King Valaghost. Horror came next to the batteries of the Duke, which fled their engynes in futility. Rushing fyre issued from that vermt belly and lit ablaze those great Authapian war engynes which all evening did sadly smoke.

So ended they the first day of bloody battle, charred corpora strewn over the winter vale, feast for dogs and birds. This is all of what the Oruscans had writ concerning that devastation, the first day, for I was not there but heard of it later from the Duke himself.

No other report was offered save the notice of a hoary snow, supposedly from the gods. Snow is sacred to the Litrurians, and its presence is ominous. It did blow athwart the pine-treetops at nyght, in recollection of the unburied, those who must now, according to Litrurian Worship, go to the Hall of Sculls for the weyghing of souls, far beyond even the northern lyghts. And now scant may they of glory seek.

Of that snowfall, we may perhaps conjecture the withdrawing of the dragon Scourg, since it is well known that such creatures soon long for the comfortess and warmth of their caverns, far from the iron clad dealings of men and the kindreds. So greate, it is held by tradition, were the numbers of the dead with the opening day of combat, and so sharpe the scent of burned flesh, that the bolgoth had to beat back with fyre-brands a den of ravenous hulk wolfen that had waited till moontide to feed upon flesh near the warm pyres of burning catapulta.

So unfolded wretched decimation unto the Legion of the Sanctuaries. Yet not all was lost. For still did noble Duke Ikonne and good King Valaghost expect to soon be joined by the Authapian horsemen of Nystol and counseled by war-sages of highest wisdom.

It was known that in the coming day must be had a feast for solemnity of the sacrifices of Numus, ancient priest of Oruscia. Yet the legion, hungry and tired, had left many supplies in the stretches of land when ceded they to their bolgoth and Devilmen foes. Nor did they have much strength in their bones but to take rest, having for many an hour hewed limbs of reeking bolgoth.

So off on the little rocky hills they encamped, but a fraction of their former number surrounded by dark thicknesses of pine forest. And they were not without longing to commend their fallen companions now silent. Campfyres sent embers up to stars where dwelt their elder gods.

Great be a warrior's anger exploding out of warre-sorrows, and worse if enemies mock when the tide of batel be theirs. On the nyght wind crept the sound of the not distant bolgoth victory bacchanal, premature though it was. So the remnant knyghts and men at arms drowned their sorrows in slumber, intent on rising early to tend to their duty, knowing thereat never would they rest well if bolgs yet tread earth.

Lack of forest creatura astir presaged bloody batel in the shadows of eclypted morn-lyght. Once again did the dawn stretch forth her glymmering fingers, and already arisen was Ikonne, Duke of Gorre, strapping on his loric of ethereal bronze, wrought of Ambrosius Ammouri, the messenger of the Divine One. It was sturdy armour which more than once kept him safe from bolg bladework or kobold knyves in darkening caves.

Considereth he now his fallen knyghts and his dear long time companions, the two sonns of Nurhors, Sir Oinod, Lord Nemesius, Lord Petrozean, and many others who now be lost. What grim enemy this day myght cross him? Scourg, the fiery dragon of war? Or Sarpolon, of the dreaded spear, best of the Dirgmen. Mayhap even the War-king Synostochs himself, Lord Admiralus of the Dirgmen, with his Hell-forged blade of sorcerel metal oft invoked by the accursed title Mochdod

Elmethodon.

Massive indeed, considereth Ikonne, was the bolgoth horde which now had welcomed the newly expected Kobold swarms and mercenary Scorc lords arisen out of deep earthen halls during the nyght. Nor was it beyond suspect that they had even sacrificed captured townsfolk to their dark gods, going as far as to drink their cheap ale from blood-stained sculls.

Such contemplation coursed through all the minds of the men at arms and knyghts hastening to fasten boots and straps in the grey dawn. For this was the shortest day of passing lyght from the Sun's circuit till measured the twelfth phase of Calduin an hundred years hence. This was called the Hollows-wake, which not all are so unblessed to see. For it is that lapse of six phases of an Aeontide when the powers of devilry and darkness may, if prayers to the gods be neglected, cast furthest their shadows over the upper lands. It is at this time that the red planet, Calduin, waxing larger than the moon, eclypses the sun continually for eighteen growing seasons, with but intermittent autumnal lyght.

It is known, that some twenty-seven Gladitorias before the Usurpation of the Romani, about eighty winters after the fall of Troy across the sea, an Oruscan King commanded that this Battel of Ghorwood be set down in record, lest memory of it be lost to men. Before that time human remembrance is scarce able to recall the Hollows-waking of the previous Aeon, which approaches the reign of King Nimrod of Holy Writ.

And so with the cock crow warre was again risen in the aer, and all the bolgoth rose out of their slumber of drunkeness, expecting to see the walled town of Sarpis deserted and abandoned out of fear. Their intentions of easy plunder failed when chief Carnox of Hogtomb, foremost consul of the horde, was informed by his kobold scouts that camp smoke had been spotted in the rocky hills to the east and was indeed the remnant legion of King Valaghost and his Champion Lord Ikonn. Moreover, to add to the insult, the Legion was cooking what smelled of bacon for breakfast. But what upset the chief even further, was report that a detatchment of Edolunt Riders were less than a day away and had with them the ancient oracle of the Tyrrhenian Senate, Elkomenon.

And now it is necessary to describe in brief the notoriety of this Mage, Elkomenon. Nay indeed, we cannot know the cause of the battle's turn if we do not recall the ancient superstitions of battle-augery. Consider thou this: who has not heard, through this wide Illystran continent, of the grand sooth of Nystol, who even once did speak with the kings of Atlantys? Herodotus, the renowned Grecian historian, in his forgotten volumes of Litrurian research, names Elkomenon one of the four high sages of the Postdiluvian Age, who learnt the writs and laws of the mysterious Vortex poem.

A story oft told of this great seer claims that just like the famous Grecian prophet, Teresias, who, though blind, syghted with prophetic eye the wyrdd deaths of men, Elkomenon also had the gift to foresee the dooms of men. It was his treacherous peer, Ammoth, a brilliant Mage, who would recommend him to the very lovely songstress Lazaria.

Perhaps thou hast heard the famous tale, how Lazaria, daughter of Emperorer Echecrates, and disciple of evil, contrived a bizarre cult of bardic initiations, and luring in Elkomenon, unfolded the secret revelation of those noxious songs of the Sirens. For know that Duke Ikonn somehow had heard the Siren's song of deadly wisdom and had defended the traitorous honor of Lazaria, even revealing unto her by intimate appeal the entirety of the song, in those days when he had fought under the command of Prince Synostochs, and, like Ulysses centuries earlier, Ikonn lived to tell of it, the Xilmurian epic, but never did he set it down, or so it is hoped. In the same way, Elkomenon was undone by a clever nexus of beauty and knowledge, the fair Lazaria, the magic mirror she gave him as a gift brought him to insanity as he promised to search through the world seeking The Orb of Potentiality.

It would have been better had he been blind like Teresias and never glanced by chance upon her passing beauty. For sight though he had, unable was he to discern his own doom, which lay neath the bloody sword of a jealous Forynth noble who relieved him of his burdensome head. Even all the learning of Atlantys and sooths of Egyptian Karnak, the contemplations of Neoplatonian Dragons and scribes of Siluria, could not save him. He was unable to shun the nemesis Lazaria, the profane love to which he woefully succumbed. Yet enough now. Let us return to the day at hand, to make account of the bloody battel in which he played so crucial a hand.

Noisy rush of preparation was made in the foolish bolgoth camp which had no time for breakfast. For axes were to be sharped and armor suited. There was a shortage of animal furs for warmth, and the kobolds became grabby with the Scorc Lords. (Scorcs, thou must know, were a kind of devilish bolgoth no longer seen today, but they were massive brutes of old). The little kobolds, how bold they truly are, made contest over the possession of the thick hides torn off the carcasses of the dead cave leons and wolves slain by bolgoth and kobold arrows during the nyght. Indeed, it is reported that they came to blows over the precious prize of a hulk-wolf pelt.

One bolg, King Arrhoc of Hellhill, with bolganth tusk and an Atlantean blade, foolishly challenged the ryght of the massive Lord Minogog, myghtiest of the huge Gog-kin who stood some twelve chords high and sported a caged helm with horsehair ridge and ancient gryphonbone. But it was Rexar the Mad, a mischievous kobold of no small intellect for evil, ally of that fool Arrhoc, Horrid bolgoth-King, who gamboled up a pine stump and pounced upon the sinewed back of Minogog, and taking hold of the long Gog-hair braid readied the hulk's guttural with a well-pointed knyfe. Minogog started and let out a troubled cry, dropping the contested wolf-pelt.

This great stir seized the attention of the horde, and all came up to investigate the ruckus. When the bolgoth captains also appeared with chief Carnox, they commanded that the issue be decided by ryght of combat. But this infuriated Minogog evenmore, who could not bear stooping to combat with a mere kobold, and who, with his honor slyghted, found his trusted Scorc-lord war-party not declaring the defense of his war-right. So Carnox decided that the yssue be taken to the Lord of the Dirgmen himself, whose devilish army was encamped in a nearby swamp, a place so rotten even the stinking bolgoth feared to visit.

Now this happening was most serious, for chief Carnox knew that the light was soon to spread athwart the forest for many hours and the Bolgoth-horde would be venerable if attacked by King Valaghost's remnant Legion. On the other hand, if Minogog were kept disgruntled long, he was sure to go berserk and might cause a mutiny. For the raging mercenary Minogog had just disabled two Bolgoth, as well as Rexar the Mad, a vocal leader respected among kobolds, whom he had cast into aer some twenty paces (upon grasp of his mangy blue fur) into a campfyre.

Fearful lest the conflict spread and the horde be broken, Carnox, rather than offer his own gold and slaves for compensation, bade that Minogog and Rexar submit to chayns until settlement was made. Yet this also was foolish, for the Gog-kin are not eased when brought to dishonor, not until their Rage is brought to full fruition and sated. Nor did the honor of scorc status quench his thirst for venging him his war-right."

The fragment ends there, unfortunately. So there I ended the song, but everyone has heard about the famous things that Ikonn and Elkomenon did subsequently, and thus the valraph prince was mightily entertained and in not anything nor in any detail of art was he even slightly displeased.

II

The Magian Dichotomies

A *light shone in the darkness, and the darkness comprehended it not.* A bright blaze of fire appeared. The finely-wrought man-elf steadied this flame before himself, in such a way that his finely wrought features were all illuminated from the burst of that tinder. He had produced the match from his secret tinder box. The flame danced about the pipe bowl and the embers glowed red upon his aquiline features. He gave a nod and passing the pipe spoke again.

"No doubt such things did truly transpire in ancient days as thou hast sung, and *thy very witness hast given great power of insight* so as to recount the deeds of heroes with such poetry. But now come, wipe away tears and think not of things so long past. Affix your mind on these my teachings."

So began he again:

"Voethius' lost history once stored these many things in my memory. I must now tear you out of the cavern of your own passions and worldly memories. As the great philosopher once taught, I must pull you into the blinding light of the lasting reality."

"Say then what thou shalt, merciful friend, and bring me away from the memorial sadness in which my soul now languishes."

"Very well, dear minstrel, and may thou be crowned with laurel or even the oak. I will do as you beseech without thought to your comfort...

We had been discussing the school of those wizards among the Eldari. We had said how they began to have problems on account of underestimating the dominance of mystic representations. They had relied overmuch on the accessibility of physical components.

Although their old language was less and less used, the Wizards became increasingly comfortable with deriving their sense knowledge merely from lore-objects. Formal distinctions were left to pass away. The substance itself became the only determinate for material components. Materiality came to the forefront of hypostatic reflections in the sub-lunar mode."

"I am seeing these things ever more clearly." I assured my teacher. "So the wizards got caught up in the categorical stuff and they lost sight of the forest through the trees. They started confusing old kitchen magic for mind magic. Indeed some of the original theory must have degenerated since the philosophical opponents deemed it too rigid. Rhistoghorst's disciples turned it into a mere science of folklore."

"It was as thou sayest," he replied. "soon the tribal imagination and emotive glyphs were no longer analyzed or abstracted into modalities or formic tonalities, but were considered harmonic with the *logos* in themselves, (since their causality was recorded). Eventually phantasms were abandoned and only tribal-material components were used, (for example, a lizard foot to represent the eclipse of Saturn). Without realizing it their system had devolved into the sub-philosophic on account of a fascination with terrestriality. It goes without saying that no planetary modalities or *logos* emanations would then need to be resolved or re-mediated. The high lore-objects were forgotten. Superstantial models were deemed insufficient.

To add to the frustration, their incantation was writ in a form of runic cursive. It had severe limitations in the field of expressing inter-elementals and the preternatural fluctuation. They also came close to positing causal grounds for a terrestrial *nous*, that is, a monadic system, which is of course implausible.

It was because of this and other problems that, a century or more later, at the beginning of the age, the Red Ascetic was able to convince the Order of Wizards that the situation had become static. It was stagnating the progress of high magic. He claimed that the long established *logos* ethic of preternatural intellection formulated by Zorcades, and the hypostatic detection (such as is manifest in Rhistogorst's sense-ground), as well as Anherm's ethic, were all but defunct. He argued that they were founded on contradictory principles inherent in *paraphysiks*. Never efficiently rejecting his position or able to disprove it during any of the disputations held for the Hyperlyptic Alignment, a great seed had been sown for doubt. It was not long afterwards that the Wizards themselves translated Scardetes' famous work *The Magian Dichotomies* into their own tongue: Thus sowed they the seeds for their own undoing, and the first crack of the great rift appeared."

"Do ye mean to tell me," I asked, "that the Red Ascetic, (a man still living by means of somatic *unicornia*), and later Scardetes, convinced everyone that all the previous magics and philosophical grounds, including those wrought by mystic contemplatives, were founded on invalid principles?"

"No, rather on misunderstood principles," he explained, "on philosophic grounds that were contrary to the natural human impulse and therefore not in accord with the *logos* ecliptic. Scardetes argued them illicit, since they required a certain somatic self-control which other men did not display. Had he merely said that they were invalid, simply fiction, he could never have convinced anyone.

But before I explain more of his system, I must first back up to a somewhat unknown but very influential Sooth. He was one who had lived years before this, (and in so doing I shall introduce thee to the Order of Sooths).

In the 1o73rd red moon before the fall of Nystol, The Sooth Anherm of Whigg, a former slave of Silurian descent, completed a voluminous work examining the secret thought-portals of the Astral axis. In his poetic style of discourse he explains the implications of Astral syllogistic productions as applied to the Zorcadian *logos*."

"Anherm of Whigg, yes, I know well the name for he came from my own beloved land. He was never much read though, being writ in the Saturnine Latin of the sons of Rumil. He was thought to be rather old fashioned."

"That is just one reason." He affirmed, "Anherm's work: *The Dragon of The Valent Imagination*, opened up exploration into many overlooked areas and eventually lead to the re-assessment of the very old Magian works, which had long been back-shelved and considered useless storage in the dusty siege-tunnels beneath Nystol. His renewal of Magian understanding brought about a founding of another order, the Order of Sooths. The Sooth employs the mysterious and prophetic language, the glyphs of Sarnas, whom few men have ever seen.

Much of the ethic of Anherm was an attempt to reconcile the old Ammouric religious laws with the *logos* of Zorcades, and so he developed a very disciplined rule of life for the Sooths. These included days of fasting and observing the selvad rituals. According to the philosophic imperatives of Anherm, the most important quality for a Sooth or any other arcane to develop is a taste for absolute Truth."

"But why was his work and method so important?' I asked. He answered with typical complexity.

"He discerned something he would call the 'Valent Imagination.' This demonstrated that the imaginative faculty contains a subtle dynamis (power) never before perceived. It not only has a filter to receive the flow of the preternatural source-founts into the terrestrial sphere and sub-lunar vortex, but it can also realize subjectively generated phantasms by receiving the *logos* ecliptic paraphrastically. Before Anherm's discernment, the faculty was only known to project into the intellect immediately analogued models of unrealized signs.

This power Anherm distinguished from the potential imagination and called it the Valent Imagination. His study found that this active power is the material cause for generating not only polar ideas but also formal tonalities that cohere with the mathematic matrices of the celestial spheres."

"Why didn't his work get noticed until late, until after the conflict with Scardetes had already begun?" I asked.

"I suppose it just turned out that way. The centuries quietly passed. After the acceptance of the new Scardesian "*Irreconcilables*" the common magian sphere-formulations became increasingly rationalistic in tone. They degraded into a hyper-idealist exaggeration.

Here now is how everything changed. No longer was the sense-ground being considered an accepted terrestrial source for reducing superstantial realities into form-modalities. Nor was the valent imagination projected into the preternatural *nous*. Those who stuck to old magian and other traditional systems, which still worked, were not seen as contributing to the advancement of the world.

After the Atlantean Wars and the grand display of power the Eldari had shown by the defeating of the sons of Atalur, it soon came to be thought that men could accomplish anything. Without adhering to gods or superstitions of some invisible "Ancientmost One," mortals could determine the nature of things. In time men had shown less and less respect for the elderly, they whose words were once considered divinely sent. Man himself, not any other kind, was to become the measure of reality. He was to "get on with his magic development and obtain illumination."

The habit of scholarly contribution and discovery that had emerged under Rhistogorstan sway (and had replaced the older way of inward contemplation) was unable to be reformed. There was much pressure to publish more and more magical discoveries. They published in order that the notable teachers might not seem obsolete. They could also protect their hierarchic positions, their Arch-seats, restraining those younger minds who tried to correct their errors. After magical discoveries were exhausted, they turned there minds into trying to formulate new ethics, but they did not rightly desire truth, nor had they developed a taste for it. The result was that much good writing by greater minds was drowned out by a flood of trash philosophy writ only for the sake worldly honour, not true knowledge. All these things would transpire after Scardetes' lifetime. In his day however, during the time of his fame, there was still considerable integrity. Those who could not defend their theories by a proper demonstration of logic still risked expulsion.

Scardetes' peculiar logic, disseminated among the new students, had sown the seeds of doubt and shattered the confidence of authoritative judgements. Most of the new Arcanes began to speak of the Rhistogorstan synthesis as outdated and incapable of demonstrating what they called the causal spirations of the *logos*. "Rhistogorst's outdated synthesis relied," wrote Scardetes, "on an inexplicable categorization of hyperstatic tonality, merely the outgrowth of vaguely expressed magian axioms used to uphold ancient and outmoded paraphysical dogmas."

Thus the entire *paraphysik* of superstantial reality was turned on its head. This revolution broke all previously accepted norms for magical method and philosophic integrity, even though Scardetes still professed conformity to the *logos*. Scardetes' new system seemed to require a detachment from the preternatural sources and their intellective capacity to flow directly into sense-objects. It was a position that he based on the innate mathematic fusions of the microcosmic *logos*. Once the preternatural sources were disembodied they would close off completely. Superstantial reality could no longer be accessed to inform the intellect. Neither could the sub-lunar modalities nor the celestial spheres be apprehended by the *nous*. Ethical derivatives could not even be conformed to the *logos*. The Hypostatic Rift was underway.

This is exactly what Scardetes wanted, so that his contrived mechanistic non-magian *paraphysik* would prevail. However he was totally incapable of devising a way to accomplish this. No one had ever closed off the psychical vortex from the valent imagination. When it is sealed, it is sealed permanently. Scardetes instead spent his energies trying to disprove the paraphysical principle of the Non-void, which of course no one had ever bothered with, since it was considered a self-evident. The melancholy of paradox had so wrought on him that he took false shadows for true substances."

"I confess that I doth not think much of that Scardetes," I reflected out loud, "he seemed to be doing a disservice to the Truth."

"Not entirely his desire, good friend," the man-elf countered. "Scardetes esteemed himself a moral man hoping to reform thought. It was Invernalius, (the impostor who cursed the holy missionaries of the Allfather and dared assume the title Magus), who first posed a deadly threat to the ethic by devising his own system.

Let me describe then the Transgressions of Simon Invernalius. It was not until the ascendency of this mortal man, self-titled the Prime Sorcerer, that the Sagian Hegemony at Nystol would capitulate. He was a dissembler and deviser of a most diabolic plan.

Up to this time, no Arcane had discerned the distinction between the spiritual and the magical spheres. No one had even heard of a spiritual "sphere," nor had ever considered accessing the spiritual goods for paraphysik purposes. Some, very early on, Arcanes like Hyrclistos, had speculated that spiritual contents could actually be applied to terrestrial intellection for philosophic purpose. Nothing came of it...until now.

Since so little was known of the spiritual, which the Ammouri claimed as their primordial right over all mankind, no Arcane would dare cross the threshold of the *logos* delineations holding in his valent imagination percepts for potential thought-vessels, especially because some spiritual entity might revoke the ancient Ammouri "*Indulgence unto the Magi*" as writ thus in *The Black Book*:

For the powers of our ancient parents as they dwelt in the gold-branched isles of blessedness flowed forth from their luminous prayers and worked every good thing. But when from the oak of knowing they fed on the acorns against the shining laws, and the unborn Son of Dust saw that he was dust, then from the vortex of his mind the All-Father withdrew the power of light. (. . .?) the Tablets and hid them away in the Sea of Immanent Waves, that they might not destroy themselves, and they no longer gazed upon the bright winds of the prayers beyond time, but fled into the dark caves athwart the vastness of the Vastess Sea. (..nor do) any of the strong offspring of the Son of Dust know how to fill their (thoughts with) the old powers, save for the ones that are lawfully chosen to war against the Sons of Darkness, the tribe of(the Magus who came) from the mountain beyond...

He paused in a sort of profound and peaceful silence for a few moments after reciting these holy verses from Ammouric scripture, and taking a deep breath continued.

"In the late second century certain Illystran poems surfaced. Some began to circulate and were recorded, and these contained a wealth of spiritual contents. Invernalius, believing that the pneumatic threshold held unimaginable power for him, devised a way to enter the proposed spiritual sphere by means of intense physical pain which reversed the source flow of the preternatural founts. When he did this he was surprised to find what he could only describe as "angelic entities brandishing swords of punishing fire" upon him, and so he returned with his tail between his legs. On subsequent re-trials Invernalius claimed that he conversed with wise and brilliant beings who told him the secrets of the *Cosmoid*, and especially the power of the unicorn's horn, and in return Invernalius adored them and offered sacrifices!"

"What a strange fellow," I said. "...was he in truth noble-hearted yet in mind deceived, or just a worker of evil?"

"A pure heart cannot be deceived!" retorted the man-elf. "When it had been gleaned by the Sages that the Veil-flame was extinguished this man was summoned before a tribunal to explain what he knew about it. In his report to the Fold of Sage Masters he not only suppressed information about the fact that he had transgressed the *logos* delineation (claiming he had entered a new sphere), but he intentionally confused the distinctions of spirit and magic. He then gave a wondrous display of what appeared were magical powers never before seen, even going so far as to resurrect the dead, or so it seemed. Although somehow word got around that he had transgressed the *logos*, the Fold of Sage Masters examined the case as custom requires. The majority of the Wizards and Mages at this time had already adopted "the new optimism" of the Scardesian metaphysic. They therefore decided, it is amazing to relate, that they need not retract their already too lenient decisions concerning discipline, but should even encourage Invernalius in his explorations!"

"How could so many wise and virtuous leaders cave into such populist pressure?" I asked.

"Because contrary to what the Ammouric holy men teach, they decided to conform to a worldly spirit, the spirit of the age in which they lived, thoughtless of the unavoidable afterlife and the final judgement of souls. They wanted to be in step and protect their positions. It was not too soon thereafter that all the adepts, wizards and mages of Nystol found that their old incantations, enchantments, and formulas, (from what seemed time immemorial), were drained and sub-active! This caused a considerable disturbance and uproar, but Invernalius covered himself by saying that his spirit-masters revealed how a new age had arrived, and indeed it had, and the Neo-Aeonic school of ethic was its shibboleth."

"So what did that mean as far as long term effects?" I asked.

"Well, for one, the psychical vortex of the valent imagination was now permanently sealed and the chromatic veil of perception burned away. Anyone able to penetrate into the sphere by means of thought-spiraling through the Astral axis found only *logos* contraries in every attempted apprehension. From this point on, anyone who would practice the arcane arts had to utilize the Etherial vortex instead, and by implication must adore the bright spirits encountered by Invernalius."

". . .and ye mean to say that this precipitated the final philosophic dissolution?"

"Thou hast spoken what came to be, the decline of Nystol. I was there and saw its last years with my own eyes. Most of Nystol accepted the new teachings and began to summon these new (or should we say old) spirits that demanded blood sacrifices in return for their amazing services. No one had ever imagined such a catastrophe would ever occur on a spiritual level. Only various groups of Sages and a few now powerless Wizards discerned the horrors of "the new magic" which, (according to the long accepted etymology of Pseudo-Mercurius), they named 'Sorcerie,' after the act of reversing the flow of the preternatural source-founts."

". . .but were there any dissenters who went against the tide and sought the one True Good?" I asked.

"Of course!" he brusquely replied, "these few dissenters looked beyond Nystol for help, realizing that trying to gain re-entrance into the non-personal sphere of superstantial realities was utterly hopeless, and they did not know how to employ spiritual contents to navigate in the Etherial Permiation and avoid unwanted demonic interference. They also needed someone formidible enough to counter the machinations and power plays of Simon Invernalius. Thus they called upon one of the greatest councelors then known, Nicodemus Blackrobe, Culdee of Sashel (just in time too). This was a recall, for he had long before, during the Hypostatic Rift, grown weary and left Nystol to retire in the manor of Morpheus Memnos."

"He was one that lived as a great-souled man," I added. "one to be reckoned with, and I even met him once," At that he paused and looked at me as if he suddenly remembered how old by count of solar years I really am.

"Indeed...now when the rulers of the great kingdoms discovered these events, many of the high level Selvas of the Ammouri were consulted and heard questions as to the meaning of these unnatural goings on. The High Patriarch Rvanus called for a general council of the Soothfold. Simon Invernalius was put under censure and his indulgence revoked. He was now an outlaw in the eyes of the ruling families of the Ammouri. He was given ninety days in which to renounce his new method and submit himself to Ammouric discipline, but everyone who knew Invernalius understood that this would merely cause him to laugh hysterically.

When the Ammouric Selvas and Sooths of Nystol concluded the council they issued a declaration titled *Terminus Astralium* which decreed that anyone who now practiced the arcane arts was of necessity consorting with evil spirits and violating divine law. Although various enchanted objects still legitimately held their powers, such as rings, staves, and wands, weapons etc... no new enchanted instruments could be fashioned or old ones renewed, and no incantations or spells designed. Now only the spiritual sphere, which held a causal immediate-relation unto the Etherial vortex, could be "supernaturally" projected. The terrestrial-and celestial spheres that once pivoted on the Astral axis were now, for all intents and purposes de-essentialized and permeated with *logos* contraries in their syllogistic productions, and could not receive the preternatural emanations.

And so there ended much of what in olden times was known as high magic, the very work of wisdom that was meant to build up the Good."

"Well that's some chunk of history, and I am not even certain that I understand it all." I said with bitter sweet.

". . .but that does not matter," he replied, just commit these things soon to writing that posterity may have some knowledge of what once was."

"After I escape this prison, I will do no other thing until all thy words are in ink," I replied, "but thou hast told me only how the Arcanes forfeit their powers, and not how the famous collection of towers which are Nystol became ruins, even whilst I was here sleeping, and how the great catastrophe and the destruction of her libraries came about."

"For that story," he said, "we need to turn briefly to another land. We must speak also of Adeuces, Archimagian monarch of Azerdon, the kingdom in the Andolyn mountains. He was accepted as ruler in 101st red moon after the death of the Sage king Thmir, a king who, who on his death bed, it is suspiciously claimed, appointed Adeuces as his heir. This "mercenary-wizard," Adeuces, they titled monarchic "Archimage" at the age of 303. His life span was promoted no doubt by his costly purchases of somatic unicornia.

Adeuces was chosen as a youth to be trained in the primeval Avestan system of Sisen. The system secured right intention and was yoked to ecliptic *logos*. Nevertheless Adeuces somehow gained permission to enter into the *scholarium* of Nystol. There he studied the "*New Magian Dichotomies*" and soon came under the perverse influence of the most infamous heresiarch: the Red Ascetic. (Not yet had that master of heresy ruptured the Ammouri synthesis or established his doctrines in full).

The Great Hypostatic Rift would devastate the Magian Authority even as it was under the watch of the great Nicodemus Blackrobe. Years later, exactly twelve prior to the Great Burning, which the Red Ascetic would help engineer, Adeuces finally accepted his teachings. He suspected the Red Ascetic possessed the codex which described in glyphs how to turn lead into gold.

Soon, as in all heresies, learning that the Red Ascetic had much more assured ways to obtain funding, he broke away from the heresiarch over what he called "solipsistic dogmas." He then contrived his own modified system.

Adeuces left Nystol and returned to Azerdon. He proclaimed the foundation of a neo-Magian falling into Sorcery, and he condemned sympathetic wizardry as rudely primitive and base, oriented toward the fallen passions that debase the nobility of the flesh.

The true sage, according to Adeuces, starts from mathematic axioms, necessarily detached from sensation. He discovers the inner psychronic and golden permeation of the Cosmiod, and so realizes that he alone must surpass himself and even the power of the son of dust. The change from lead into gold is a spiritual process. For this to happen, the entire matrix must be willed into his service by devoted followers. Only then can the Cosmiodic Spheres be tuned to the proper hypostatic modality. This synthesis involved star-light modalities, tuned to traditional Ammouric glyphs, pivoted around "the telegenesis of Quintessential Permeations, according to the standards of the Khitai."

This Adeuces even now claims to be in possession of the ninth book of *the Xilmurian Epic*, or at least has knowledge of its whereabouts. He professes that the secrets therein are too sacred or perhaps too arcane to be disclosed to the general public.

Although his work never degenerated into Sorcery or Necromancy, his system only was maintained by rigid applications. They are the kind that distort any integral diffusion that its valid potentialities might have offered. His synthetic vision is inherently flawed. It teaches that the final purpose of Man is his own mental and physical health. In highest state it is the ease of mind wealth and fortune can yield. According to his utilitarian path, spirit and flesh are so indistinguishable that, as he writes "those Arcanes who know how to maintain perfect health under mathematic fusion cannot die, and he whose supply of coin is greatest has divine favour."

In his system, the utmost mode of human life is not spiritual, but transcendent conformity to matter. Through this he hopes to reach the state which the Dark Shepherd called the "Cathartic Titan." or *scholocrystalon*. Adeuces asserts that this might be entered through the deep learning of his work, *The Psychronic Gate of Astral Metaphysics*. It is a gaudily decorated book of his doctrines which contains elements from *the Black Books*. A copy of the book is a very expensive purchase. All his bureaucrats labour at making copies to sell to the unsuspecting populus.

In this work he makes the vague claim that all moral calculation should be mindful of "the health mode of each, for health is wealth." He does not explain how this should be applied or what constitutes moral health. Adeuces took the title for himself as the "Prime Physician," and instituted the study of herbology, ointments, and medical lore with a pseudo-traditional set of incantations calling upon the "One Cosmic Physician" for healing.

Ammouric worship and even the pagan cults in his kingdom have been suppressed. His sovereignty in Azerdon has been oriented toward the continuation of his sect rather than the common good of the people. He actually requires payment from initiates to advance in spiritual enlightenment. The tyrant is no longer taken seriously and has resorted to establishing laws which suppress open dialogues. He claims that his novel absolutism over the social order is based on an innate Magian illumination of axioms. He assures us that these axioms are rightfully detached from the strictures of natural reason.

Adding to this vexation has been his heavy taxation for the funding his quest knights who seek a lost stash of somatic *unicornia*. They have been seen in the Tomb Labyrinths of Garmsir. By extending his life with the forbidden elixir he gains more time to achieve the state of Cathartic Titan. Adeuces still lives. The few Eldari who survived the fall of Nystol know of his hand in the destruction of their homes.

Return thou in mind to that time which I have been describing, when the revelations concerning dissolution of the magic systems had already transpired. No new magic in Nystol was being contemplated. Soon there came to the attentions of all that barbaric horsemen of the north were on the move, the Maharim. They were looking for a way to enter below the frontier.

When I sojourned in Nystol at that time I was often out on the Sardu Mesa helping to chart enemy movements. We assembled information from scouts sent around all the furthlands. Much time passed, and it seemed that the Maharim had given up finding some way though. During this time I was permitted to return to Nystol and resume my search in the Library of Hennsooth. I knew one of *The Black Books of Melancholia* must be stored there, buried no doubt under a thousand other books in some remote chamber.

I searched references in other books to track down the *Black Book*, but these availed little. There were no lists of books and scrolls compiled. When I disclosed my quest for the book to the Head Librarian, he laughed and shook his head, for none of these uncounted books were arranged by subject or author. All he could say was "Most of the books and scrolls from the second age which deal with metaphysical or paraphysical excavation are on the third floor in the West, that leaves you with perhaps ten rooms containing about eight hundred books each, and even then, it may have been moved, for several men have sought the book. However it never left our library, for it is forbidden to carry such books out of these chambers. So now if you have some years, you may indeed find it. In the worst case it may have been stored in the basements, the siege-tunnels, labyrinths four times the size of the tower." This at first grieved me, but I determined to resume searching.

The Maharim meanwhile could not enter the civil lands by way of Aram. Its Hills of Fire and the undefeated feudal regiments of Ulthuring kept an impassable gauntlet even for the fiercest armies. Instead they rode unto Thasos and followed the coast to Hyrcanth. They came at last to make camp in the Pass of Dariel. There they sat for many weeks by their fires in front of the colossal bronze gate. The gates rise like a titan forty feet into the air. They were fashioned long ago by Hermius the Conqueror in order to keep out barbaric tribes or troll hordes from the civil lands. There the barbarian horde, (among whose ancestral relatives was Cromhur), camped for many moons. They were vexed as to how they might burst through the foot-thick brazen bars, and it seemed they would soon turn back for the hunting season on the steppes.

Civilization was next betrayed by an unwitting gelf, Gulathar, a weirdling. He it was that found the key and did open the gates for the

Maharim, trusting in a false and misdirected pity.

Of course Nystol had sat for thousands of years and had never fought a war or raised an army, relying for their defense on the mercenary horsemen of Urguard. The scribes never thought of removing and storing safely the great volumes. Of these were included the Mage authors from the Library of the Arkand, the grandest collection of magic scrolls in all the world. The safest place, it was determined by an experienced war counselor from Urguard, was the foundation chambers under the massive Tower of Manihord.

The Mages however, by some strange act of destiny, would not forego their autonomy and store their works with other writings in Hennsooth. They feared it would give rise to a pattern of mixing their sacred works with common writings, for the Mages still held to primordial superstition. The orders of Sages, Wizards, and other Arcanes took offence at this, for they had stored many works in the Library of Hennsooth.

Now listen, for great shock well may come upon thee. Much fiction has been spoken about that cataclysmic year...but I was there and saw all the events transpire.

On the third moon arrived the five tribes of the Maharim, that vanguard of the Devil (or else the very Scourge of God by His Divine Hand): for some say that the five antiquate kings who originally exiled the early wizards to Nystol in the second age were the five fingers of God against experimental magic, and the five cheiftans of the Maharim in the fourth age were his five fingers against Sorcery). But which ever insight ye esteem, they stood on the rim of the Sardu before the Ancient Rises of Nystol, together with the Tungoth of the Steppes. We never imagined so many barbarians could enter into the civil lands or find a way through the pass of Dariel. We awoke one morning and there they were, assembling their siege.

How had the Arcane haruspex failed to notice the obscuring of the sun, or the increased howls of desert framexes? Why did the watchers not take alarm at the alteration of the unicorn galaxy, or withering of oracular fig trees by the shrine of Zorast? These things had amply attempted to forewarn us of this disaster. The greatest omen by far was a mazzaroth of the southern sky, a massive comet that had appeared, streaking slowly past the Leaping Rabbit constellation. There can only be one explanation by him who looks back and sees all events: the orders were too caught up in the self-willed furies of dispute.

The Mahark chiefs, quite pleased with their surprise appearance, next sent an envoy to the Council of the Seven Thoughts. The Council was then assembled in the open Hall of Infinite Ceiling, which was simply called "the pantheon."

The atmosphere was very tense, some of that initial sense of security from being high aloft upon cliffs was soon lost. The Sages had now seen from their own towers the great mass of warriors and Authapian war machines. The enemy had prepared for a devastating sack. Huge iron pots were drawn up ready to melt down all precious silver and gold.

It had been long disputed among Sage historians concerning the Maharim. Some have said that they came from beyond the Sea of Shirvav, but this is an error. They clearly do not have such a complexion. Others assure us that they are of the Dark Orkhan, (a possessed and tyrannic warlord of the eastern steppe), and this is possible, although they worship the open sky. They are without doubt the descendants of Mahar, son of Maceon, who "went North, seeking game, and never returned thereafter, except in the shadows of the moon."

It soon became known that each of the five tribal regiments had agreed to refuse tribute or ransom from the Eldari. They had made blood oaths to destroy Nystol and rid Illystra of her accursed Sorcerers, beginning with Simon Invernalius.

A siege was protracted for twelve days. The great Authapian war machines were moved into place. On the third day our mercenaries launched flaming fire bombs at them. Five of the seven towering machines burnt to the ground. We celebrated that evening with a feast. Though I was only a guest, I could see that everyone there was denying the inevitable. Hopes were very high. There was talk of "showing the smelly barbarians their place."

The Council of the Seven Towers had brought news to the pantheon that The Kalar Army of the Fifteen Sheiks had been spotted by the hawks of The Eldark away near the Lake of Titans, traveling West into the Dry Blood Sea. The Eastern Kalar and Shalay Empires have always revered Sagedom, unlike countries such as Ardeheim and Osring which have descended into the rule of the violence. Perhaps the Kalar had meant to fight in our defense, but they never arrived. Nor would any other nation of Illystra come to Nystol's aid. Her political reputation was terribly marred. Only a year earlier she had betrayed Dwarf-Emperor Nergalf. Though wealthy and powerful, she was no longer trusted. She had promised the mad dwarf-emperor battle-wizards but then consigned his army to defeat by a no-show at the Grand Battle at Gederon in Arahom.

Our missile attacks against the enemy continued.

On the fifth day one could look down from the high towers of the Library of Forgotten Words and see the corpses of painted and shirtless Mahark and Tung warriors strewn here and there all over the rocky feet of the great Rises. They were many, too many to be counted, for our few Urguard troops had a great strategic advantage over them. The Ataluran bow from above is devastating. I reckon that at least a fifth of their forces had been expended at that time.

It sorely injured the hearts of many a wise man to behold such gloomy expenditure of life. The Maharim were willing to pay with their own young warriors, but little did any suppose how even less value the enemy placed on scribes and Arcanes.

I must now speak of the great division which has been said to be the foremost cause of the triumph of the barbarians. Many Sages saw beforehand that the four days of Red Moon forbade crucial war. These days were seriously recognized by all Patriarchad Nations and Sagedom to be days of non-war. Furthermore, the Soothfold had decided over six-hundred passings ago that the use of Mage-lore be forbidden on those days. It came to pass that according to very ancient records, all prayer was said to negate the use of magic during the first four of the seven days, for better or for worse. The tradition developed out of the festival known as the *Magophonia*, or "killing of the Magi", which commemorates the massacre of seven Magi in eld Persia during the Second Age. Herodotus of Halicarnassus, the Grecian historian, gives a full account of this incident in his third book of *Researches*. The rule states that no adept of the order of Magus may be seen on that day, and by implication, may not employ the art. Those who disobey shall be execrated accordingly with the proper rite. The Indulgence of the Soothfold was later considered a compensation for Nystol's pious observance of these sacred days.

Today we see many a treasure-seeking man venture into the Underdyrth during those particular days. It's all for naught, since the subterraneous Arcanes do not reckon such a commemoration. The tradition has it that any who durst hurl a spell on those days would lose their own memory, or, if the offence were grave enough, the offender would turn to stone.

Allow me a brief digression lest a wondrous tale be forgot. There is a tragic song handed down from the second world-age of the heathen dispensation. It is called the bane of Myrmyrd, the greatest Mage-hero and lover of his time. He sailed with King Ikonn athwart the vast stretches of Windy Lake, and he prayed to the goddess of Desire that he might win the hand of the beautiful maiden Thymesilea. He had loved her for many years, but she in turn had denied kisses or any other of love's consolations, in accord with venerable custom.

The goddess granted his wish, but kept it unknown to Myrmyrd that the maiden was near death. However, the goddess also knew that the Mage would be tempted. He would break the sacred law by his uncontrollable passion. Others say the goddess desired a martyr for her cause.

When he arrived at the habour fort of Ardeheim, a funeral rite for

Thymesilea was already underway. Upon discovering the corpse of his beloved upon the funeral pyre, Myrmyrd was unable to put out the flames, for in his forlorn love-mania he wished to spend many hours gazing upon her face. The face was become cold. So Myrmyrd hurled a spell upon the flames. Being one of the Magi, whose cult was founded in the worship of divine fire, he had great influence over that element. Myrmyrd knew that he would lose his memory for transgressing the sacred law which applied on that day. He nevertheless used his arcane intonation.

The flames died down and he climbed the smoldering pyre. He gazed into the face of his love for a time, placing the Lothlavas flowers upon her. When he climbed back down King Ikonn approached him and said, "my friend, why not stay a while longer with Thymesilea?" But Myrmyrd with a lost and incomprehensible look replied "...with who?"

After this the once great Mage could not even recall his own homeland, not to mention any spells whereby to aid the great king in his quest. He spent the rest of his years in a lost daze, trying to recall who was the beautiful maiden whom he had seen."

"An intriguing tale, my dear elf, which I should have known since it involves ancient companions, but I have never before heard any of it. I must write out an epic rhyme for it some day. Did you learn of that in the library of many towered city?"

He nodded in the affirmative. "Even while the events heralding doom transpired before me! Now let us return to further recount the end of Nystol.

So the great scholars, mages, and philosophers were divided in their meeting hall. Some argued that the period of non-violence and non-magic be overlooked and an army be purchased, that messenger pigeons be sent to Urguard. Many pious Arcanes were appalled at the thought, and rightly argued the case that such an act it is strictly forbidden, according to the agreed Sagian ethic, and affirmed by the Eldark. No sentient being or power, let alone the city-state Nystol, may commit some evil in order that a greater good come of it. The evil of not observing the sacred days of magic abstinence, known to all from the very beginning, may not be accepted in order that Nystol be preserved from annihilation. If the gods willed the end of the great towers, and all written knowledge, then so be. For this argument they were harshly rebuffed by the Sorcerers. Having spoken these things, some Arcanes retired from the pantheon to enjoy the few hours of peace before the end.

The ruling Order of Sages at last pronounced that the ancient magic restriction be rigorously observed...even under pain of the city's destruction. When the Mages proposed that they alone determine what combat spells may be cast, since they had warred against the dark sooths of Sarnas in ancientmost days, the Sages and Wizards became infuriated, having recently suffered the slight about storing books in Hennsooth. This aggravated the meeting even more.

Young apprentices claimed the Ammouric law was superstitious, that spells must be cast regardless. Most of these young mages had thrown in with the new philosophy of Scardetes. They had enrolled in the Sorcerel fold of Invernalius. Factions arose, the outrecuidance of the students in various orders gave way to opprobrious verbal fights.

As I watched all this I began to see. I began to see that the doom of Nystol was casting its shadow. When they had spent all their physical and mental energy in verbose debate, a lull somehow found way. I saw my chance and rose up to speak.

"Forgive me, grand council. I am hoping that you might gain some insight from the voice of one who stands apart, one free of any faction. I am a guest here, a stranger to this land and to your ways. My dear and generous hosts, know that I seek only to benefit the wisdom already here. Can any highly placed lords of furthreach suppose that they are beyond the censure of the greater world of men? My intention is only for the good of the souls who dwell here and guard the secrets of the ancient magic. Beautiful are the eld towers that stand as signs of learning and transcendence throughout all the Illystran lands. But now harken to this and consider it well, o men, how fragile ye now stand this night when the greatest danger is very near. Huge affliction is bearing down upon this realm and upon the furthworld entire. I am a man of few ambitions, but since I am part elf, I can see many things hidden from the eyes of mortals. So now I utter this: if the many towers fall beneath savage sword and fire, the furthworld shall slip into chaos, into darkness visible. I do not see that you can avoid this by war. So it is, so has the Allfather let things unfold. Yet nothing is fated, and He always gives a way out. Therefore I offer this advice which ye may take into council. Contention has of recent marked this pantheon. No sound war-plan can be carried out. Therefore, since no agreement is yielded, ask help of the blessed Eldari, the embassy of the Soothfold in yonder tower. Go before them and let each side speak in full. Let them consider and pray, interceding, and so render a judgement, ratified by the Ancientmost. This will put to proof the ancient prohibition and perhaps even win the divine favor. Send heralds then to their tower to declare that you come with trust and hope. It is known through all the furthlands: blessed is the one who heeds the council of the Soothfold."

So I spake and sitting down bowed my head. Most of the council rose up in affirmation, including Nicodemus Blackrobe. However not all were pleased. It came to pass in those particular years that Zuphagen Wren was appointed Exalt of Exterior Affairs. This ambassorial office was part of the *absolvid*, meaning that their decisions could not be contested. According to law, Zuphagen Wren would have to agree to allow heralds to be sent. Someone brought this matter up. All the heads of the Arcanes now looked to Zuphagen who sat in one of the eight ordinarial seats. He looked up, closed his eyes in brief thought, and spoke.

"The Soothfold is a venerable council. Yet not all in this pantheon are persuaded by the old Ammouric superstitions. The times are new. To go to the Soothfold seeking answers from the Eldark would seem a step backward to an era when the Mages were dominating these towers. Let us be ourselves ware of such a reversal. Yet their words should be welcome. Therefore, yea, let them report what their divines utter. But send no herald, let them instead come hence and stoop to appear before us."

Nicodemus Blackrobe, also seated in one of the ordinarial chairs, looked with a certain fury at this. At once he glanced up to speak.

"What is this? Is this not obdurate pride? We durst elevate ourselves to voice a summons to the Divines of the Soothfold, servants of the sublime Creator? It has never been done! That is unseemly, most shameful, the thought itself a dreadful omen! No, we must with suppliant knee appear before them."

"I will not debate this point, Archisage," muttered Zuphagen. No one else voiced dissent.

At that point Nicodemus Blackrobe arose from his ordinarial seat. He was visibly disturbed. Silence gripped the hall. He brought forth the wizardic staff of Archons from its place in the stall and stepped down to enter the central floor. He turned round once and looked upon each member. Each lowered their gaze in shame. Then he moved about no more. The crashing sound of his staff, as he let it fall from his hands and hit the wood floor, was soul-wracking. I will never forget it. It was as if a door had been slammed shut. Nicodemus Blackrobe, Archisage, then departed the hall without further word.

Little did anyone know that just a few days earlier, when the horde had first appeared on the rim of Dry Blood Dunes, the entire retinue of the Eldari had set out from the Eastern Plateau for the pantheon to warn the Archisages that the gods were punishing Nystol for having permitted the summoning of spirits and consort with demons. The Eldari were calling the barbarians "the Scourge of God." The fold of Sorcerers, outraged that a religious power would dare interfere, anticipated their route and intercepted them. They apprehended them illegaly and conducted them through the lower forests into the deserts, abandoning the old men without water to the dune wastes. Nemesis, they say, would exact a severe punishment on that particularly wicked deed.

No heralds were sent. Only a messenger with a letter. The letter requested the presence of the High Archon and his retinue for the purpose of " offering recommendations." The messenger never made it to the Tower of Soothfold. The idea of being the dishonourable conveyer of such an outrage had taken hold of his soul. He disappeared instead into the libraries.

Few slept well that night. Before dawn we were awoken with the news that seventeen priests and acolytes who had been journeying to the shrine of Zorast to receive blessing had been massacred by unknown masked assailants. Some were simply left to die on the path, whereas others had their heads left on lances. This brought fears to a great upsurge. Could anyone be trusted? The saying *Quis custodiet ipsos custodes?* (Who will guard the guards?) echoed disturbingly in my thoughts.

With this news, two highly placed and now indignant Magi, Prexasbes, Ozanes, and a wizard, Valring, made way together toward the marble balconies (gifts of Bamusk II) overlooking enemy battlements and armies far below. Several of the elders and a few others took notice of them as they dashed through pillars down the hall of gryphonheads over a long parapet to the Tower of Earthly Vision. It was so called because the parapet was so lofty that one could gaze far out upon the entire expanse of earth and see what seemed all the kingdoms of Whitehawk.

They stood there on the balconies bellowing deeply intoned utterances not often heard. They had taken up with the fold of sorcery. In rage they hurled combative spells upon the enemy, balls and torrents of fire, rays of destruction, hail missiles, bindings and imprisonments, confusion. They accomplished much damage and woe unto the enemy, weakening them severely.

A few others and I tried to talk sense into these overbold adepts. They angrily ignored the others who were chastising them much for breaking a sacred law. Since I was a guest, I might have a better hope of talking sense into them. Against me they harboured no rivalry. Even the law of hospitality should have caused them to at least hear my reasonings, but these were ignored. It was as if an insult. We followed them about the broad balcony, fearing for their lives and the curse that might come upon this tower. We kept beseeching them to obey the sacred law. Then upon a sudden we watched in horror as their bodies stiffened and crystalized where they stood. Statues now they were become, portents dark, omens dreadful, reminders of the remnant power of the ancestral fathers.

At this moment it became evident to me and especially to the few others standing there that a new age was being ushered in. It was the both bloody work of the Maharim and the destiny uttered by the forefathers.

We stood there and I touched with my fingers the still warm stone statue of Valring, so late through whose veins blood had coursed. I was both amazed and filled with dread at the sight of an ancientmost nemesis having executed judgement on the transgressors.

I am not one to be called follower of Fates' beckoning. After a pause I straightway spake to the Head of the Libraries who was standing beside me.

"Lo, the times of divergence now hasten by. The day of destruction was prophesied by Mercurius Yod. It swiftly approaches unto consummation. No more time is left to turn away from what now must unfold. Let us make arrangements quickly for the collection and storage of tomes and codices, before the others notice. We few that here today have witnessed this punishment have been granted it as an insight: these very towers will not stand for many more dawns".

All consented and agreed with my interpretation of the signs. The meaning of what had just befallen could not have been deliberated. It was indeed in accord with eld prophecy. The others left quickly to spread the sorrowful news and attend to their responsibility. I stayed there, on that utmost balcony, alone and silent. I gazed out over the vast expanse of the Whitehawk kingdoms.

After some time in deep and troubling thought I began listening. I heard the voice of the wind, as I always do, but no answer came. I was considering the horrid statues beside me. Then I began regarding the slain below. And I sensed the presence of someone. Someone had been standing there the whole time.

I turned to look. There stood Simon Invernalius, the Prime Sorcerer. He was dressed in his crimson and silver robes. The high-arching collar gave him an air of superiority. His close-cut goat-beard and bald head marked him as the tonsured elect of the fully committed sorcerer-fold. He stood there looking out upon the vastness. His eyes glinted like diamonds in what seemed a profound vision. It was a look of longing. He had been one of those who had witnessed with us the tremendous punishment which had just transpired on that balcony. These were men who had been initiates in his own fold, his closest allies. Why had he not ordered them to cease?

"My friend," he began, "you look upon me as if you had seen a ghost. Perhaps you wonder why I did not prevent my followers." He gazed upon the image of petrified Ozanes. "It is true that I did not believe the ancient censure would still be in effect. Yet I did not see all until after they had finished and vented their wrath, but they were rash men anyway, unsuitable for the fold of Sorcerers." He turned and looked upon the horizon. The stillness yet unlit by the dawn. "I am glad you have chosen to stay here a while and grieve with me on behalf of these men. I never had thought highly of your remote elven feudatories in the north, but now it seems I have missed the truth. It seems your kind has a deep felt power of sentiment."

I had not before spoken with Invernalius. I knew full well of his seductive power and influence.

"Elf kind are not subject to emotion after the manner of men," I explained. "but they express longing by way of the natural world. Myself, however, being a valraph sharing humanity I do indeed experience that sort of pain. Once I laughed with these men, while they were living. I cannot weep for them now. Yet in the distance I do hear some song bird far below in the southern forest. It is a song which I know, and the bird sings mourning for one of them. "Recall thou Valring as he was when a child," it sings. That is what the Allfather prefers in all men. He sees them as they were as children, yes, pure, filled with love."

The moment I spoke the word "Allfather" the diamond eyes of Invernalius jerked and suggested impropriety. Then his glinting seemed to fade like candles. He breathed deeply through his nostrils, and held his head up high, again looking now with wrathful eyes upon the horizon.

"The old faith that men still cling too, after all these years... It has caused so much dissension and discord in the world. Would you not grant that? Men fear to stand alone without a god. They fear to bravely face the nocturnal unknown. I know that my teachings are scorned by many noteworthy sages, and I accept this. Please, humour me and hear my message, at least in honour of those here frozen before you, martyrs for my faith. I tell you, and you know it yourself, a new time cometh, friend, an era when new powers will arise. The old ways of Mage-craft and Sage wisdom passes. Those who cannot conform their minds to rise above the new system of belief will remain ineffectual. They will be unable to avail the common mishap of the human condition. Even that authority and spirit you just spoke of, whose seat is high upon the mountain, that one does not change nor alter his will. He allows evils to rain down upon men and does nothing, sitting there with his edicts gone throughout the world and passing judgement on souls."

At this point I judged myself compelled to speak.

"...That divinity is one of mercy. He is the father of all created things..."

Invernalius interrupted the attempted sermon.

"--he is NOT like men. Let his absurdities be forgotten. Have you not thought that all the needless suffering out there is something you might put to an end? Are not your very hands appointed to mend the world? You are so gifted, one who could learn so much of the sorcerel way. I admit....I have been considering you for a long time. I was hoping that you would talk with me about our path. Surely you would surpass even me in your power over the spiritual domain. Look out there..." he pointed to the horizon.

"Behold, think upon all those kingdoms out there, filled with their petty rulers. It continues punishing innocent men and rewarding the evil doers. And now, in this time, along cometh thee, of highest nobility and spirit, a merging of two races in one man, elf nature and human, in one fused. Yet your old faith, devoid of reason, tells thee to "be silent and still"?

Now all this was becoming a devastation unto my spirit. The mood of the times was such that, everything he was saying, all these doubts, had been churning already in my heart for some time. Invernalius had treated on it in such a way that it seemed mad knavery to cling to an old rigid deity few understand. I even learned sympathy for him. It was as if he had some vast understanding other men, even the wise, had overlooked.

Above all the heart deceiveth. A cold sadness came over me. Invernalius continued.

"I am sure that such a censure upon broken men should not apply to you," he said, "for you were meant for great things. All these kingdoms are before you for your care and wise rulership, to rule over and accomplish wonders. I can give you this! My tomes hide the secrets of ages, powers untapped. This very citadel and these towers all, all these libraries of Nystol and pools and gardens of serenity, together we can save all this. In thy veins flows blood that is neither elven nor manling, but of some rare combination, valraph. The ancient prohibitions do not apply to those whose blood is not human. This very day I can teach you the words of power that will cut down the sea of Maharim like a harvester's scythe does with shafts of wheat. The spell is an invocation of the spirit of death who can cut down entire armies as was done in ancient days. So would begin thy new magic reign upon the earth, to usher in a golden age....come then, join me, enter into my fold and learn this new art..." I gazed upon him. His diamond eyes glinted with a gladsome hope.

He took from his robe a scroll in a bone scrinium-case. It was the powerful mass-death spell. He held it out for me to take. My heart consented. Just as I began to reach out to take hold of the scroll and begin, an uncommon memory flashed before my mind's eye and took hold of me.

I recalled how as a youth my father the Valraph-king had waged bloody war against the kingdom of Plathonis to the east. We were sailing with a force of thirty griffon-prowed war galleys all adorned with the bright long-flags and banners unfurled in the wind. I stood there on the deck with my father. I had asked him if the Allfather was displeased with elves, or even a half-elf, going to war. He explained it in this way:

"My Son, this is the way of things which the great Father has always known. He forbids no nation to make war when under necessity. These men, they will not merely die for their king. They will die for one another in grim combat. So now each moment of life, each bounce of the ship's prow they savor, but they have no fear because they die singing as they fight. They know that the Allfather will greet them with song in the Halls of Evening. The Allfather allows many to suffer that he might bring them worthily into his feasting chamber. He loves not just part of each, but the full..."

What my father was trying to relate to me was a mystery, especially those last words. I remember that in the battle of the Petrozean Monarchy, which followed the next day, it was reported that King Petrozeus had died in combat bearing the sacred image of the Seven Rays of the Eastborn Horizon on his back, the famous sign of the Ammouri. That night the victory feast was filled with strange joy. Though the defeated and slain king, a mortal, was burnt on a pyre, we gave wine even to the captured enemy. Their King Petrozeus, prior to battle, had commanded them that they must make merry see they victory or defeat.

So I had instantaneously thought of these things. They went through me like a bolt of lightening. I am not certain why, or how, but I pulled my hand back from Invernalius' scroll. He looked at me. He was appalled. There was a silence as I gazed into his bright eyes. I knew that he spoke with a forked tongue. He looked askance at me and squinted coldly, and said "Very well, I suppose every absurdity has a champion." Then he quickly turned and hurried down the cold hall. I turned back and I set eyes again upon the horizon. Seven rays of light beamed up from the rising sun.

Sometime after these events word came to me that Simon Invernalius had left the Whitehawk kingdoms. He had sailed the intermudian sea. Into some other continent he is said to have ventured. There were many thoughtless mortals and even an emperor who feared his power, and he was officially proclaimed a god in another world!

So that very day we began the impossibly huge task of gathering and storing books and scrolls deep below in the vaults. The most famous and rare books were grabbed first, Dune's *Percepts of the Dream World*, Articles for Beginning Somatics, *The Vaultbook of Thulez*, Poems of the Wild Ox, *The Goat Meditations* of Zorcades, The Morphean Jewels, The Song of Padishah Bamusk II, *The Dragon of the Valent Imagination* by Anherm, *The Travels of Aetholus*, and many more.

We concealed these books and many more in the basements. There were several hundred, a mere fraction compared with the tens of thousands that were left above. Deep into the long abandoned basements of Hennsooth we journeyed by lantern. Distraught, some in anger, others resigned, we knew that we could only hope to save a small portion of precious books. Most of the books had few or no known copies. And the ones that we were save? How long would they last down in those dusty basements?

The rest of us had to bring as many books down from the upper levels of Hennsooth as we could.

"We will surely die or abandon Nystol, after this sacking," I said, "and we are unable to carry many loads of books."

"True," said Artaphract, "the only caretakers of the surviving books left behind will not be men, but rather worms and dust."

"We cannot store them all safely in the deep areas of the Labyrinth, that will take too much time. Who among us will dare to remain here after the barbarians have left?"

"Stay here, I tell you, the towers WILL burn."

"I know there must be some of you bold enough to stay and hide in the basements of the Sardu, to guard the most precious tomes until the ignorant go their way. Surely those without relatives, men who understand sacrifice for the greater good."

An melancholy silence intruded.

"I shall do it." said Farron, a Sage. "Assign me to the task for the few books of precious wisdom, even if I were to offer up my life: I dare to stay hidden in the basements after the sack. It is a task I desire with vigor."

"All for naught, if your superior refuses. It is not very practical."

"The time for practicality has ended. An act of fury proposes an equally hot answer by the righteous."

"You are an Eldark."

"One of the last, and secretly so. I will guard the Rythopylean Passage, the only passage into deep Astodan, the necropolis where the great ones of old sleep. It is a narrow stone hall, large enough for but a single man, but not too narrow for spear or sword. A single warrior could stave off an entire army there. In this narrow and dark passage descending, even the mightiest of the Maharim will fail against my bracers of might and spells of stumbling, I shall rain down destruction upon them."

"The Eldark have refused carnage."

"Oaths sworn in a time of servile peace. Men are not bound to the absurd and fruitless. It is written that we may defend the truth."

"It is unwise. I will not go with you.

"You should stand behind me in battle. If one of the barbarians has a stroke of luck, I would fall and my sacrifice would be in vain. If you stood behind me, he would then face another difficulty just as terrible."

"It is madness"

"So be. We men live but once."

"But why would those untaught northmen wish to enter below into Astodan?"

"There are well known legends of its treasures. They will come."

"There is strong suspicion that they have come to Nystol for that very purpose." I added, "When they do not find the spoils they are seeking in the towers, they will go below the towers, knowing well that the greatest treasures are stored deep. Neither do they fear ghosts nor liches."

"Farron, your superior will refuse."

"How can he refuse? He will be speechless under the axe blade of the Mahark warrior before this day closes. Will you stand with me, Artaphract of the Order of Mages?"

There was a long pause as the Mage frowned and touched his beard.

"You ask much...but yes I will stand with you till the end. I will use my staff of desertwind to send them home to their mothers."

"If it is agreed, we must then carry the books further down, into necropolis Astodan." I said.

"We have no time." Farron replied, "We must carry only the most precious of the precious, already deemed the most powerful. There remain not enough hours to save many more. We shall store the great scrolls and tomes in the very tombs of the ancients."

"That is folly. No one should dare risk entering into the ultimate chambers of the ancient Arcanes. Those areas are guarded with powerful glyphs, even curses...and were you to awaken a lich...may the holy ones help you."

"Come, we shall go there at once," said Farron, "to prepare and to find a path and the chambers free for storage. You can judge for yourselves this hall. I am certain that the sleepers shall not waken. The rest of you make ready the precious books and scrolls, choosing the best and most precious among them."

So they left and went off following further deep descending passages into the Sardu mesa.

While I was rushing up and down stairs looking after these

things, there came upon me a certain sorrow of frustration. The particularly mysterious tome of *The Black Books of Melancholy*, for which I had spent so long searching the libraries, would remain lost under the myriad piles, very likely to be destroyed in the flames.

Just as I was about set down a stack of books upon another stack in the basement forecourts, (where several others scribes stood about determining which texts should be saved by deeper entombment), I noticed something. In the back, behind many other books, an unusual book bound in black with geometric design lodged in the stack. Could it possibly be the one?

I turned away and going up the winding tower stairs, I could no longer fight my supposition that the black book of geometric design I had spotted was what I sought. Could another book with a similar cover exist? Of course, it is no doubt a minor philosophic tract or a glossarium, perhaps a mathematic work or some sort of law book, all of which are known to prefer geometric design.

As I finally reached halfway to my destination on the stairs, half way up to the twelfth floor, that inner voice whispered, that I even take the risk of wasting time and return back down to that dismal place alone, and check to make certain. There was the danger that I would get locked down there in those labyrinths, forever, and so sleep, and at last succumb to the miserable dream-bane of the elves. If I waited till after the invaders finished the sack, I might never be able to return, it might be left buried among other texts or taken into deeper Astodan. Just for one book I would have to turn around again and go all that ways, and this might simply be an old scholarium text. Only this last chance was given.

It took me three sand-glasses or more to go back down the tower and unstack several layers of books to get to it. At first, paging through it, I could not understand the dialect, for it was mostly what seemed pastoral poetry about shepherds and sheep. There was no title page as most books, and the arrangement of compiled authors was random. Then I turned to a page writ in Greek, a translation of the Spartiad from the second age. This excited me, I went through some other pages and found fragments of the *Vortex Poem*. Although I could not read most of the book since much was Outhapian script, I realized that I held in my hands what I long had quested. Who knows what other excellent tomes would be sacrificed to the flames, not only because of the imperfect knowledge of those who were choosing the books to be saved, but also out of lack of time to save many.

I closed the book and we went back to our toil.

Word came to our small crew that a certain Archisage and influential colleague of the Head Librarian, one Arizel, the Viridian Robe of Azerdon the palace kingdom, forbade us from entering the upper towers of Magian and Sagian Libraries. He claimed that we might use the books to hurl some war magic, which, for now, was still forbidden. Only now do I see clearly through this ruse...

Hraxor

THE FALL OF NYSTOL

We all wept, and wept the more for what would surely transpire, foreseeing the flames. Arizel denied us still, refusing to discuss. And it was him I saw while I watched from the hoarding that overlooked the inferior courtyard which leads down to base tunnel complexes and into Astodan. He had spoken with the herald of the Maharim before the guards let him pass out of the postern gate.

We all now realize what he really was doing, Arizel, the one who accomplished damned treachery. For this man conceived that the infernal ghost of Nuzzib was directing events. Arizel imagined how the Red Ascetic, once Nuzzib's disciple, the man who had inherited the cult's office of "the Divine Judge," was being directed by the shade of the "divine" Shahi Nuzzib himself. Arizel abhorred the rise of "decadent Sorcery" and his influence in Azerdon had been destroyed by the Red Ascetic's doctrines. He now had a chance to reek revenge.

The Red Ascetic had poured all his monies into gaining control and influence over both the Soothfold and The Great Sage Council of Nystol. He had long before sent armies of Librarians to all the furthlands even as far as beyond the Sea of Shirvav, to collect all the books he could find, on all subjects, paying a small ransom for them, saying to the owners, "Let us borrow the cherished book and convey it with all care to Nystol, that we may make copies of it, and vouchsafe its preservation, for this thing was promised to the leaders of Nystol when they aided the Maceonid alliance against the Atalur, and now we lay claim to that promise which was secured."

When some kings refused to yield up their most important

treasures, professional thieves were secretly hired. In this way almost all writings of Illystra vanished over a period of eight years into the Libraries of Nystol, which are, for the most part, inaccessible to common men.

Why did the Red Ascetic, lusting for power, do this? The Red Ascetic believed that a monopoly on all knowledge would assure that the twisted devotion begun by Shahi Nuzzib (and fully realized by himself) would eventually become the sure font of all knowledge. No other competing philosophies and faiths would be left to offer alternate answers to life's riddles. With all others submitting to the doctrine that carnal pleasure is the highest good, he would be able to manipulate knowledge and make all others subject to his commands. The infernal labyrinth of his heretical doctrine would also insure that future souls would die stranded in spiritual confusion, prey to his lust and the horned devil's axe. Where would men go for knowledge but to the local Red Priest?

Such was his diabolic design. There was another reason as well. I learned of this during a conversation with Nicodemus Blackrobe, as he stood there in his tower-laboratory having prepared himself with meditations for what was to come. He had told me that he was very uncertain whether he would give himself up to the enemy blades without a fight, or if he might attempt to escape. He said that he could not envision himself without his beloved Nystol, eventhough it had become corrupt and deserved destruction. A great melancholy had come over him. I had gone to him and voiced my suspicions about the Red Ascetic the evening prior.

"The Red Ascetic desires to obtain the Nagamaud Amulet," he explained to me. "This treasure encases the very crystal which imprisons the Demoness of Ashkehon, a nephilung. He perversely has concluded that by releasing the entity within he will be able to gaze upon her utmost physic beauty and in his lust possess her. This experience he vainly hopes will bring him to the state of Cathartic Titan."

"Cathartic Titan?"

"It is a legendary state of pleasure, both of mind and body, rumoured to cause a catharsis, a cleansing, a purging of uncleanness, allowing one to transcend the limits of human weakness, to restore the power of the preternatural, making one "godlike." It is a rather unseemly legend."

"Will this hope materialize?"

"There has been a serious obstacle. It is thought that the Nagamaud Amulet was seized by an Ammouric Ranger who found it in the intermundane caverns hundreds of years ago. At the same time another rumour surfaced, that Hermius' general, Nergalf the dwarf, had stolen the amulet from Hermius and replaced it with a fake, hoping to give the real amulet as a gift to his beloved elven queen. The supposed fake, which may not have really been fake, was by order of the Patriarch sent here and locked up with *The Anathemazine Corpus* in the Ammouric Vault below our Hall of Infinite Ceiling. No visitors or others have been allowed to pass into those chambers. Rumcur has it that a guardian Creosphynx patrols the tunnels that lead to the Vault. Anyone other than an Ammouric High Selva who would dare make way to that locked chamber better be extremely clever at answering riddles or he will pay the price with his life."

"That is news indeed. It seems that the Red Ascetic also may be seeking the *Black Book*?"

"You have guessed correctly, the Red Ascetic also needs that tome as well, especially the compilation which contains certain Ammouric formulas, which can exorcize the demoness from the jewel, but not for banishment as a priest would if continuing the prayer, but rather to gaze upon illusion and reach the state of Cathartic Titan. That is why he was cooperating with Arizel, who in turn will betray his own fellow conspirator. Arizel, Master of Planets, has vowed vengeance upon the Red Ascetic."

"He could not accomplish such a feat."

"As it seems...but he knew that such a High druidic Priest would be under the protection of very strong magic, almost impervious to assassination, not to mention his stunning popularity. The only way Arizel could strike back was to foil the Red Ascetic's diabolic power play."

"Then it was the Red Ascetic who had ordered the assassination of the seventeen priests and acolytes in Nystol."

"It was...these were ambassadors from Vesulum who were acting as mediators concerning the Sorcery question. In their researches these men had come athwart knowledge of these schemes, so they were done away with, but not before they came to me. Now I too am in danger, not only from the onslaught of the savages preparing to destroy us, but from within."

"I also have learned of these many conspiracies from these men," I explained, "that is why I came to you. As one of these acolytes lay upon the stone paths of Nystol in his final position, still yet clinging to life and with breath, I found him and he told me many things that he had discovered, all the while his life-blood seeping away. He trusted this information to me because I was a guest, and did not belong to one of the factious orders of Nystol."

"Arizel also knew only half-truths, whispers," added Nicodemus, "he knew because he had been told by a drunken man, Adeuces, the Golden Robe in Azerdon."

Adeuces had once long ago told of how that red Heresiarch's plan for power involved a monopoly over a huge library. Adeuces however had his own designs. He had made a bargain with the centaurs of Mahanaxar to let them participate in the sack of Nystol on which he had gained intelligence through Arizel, for Adeuces also had quested for *The Black Books* and an important volume had wound up in the hands of the Centaurs, who also let him live under this deal. In other words, Adeuces sold the security of Nystol for the Centaur's volume of *The Black Book*. He obtained an excellent price."

"How did he involve the Red Ascetic in this intrigue?"

"It seems that Adeuces realized that a Maharim invasion might not occur because the horde was stalled up at the Bronze Gates, in the Pass of Dariel. He began to worry that the Mahanaxarean centaurs would consider themselves cheated and wrathfully put him to the sword. So Adeuces, guessing the designs of his adversaries, secretly visited the Red Ascetic in order to discuss how to fix the dilemma."

"What would he yield in conspiring against your beloved Nystol?"

"The Red Ascetic planned to let the whole thing go up in smoke by opening the Gates of Dariel (Hermius' bronze gates) to the invading Mahark barbarians, for he no longer cared about the meager monies he would collect from Nystol, but had fixed his eye on the Exarchic throne of Tyrnople. Nystol had always been a rival of Tyrnople, so divesting us of the greater treasures and power was thought justifiable by many. Even more important was the threat of learning which Nystol posed. Were Nystol to burn from the torches of the barbarians, true learning would vanish, and it would secure forever his final monopoly on spiritual doctrines."

"And how was this accomplished? What would the savage Maharim have to do with the refined corruptions of the Red Ascetic?"

"It was not too difficult. A message was sent to the cheiftan Yurthmahar, Master of the Horde. It read something like this: that if the horde could plunder Nystol every tower should be put to the torch. That they would be rewarded for this service, not only with loot, but they could earn the friendship of the coming emperor, and free range throughout the civil lands. These towers were made mostly of dorn wood, which when moist is like stone, but in a dry desert like Nystol would burn fiercely, (as you know physic fire is not permitted here)."

"The Red Ascetic surely did not leave his seat of cultic power beneath The Yezez Desert," I wondered aloud, "the awesome home where Shahi Nuzzib the Divine once dwelt on a satin couch? His absence would not go unnoticed. Yet would Yurthmahar heed the note of a herald? Barbarians like they cannot even read."

"Instead of delivering the message himself the Red Ascetic bade Adeuces of Azerdon to find someone who could do the job. Adeuces enlisted the aid of Gulathar, the famous gelf of the old stories. Now old and tired, Gulathar had spent a five hundred year span as a scout and dungeoneer, clearing out the many infested Intermundane caverns and rescuing trapped warriors. Now he was eager to do some last memorable good before his spirit left the world."

"Such a noble gelf would not submit to craven affairs."

"True, but clever Adeuces with his charm deceived Gulathar and took advantage. Gulathar was the best choice for this mission, for his skills at dungeoneering were the finest, and the gelf suspected no conspiracy. He told the trusting Gulathar a pack of half truths: that a great and terrible storm had driven the horde of Mahark hunters Southward and that they had heard of refuge in the mage-city, that the horde was stranded in the mountains and faced starvation."

"How could he have fallen for such deception?"

"Gulathar was old and remembered only the good men of simpler times. Before our day, most folk had heard only good things about the Maharim. No one had guessed how they had fallen under the spell of the Ogodar, Ur-khan of the blood-law. Most folk had pity for them because, like the Cimmerians and Hyperborians of which the Grecian sagas tell, the Maharim spend most of the year in cold weather.

Gulathar was to enter into the catacombs of Garmsir and find the key of Hermius, a special platinum make by which one might open the great bronze gates. He then must travel directly to Dariel and open the titanic gates, having been kept shut for almost a thousand years, so that the Maharim might not perish in the mountains. Further, he was to tell no one of his merciful mission, lest those in authority change their minds. Such was the treacherous lie of Adeuces."

"Surely Yurthmahar would not have fallen for the ruse. The Red Ascetic is no Emperor. He can make no such promises. Besides Gulathar would learn of the deception upon reading aloud the message."

"These difficulties were overcome, for their strategy was elaborate and sinister. Adeuces gave Gulathar the sealed message for Yurthmahar, master of the Horde, second only to the dark Orkhan himself. The scroll was writ as if by the real Emperor but enclosed instructions to slay Gulathar and burn withall the city of the Arcanes, promising all the lands West of the Washir to the Maharim. Thus would poor Gulathar unwittingly carry the message of his own doom. On this scroll Adeuces set the seal of the Exarch of Tyrnople, which the Red Ascetic had secretly forged while he stayed as a guest in the Emperor's palace."

"But no one is allowed into the emperor's inner chambers."

"It is thought that somehow, using his druidic charms the Red Ascetic gained access to the inner chambers of the Imperial Palace."

"Was Gulathar successful in finding the key?"

"Yes, Gulathar acted and entered into the lower depths of Garmsir. He found the miserable Vermillion Worm that slithered there, which legend taught swallowed the key in ages long past."

"What legend is that?"

"It is said that the dwarf Nergalf, who carried the key that Hermius had fashioned, in his spite against all the northern peoples who had aided against him and defeated him at the old Battle of Gederon, cast the key into the worm's mouth, assuring that it would never be found for at least a thousand years. Hah, the key was in that belly but a year!"

"How did the gelf at last find the Vermillion Worm? I hear that there are many more than just one."

"It is said that Nergalf still wanders the underworld. Gulathar claimed that he tracked Nergalf down and forced him to describe the worm's unique markings."

"How grand his effort must have been against that battle-hungry dwarf."

"No one knows how he managed it. He did find the worm at long last. Gulathar however was luckless in battle against the tremendous beast, his companions fled and he himself was swallowed by the beast. But because of his strange gelf-flesh the worm could not digest him! Instead he said that he cut asunder the great worm from inside out and even recovered the key from its belly."

"Was not the message-scroll also digested?"

"Were that it had been. Gulathar, an experienced spelunker and adventurer, understood the dangers of water and acids in the deep. He had kept the scroll well hidden on the surface as he journeyed in search of the worm."

"And did he return from the depths?"

"After harrowing trials, he returned to the surface and journeyed on foot for weeks until he reached the great bronze gates of Dariel, arriving under a starlit sky."

"Did he use the key and open the gates?"

"He opened them, to the great gladness of the Maharim."

"And the message?"

"Gulathar appeared before Yurthmahar in his master pavilion that night with the scroll. Yurthmahar, not having a reader at hand, bade Gulathar to read aloud the message, which included instruction for his own execution. He read aloud the words to his own utmost chilling irony and horror. The great horde mounted their horses that night and went thundering through the pass, trampling the gelf hero under their horse hooves. So long was the line of mounted horse passing over his mangled corpse, that his very bones were nothing but dust after the last horse hooves passed over."

"Did Yurthmahar, a great warlord, have no suspicion?"

"Not at first, so great was his sense of relief that his horsemen would not mutiny for being further stranded. It is said that on the rising of the sun in the morning, when the new era had commenced, Yurthmahar regreted the execution of Gulathar and bade the mangled dust-body be set under the earth, and a rock tomb be erected. Upon the head stone Yurthmahar had an inscription carved in the ancient script of his ancestors, which he did not even know how to read.

The inscription is said to be a formulaic commemoration of the dead, probably memorized from some ancient Mahark poem: "Speak not of the numberless dead, they await the desire of the everlasting mountains"

"I have heard that this be the same morning that the Hycmen warriors under the leadership of the general Throash made their famous stand in the mountain pass, a few hundred warrior-knights against ten-thousand-thousand horseman. The whole civil world had heard about that bravery, though remaining ignorant of a conspiracy."

"The fact that the immense gates, locked for a thousand of years, were actually opened, proves that what I have described did indeed transpire. For everyone knows that no other key was made by the smithies of Hermius. Furthermore, no human could have retrieved a key from a vermillion worm's belly, only a gelf."

"That is fair reasoning, and it is unfortunate that the Hycmen could not have turned the horde back at the pass." I said. "There they died under the spears and axes of the overwhelming onslaught of the Maharim, but before they passed they made the boldest stand any had ever made in defense of the civil lands."

"And now the fatal hour has come, and the conspiracy of ages has begun to unravel. Indeed, my elven friend, I foresee that the fall of this grand collegium of towers will initiate a darkness that will cover many lands, allowing for a great war, and seeing further into years after that, in an age yet to come, there will usher forth an iniquity of ages that has long been waiting to ferment. May the Allfather help the men of that era yet to come, for were it not that he cut the time short, all flesh would perish."

So did our conversation end, and we parted to our respective destinies. I never learned what happened to the great Nicodemus

Blackrobe, a man perceptive enough to see into the secret workings of many powers.

ჩჯsxzᕂ

It is well known that the mind of the Red Ascetic has the faculty of unnatural memory. Even today the Heresiarch could write out accurately several hundred of the library's great tomes. Nor did he ever forget a name, not even his most seldomly met acquaintance.

I now await in this prison still hoping to reveal Truth to those who will listen, for his spell has darkened the minds of many. Now, like many other errors, his devotions have flourished because of the fall of Nystol, contrary to the hopeful envy of Arizel.

The flaming arrows were not doused by magic as before. No, they hit their marks. Divine Justice commenced.

The misled Arizel himself opened the lower gate in Sardu for the Maharim so that they might climb through the secret tunnel-passages that lead to the interior of Nystol from the lower mesa. The postern gate had inscribed upon it the ambiguous words of the Ammouric Soothfold who had forged it long ago and gifted it to Nystol. It read: *Porto patens esto nulli claudaris honesto* (it can have either of two meanings: *Gate be thou open, closed to no honest man*; or: *Gate be thou open to no one, but be closed to the honest man*. Either destiny Nystol might have chosen!

I can only say that I am alive because I was favored from on high. While all the other scribes and a few soldiers surrendered and were executed without purpose on that last day, I scurried amid the flaming chaos unseen as elves often are. I grabbed that rare tome of *The Black Books*, for which I had originally come, as well as Rumil's *Voyages* and *the Oceanicon* which happened to be placed next to each other.

Had I chosen to die in battle that day, a thing which strongly tempted me, the knowledge of Allfather and the Truth may have been lost perhaps for many ages.

Before I left, I passed two Mahark axemen, huge warriors with long hair, shirtless, with griffons painted upon their torsos, bearing mighty spears. They were descending the circular stairs leading to the basement vaults and so carried torches. They would have easily cut me down had I tried to check them.

Who knows why barbarians slaughter some and spare others?

I came up onto the lower decks and complexes, there were fires blazing on all sides, every tower an inferno.

The centaurs of Mahanaxar whom Adeuces had promised a share in the destruction of Nystol must never have shown up, and it seems that after they released Adeuces they became embroiled again in their war against the Regulians.

That day, it was a clear bright blue day, I traversed the lower forests alone, hearing the screams and death cries far above in the towers and ramparts. Several explosive blasts went off, very powerful, which I now understand were the bombs planted by Arizel.

I spotted the figure of Nicodemus Blackrobe above by the walls. He had been captured and brought before the famous warrior Hrathor, brother of Yurthmahar and mastermind of slaughter. Hrathor, massive in stature, stepped forward and was about to cleave the great magus in two with a stroke of his wing axe, a work of mercy from a barbarian's perspective.

But an angel, or some gentle soul, must have prevailed upon him to summon the Tungoth archers do the work instead, thereby supplying a death less gruesome. For some reason, eventhough ignorant, the barbarians detected nobility in Nicodemus, and refused to mutilate him or set him on fire as do all nations who abhor wizardry. So did the Blackrobe die, his torso filled with arrows.

We heard the jeering laughter of the Maharim. Most of the enemy host had left the level plateau and were up in the towers and palisades on the mesa bringing havoc.

Everything was being wrecked and razed, every metal statue between the Solitarium and the Elemental Stairs of Entrance fell. They would climb up, rope the bronze statues, and pull them down with the might of their hurth horses. Precious works of art they were and gifts from every land. Statues of sages, elf monasts, solemn unicorns and equestrian statues from Urguard, Gohhan sphynxes gilt with gold, and dragon and statues of dwarven mastery. And even the great bronze colossal statue of Hermius the Conqueror, which took them hours to haul down, came crashing into the Tower of Earthly Vision.

A few bands of men were in the southern lower forests where a few other escapees and I sought cover. The invaders were more interested in collecting treasure than seeking thrills by butchery. There we saw that the Maharim had even left unburied the bodies that Nystol archers had previously slain the day before from high towers.

Others, more interested in war-honours than gold, were tying the decapitated heads of Mages and other Arcanes to their chariot chasses.

We also saw among them our own slain Urguard mercenaries and some valiant men of the Kalar.

The Maharim had once been known for their kind treatment to prisoners and their burial of the enemy dead, but no longer, for their year or so of corrupting delights in the city Authapis had taught them vice and hardened their hearts.

Arizel I spotted with the Mahark barbarians, and they had given him a horse. It is clear now that Arizel knew of Adeuces' scheme, and even though he hated the Red Ascetic, he despised even more the Sorceries of Simon Invernalius. Arizel's plan was to encourage the Maharim to destroy only seven towers, preserving the tower of the Sagian and Magian libraries only, in hopes that remaining unmolested the ancient knowledge of the Sages and Mages would someday be revived in purity.

It was not to happen this way, for the Warlord Yurthmahar feared his master Ogodar the dark khan greatly indeed and would not consent to leaving the task unfinished.

Profound grief struck Arizel when he saw his beloved libraries burn and so many wise men who had once held him in high esteem put to the sword. Images of that memory in his mind would never lose their remorseful clarity, and he began to lose touch with reality, a tempest took his mind, becoming very much effected by some sort of despondent lunacy.

On the evening of the burning, while the Maharim were encamped on the Sardu Plateau enjoying their victory feast, Arizel was found screaming in horror rushing out of his own tent.

The Maharim found him to have poured a strange magical potion into his own eyes.

The potion must have reacted adversely and brought about a horrible side effect: one of Arizel's eyes was totally burned away and was destroyed, while the other now barely functioned.

The Maharim did the best they could for him with their primitive medicines. They all worried what he might try next. They knew his native greatness and they set a guard for him, for "madness in great souls should not unwatched go."

The sky was turning black with smoke, and I watched at a distance, far into the open Sardu Mesa now, I saw how Nystol burned. It was like a great storm passing over the entire world. Darkness covering all the broad lands.

It is said, and I think it true, that the fire which burned Nystol was a sacred fire, whose initial flame was brought by torch from Vesulum where long had been kept the sacred Ammouric fire.

In the first age when the earliest priests of Allfather came to Vesulum, they brought with them the sacred veil-fire that burned upon Mt. Argunizial in the upward sanctuary.

The same flame was kept burning in the holy city for three thousand years or more.

In the third age, the companions of Nergalf the dwarf stole it away into the underworld when Shahi Nuzzib and his cult had overcome Vesulum with their heresies. They traveled under the earth with the torch of the flame, and when they came up through accursed Astodan hundreds of years later, when time had escaped them, (or rather they had escaped time), the flame struck terror in the ghosts that dwell there. In the end the adventurers passed the torch to Yurthmahar ascending the mesa at the dawn of the last day.

The Ancient Rises of Nystol burned ferociously for twenty two hours unceasing.

On the fifth day afterwards I was far off. From atop Eagar Dog's cliff I saw with my elven eye Maharim celebrate their victory with Authapian style burning of captives. Such was the end of Nystol, and the end of an era.

The integrity of the Nystoli synthesis, in the end, my friend, was at last compromised. The city was set ablaze by barbarians from beyond the civil lands, an infamous act which at once represented some profound betrayal and a divine nemesis upon the lawless.

All source records of the true knowledge went up in flames together with the false. How all this transpired and what may come of it I am not at liberty to reveal, since the great conspiracy of iniquity is still at work in the world, and were they to become alerted to my knowledge of their identities and dealings, those responsible would surely pay an assassin to harm those dear to me. Therefore I must remain silent in this regards, however I urge those who are free of such threats to seek through the remaining histories of the Furth and piece together their dark riddles, lest the world entire, like Nystol, be swallowed in darkness.

Therefore consider it well in thy heart, Gnome, how deep the world must have fallen into chaos in these past years since Nystol burned".

Then having finally taken in all this news, in horror I spake.

"Great and dreadful indeed, high one, are these tidings. If only I had not closed my eyes for but one moment when I first arrived here when perhaps I was hoping for some meditating. Alas that I would not have slipped in that nap of ages. With my great Gnomish abilities and knowledge of things, this ruin may have been averted."

"Have you not yet learned the one simple lesson of this history?" he said. "It were thoughts like that which brought about the grand calamity upon the world, an imagining that mere flesh and blood can by magics direct the course of things. Allfather has allowed this; that is what I believe, to free the world of the burden of magic. Even a gnome cannot thwart his will.

How then, after all, did ye arrive here in this miserable place, friend, after your escape from the Maharim?"

So the rest of the conversation you would guess from what I have already explained about my own capture by Nuzzib. The man-elf however had not finished the conversation, and had much yet to explain, so after some quiet time we continued.

IV

The Scroll of Illumination

Hear ye more discourse of the kind man-elf, and first know thou, gentle reader, that Ynolls, creatures of which ye must now read, are tall ugly man-limbed bipeds with hairy hyena-snouts who inhabit the wilderness and various underworld regions. They are usually heavily armoured, preferring banded mail, carry long ash spears and halberds, and they are always dangerous.

The man-elf took back his pipe and puffed, then spake: "So did I make distance from that accursed burning. Traveling alone through the Canyon of Hermius I was surprised by the great amount and variety of whitened bones laying about in several areas. I later realized that these had been victims of the raiding parties. Of course most of the abandoned weapons, I noted, were left by Ynolls from the site of an obscure place of carnage: Battle of Clawg.

These Ynolls now occupied the area I was passing through, and they guarded their Moho (prince) from any possible intruders. This Moho was actually a human, one Hawd Ukhanig the Bloody Mouthed (Muur-urhad), and he is called simply Mohohad for short.

Men have searched that vast canyon for years and years looking for the Tomb of Hermius, where legend has heaped untold treasure, yet all have failed. How many skeletons of slain or injured *gazalir*, (having slipped and fallen from the canyon cliffs), might one who visits the canyon be able to count?

I counted over an hundred skulls alone, and I had not even traversed a fourth of the Eager Dog Trail. There are so many bones scattered here and there, that the place has also earned the name Skeleton Canyon.

While I traveled secretly at night up the river towards Vesulum I could see the snout-headed Ynolls lighting campfires in the cliffs.

In the next several days I met scribes wandering along the edge of the river. They were refugees from the Burning of Nystol, mostly apprentices and students, a few tradesmen, but no ordained Arcane or Eldark. Suddenly all took cover and hid behind rocks.

One particular scribe, who had been separated, was torn, burned and battered, was being pursued by the brutal Mahark horsemen of horde, for what reason we do not know. It was difficult to cross the swift river after the bloody horsemen left, but nevertheless we buried the man where he fell.

It was not long after that the Ynolls finally sniffed us out. Instead of slaughtering us, which is what should be expected of their kind, they divided us up among each other by throwing lots as is customary for war-booty. The Ynoll-master who won me had us tied up, three of us, and led us through narrow defiles and tunnels in the canyon walls.

But suddenly he was commanded to take us a different route, toward their headquarters. Surely news had spread of Nystol's demise and hostages were to be interrogated.

Finally we came to the chamber and throne room of the Moho. Beside him two Mahark barbarians and another scribe stood discussing, as they were purchasing refugees for slavery. The captors soon bound us head and foot, thrown over mules and taken far away. Soon it was my turn, and I was sold to the Maharim.

I recall now how the Maharim began to do the bidding of the Red Ascetic. For on the very same day that Nystol burned, the noble Emperor Florians was assassinated not far from Regulum. Many insiders knew that all this was the design of the Red Ascetic, who had paid off the Praetorian Guard by promising them access to his palace harem. (He intended, once in power, to force his senators into giving the bodies of their wives over to the lusts of the imperial court).

Now we soon heard that the Red Ascetic had "temporarily" seized the vicarate and administration of the Principate "on behalf of restoring order." He employed the reckless Maharim to strike terror and bloodshed in many lands, at any time, to keep the people in fear. The untaught warlords spread the darkness of violence throughout the world, foolishly trusting in their even less capable leaders.

Yurthmahar, for example, had never let his captains know that he took orders from the Emperor, though he continued to receive Imperial posts, and let his warriors suppose that the many cities which submitted to him did so out of fear, not respect for the imperial seal. Yurthmahar at least showed cleverness, since such knowledge among his generals would have made them all seem mere servants to a corrupt city-lord, a thing revolting to barbarian sentiment and productive of grave suspicion.

The Dark Orkhan, it seems, had often described Emperor Florians as his dear ally, sending word that, after the sixth moon Yurthmahar should take all orders from the Emperor instead of himself, since the Orkhan would be too far afield.

Of course even the Orkhan had long before conspired with the Red Ascetic in this awful scheme. In earlier decades, during a conspiracy which bore no fruit, the Northing had once even used the philosophy of the Red Ascetic to convince the Mahark tribes and Tung to be loyal to him, for the creature admitted that such a philosophy was better than anything a ghostly creature like himself could contrive. The Maharim had even naively thought they were about to save the world from evil.

I soon became scribal servant of the chief of the Third Tribe of Maharim, the third regiment "Ashoth-di." It was my task to write down the correspondences between the rival chiefs who had divided up their conquered territories. I saw how old jealousies resurfaced among them, grudges unchecked, which eventually split the five tribes. The Tungoth had returned to their homeland in the furth East, satisfied with a moderate load of booty.

Not so the Maharim... Unable to unify because of bickering over spoils, the Kalar captured them all at the Battle of Yellow Banners and crucified the five Mahark chiefs. Ten thousand warriors were to be executed by beheading if they refused the creed of Bah Ukah. Only the masterful Hraxor and a handful of others escaped.

All that remain now of the once great horde are a few villages of kurts far off across the Sea of Shirvav. I escaped death many times, but I will not forget my main theme, that is, the recovery of *The Black Book*.

When the foul Ynoll creatures of Hermius' Canyon finally captured me shortly after The Conflagration, they brought me in chains before the Mohohad their leader. The Moho amassed many riches for himself over the years and had become a rather sedate and fattened king.

It was obvious that his prime interest lay in self-indulgence, and so he dwelt with the snout-heads who would serve him various tasty meats. He did not care for books, nor the grip of cold iron in the hand, and the thrill of the arena did not much for him, but only all manner of dining and food tasting, sating himself with every delight beyond what is lawful. Bulging grotesquely, he weighed as perhaps an equal measure of an entire horse.

In order to obtain the richest and most rare of foods the Moho needed more and more coin, as his belly was expanding. He had ordered his Ynolls to be employed in finding the treasure of Hermius, which also kept them too busy to bother with attempting mutiny. However, looking back to those days it becomes apparent to me that Mohohad was in cahoots with the Infernal Monks. For not only had he accepted payment from the Maharim to capture all holy men, priests, scribes and Arcanes who escaped, but he also tortured me cruelly for information on the whereabouts of several magical tomes, which he hoped either to sell or put to use under an enslaved Sorcerer.

They brought me before his seat and Mohohad questioned me himself. Even as his mouth was full of horse-meat, he ordered the guards to pummel me each time I gave an unsatisfactory answer. The guards had seized my rescued books and presented them to Mohohad who examined them, and he showed great interest in my rescued copy of Rumil's *Voyages* with all its finely drawn maps.

The horrid king interrogated me about the book and began to rip the maps out. Afterwards he picked up *The Black Book* itself, the very tome in which had been writ the key to translating the ancientmost *Scroll of Illumination*.

This *Scroll of Illumination* is said to be a copy of the prophecies uttered in the first Age by Seth, brother of Anathron, He had engraved these on a massive obsidian Pillar which was intended to survive the Great Deluge. The Pillar of Seth was lost far across the Vastess Sea, but a copy of the engravings reached Whitehawk. Aramaic peoples of the lands across the Vastess Sea are said actually to possess the doctrines of Allfather himself in his own words.

The first part of the scroll is the prophetic utterance by the first man, the Son of Dust, Seth's own father, concerning the Great Deluge and the coming Desire of the Everlasting Hills, the fulfillment of the Age, and the Last Days. The second part is a spell which divulges the doctrines of the holiest man who ever lived.

Now Mohohad was likely unable to read. He must have supposed the charts of Rumil would help him quell the vast world, who knows what he saw in that. He foolishly thought *the Black Book* to be some inane history lesson, and he passed it to his scribe. The scribe who stood there next to Mohohad held the book in his hands and looked curiously at it while Mohohad kept barking orders at his lieutenants, being so fat that he was unable to move himself.

Cast to my knees violently by the snout-headed guards and shackled fast, I lifted up my bruised head slightly and watched the scribe. This scribe, obviously a former student of Nystol who had ransomed his life with slavery, now began to read the book to himself. His eyes soon began to widen and he began to tremble as if ready to explode with excitement, for he knew well what book he now held. Then Mohohad holding Rumil's *Voyages* barked in his own guttural tongue from: "Cast into the flames those other books." Why he would do this I know not, but let it suffice to say uneasily did his fattened head wear the crown.

The shade of the scribe's face turned white and he abruptly said:

"My master and great *moho*, please, let me keep this one book, as well as that book with charts, for I am thinking that the whereabouts of Hermius' treasure may be recorded within." Mohohad looked disturbed at this sudden contravening of his commands, but realizing that the scribe was immeasurably beyond him in knowledge, he reluctantly assented by a nod.

To my horror the other precious books were burned before my eyes by the snout-headed guards placed them calmly in the fireplace as if they were logs. After this I was beaten again and dragged back to my cell.

It was during that night on the floor of the jail cell that I had begun to put certain pieces of the conspiracy together. I realized that the scribe whom I had seen working in the Moho's chamber and who had recognized *The Black Book* was no scribe at all, but indeed Adeuces himself. Adeuces shortly thereafter fled away with *the Black Book*, not because he wished to put the knowledge to good use, but to satisfy his own vain curiosity and use it for his novel cult.

The Mohohad demanded a new scribe be provided him, and I was the obvious candidate. For years they almost treated me decently and even released me after the wretched king died of mordid obesity. Mohohad was struck down with dystheria and choked up having disemboweled himself in a sickness which resulted from eating a thousand sand-shrimp in one sitting.

Cronach Longsnout, a snout-head, now rules over the Ynoll Kingdom with an iron rod.

It was not until some 13 years later, after the Maharim were long broken, and the ruins of Nystol came to be considered haunted, and when it had grown red with *Hellopian Ivy*, that I happened across a different volume of *The Black Book*. It was in a Wizard's shop in Regulum. This was the twenty-second volume and included the Outhapian *Astronomicon* as well as excerpts from The Codex of the Angelic City. It had the stamp of Nystol on the inside of the binding. Some of these tomes have strange tendency of avoiding sure destruction, so it is said, and it seems true. Blood stains were all over the cover, but it was still in fine reading condition. The book had somehow come into the hands of bandits perhaps, or ignorant folk like the wizard shop owner who had labeled it *"Anonymous Book of Children's Fairytales."*

He sold it to me for the price of four gold, but I had to be honest and admit to him it was worth much more, and he only laughed. I did not wish to buy this at such an unfair price, but I had no choice for he would eventually have used it for tinder. Although this finding was some consolation, it did not make up for my previous loss.

Indeed much gladness came to me, I had rediscovered a most

important book of poems and legends for men remaining from remotest antiquity.

The furthworld was entering a dark time, a time of confusion and uncertainty, the Dark Orkhan was on the move again, the seat of empire at Regulum, capital of the old Principate had been moved east to the teeming shores of The Sea of Goldyndol, to Tyrnople, which soon rivaled its own parent city and angered the Regulians by rejecting all offers of compromise in matters of trade.

There was later much violent news and hostile talk, and finally, that very year, the Regulian Legions accomplished the devastating sack of Tyrnople.

It was just this past year I learned that Adeuces almost perished. In the dark hallways of his palace in Azedon, while Adeuces in his golden slippers was returning to retire to his silken bed after calculating his treasure, he heard a movement in shadow. A hooded figure appeared from behind the arches. Adeuces could see a wavy-shaped dagger blade glinting from the light of his lantern.

"Who are ye," he asked in desperation, "why have ye come thusly, to steal my life?"

Under a dark cowl the figure spake.

"I am the angel Azrael to you. The angel of death. Your span of days has ended. Even an angel must use a weapon, so look ye well upon this serpentine dagger. But now come, your life blood shall now stain the golden robes"

"No, please, I shall pay you a vast amount!"

"You try to bribe Death himself? Were you to pay a great number of your coins, a great number would doubtless remain. Let me not by further discussion deceive you with false hope that such would be accepted. What can a man offer in exchange for his very life? But come, Death is no respecter of persons, this very night shall see the palace cook taken as well. Ready yourself to receive your cruel life's reward."

"No, I beg you."

It is told that Adeuces now went to his knees. "I shall give you every last coin of my horde!"

"Pity," replied the dark figure, "To see a man so groveling to hang on to the life of this world. And here I had heard that you had contrived many spiritual doctrines... This very night your life is required of you, and even the fine robes and slippers that you are wearing will be forfeit. Now be silent, the time has come and cannot be avoided."

With that the hooded figure rushed and struck three blows to

Adeuces' frame as he knelt there in the middle of his palace's corridor. With cries of pain Adeuces struck the floor.

In this way, Arizel, in a fit of envy, endeavored to slay Adeuces. Arizel left him for dead, taking only the slippers, but the poor sinner somehow lived and has been given a second chance.

The Black Book containing the translation key to the *Scroll of Illumination* had been taken. Arizel set out on the journey to Yrbath in the North, where he hoped to become anonymous.

At this point Shahi Nuzzib appeared, a man whom historians and other minds thought had died two hundred years ago, but it turned out that rather he had disappeared into the Underdyrth, and then slipped into a time distortion. He reappeared just last year to reclaim his lost time, and his former seat of power here outside Vesulum in the Yezez desert.

The Red Ascetic, once the Shahi's disciple, was shocked and amazed at the awesome sight of his teacher, so long thought to be in the grave, now alive and stronger.

The Red Ascetic then left Shahi to his own devices and went to Tyrnople to stir up trouble there and he was very successful.

When the imperial city of the east, Tyrnople the bride of the Principate, was sacked in the civil war against Regulum, Mercurius Yod, the famous legend keeper and pagan seer, was slain by Regulian Imperial troops in his study."

"How possibly could he have gotten away with that?" I asked in amazement.

"In the ensuing chaos that enveloped the city, the legionaries of Regulian invaders broke into Mercurius Yod's study in the tower of Vyst. There they saw him gazing into his tripod receiving some sort of vision. The centurion unsheathed his short sword said: "Scribe, turn around and submit to the Red Asceticism!" The old man did not turn around or in any way cease from what he believed was his duty. Instead he replied: "Not now, soldier, I am busy with things beyond your skein."

Of course the centurion acted without constraint.

The Red Ascetic of course had provided for this execution in his proscription lists. He goes by the old adage of an Athenian tyrant, Peisistratus, "first cut down the highest of the stalks of wheat that you might rule more easily."

The Red Ascetic used the new chaos of civil war to gain power by claiming to hold the design for a new order in the world. In response, to everyone's amazement, the bright city defended itself, and though it was sacked, they nevertheless expelled the occupying legions and even put many to the merciless sword. The Red Ascetic took credit for rousing the people to re-arm themselves.

A bloody and dreadful civil war it was, and even now the people weep when they consider how terrible it all was. There was talk of furthlands entire lapsing into anarchy. The Red Ascetic, desiring once and for all to subdue the rival capital of the Principate, gathered a huge army of disciples and marched on Regulum.

And now my friend, grip thyself, for thou must know that the very seat of pristine Regulum, and all what was her venerable Principate is tyrannized over by "The Red Emperor."

Hear me, friend, the city of brazen domes is destined and rebuilds itself even now. The Principate thrives in a perverse way and is strong. Its people do not bother with the old ways or the Ammouric customs, and many there look down on the worship ways of Vesulum with a tolerance bordering on contempt. Marriage has been outlawed and children are taken from their mothers at birth to be raised by the state. Many of these, upon reaching adulthood, must become pleasure-slaves for the members of his now public cult, and those of best physical make up are made to become breeders for 'the new race.'

Those who do not practice the Red Asceticism proclaiming the emperor a god are left destitute, unable to buy or sell without the red mark on their flesh.

Regulum has become an eerie place, its grand temples and markets uncared for, the ghostly streets empty save for an occasional farmer, fisherman, or retired senator. Weeds overgrow the Forynth capital on the Atlantean Hill. The Red Emperor has maintained his seat of rule in the Principate.

What befell Nystol had repercussion throughout all the furthlands. Men's lives are short, seventy years, eighty, so the young ones that live now no longer remember the greatness that was, but the other kinds remember, elves, gnomes, and others such as we.

Unfortunately the minions of darkness have certain seeing abilities and are able to note some of the movements and thoughts of the good.

Arizel, going blind but making his way to Yrbath in Ulthuring, (the only true remnant of the great civilization that was), was accosted by bandits. *The Black Book*, which Adeuces had once entrusted to him for surety that Arizel make no further attempt at his assassination, was stolen.

Yes, stolen again it was...alas. The marauders sped away with his saddlebags and horse.

My own disciples found him bleeding and raging with madness

on the Serrian Way in Ulthuring, stumbling around on the road reciting poetry, for I had bade my men to follow him at a distance. My disciples and I took him back to Tyrnople in the upper room where we were staying, and we fed and bandaged Arizel, forgiving him of all the evils he had caused.

As a penance in return he provided us with a slight clue, and how so very slight and enigmatic.

We had at first thought that the Nystol had hired thugs to do this. But when Arizel was wrestling against one of the marauding thieves, he saw the man's brooch with an inscription of the word, in some kind of Latin but in pseudo-greek script, "*homoanimo.*"

I knew no proper translation of the word so I brought this to the attention of Morpheus Memnos, the illustrious scribe in his last years who was well acquainted with my original quest, a subject of highest secrecy.

The old man told me that *homoanimo* is a Latin term possibly meaning "the Man-Soul" which is an old salute demanded by Minogog for many centuries. Minogog often sensed inferiority to men, who tended looked upon him as a beast, so he ordered his army to salute him as Man-Soul, so they would not suppose he was lesser.

He never truly accepted who he was, that he was a flawed creature like others. The knowledge of the brokeness of his own self did not bring feelings of pity or hope for mercy, but rather rage, self-loathing, and hatred of the Creator. He only held sacred the perverse desire to vent this rage on other living beings, poor monstrous creatures not unlike himself.

It was rumoured abroad that when Shahi Nuzzib disappeared into the Underdyrth two hundred years ago he had encountered Minogog, (now several hundred years old but in the bloom of his youth), attending the gladiatorial games of the Uriod. Minogog had become a gladiatorial champion and was beloved by all the underworlders, save for those he slaughtered in the arena with his double-bladed axe.

He had made huge betting sums for the Anarchs of Uriod and they insured the continuance of this profit by supplying him with expensive doses of somatic *unicornia*, which extended his natural Gog lifetime by ten times or more. There in the frenzy of the Uriod Shahi Nuzzib befriended the creature and convinced him to rest from his labours. By his sloth-spell he infiltrated the gog's bestial mind with his bizarre faith.

He convinced the Minotaur to serve in his new inverted hierarchy.

Minogog had grown weary of the games and his victories had

become far too easy, life and death in the arena had lost distinction.

The Shahi offered him a new vision and purpose to live. He wanted the beast-man to work as a personal guard. Using the coin collected from his cult services he bought Minogog's freedom at a high price. The minotaur, having no spiritual awareness since the death of his prince so long ago, agreed, and together they raised an army of underworld devotees.

The Shahi now has employed Minogog to guard the *Scroll of Illumination*, a most dangerous prophetic scroll which he had captured and feared greatly. Queen Arva the Prophetess was once prophesied unto the Shahi when he sojourned in the underworld. She uttered how he would someday come across a scroll of great power and how the wisdom recorded in the Scroll could unravel the evils of his mystic doctrines and unshackle his own soul.

Years later, when The Shahi had entered the city of Sahkania and stayed to learn the Sorceries of the Drow, he found this scroll buried deep in the belly of a bronze dragon in the Forbidden Garden. He saw that the scroll was of finest make, edged with gold, and wondered he what powers it concealed, and so decided to steal away with it. When later he returned to Vesulum with the scroll he remembered Queen Arva's prophecy and was greatly disturbed, fearing that even if he could read the scroll (and his soul consequently unshackled from his own evil contrivances), he would nevertheless lose his power as The Divine Master of Dreams and Hegemon of Sleep and be thus scorned by men.

The Shahi chose to keep his soul enslaved to his dream gods, as well as the souls of his monks and priests, ensnared in the bizarre doctrines of his twisted devotion. So it is that the Shahi surrendered himself unto evil. And so it is that men are often eager to trade away spiritual responsibilities of highest import for worldly advancement and leisure. We may indeed ask what doth it profit a man that he gain the world and lose his eternal soul?

The Shahi's curiosity had got the better of him, and he was dying to know what wisdom lay in the scroll. He needed to find some one who might be able to translate the scroll and learn its wisdom, someone small, whom he could easily get rid of after reading the scroll. On the cover of the scroll someone had written "Key of Outhapis", which as ye know refers to *The Black Book*. The Shahi revealed these things to Adeuces who knew much about *The Black Book*, and together they planned to publish the fiction abroad that the eleventh volume of *The Black Book* had survived Nystol and was known to be kept in the Chamber of the Well of Empty Dreams in the cryptoporticos of The Divine Shahi. This rumour they hoped would draw someone who had the ability to understand the Outhapian Key and could translate the scroll.

This is where ye come into this maze of conspiracy, my little friend, drawn as you were to find *The Black Book*. They captured thee and locked thee away here in Vesulum, intending to use thee later, but they were uncertain if they could contain thee, since ye are a Gnome and have a magical nature.

The Shahi outgrew his curiosity when Adeuces began to translate the scroll using *The Black Book*, but grew terribly ill. Shahi Nuzzib determined to "dream away" the scroll. When that did not work he tried to simply forget about it. First hiding the scroll locked away in his iron box, he found that certain of his initiates kept trying to unlock the box. Unable to explain their actions, the Shahi suspected that the scroll had some sort of magnetic pull upon certain persons.

The Shahi tried to destroy the Scroll but found that it was somehow blessed with a power of indestructibility. So Shahi has hid the Scroll in an unlikely place where he hoped it would be lost among a myriad of other unread scrolls, the inmost chamber of the vast basements in the mesa of Nystol, the labyrinthine ruins of the Library of Hennsooth. He sent Minogog there with the order to keep guard on it for a few days, but the beast found himself having to continually dispatch wanderers who had come into the library "searching for something."

Minogog dismissed the other guards with the message to Shahi that he would continue both to guard the scroll alone and meditate not on the Scroll but on an absurd concept: The Void. The scroll must be guarded at all times, for it doth radiate goodness and holy men are unwittingly drawn to it from distant lands.

Thus, as it has happened, pilgrims from far shores find themselves traveling across the Yezez desert or Dry Blood Sea to the ruins of Nystol and making camp on her red cliffs. Later they find the basement of Hennsooth and enter it, only to be weakened and frustrated by the extent of the incomprehensible maze. Many come to frustration. They become so worn out that they go into a panic. Eventually, nearly starved, they are found by Minogog who dispatches them to their foreign grave.

The Black Book says that anyone who reads the scroll is filled with a Holy Truth and can by preaching not only revitalize the Ammouric Worship, but bring about the return of the divine king.

I decided to follow this quest for the sake of men, for as ye know, many of the old families, even though they claim adherence to the Ammouric faith, do not conceive of the reality of the Allfather. They live their lives according to the world and the flesh. Even many of the clerics now, counselors of the Soothfold and minor patriarchs, have been poisoned with the heresies of the Nystol and actually are trying to change the Ammouric doctrines. They are working secretly within the hierarchy and altering the prayer ceremonies as well as corrupting the folk with strange sermons.

So it is that the Ammouric faith is no longer understood in its fullness, and many only see the difficulties of following such a faith, being without understanding.

Now they are choosing to follow the ideologies of the Nystol instead. The original Ammouric doctrines are broadly considered old superstitions, but a few true believers hold fast, only a handful. This remnant consists of a many farmers, a few Knights, Selvas and religious brothers, some illuminated sisters and prophetesses, and some learned teachers.

I spent much time with this remnant in Ulthuring and learned many of their spiritual practices, as well as teaching them some of my own.

One day, during my sojourn in Ulthuring, when I was helping the brothers milk the cows very early in the morning, a celestial being appeared me. He came out of the morning mists which hung about the barn. There were huge eagle wings and he had the head of a lion. Seven horns radiated from this head like the rising sun. In one hand he bore a great staff upon which seemed to be a glowing oval gem, perhaps a sapphire. An unearthly bluish light was not reflected but arose from within the gem itself, or from some place of peace that souls long to visit.

Strangely, I recall noticing he also stood on a peg-leg enameled with mother of pearl.

He imparted to my mind that he was Ambrosius Ammouri, the mystical guardian of Intermundane travelers. He told me that I must go unto the place of ashes and face the horned god in furious battle, for there would I find what I sought.

When I revealed to the *selva* what I had seen and heard, he was very interested. He was not certain as to whether I should go, for often times a demon may appear as a being of light. He bade me wait for a time and see if the spirit re-appeared.

This I obeyed. A week later when again I was milking the cows this Ambrosius Ammouri appeared to me. This time he spoke assuredly.

"Let the selva not suspect me an apostate spirit, and so that I might assure him of this take ye this wondrous gift from Heaven"

The being presented unto me a bright helm, the likes of which I cannot well describe. It was beautifully adorned with daedal griffons engraved on the flanks with the radiant of the seven beamed sun of Ammouri upon the crest, and it boasted a red horsehair plum. Ambrosius communicated this to me.

"When ye confront the horned beast-man, don this fine helm, for it shall make ye thwart the smite of his double axe."

Then Ambrosius bade me make haste and passed away into the Aether. I showed this helm to the selva. The priest pondered and went off to pray for several hours. When he returned he confirmed without doubt that the helm was of divine craftmanship and that I must journey to Nystol alone.

I packed up my mule that very day. The brothers supplied me with many good provisions for my journey south across Kithom and the Canyon, with all the hills and deserts and hostiles. I had been warned that the terrain was most arduous. They gave me an Ammouric blessing and promised to pray for my success.

On the way I came unto Tyrnople the city of the brilliant domes, exarchate of old Aideen. There I saw many poor folk who had been down trodden by the great devastation of our age. They were forgotten by the worldly. This moved me and I could not bear to see men, some surely as noble in spirit as Duke Ikonn, but sitting in the streets among the rats eating garbage. I begged Allfather in prayer. Let me forestall the quest until I had helped them. I sensed that Allfather, though reluctant lest I be distracted, had permitted me this. I knew that the dark spirits would exact a cost.

I provided these souls much food and we drank wine together. They demanded that they be allowed to serve me in return. At first I declined, but they persisted. I told them that they must pray, and go about and learn the whereabouts of the wizard Arizel for me, for I suspected him of conspiracy.

The quest however still haunted me. A month passed and that day came when Arizel had fled the city and was subsequently robbed on the Serrian Way. We located and took wounded Arizel in. We looked after him following his misfortune and robbery. Most criminals were mere men driven to banditry by cruel lords or slavers that had gone unchecked since the Red Emperor.

Arizel, in a seeming repentance, divulged unto me everything he knew about the conspiracy, and these are all the things which I have previously related to you. His greatest regret was having revealed to the conspirators the sacred days of abstinence from magic observed by all Nystoli.

The greatest legacy of this conspiracy is the Hypostatic Rift. The Sages became confused about the philosophic ground, and could no longer ascertain how to define a substance or superstantial power. They could not determine even if such doctrines should be maintained or cast into the ash heap of history. They were truly *in nubibus*. Unable to trust their senses, the Mages and scribes, and later other men, could no longer focus on the vibrationals of objects. They became disoriented in a maze of *irreconcilables* to the extent that the syllogistic productions were useless. Without a philosophic ground whereby to know a substance, it is impossible to project a superstantial. In this way all formal intellective productions were reduced to mere sense data.

Arizel had been affected by this Rift much more than anyone. His madness is partially symptomatic of the inward schism. He could no longer put reliance on his experiences, and soon doubted the reality of simple matter and even living objects like a dog, not to mention universals like the canine species. It was because he did not want to believe the reality that some people had it better than he, or knew more than he, or were more esteemed than he. One may conjecture that the bizarre irony of losing his eyesight kept him from coveting that which was not meant for him. It also caused him to force more reliance on his sense of touch than is normal. This in truth may have been the merciful hand of divine correction.

So I bade farewell to my disciples. Across the Sardu I traveled to visit the house of Morpheus Memnos, the old Ammouric Saga-sayer. I was hoping that he could determine for me the interior meaning of the word *homoanimo*, and his explanation I have already told about.

At last, after many trials, I entered into Nystol and the basements of Hennsooth. I made my way through the dark maze.

Now this maze "Astodan" is the greatest in all the world. It is of vast size, stretching miles through the bedrock of Nystol's Rises. It took many hours of great patience for me to navigate this maze. I did so calmly without losing my senses, trusting in prayer.

I tracked down Minogog. Perhaps he had himself been listening for me. I slew him. I will not boast here with a battle account. The skill is not mine. It is a divine gift which I would rather not have used. Suffice it to say that, added to the natural dexterity of the elven race, the gift made it easy to outmaneuver the enraged assault of Minogog's heavy double-bladed axe.

At last then I used the translation key recorded in *The Black Book*. I intended to read *the Scroll of Illumination*.

At first I wiped the minotaur's blood off the leather scroll case. I was about to turn and to trace my way with the ball of thread back to the cliff surface. There were many other books down there which I found worthy of rescue and I intended to load my donkey down with them. My thoughts were that in the physic sun the scroll's strange script would be easier to read than by torch or lantern.

Then I reconsidered. I had been down in the Labyrinth for perhaps three days, what if Shahi Nuzzib's henchmen picked up my trail and were waiting to capture me as soon as I exited the basement? They would take the scroll and I would never read it, and the scroll would be buried down deep in some hellish lair for a thousand years or more.

I opened the scroll right then and read as much as I could by lantern. Taking out *The Black Book* which held the key of translation, I set down the sacred scroll on an old uneven table which Minogog had been using and knelt down before it. Then did I remove the scroll from the blood-stained leather case and the saw the it was made of finest quality *bembus* leaf. It was like other papyrus but protected by a light pearl glaze of some sort. Then, resting my lantern on a fallen stone block, I unrolled the wondrous scroll. When it was almost completely unrolled the pearl-colored papyrus began to unveil unnatural power. It was as if it were living. The scroll radiated white light and the entire chamber was filled with a holy and sublime brightness. It was shining forth from the scroll, so bright it was, brighter than the physic sun. Nevertheless my eyes did not squint.

These were not like natural rays of the solar illumining. Those rays may pain the eyes. Rather it was a sort of spiritual luminosity. I had set the lantern and planted a torch in the sand, but these now seemed dark in comparison. I held the sacred scroll. *The Black Book* I also opened on the stone block. Then I undertook to translate. This was many hours for the script is ancient and in many places abbreviated. My familiarity with Aramaic leaves much that is wanting.

What I read metamorphisized my living spirit wholly and infused with sacred knowledge my understanding of reality. The sacred signs of the most High God were engraved into my being and any darkness that had once plagued me from my past was healed, and I was shown how my life was being used to avail others reach a Heavenly City, one immeasurably more grand than the lost city that worldly scholars weep over.

When I was finished reading, I rolled up the scroll with great reverence. I understood that the words of the scroll had filled me with a kind of spirit beyond what is natural. After many more hours I finally returned to the surface. I did not even recall any fear of being seized by Shahi's henchmen. I simply returned to my tent and retired without supper.

That night had I a wondrous dream. Know at the same time that there was something not of dream, for I was aware. Celestial Beings roused me and brought me through the Yezez until I thirsted greatly. Finally they allowed me rest. Then was I taken up in spirit to the singing Heavens. There was I shown many mysteries of which I cannot speak. I beheld a Celestial City, a place beyond profoundest imagination built nigh the summit of a beautiful mountain.

There I met a Shepherd clothed in Light who spoke many beneficent and mysterious doctrines. He bade me impart these to men upon earth. He told me that little time was left for me. This Shepherd revealed to me how all the cities and libraries of men are but passing as dust, vanity in sight of Eternity. If souls would only begin to seek after the true Good and long for the unearthly Peace of the Celestial City, the courts of the Palaces of Heaven, they would not so greatly bewail their misfortunes. The destruction of their own cities, such as Nystol of the nine towers, would seem no more than a passing thing. The lives of men, said he, are but a brief span. The world is a test for those who wish to be worthy of entrance into the inmost chambers of Heaven's Palace.

The Shepherd had chosen me to spread this doctrine. Even he had once walked among men knowing their ways, far off across the Vastess Sea. He had tried to teach men this way, but most refused to heed him.

This was the same man whom I had read about in The Scroll of Illumination, the one whose teachings were true. Ye have surely heard men remark about the rumour, that the Allpower had taken on flesh and become a man to somehow save human souls, a thing which occurred about the same time as the Hypostatic Rift. Although we know very little about this man-god, I propose that he actually appeared to me in my dreaming state.

The Soothfold of the Ammouric Canons are said to have some knowledge of this and still await sacred writings from beyond the Vastess Sea. No doubt, they were awaiting *the Scroll of Illumination*, but the scroll was intercepted by Shahi Nuzzib.

Various powers of mysterious iniquity are at work in the world to suppress this knowledge, so I have safely hidden the scroll beneath city of Vesulum, and I shall now divulge unto thee how to obtain it once ye have *The Black Book*.

The day after the dreaming vision, I awoke to my amazement far away from Nystol, at the Chumnut oasis only a couple of days from Vesulum. My mule had been following me, mysteriously all packed up. The Celestial Beings had placed me near a pool of water and from my mouth I leaned over and drank, since it was terribly dry, for not yet had I gathered my thoughts.

After some major draughts of cool water swallowed down, I looked up at the palm trees and thought how like such a tree is the just man, the man who gives worship to the Holy One. He is like a tree planted next to a stream of cool water like the waters from which I had drank, so say *the psalms*. Not so the wicked man. He instead is driven like chaff in the desert wind or rats in dungeon shadows. I bent down and took up more fresh water in my mouth. As I did I heard an unearthly voice and knew it to be the voice of the Shepherd clothed in Light.

The Chumnut oasis is beautiful, and reflects a little of the paradisial visions I had seen. But I had to go. I returned to sacred city Vesulum and began to preach the truth and turn people back toward a holy way of life, the way of divine law. This angered the High Priests and they paid Arizel a handsome price to betray me. He handed me over to the Shahi Nuzzib, in this way avoiding the embarrassment of condemning an innocent man. I have heard that Arizel is back to his old self, though still on the verge of insanity. He has been able to pay the Wyrmlords to enter the Tower of Zenops and locate an old and magical glass orb fashioned by dwarves in the third world-age. He can use this orb in the socket where his corrupted eye had been and thus see, though imperfectly...but there has been a terrible side effect.

Now the Shahi does not want anything to do with me either, for I have appeared before him and spoken the Truth about Allfather. He is going to send me to the Red Ascetic, that is, The Red Emperor, who will without question put me to death. That great heresiarch I hear is now very close to finding the Nagamaud Amulet. He has even gone so far as to employ the Wyrmlords of the Underdyrth to seek through the vast and cavernous expanse of the intermundane world to find it. They search in every place, not only subterranean cities but also deep libraries, hoping to find some reference to it in a tome.

Now Kruthendel, I tell thee, go thou on and seize that particular tome of *The Black Books of Melancholia*, recopy it in the ink of Gnotus the dragon. The work is sealed in an enclave in the Hall of Celestial Tusks, the great hall that overlooks the shores of the High Seas of the Pagan upon the cliffs of Bah Ukah's Song in the closed city of Kalar. You must go disguised. No person from beyond the great desert may pass into that land.

Recall thou how there is a prophecy recorded by Mercurius Yod, that when the dragon Gnotus lay dying, how a strange deep golden-coloured fluid poured forth from his heart and swirled with his blood. Morpheus Memnos believed the fluid to be the remedy for the humour of Melancholia, the black bile which he prophesied would someday be the predominate humour over the race of men whose sins lead to sadness. He who writes down the words of Gnotus recorded in *The Black Book* shall find, in the Chapters of the 7700 verses, if by moonlight examined, then.... wait, listen, do you hear the footsteps? They are coming for me, do as I have said...!"

The latch clanged loudly and the rusty iron door burst open. Two Exarchial guards of Tyrnople entered. They grabbed up the frail man-elf. The guards laid violent hands on this holy one. The brutes took him away, slamming the door which resounded like an ironclad tomb. I yelled out at the guards and was heard only by mice.

What these Tyrnopolitan troops were doing in Vesulum I do not know, but later to my dismay I learned that the Exarchate of Tyrnople had, within a span of ten years, occupied all Vesulum, Nystol, Echorias, Ulthuring, Regulia and more).

As they took him away down the dimly lit corridor he yelled out "....Gnome! Mark and remember, the Sphynx eateth the Scroll...!" I heard later that the man-elf, who never thought to impart unto me his name, was conveyed in chains to Tyrnople and strung up to die on a dead tree, that very day, with thieves and other enemies of the state.. He died like a criminal on the Echecratian Way, for "crimes against the people's pleasure."

And now, good Guild-masters, I am too weary to continue. So let it be thy chief concern to find out the meaning of these mysteries, for there were many other terrible things which he imparted to me and I am bound not to divulge them. Apply thy mind to these enigmas, lest ye also drift into all-conquering sleep, and the world entire collapse into oblivion.

Appendix A

INACCURACIES OF A FORBIDDEN TEXT

Here is a mysterious portion of text from the Neoplatonic Archiscribe Epinanaus. The corrupted Authorities had required Epinanaus to extract these paragraphs from his demonstrations daemonicae, "the Demon Proof" on account of "fantastical opinions," and "inaccurate political content," especially "impolite references" to public personalities and various religions esteemed among men. What was even more threatening, was that his history of the second age, the postdeluvium, suggests the factual basis of Ammouric metahistory. These things were provided as evidence in the trial that lead to his exile.

....which begins with the story of Maceon and Giant Edamnuch and ends with the Battle of Suar Bille. The epic consists of a combination of memorized verses and synopses. Hepthe memorized them, like a trained bard, when in possession of the Black Book. It was a feat he pursued during his three year imprisonment in the rock prisons of Gohha).

The ancient script is difficult and the grammar most arcane. For example, with great difficulty I determined the doubtful Akratic phrase, *vithze segur*, to mean "bitter axe" rather than dripping axe. Holernus the Pellamant Archscribe concurs with the latter. Thus the scaldsong could read: "A bitter axe crushes, a chance battle occurs, under Mount Akinusikul they lay.." As well as Epinanaus' own obscure poem attached at the end "..a more bitter axe to cut the tongue of Epinanaus doth he (Vistonn?) aspire to.." Of course this translation makes the reading easier and sensible. Recall that the lost *Lays of Illystra* also told of the early frontier wars of the first ages and the coming of the Maceonids to Ulthor (as recounted in the fifth book).

We can infer that indeed the venerable Maceon, survivor of the deluge, followed the *havercanth*, a trail which in the fallen tongue means "axe-cut trail." This is understood to be the major axe-marked trail leading northward. It runs through the cold swamps of Hithgroth infested with grisly bloodbears. Innumerable axe heads from some unknown time dating back several millennia are known to lay buried there along the trail. It is said that they date to a time when a flood covered the world, a notion which seems fantastic.

Though as a youth I took this to be a foolish folktale, I have in my life's twisting journey come to see with my own eyes one of those axe heads. They have the most unusual shape and are forged of some unearthly metal. The civilized townsfolk of Regulum have always regarded the burnt and scathed swamp-forests of Hithgroth and the cave-riddled forests of Kath and the

Deepwold with fear and hatred. The Illystra books, as Holernus recounts, spoke of this place as if it were some lost paradise. The sound of Calleth lake is described as waves resounding upon shores with the "roar of immortals." This is of course Wilder Lake as we title it today (few men have been able to see it without an army to protect them). It is a lake, they say, filled with the bones of the men who fell in the "occurrence of war" on the Axecut trail.

Nerses of Temas, (a worthy geographer who mapped the sub-polar wastes (and other areas) on the campaigns of of Hermius the Conqueror, claims that in those days he was able to see the many piles of bones submerged in the shallow lakes of the battle site. Durgoth guides had known of it through tradition and brought him there. Nerses claimed that, upon his examination, he determined that they were not ancient warriors, but rather winged creatures of some sort.

Perhaps then this is what is intended: Maceon was the first man to have entered Illystra in the dawning ages when the flood receded. That time was even after the winds had ceased, and Maceon does not wield a dripping axe, but has followed a trail "cut by axes." This also takes the poetic description "bitter." Indeed, I have heard from a monk who visited Nystol that an eld folktale of the Durgoth recounts how Maceon had been suddenly ambushed by the winged creatures.

According to legend, it was in this conflict that Maceon's son, Mahar, proved how he was greatest in war among the five sons. Even though he oft before had been challenged by Rumil, the eldest, heir of authority and power. Against both, it was understood by the Eldari, the third son Maurob became jealous and especially hated Mahar for the glory of his warcraft. Strife arose among the brethren. It was thereafter that Maceon the Patriarch bade Mahar and Maurob both in contrary directions go, departing the primordial clan. But Mahar returned to the north, to Duur and Ard, Maurob to the east and south; the shores of the sea of Ymmin. Yet Kutaal the youngest refused that Maurob walk alone in the wilderness, and begging the will of the Patriarch accompanied his brother. Mahar and Elod stayed with Maceon until the time that the tablets give.

Arminius, three thousand years later, commander of the Regulian Legions, popularised the name Axecut Trail, having known *the Lays of Illystra*. So it is nevertheless properly titled, since axes give a sign of the imperial power of the sons of Maceon, as you find sometimes painted on the banners of our legions.

What is even more telling is that the word for *bitter* is found repeatedly throughout the epic poem. It is found only once in the history. The implications for the histories are undeniable. Menaced again by winged creatures, Maceon and his two remaining sons fled West. They fled away from the bitter lands. The mysterious "northern colonies" are actually what we have named the western colonies. Indeed, Maceon did settle the region... "Red Hills he found near a sea, and they kept the worship, He and his descendants."

The Ammouri, superstitious and unlearned as they be, are again, it must be confessed, found to be unwavering in their strict legend keeping, thanks to their saga-sayers.

These Illystra books tell of a time that predates the fall of Alantys, almost to the time when the great deluge submerged the wicked cities. You must imagine a time when iron work was unknown, and bronze smelting was the highest art, when the Rumilian laws were unwrit, and when no vast stretches of pleasant villas and resort towns stretched across the shores of the Diamond coasts. Allapis was still just a Tartessian colony and the sacred philosophy of the Ammouri was sung of only in song. The Tyrrhenian colony of Orusca on the watered plains of Pasos alone could rival Allapis in trade and wealth.

In this time Maceon's spirit had not yet passed into the deep reality and reckoned with the All-power. For he was now some 655 solar passings. Men of high antiquity lived naturally much longer in those days. The dead flesh of animals was not usually eaten and the sins of mortal men had not so overflowed the soul and flooded into the body, as today. Ours is an age of iron, and it is to our sorrow, and would that the Allfather had appointed my birth before this age, or in some age long past, when men still feared the gods and descended not into the evils of wars massive, of treacheries, and dark magic.

In his mercy the All-ruler did consent to shorten the lives of men, and this came to be after the passing of the five sons. Lest brazen men offend Truth the more, their lives were cut short, for it is better to live a short life with no or only a few sins, than to enter the next life burdened down with innumerable sins of an extended mortal span.

In contrast, the previous age before Maceon had seen wrongs done by the seed of Anathron, and those simpletons nevertheless lived long upon the groaning earth, and in the end they perished with the water when the world entire was punished. Their misdeeds seem as mere slight omissions in comparison to what is done in our day, the work that the plotters of iniquity have designed.

Yet these things too will pass away, just as the silver age gave way to the bronze age of heroes. One age passes and is overcome by dominion of another, and in some future age the All-Father will allow all the furthreach to be consumed by fire, since men will cease to give thanks and venerate. For this was prophesied by Maceon, who had received it in a mystic dream concerning the unborn man (the son of dust) who disclosed to him forgotten truths of the Highest One.

Maceon the prophet dwelt in Ulthor of windy shores, his long locks and white beard daily caressed by the westward breezes from the Sea of Immanent Waves. There he would look off into the distant east from dawn to dusk with his arms outstretched, praying for the return of the ancientmost god, preaching, and doing penance for his sons and their offences against the Peace that emanates from the heart of burning Reality.

In no way at this time was any man without some knowledge of the rites passed down from the sons of the unborn man nor could any of the great chieftains claim ignorance of the five ways of sacred knowing. The idolatries of the Nzulg were unmentionable and that such a place could exist would have been beyond belief.

Such sorrowful half-beasts as the centaurs (who now scourge the land Mahanaxar with chaos) were not to be found in those days, for the offences of men had not yet merited such. Centaurs, I have heard, were later fashioned in the clouds by some evil demi-god, with the permission of the All-Father, for the chastisement of men. But know that no beings by fact of their being among the living are evil by nature, though prone to violence they may be. A few centaurs by disciplined life have even accomplished good work, as is told by the Greeks of the Centaur Chiron who dwelt among the Arcadians. There were other beings arisen from the cosmodic order, both intellectives and beasts, as for example, the leviathan and the huge dragons of the wilderness, and such beings that you might see in other lands thriving. Also were there giants in those days, before the earth was rent asunder, mighty demonians they were and feared by all.

Now it was giants who had descended from Gog who found refuge in Whitehawk at the time of the world-flood. In our time we have seen no giants but report is often heard from the mariners and the tradesmen of Ael Lot how in the past ages the giants burrowed deep into the Hinterhills of Naxicanis and erected the great boundry-stones.

The gogs were, says the Xilmurian epic, beings of rebellious spirit who sought to vie with the gods, as you doubtless have heard, long before they were driven into Thasos and the hinterlands beyond the Hyperborian Sea. Yet wandered they in the past ages of the world causing strife and mercilessly hunting animals for mere sport (with far greater ease than men), or plotting wars against the celestial host.

Also gave the Ancientmost gave strength to the sons of Maceon, that they might make war with the giants. In the twelvth year after the expulsion of the sons of Maceon from Ulthuring, Maceon beseeched the High One that he be protected from the wrath of the Gog-kin, especially the giant Edamnuch, who carried with him the fury of devasting Stormwind and the flashing fire of the Sky, which he had stolen from the gods.

The ships of Kutaal had brought tidings of that mighty evil brow, seen off the coasts of Arahom heading south to Ulthuring. The creature had spent years, it is said, trying to climb the steepest heights of sacred Mt. Akunyskul to ravage the sacred treasuries of the nations, and the Blessed Oracle Diviniton, and to slay the sacred black-necked Swans of Destiny.

Yet all stories must have a beginning, and this tale must be told, for it is testimony to the Allfather. There must now be attached the tale which you heard mentioned of Maceon and Edamnuch, the excerpt from the Xilmurian epic which concerns us, and which, I conjecture, records the seed of many mysteries. It begins the Epic of the Amourim, the precious 33rd book, which my account has set in translated prose, listening to Hepth's broken Atlantean hexameters, for the work was originally told in a Phoenician dialect, and later modified with Atlantean archaisms. Now the tale begins with Maceon, who does penance on the shore of the Furthsea, for, the Illystran thus describes him:

"There was one found obedient before the All-father, who did not shake his head at the troubles of the day or crouch in fear before the axes of the fallen kind.

Came the son of Maceon forth unto his father's abode riding proudly on a pale stallion and his brilliant bronze armour flashed, behind him ran servants leading a heifer for sacrifice on the shore of the wave-crashing sea. At a distance his well-armoured horsemen rode by the waves, eight-score heavy hooves thundered and splashed upon broad Earth's countless stones. King Mahar of the subtle council he was, the grim father of the tents of Kalar, who knew the plans of the distant tribes.

The Grey-haired Patriarch with arms outstretched offered thanks to heaven. There beside him perched one of the mighty Rord-hawks, for the three others were on distant journey aloft, gifts of the Allfather they were, who upon the four winds ever-blowing glide, so trained were they by Ambrosios the Diviniton, oracle of the Ancientmost, that with keenest eye they might perceive the ceaseless movements of men. To and fro went these far-calling birds above broad vastness of earth, to search out news for the great patriarch. And with their-own bird-sight the prophet saw when, grasping the staff of the four winds, he prayed, as he did now, gazing upon the distant tents of Rumil to the west, the land were he rested his hope. The hawk called Grenzar, who searches out the eastlands, not far above rested on the branch of the oak tree, a guard for the old one.

Nor did Maceon cease to pray for his sons, --(*remainder of text missing*)

...Even as I write, the historic consequences of the legendary Maceon are upon us, for had not the sons built the roads out of the Northern Wastes we would not invite dangers from the frigid Hithgroth vastness, (which has brought us all nothing but ruin and put the very order of civilization nigh the verge of final dissolution)."

In later years men built the mighty Horg Wall, and Hermius raised up his bronze Gate of Dariel, so were the lawless breeds and savage races kept out of the civil lands.

Abaddon, Mt: In stark contrast to the numinous Mt. Arguzinial, Mt Abaddon has long been called the mountain of fury. Here it is said dark storms are ever present and wind and hail, as well as fire and smoke from the innards of the mountain. It is known to be a habitation of unnatural beasts as well. Yet the most frightening tale concerns the evil spirit associated with the huge mountain. It is told by the Ammouric Saga-sayers, that when the Time of the Harvester comes, Mount Abaddon will spew forth an awesome cloud of dust and fire that shall engulf the earth, causing men to flee into the caverns for cover. The mountain spreads its arms north and south with very treacherous cracked stone, similar to the Cracked Mountains themselves. There are no known passes through these huge walls of rock, through which flows the raging river Hyphasis.

Aels: Maceon, survivor of the deluge, had five sons: Ael, Maurob, Rumil, Mahar, and Kutaal. Ael was alloted the icey sea shores of the Northern Warm Sea and the glacial mountains, "for the harvest of sea." Maurob was given the East, all the shores of Ymmin and beyond. Rumil was given the temperate forests of the Echoriath for hunting and shores of the Vastess Sea, while Mahar and his son Mahanax was given all the Southern stretches of tropical lands, for fruit and plow. Kutaal, for his sin, was given all the middle waste, the great deserts, which was a blessing in disguise. Later Mahar returned on the Axe-cut trail to his father's home in the Northern woods, leaving Mahanax in the South. Mahar stayed there with Maceon until his death, and had further sons who would become the Maharim.

Aeon: A period of time, possibly reaching into centuries or even millennia, but usually designated by some spiritual hegemony or the metahistoric condition of the human relation to the Ancientmost source of All. For example, though a period of time such as the Ziah is said to have occurred during the first world age, in reality it was an Aeon. The long tyranny of the Demon-gods is also called an Aeon.

Aethuria: See *Ayrs.*

Agathodaemon (Oruscan Gr): mysterious word meaning "good spirit." –and not necessarily a demon.

Aidenn: The Greek-speaking empire founded by Hermius which stretched from the shores of Xasbur all the way to Turnople.

Akaratic: Glyphic writings left over from the first world-age. These are thought to be the oldest of all writings in the Furthworld, representing a celestial language used by God himself.

Allapis: A peaceful, short lived and vanished trade-empire of unknown origin from the second age. Its considerable unwalled- ruins are on the coast near Regulis. It is said that Hermius' vision for Aideen re-awoke the dream of the Allapians.

Ammouri (used as a noun when in plural; adj. Ammouric) (possibly fr. French amour): A rite of ancient Christianity, comparable to the early Celtic rites of Cambria and Hibernia, which in some places remained independent from Roman governance on account of the vast distance. The clarity and association of Latin with Christ's era was highly valued, however there is evidence that a few Hebrew and Greek scriptures, such as Leviticus, Luke, St. John's Apocalypse, the Psalms, and one or two others, had been provided them. More warlike than any other form, the Ammouric faith also featured an emphasis on cave exploration for the purpose of "releasing for Christ the souls captive in the underworld," to this end it developed an aggressive order of Paladins, the Ammouric Knights. It was widely held that the only genuine kings of the Furth were the Maceonid kings sworn by sacred anointing to defend the Ammouric Faith. After the Furth became swallowed by sands and sunk into earth and sea, the Catholic Faith from Europe easily replaced the remnant shrines of the Ammouri.

Anosh, Sea of: The great sea that is the bounds of eastern Whitehawk.

anthrai: exact record of these creatures is lost, but local rumour of Hermius's Canyon suggests that they were many-armed Cyclopes that were hired to build a number of colossal architectures in the third and fourth ages, including the horg-wall.

Anshan: The great and far-away oriental kingdom of easternmost Furth.

Aquilaris: The great sea-bound kingdom of Maceonid monarchs which stretches from Rumilia all the way to Mahanaxar on the Vastess Sea. Bordered by the Vastess Sea in the west and the Murmrik River to the east, this Regulian Province became known as the hub of the civilized order.

Arahom (Aram): A northern "no-man's land" of swamp, plains, and hills, and some fertile land beneath sacred Mt. Argunizial. Site of many battles against the Nazageist.

Aragac Mountains: Mountain chain of Xasbur that borders the Sea of Sirvav to the west.

Arcodon peninsula: Southernmost arid and semi-tropical lands extending south and west from Gohha. It is a remote and untamed wilderness south of central Illystra.

Arcane Histories: There have been many Arcane Histories written, especially in the days of Nystol's waxing. This was because the various arcane systems required explanation for initiates. However, most of the old histories vanished in the flames of the Great Burning. Now only fragments survive, but most notably the histories of Voethius written after the burning in his attempt to give an impression of what was lost.

Arcavir: a mysterious office of elphic origin who were watcher-guardians over the Illystra continent, reputed to be half-gnomes.

Archsin: A term denoting the original transgression of the first humans, (the primordial couple). This was accomplished by encouragement of the devil, whom God permitted to take the form of a serpent and who communicated by *telepathica,* with false promise of promotion, (*"ye shall be as gods"*). Consequently the immediate communication with the divine Creator was forfeit, so expulsion from the earthly Paradise; the Archsin was serious, and also by law incurred the penalty of death to all the human race. The deadly curse of the Archsin was to be passed down to all subsequent generations. In Furthlore it is also recorded in *The Golden Pages of the Wind.*

Ardeheim: A great and ancient land of brown dusts storms and terrible rocky wastelands in the central and northern bounds of Illystra. This vast land, now called Kargiwall, has fought many wars a with Ulthuring. Its dangerous vastness is a refuge for mauraders and evil doers.

Arguzinial: Various spellings and pronunciations are found: Argunizial, Acusynicul, Achozinaal, Akkyrzal, etc. This mountain is considered sacred by all the nations of Illystra. It is located in the south of the Niruz Peninsula in remote forests.

Arraf: Meaning "East". . . a general designation referring to mideastern desert realms, such as Kithom, Kutaal, Vesulum, Vath, Namaliel, Sarnas, Atalur, Succon, and Gohha, all of which speak a variant of the Kutaal.

Arvad, Sea of, Isle of Arvad: The Isle in the Sea of Goldindol which was settled by hycmen in the seventh century before the great burning.

Ashkehon: (read also Isle of Arvad entry) Long ago, an Ammouric prophetess who dwelt among the Atlanteans spake unto the mothers of the hycman race, and bade them pressure the Atlantean lords to build a stronghold for their half-breed descendants who would return in a distant time and even "help to save the furthworld from darkness," The day would come, they warned, when the Atlantean blood would run out and cease to rear mighty men, save for the hycmen scion. Wherefore consenting did the Atlanteans built the mighty fortress Ashkehon on the isle of Arvad, fortified with giant slabs of Kobbite stone from the Andolyn Mountains, and concealed it in a cloud of mist "until the time of the new race would come".

Ashkhar: The divine kingdom of Allfather which surrounded mount Argunizial in the first age.

Asphyl, Lake: A great inland swampy but half-dead sea south of the sea of Immanent waves and bordering Atalur.

Asosmos: The wild and impossible-to-rule hill-lands north of Rumilia.

Andolyn Mts: The older name and central part of the Antelynk Range.

Antilynk range: The great chain of young mountains which divides western Illystra from the eastern plains and deserts.

Azerdon: A feudal kingdom tucked safely away in the Andolyn mountains. The palaces and halls of Azerdon are noted for their beauty. A sanctuary for wizards from very early times, it is said to have once rivaled Nystol in learning.

Atalur: A land of many minor city-states or western principalities in Arraf, founded of the Atlantean colonists in the second age. Eleven castles lie astride the pass from Namaliel on the east shore of the Sea of Goldindol.. The secret of Ataluran arms and especially armour is unknown, but they are famous and highly prized by royal and noble families throughout Illystra.

Auroran Wars: "dawn-wars," archaic title for a number of conflicts and battles fought at the dawn of time, the first being the expulsion of Lucifer from Heaven.

Authapian: qv. *Outhapis*

Authapis: The city-state founded in the west by orientals who migrated from Anshan in the second age. Authapis was built over the post-volcanic submerged ruins of the very ancient city Outhapis, (a semi-phonetic namesake). The city has defensive walls second only to its neighbor Urguard. Colonists from oriental Anshan built Authapis upon the ruins of buried Outhapis during the end 0f the second world age. The walled city of "Imperial Authapis" is generally self-sufficient and strongly discourages cultural mixing with western peoples.

Ayrs (Aethuria): The forgotten kingdom of half-elves, valraphs, in the sub-arctic pine regions of the Great Northern Forests. Ayrs was destroyed in the *Bellum Diabolicum* by the Mulcifer the Elder and his massive armies. Her castles now stand empty. The surviving bands of valraphs encountered in the furth are permanent refugees from their homeland.

Bamusk, straits of: These straits are believed to separate the southern Illystra seas from the far eastern sea of Anosh

Banelord: See *Nimrul*.

Bannock: Furth-name for Arizel the wizard.

Bardelith: The wild and remote sub-arctic lands of northern central Illystra. Legendary home of Illystra bards.

Bellum Diabolicum: "The diabolic war." Prosecuted principally by Nimrul the Banelord, this war changed the face of all Illystra. The orcan and barbaric human armies, united under the banner of the Black Claw of Mulg, invaded all the civil lands.

Black Books of Melancholia. The contents of these mysterious tomes only are left in fragments. Thought to be compendiums including histories of Illystra and arcane studies, these are records of kings, wisdom and lore, and sacred poems, coded keys and enigmas all bound up with the world-destiny.

Bolg, Horg: Ancient terms, sometimes confused, referring to the considerably warlike and fallen elphic races who form armies and raid the surface of earth. The teaching of the wise identifies them as fallen spirits incarnated. According to legend all fairy were the result of angels who failed to take sides during the holy war against Lucifer.

Bolg Wall: fortified and monumental work of architecture rising some hundreds of feet into the sky of Arahom. It was built by the Ulthurings in the fourth world age to keep out the bolg armies of Nzulg.

Book of Bloody Battles: Duke Ikonn's own words describing collected events his dungeoneering campaigns throughout Illystra in ancient times.

Bzebus leaf: the wide fronds of the plant used for manufacture of scrolls which deal with magic. The flowers are an unusual scarlet colour and emit a rotting smell, which entraps and digests flys. *Bemble leaf* on the other hand is similarly shaped but the flowers are white and saffron, attracting bumble bees. It nourishes the bees with nectar and in turn they protect the plant from larvae and other pests. It provides the preferred leaves for thaumaturgical scrolls and the works of poets and theologians.

Budderham: A grandfatherly figure who dwells in the *Vale of Chimera* in a little villa tending his garden and supplying baked goods for wayfarers. He has been a key player in political dramas of the continent, and his wisdom is sought even by Emperors and Patriarchs. It is said that he is over 500 years old.

Canyon of Hermius: The canyon was forged by the Alph river, sacred to the Ammouri, which flows southward from a place in the Antylynk mountain range. Some even say that the Alph river connects by underground flows not to the Lesser Mountains, but to mount Argunizial. "Where Alph the sacred river ran, through caverns measureless to Man..." Hermius disappeared into the canyon with his legions and legend asserts that he was defeated on "the Isle of the Harpies." His vast treasure horde is said to be hidden away somewhere within his tomb in those parts.

Cathon: A region of hills east and south of Kithom

Chyldirwood: This vast deciduous forest once extended all the way from western Ardeheim down into Aquilaris. On account of Imperial Forestation however, most of the forest now only extends into central Rumilia. *Chyldishire Forest*: lit. "Children's shire-Forest"; a vast and mysterious deciduous forest west of the Antylink range...once home of the WoodElves.

Chumnut Oasis

Crach Mountains: Also called *The Cracked Mountains* because of their appearance; these merciless and desolate northern mountains are avoided by all except the most daring.

Chronian Sea: some geographers say it is an old name for the southern stretches of Vastess Ocean, while others have insisted that it includes all the seas of the far eastern shores of Illystra as well.

Chymera,Vale of: A valley of the Andolyn mountains long rumoured to be haunted by a chimera beast. This peaceful valley is a commonly used passage for those going east. Here also is found the house of old Budderham, a friendly mountaineer.

crizet: A unit of gold or platinum coin. Ten silver crizets equal a gold piece (croat). One croat buys a skin of vanic wine. Sixty croats buys a good pack-horse.

Culduin (alt., Calduin): A planet of unknown identification, possibly Mars, but certainly not the moon, often used by Illystras but especially travelers of intermundane lands to keep time. Most scholars insist that this planet or heavenly body was once quite visible in the ages of Illystra, but centuries ago strayed from its orbit and was forever lost.

darfur: a kind of deep grey tinged with red.

Dice of Golgotha; also called "The Bone Dice of the Legionaries." These relics, four Roman six-sided dice, are the same which Roman legionaries used to cast lots for Christ's garment at the crucifixion. They are recorded in Illystra at the end of the fourth age. It is unknown why they came, or who brought them, but they are among the most important of the relics sought. The Guild of St. Dismas claims the dice. They say that a certain cleric, "Marconius" has stolen away with them. The powers of the dice are mysterious and unknown. It is insisted by Church officials that they not be rolled. They have funded guild expeditions to find them.

Dragons: "the seed of Ocean" all dragons are sprung from Vorthragna mother of dragons, who according to the myth embraced Oceanus the titan. Guy of Xaragia claims that chromatic dragons, red, green, white, black ect, are an evil brood, and good are the metallic such as copper, bronze, and silver, gold. According to Morpheus Memnos however, only Neoplatonian Dragons are earnestly righteous.

Draker (dungeoneer's slang), fr. Gk. drakon (and later drake, denoting a winged dragon): The word draker is a pejorative: a coward.

Drakodemon: Greek transliteration for -spirit.

Dry Blood Sea: (Dry Blood Dunes) part of the Great Southern Desert, the Dry Blood Sea has the appearance of a sea of red sands and stretches from Atalur to The Deadly Hills and Nystol, and from Namaliel to Sarnas. See entry on *Mercurius Yod* for further lore on the Dry Blood Sea.

Duke Ikonn: "the Maurader of Worlds" the title was unfairly given to this high adventurer who first arrived in Illystra in the Second world-age and was the first "Conquistador" from the Western Reaches to explore all the lands. He was accompanied by such noteworthies as Kruth the gnome, Elkomenon the wizard, Petrozean the dauntless, and Godiun Foute the thief. Records of their adventures, such as the *Xilmurian Epic*, (the contest against the Banelord Synostochs and their exploration of the dome-city Qui), and the *Oceanicon*, (explorations of Thule, the Northern Warm Sea, and Golden Coasts) existed for hundreds of years as bardic entertainment and but the writings have yet to be recovered.

Durgoth: The northern wooded lands beyond the great lakes is inhabited by the Durgoth barbarians. They were once a noble-hearted and independent breed of righteous men who live beyond the civil lands. They have now become Arian heretics.

Dwarf; Closer to men than the ancient elves, the dwarves have even been identified as stunted valraphs. This insult to them however is to be avoided. Their culture, histories and talents are quite distinct from both men and elves, for there are never any credible reports of half-dwarves. They are however surely a kind of *elphim*, and are famous in legend for having brought low the giants of old. One evil dwarf, Nergalf, even claimed royal descent from a Maceonid king (likely a falsity) and by warfare became Emperor of all the Furth for a time.

Ebberhar River flows north out of the Lessarlik Mounatins and is extremely twisting and difficult to navigate.

Edolunt Rangers: originally an order of lawful good Rangers who patrolled the Furthlands and the Frontier. Some of these were Ammoutic knights. After the fall of the old republic, the empire co-opted the order, expelled the Ammouric grand knight, and changed them to lawful neutral.

Eleusinion: see *Kruth*

Eldark (adj.): On account of the famous wisdom of the Eldari, the adjective *Eldark* came into general usage denoting anything displaying an ancient and seemingly dark (ie. pre-Christian) or arcane wisdom. *Eldari* (also adj.; Eldaric, Eldark, Eldrist, and n. in sindari tongue, *Elthildor*): The foremost authorities of wisdom available before the revelation of the All-law. Their theology was henotheistic, positing many gods emanating from a non-personal deity, a supernal force. This group cannot be pinned down to a certain location or culture, and many believe that it was a secret society who has preserved lore from the first age, even tracing their name back to the race of Elthildor. Their religious system was based on a philosophy having many similarities with Neoplatonic theurgy. Later, certain Arcanes adopted the system and kept to the old wisdom, (eventhough it was thought defunct by the latter day Archsages). Such throwbacks were called the Eldari and they gained a reputation for great transcendental magic. Some of these survived the great burning and later came to embrace the All-law, Anherm of Whigg being the most noteworthy of these.

Elfshade: A pervasive vine which strangles trees. The vines have spread out though forests across northern Illystra and its leaves, it is said, can hear the talk of men.

Elkomenon (Al-comemnon): reputed to be the founder of the Order of Mages, a descendent of the idolater Chus. It is on account of his instruction that magic-users wear the conical hat with astrological signs. A ancient report exists that this mage died of a parasitic infection on the distant Isle of Dreadful Afternoons. His corpse holds some sort of magic mirror. Another epic tale asserts that he was seized with ardor by the *belle Dame sans merci,* Lazaria, and died of a poet's heartbreak, but this is apocryphal.

Elphim: A general term for all rational races other than humans and angels.

Elthildor: See *Eldari* above.

Elves-high elves: they left the furth, and all the world, because of the overwhelming injustice of men.

Erelim (Akaratic *erelim): the holy angels from Heaven

Folia (Latin): leaves or pages of a book folia (Latin) "leaves"; most often refers to the leaves of a book, ie. the pages, which are likened to leaves on a tree. Great books are often called "trees" in the intermundia, to disguise their presence from the unlearned and hostile.

Furth High King: Most consider this title to belong to Christ himself, ruling from afar upon Mt Argunizial, until wickedness becomes too great and he returns to the middle earth to set things right. The title is also associated with the highest of the celestial spheres.

Furthreach, furthworld, furthlands, (furthlore): A name for the great Illystra continent. A name for the great Illystra continent. The word Furth is the most ancient known appellation for the continent, far older than Illystra, and has been found in a manuscript dating to the early second age. This manuscript has various diagrams of celestial bodies, namely "the wheels of the sky which only the elf-kin can see, and which only the righteous can hear" the most sublime of which is called "The Furth High Wheel." How it came to designate the continent is unknown.

Furthsea: includes all conjoined interior seas: the Sea of Goldyndol, the Sea of Ymmin, and the Sea of Shirvav.

Friars of Whigg: reputedly the greatest theologians of all the western Furth, they nevertheless accepted the novel, much disputed, and quite clearly erroneous proposition that the ancient wizards of Nystol may be lawfully resurrected.

Gandolon: The wondrous and prosperous capital of Isauria. Trade-goods from all over the furthworld may be found in market places of towering Gandolon

Garmsir: A vast network of tomb-labyrinths somewhere east of the Deadly Hills.

Gates of Dariel: Colossal gates of bronze and adamantine construction built by Hermius the Conqueror in the third age. These gates block the sole passage through the Valaghir mountains on the Isthmus of Hyrcanth

Gederon, Plain of: The site in Arahom identified as the fields of battle for the wars of the Allfather against the drakodemon. Prophecy also names it the place of the final battle between the wicked and the just.

Gelf; the name is a contraction Ge+elf (Lit. "Earth-elf," also called Cave-elves). Originally a breed of wood-elf but their clans inhabit the caves of earth and they often traverse the intermundane regions. Unlike the Drow or Grey Elves from the deepest regions, the gelves are not morally ambivalent or mischievous. Explorers of the caverns put a high value on taking along these "Rangers of the Deep," who are expert at spelunking and rescue, and have a keen knowledge of all things intermundane.

Guy of Xaragia: an encyclopediast of the sixth age whose "gaming manuals" cover "the worlds," giving in mathematical terms the relative and statistical probabilities for all things; but especially entities of the intermundane regions, as well as spellcraft and demonology, of which he had suspiciously keen knowledge. Some speculate that he was a wizard.

Gnostic: An early heresy which blends Christian teachings with Platonic philosophy and traditional myth. Condemned by the Ammouric Church, the dualist theology is applied to many pagan religions as well; for example, the Egyptian cultus of *Hearers of the Dead in Ashkehon q.v.* The outcome of this for the cosmology is a kind of spiritual inversion of roles: the Creator of all things must be considered an evil puppet master, since matter/flesh/darkness, which he created, is opposed to form/spirit/light. This inversion must appoint demons as liberators and heavenly angels as jailors, *"archons"*. The various cults, the most notable here be the infernal monks of Intermundia, *monachi infernales de mundo subterraneo* generally install strict hierarchies of masters claiming possession of the secret knowledge, knowledge necessary for the soul's escape at death from the world-prison. The heresy also denies that Christ died and resurrected physically from the tomb, instead claiming only his spirit rose.

Gnome: a mysterious being of elphic nature who is a watcher-guardian over the Illystra continent. Originally the mischievous race of "gnomes" inhabited various woodlands and caverns. First mentioned by a Roman legionary in the 2nd century, their presence in modern gardens, albeit in a state of petrifaction, is symbolic and noteworthy. It has been suggested that these little statues are reminders of the old trickster lurking in the garden paradisial. Contrary interpretations have been proposed; the most notable is this one: when depicted in Christian iconography, they are *apotropaic*; righteous guardians *turning away* evil spirits, as do the monstrous gargoyles. At any rate, their conical hats do connote magical abilities, and as lore-keepers they carry all the memory (*arcae*) of the furthlands.

Gnotus (Notus): The famous bronze dragon, the first Neoplatonian, whose wisdom angered other dragons. Also a friend of Fendil the elf.

Golden Pages of the Wind A mysterious and sacred work of most ancient Akaratic script. Its divine science tells the story of the Wind which moved over the face of the primordial waters, the prophecy of the cosmoid, and many other inexpressible things.

Godiun Fout: A famous rogue and thief whose exploits are the stuff of high entertainment throughout all the Furth. Godiun Fout lived in the time of legendary King Ikonn and is reputed to have been hired by the Duke for various "expeditions".

Gohha: A kingdom settled by Egyptian explorers in the second age. Gohha consists of two princedoms: Sarnas and Succon. Of old Gohha was called Mizraim.

Goldyndol, Sea of: Bounded by the Isle of Arvad in the south and the shores of Mulrud, Hyrticum, and Baradeium to the west, Niruz to the east, this stormy sea is said to radiate a golden color during the moonrises of autumn. Throughout the entire shores of this sea are found various villages of different varieties of men, including the hycsoth, who, having been marginalized, set up a kingdom on the Isle of Arvad.

Gulconda: A winding network of natural caves, tunnels, and chambers that are beneath the deserts leading to the Sardu Mesa and Nystol. Many of the tunnels were dug out by giant vermilion sand worms in early ages. It is said to be extremely dangerous, but hides many treasures, especially diamonds. The word is also used for the immortal speech of dragons, since it was in Gulconda that Gnotus, first to use the speech, was buried. Some say that it is a form of telepathica.

Harpies, Isle of: mysterious rock islands in the sea of Ymmin. Haunted by the terrible man-eaters, it is forbidden by the rule of the Kalar Empire to go there.

Hellopian Ivy: once native only to Mullith, the ivy is widely considered magical and its properties are unknown, Its buds, branch-spindles, and stalks are reddish and the leaf shape and markings resemble red eyes. Hence its alternate name 'watcher ivy". It is not known in the norther continent, and is found mostly in Mullith, Authapis, and the ivy is dominant on the Sardu Plateau, where it has overgrown the ruins of Nystol. It is called Hellopian "Hell-eyes" because legend has it that its roots go as deep as Hell and are connected to that underworld realm to which its watching leaves give report of all that transpires in the world of men.

Hermopolis: far bordering the east of Kalar Maurob, founded by Hermius the great, once boasted the greatest collection of scrolls east of Nystol and in its zenith was called the jewel of all Arraf (the East). After the wars with Xartizan and the ascendency of the Kalar Empire, the city, mostly cut off from western trade, rapidly declined. Hermopolis now is lawless and mostly in ruins, its great halls and temples, not far from the sea, are the haunts of bandits, thieves, and other underworld elements.

Hermit's hills

Homonculous: an automaton or subcreature designed by a wizard, sometimes humanoid in shape, with wings. The are remote controlled and used for spying.

Horg; also, *Bolg* (pl.*Horgrim, Bolgrim*; spelling varies) (adj. *horgoth, bolgoth):* Shortened form of "Hobgoblin." See "Bolg"

HorgWall: This fortified and monumental work of architecture rises some hundreds of feet into the sky of Arahom. It was built by the Ulthurings in the fourth world age to keep out the horg armies of Baffay.

Hyperlyptic Alignment: An alignment of the planets well known and used by Arcanes but no longer able to be determined.

Hypostatic Rift: This was a world-changing rift in the fabric of the Cosmoid which occurred on account of space, time and cause—being idealized beyond the metaphysical predeterminates of the known. Voethius claims it was the result of a conspiracy. It first took shape in two opposed camps of Arcanes on disagreement over how matter and form combine in a substantial (and corresponding superstantial). The Arcane of infamous repute, Scardetes, tried to resolve the issue in his work *Irreconcilables*, but made the rift even worse. At last the dilemma was projected and the rift itself incremented just like a virus contaminating all superstantial reality. Attempts at reconciliation by the Soothfold merely resulted in closing off the psychical vortex from the valent imagination. The Sorcerers took advantage of the chaotic situation and obtained the Arcane hegemony. All elemental and modal casting was superceded by spiritual and illusory spells.

Hyrcanth: One of the heretical Arian Kingdoms. The lowlands connecting the Valaghir and Ptur with the Arahom and the northern lands. Covered over by the Sea of Goldyndol in ancient times, this allowed the civil lands to develop without being harassed by the northern barbarians. Later, when the sea withdrew, Hermius the Conqueror had to build the great bronze gates at the Pass of Dariel to keep them out. The barbarians claim to have originated from the ancient mountainous land of North Hyrcanthia (Nathycanis) in the west.

Hzothic Peninsula: The semi-arctic peninsula which juts northward from Nathycanis; its main city is the port Ael Lot.

Illystra (variant in Osril: Yllistra, Ilyster): The continent was originally called "*Illystrax*" or "*Illystrias*" which translates "Whitehawk." This was the ancient name and is still kept untranslated in the oldest accounts. "Whitehawk" eventually came to designate all the Christian kingdoms of the Furth, indeed the entire world-age, and again as the faith spread was expanded to mean the entire continent.

Immanent Waves, Sea of: also called Sea of Ymmin (q.v)

Intermundian, intermundane: Latin "between the worlds" It is often claimed that the philosopher Lucretius coined the word "intermundia," a space between the worlds, in his infamous work De Rerum Natura, in order to describe the material plane's intersection with the etherial. Although it is true that he made the word famous, and that the term is indeed from the fourth age, it was in use (mostly as an adjective describing the underworld) throughout the Regulian Empire long before. The most perplexing of all intermundane spaces is Purgatory, since it somehow is not quite timeless as Eternity, yet at the same time must be a temporally qualified reality. Its holy fires effect a spiritual change (purification, purgation), and yet change is not thought to happen outside of created time. Nevertheless, not only is Purgatory attested to by all the saints, but it would be logically inconceivable for such not to exist, considering the imperfection of the human race in contrast to the divine mandate to *be perfect*, notwithstanding the revelation of God's mercy.

Irbath (Yrbath): Naval port and principle city of Ulthor, also called Ulthor upon-the-Sea.

Itruria: A contested political region of the second world ruled by the cities which later became the Itrurian federation: Orusca, Urguard, and Authapis. The region was of unknown extent: possibly stretching from the shores of the Vastess sea as far as the Sardu Mesa.

Isauria: The kingdom of the diamond cities and Gandolon. Mostly tropical mountains, its interior is not well patrolled and much is impenetrable. Travelors to Gandolon must sail along the coast.

Isle of Vath: A city carved into a Rock-island in The Dry Blood Sea. Its original inhabitants were possibly Vri, but Hycmen fugitives from Gohha took it over at the end of the third age.

Iquizan: A wondrous city of a pyramidal temples in unknown but wealthy people from the second age in the fertile region of the Arcodon peninsula. Now it is in ruins and difficult to find.

Kanats, plain of: The arid rocky land which separates Atalur and the dry Blood Sea from Kalar and Gohha

Kalar Maurob: The great city of the Kalar Empire which is closed to westerners.
Kalaralu: in the land of Lud, meadows sacred to all Illystra for incense harvest.

Kasgir (Xasbur): One of the furthest known eastern lands which is bounded by the Arms of Mt Abaddon to the North and the Sea of Shirvav to the West. Aetholus records that the people are distantly related to breakaways from the Atlantean Army of Turbolion. Their Atlantean physique, bright hair, brown skin and bluish lips give them a distinctive look. Unlike the Trubolite lords they dwell as horsemen on the plains and are peaceful. In the middle centuries of third age they were compelled to take up the heretical devotion of the Bah Ukah and worship the emblem of Green Eagle, but it is said that they think little of such rites and only practice in order to appease their conquerors the Kalar Maurob.

Kedemoth: The semi-arid bush-forests and desert which surrounds and includes the Sardu mesa. Home of Morpheus Memnos.

Kiluria (see *Siluria*)

Kithom: The semi-arid plains north of the Dry Blood Sea where many bandits and lawless types have found habitations.

Kleptarch: A master thief and ruler of an underworld gang of thieves. The most notorius of these was Kluxatta, and later Godiun Fout (Quodiun). Some claimed that the gelf Gulathar, who opened the bronze gates of Hermius, was a kleptarch, but this accusation is unfounded and probably based on hostility to the foolishness of his senility. The "reigns" of kleptarchs are commonly rather short, and Gulathar was said to have lived several hundred years.

Krithusel: see Kruth

Koph Southern jungles of: mystery south of Mullith, where is found the pyramid of the Scull

Kutaal: vast region of semi-arid grasslands that in the north borders the desert of Kithom (Kathon). The capital of Kutaal was the coastal city Namaliel in ancient times. This region is also the name of the great race sprung of the youngest son of Maceon, Kutaal, who refused to leave his brother go alone into exile. He was given reign of the vast region of semi-arid grasslands that in the north borders the desert of Kithom (Kathon) The capital of Kutaal was the coastal city Namaliel in ancient times, until it was devastated by successive raids of the Atalur, Kalar, Dark Orkhan and the Imperial Armies. The Kutaal do not mix with other races, and droves of various foreigners in their beloved city made it too dangerous for them to live there.   But another city would arise for them.

Kruth: name in usage among the nations of men for the Arcavir and gnome Krithusel Eloniah. Anciently the name was short for Kruthius, or Kruthulus Eleusinion, perhaps a reference to the Eleusinian mysteries of ancient Greece, of which some suggest he was wont to attend. However other scholars assert that this was a mistranscription of his prophetic Hebrew name Eloniah, upon which the Ammouri associated his gnomish sub-religion.The Elves and Dwarves call him Kruthendel in accord with linguistic need.

Lamessia: ancient town of the Orcodoth peninsula

Lazaria: the most notorious temptress of the ancient world. It is proposed that she may have been a witch, but this is unsubstantiated. Men from all around the Illystra continent desired her, even fought over her, but she had little virtue other than her alluring beauty. The greatest legend, probably true, asserts that the army of Hermius the Conqueror saw her and they asked that she dance for them. An quarrel over which general she would sit at table with shortly ensued and broke out into rash killing, ending with the internecine slaughter of almost the entire army.

Lessarlik Mountains; northern reach of the Antylink chain, home of the dwarven-city of Ebberhar.

Lokken: a wilderness of forests, hills, lakes, and barren wolds which comprises most of the grand isle St. Aldemar. The vast and hilly coniferous forest is known as the Timberhills. There is also a mysterious Ringwood, and the St. Sarak mnts. with their Chestnut Vale and the Long Valchines in the North.

Maboloth, an ancient pine forest of vast extent: location now uncertain, but believed to be somewhere in Aramthe.

Maharim (pl.), (sing adj.=Mahark): the great confederacy of five barbaric tribes of the north, all of whom claim descent from Mahar. Their dominion stretches from Knum and the Eastern plains as far West as Arahom.

Maceonids: The descendants of Maceon, survivor of the great deluge of the first age. They became dynastic monarchs throughout the Illystra continent. and ruled from age to age, although at times they temporarily forfeited sovereignty, such as under the Atalur, and the Aideen and Regulian empires. The Maceonid League of Kings was sometimes formed to fight against such overwhelming powers. Not all Maceonids became Ammouric, "white-robed" kings, but some, such as the Maharim and the King of Kargiwall, and a few other apostates, remained heathen.

Mahanaxar: The great arid tropical country of western Illystra, wild and dangerous.

Mahar: The third Son of Maceon described as one "who was filled with violence." He was apportioned "the wild places and wastes, impenetrable forests of the continent's furth bounds..." So did he go to dwell in the great northern forest and became the patriarch of the barbaric races.

Magi: mages pl. for *Magus.* The order of Mages in Nystol was the foundational order. Magi (pl. for Magus): *descr. from Voethius' Arcane Histories, (an interview with Kruthendel Eleusinion)* The Magus was an adept in the first magic, the proto-Avestic system initiated during the Antideluvian Era, which combines an archaic glyph system of Astral tuning with light-manipulations generating in degrees radiant matter from the preternatural fonts.

Mercurius Yod: see the Incomprehensible Scroll of Yod (appendix) a heathen seer of the Third Age of the world. He claimed to have seen visions of past, present, and future events. There is a vast desert of incarnadine sand dunes which dominates the center of the Illystra continent. Tradition holds that the sands became reddish in colour during the second age. The story claims that Gnotus (also sp. Notus), lay upon the sands bleeding for nigh a century. The sage Morpheus Memnos recorded the wisdom which he sang, the mysterious *Vortex Poem* also called "the meta prophecies" which the great one recited, which is said to be lost somewhere in the nine thousand and ninety-nine pages of the books of melancholy. Mercurius Yod preserved this lore in the first encyclopedia of all the Furth.

Morpheus Memnos: A great sage of Nystol, see above entry on Mercurius Yod.

Monad: A Pythagorean conception of ultimate reality as the one ground of undivided being from which comes all things and to which all things must return.

Mulg (Mulcifer) Warlord and Anarch of the Troll Horde, vassal to Nimrul and intensely loyal and ferocious, he is said to be part giant.

Murmrik river

Namaliel: Eastern city-states on the western shore of the Sea of Ymmin. Namaliel is renowned for its fine horses. It has had to fight wars on occasion against the Kalar Empire over sea-trading rights.

Narcissus Text: A number of texts, scrolls, and/or codices, manufactured in the fourth age by the infernal monks. These have the power to entrap the reader with the allurement of enchanted and forbidden knowledge, whereby the soul is ensnared gazing at the text, reading and re-reading, and with the consequent neglect of all else. The reader is typically found dead, his boney fingers gripping the book, overcome by self-neglect of nourishment or dehydration.

Nathycanthe, Northyrcanth: Originally the province North Hyrcanthia. Once a mountainous and forested kingdom of reclusive elf-kin in the second age, no one any longer dares to enter into the great round mountains of Nathycanis. It is said that the mountains of misty forests are quiet and unsettling to most humans. There are known to be subterraneous complexes in the mountains from which no one has returned.

Nazageist (dwarven): See *Nimrul, note.*

Non-void: the fact that there was no primordial nothingness, no chaos-void from which things mysteriously arose, for there is no such thing as nothing, and before all things were there was light from light, God. This contemplation is a remedy for Melancholia.

Nephilung: Kruth the Eleusinion (Eloniah) wrote a bestiary and travelogue for underworld explorers, which he titled the Enchiridion or "handbook." The following I took from an entry found therein: NEPHILUNG (Subaetherialis Nephilung, Anahit): These fallen beings, unlike angels or demons, are visible and physic powers. By the men of Kargiwall, old Ardeheim, they call them nebilung, creature of the mist, in the East they know them as Anahit or Djinn. Some appear as beautiful divinities and they shall bid that ye worship them and assent to their spiritual service. Others take on the semblance of gargoyles. They are the mysterious nephilim of old who once defended the Kingdom of the Holy against the rebel elves of shadow. These beings, unlike angels and demons, have visible non-generative bodies which are made of the most subtle hypotomica, of material physic sourced in superstantial aether. Some sources say they numbered nine, others twelve and twenty-four, being divided into lesser and greater.   *Nephilung (nephilim=pl.)* These entities, unlike angels and demons, have visible non-generative bodies made of the most subtle *hypotomica*, of material physic sourced in superstantial aether. Some sources say they numbered nine, others twelve and twenty-four, being divided into lesser and greater, which pagans esteemed as gods. The only nephilung who has remained loyal to God, as far as is known, is the Agathodaemonian Prince of the Nephilim himself, Ambrosius the lion-head, guardian of the Ammouri. In time the others all betrayed the Ancientmost and they fled into the dark places of the world. They have many powers but must remain locked in the physical world, and though their bodies are of ethereal mould, they can still be wounded by employing blessed weapons. See entry *Nephilung* in appendix for more.

In the Age of Heroes the Anahit greatly vexed the upper world in the form of titanic Netherbeasts, to the extent that men even built great garrisoned walls and forts at the entrances to the deeper regions to block their passage. The gorgon Medusa of the ancient Greek accounts seems to have been in reality one of these Anahit. They have many powers but must remain locked in the physical world, and though their bodies are of ethereal moulde, they can still be wounded by employing blessed weapons.

Neoplatonian Dragon: A special fold of dragons who had reformed themselves and who wisdom closely corresponded to the philosophy of the Neoplatonian Sages of the ancient world. The dragons convicted of corrupting dragon nature and slain in aerial combats in the second age.

Nimrul: the elf who led a great rebellion against the Furth High King. His punishment is to never die. He was assigned as elemental archon to the northern darkness, and became the *Dire of Melancholia*. –also called *Northing*.

Nine Feudatories: Another name for Osring. These minor feudal Ammouric kingdoms share a common northern language and culture as well as Rumilian laws and learning.

Niruz: The peninsula that extends south from Thasos unto the Sea of Goldindol. It is mountainous, heavily forested, and mostly unexplored, having several rivers that create massive cataracts in the mountains. The mountains are bare and usually without snow. There has been reported at least four strongholds deep in the mountains which are of cyclopean architecture, probably the work of Stone Giants. No orcs or kobolds dwell there, or any other intellectons. However, there are fearsome direwolves, bears and cavecats. It is believed that a race of cannibals known as the Yssedones lived in ancient times on the western shore but were utterly destroyed by the Tyrbolite warlords. From hither come the race of men known as the Hulken or Hulders, these huge men measure on average seven to eight feet tall and are of massive build, adapted well for their mountanous villages.

Notus (archaic spelling): See *Gnotus*.

Northing: common name for "thing of the north," the Dire of Melancholy.

Nystol (Nyzium): Concerning this usage below *Nyzium.* Nystol (Nyzium) the older form of the college's name commonly used by non-Latin speakers. Although originally in the eldark usage it was always Nystol, this probably is a contraction from the Greek, Nystopolis, ie. "city of Nystul". The name Nystul perhaps can be attributed to a great wizard of dungeoneering lore, the fanciful tales about whom claim that he was author of many dangerous spells. Whatever the case, he was associated with the founding of the city in the second age, according to the ancient writer Guy of Xaragia.

Nystoli: Term referring to those Arcanes of Nystol whose memory or knowledge stretched back to the very founding of the same remote college itself.

Nystopolis: See *Nystol* above.

Nyzium (Latinized form of Nystopolis, "Nystol" commonly used): This is the ancient tower-complex of wizardic colleges which once sat atop the sheer Sardu mesa. In some ancient texts, such as the scrolls Of Mercurius Yod, the name is spelled "Gnostul" which would suggest a connection with the Greek word for knowledge, *gnosis,* hence Gnosticism. Gnosticism is the principal heresy associated with wizardry and is a source of many scroll-spells. Another etymology points to the legend of a certain wizard of the second world-age, Nystul, who is said to have been an advisor in the building of the city's wondrous architecture. (See also above entry: *Nystol).*

Nzul: the dark kingdom of the Northing, with its fiefdoms in Bardelith. Zabul (Zabolg, Nzulg): The super-fortress of the Nazageist located somewhere in the Crach mountains. It is said to be a horrible place of smoke, iron, black towers and unthinkably huge architecture, a typical dwelling for any master of evil. No one save Argoth and a few survivors of the Bladetongue have ever returned from there, so there is little to report. It was built by Thendyl the Archdeceiver to be higher than the throneroom of Mt. Argunizial. Trolls, goblins, and other hideous creatures patrol its walls and territories. Legend asserts that its library is in the shape of a horrible maze of book-stacks whose texts curse those who read them with insanity. Further descriptions were recorded in the final chapters of the Bladetongue, but the dark powers have managed to destroy those chapters.

Notus (archaic spelling) see *Gnotus.*

Oceanicon: The journal of Duke Ikonn detailing the events of his sailing around the Furthshores.

Oceanicyng, (Oceanicyng Oceanicurst) Duke Ikonn's heirloom sword, supposedly forged in the first age by the Vanir (Nephilim)

Oneghern: A volcanic mountain in the north-eastern bounds of Kargiwall

Orusca: An ancient city state of Greek-speakers south of the Anylynk mtns.

Osring: See the Nine Feudatories (above)

Othgog: a huge tower-prison on the isle of Cranits in the sea of Goldyndol, reserved for the worst criminals of the furth. It is said to be a stronghold from which it is impossible to escape.

Olophyxus: A famous Rumilian astronomer who wrote prophetic treatises at the end of the third world-age.

Old Budderham: Little is known about this enigmatic figure. He is called "Grandfather of All the Furth," and is considered the wisest man of all Whitehawk and the Furthreaches. He has lived from seemingly time immemoral in a cane-zigur roundhouse somewhere in the forgotten and unpatrolled Vale of Chymera in the Andolyn Mountains. It is said that he is hundreds of years old. Often patriarchs, kings, and heroes will journey to visit him and ask for advice, which he gives while chopping wood, sheering sheep, tending his garden, or household chores (his wife passed on centuries ago). Strangely, this has never in any way come off as rude. He also looks after some sort of special Nautilus shell that magically floats in a meadow of the vicinity, within which the performances and ancient lore of the great bards have been somehow rolled up and preserved.

Outhapis (also Authaphis) perhaps the most ancient of Illystra city-states which, like Pompei of the Romans, was completely covered in volcanic ash in the second age.

Passings: Refers to the orbit of the planet Calduin or the sky ring associated with it, as a calculation of time, perhaps similar to the Martian year.

Plathonis: A far northern kingdom of the west, bordering the North Sea. Once famously inhabited by the high elves who ruled the forests with ruthless dominion, but now entirely mysterious. Human population is scarce, found only in fishing communities upon the shores of the sea, and no great cities are found there.

Prime Mover: Some wisemen maintain that certitudes can be deduced by reason concerning the originator of all reality. the philosophers call an "uncreated and only necessary being and power," though according to them, it has no discernible personality. Schools of philosophy arose which posited the absurdity that there could be more than one Prime Mover. In their obstinacy, they began to call upon "powers" which they called "The Black Prime Movers." Thus, they added witness to the apothegm, "philosophy is the mother of all heresies." The orders of Infernal Monks were originally begun by these philosophers.

Ptur: a powerful city state and miltocracy governing the Valaghir Mountains. The ancient fortress was built neath the eaves of the Valaghir mountains by Cromhur.

Pyramid of the Skull: A frightening pyramid that seems to suggest a skull upon its north face. It is located in the jungles south of Mullith. Mercurius Yod says that Duke Ikonn pursued the villain Synostochs into the pyramid and confronted him in combat on a bridge over something called the abysmal gap. Other expeditions have gone there and never returned.

Red Dwarves: (And The Wells of Fire): Also called the Hills of fire, these mountains are volcanic and known to often erupt spewing forth a mixture of lava and fiery ashes that float upward covering the entire dome of Heaven and darkening the coasts of the Sea of Goldyndol. The sea-bound Lava is very quick flowing and no man or beast may easily out run the devastation. The mountains themselves are deep red in colour. A tribe of dwarves with ruddy skin, known as the Rhypaeans (the Red Dwarves) actually inhabit several mountain cliff-villages not far from the lava rivers.

Regulia: The imperial dominion of the city Regulis, which long remained in the power of a Senatorial Hegemony, until the time of the Emperors. This domain extended south as far as Gorre and was bordered by the great River Washir and the Kingdom of Rumilia, which extended as far north as Nathycanis.

Regulis (Regulum): A Roman colony of the third age. After the expulsion of the Kings of Rome in Italy, eighty years from the collapse of the Aideen, the exiled kings entered Illystra and built Regulum on the Washir River, which pours into The Intermundane Sea in the temperate zone. They began establishing Roman law and engineering and the Latin language. After the expulsion of the Kings of Rome in Italy, and after the collapse of the Aideen, the exiled kings entered Illystra and built Regulis on the Washir River, which pours into intermundane sea in the temperate zone. The began establishing Roman Law and engineering. The city grew rapidly and overthrew many neighboring cities, establishing a commonwealth of Nord-Western lands. Interestingly, although the Latin language remained intact and the old Roman culture was preserved, nevertheless a rebellion did come on account of the abuse of power, and the Royal descendants of the Kings of Rome were, like their fathers, expelled, and a republic was founded. After years of warfare the Reguli finally conquered Rumilia and built a Principate, Regulia. They established roads and commerce throughout Illystra, as well as traditional veneration of the gods. Their Emperors, such as Echecrates, vastly improved the city, including libraries, plumbing, and theatre. After death some were venerated as gods. The city grew rapidly and overthrew many neighboring cities finally becoming the Empire.

Rumil: The Sons of Rumil founded this kingdomof diminutive size but huge inportance after conquering the Atlantean Allapis in the Second Age.

Scriptorium: Hall of a monastery in which monks do the sacred work of copying down or writing manuscripts.

Selva (fr. Gohhan): Originally meant simply "priest," of the Ammouric rite, but became most common term for "Christian priest" in Illystra (meaning "sacrificer").

Seed of Ocean: see *dragons*.

Serrian Way: This important trade road of highest construction was built by the Regulians under the councilship of Serrius. It ran from Regulian Allapis north along the shore of the Vastess Sea into Nathicanis, cuts through the Mountains of the Pleasant Rain as far as the Ruins of the Castle of Petroizean.

Soothfold: The conciliar body of Ammouric Sages in Illystra.

Sodd Bloodman: famous monk and warrior-poet from the period of Emerald Warriors. He vowed never to shed blood and was victorious in all his one hundred duels, save the last, in which he did shed blood. On that account he refused to fight anymore, and he ended in misery, having unsuccessfully wooed the temptress Lazaria.

Siluria:(also: *Kiluria*) A region of the second world-age, originally thought to refer to the coasts of Nathycanis, but now confirmed to be the original inhabitants of the dominion of Ael Lot and the island Aldemars

Shirvav, Sea of: The Eastern Sea of the central pontus

Sinostox, Prince (Sinostocs, Synostochs): A Banelord, reputed descendent of Maurob, the son of Maceon. The *Katabasid Sinostoxou*, an epic poem describing his dark quest and seizure of power, claims he is the son of Tithonus. Originally an Ammouric Knight, Prince Sinostox blamed Duke Ikonn for the slaughter of his family, and swore vengeance. Pursued by a gigantic Praying Mantis, this anti-hero fled into the underworld, where he obtained the accursed sword Elmethodon. Sworn archfoe of Duke Ikonn, Prince Sinostox also became master of the Wyrmheld who patrol the great caverns. In the second age, Sinostox consecrated himself to the *drakodemon* in an unholy ceremony and is supposedly cursed to never die, still walking the earth questing for the Chalice of Infernal Consumption. In the epics he is depicted as luring the Duke into the forbidden Pyramid of the Skull in Mullinth, in order to fight the Duke on a bridge over the Abyss. Unable to cast the Duke into the abyss, he does the unthinkable and calls forth the Beast of The Apocalypse. He also appears in *The Bladetongue*, as an exile plotting against Norgonce the Grand Knight.

State of Cathartic Titan: in the pagan cult of the Red Asceticism, this is a state of consciousness is the perfection of the initiate, comprising three of Plato's four manias: intoxication, prophecy, eros. It is reached by extreme indulgence in pleasure of any sort and is believed to confer god-like status.

Tablets of Destiny: the most primordial code of Divine Law given by Heaven; said to be buried in somewhere in Setet or hidden within the Sea of Immanent waves.

Thanato Excorpus: A writer and historian of the seventeenth century who by his depth-research was among the first of the modern era to become aware of the existence of the lost Illystra epics.

Thasos: A region extending from the eastern shores of the Niruz peninsula to the borders of the swamps of Hithgroth south to southern bounds of the Hills of

Fire. The region has been settled by various tribes of dwarves but for the most part is wild.

Thaumaturgy (lit: "wonder-working"): the transcendent spells of clerics.

Tyrnople (also Turnopolis): The eastern exarchate of the Regulian Principate. Tyrnople lies in a strategic location, not only having ports and access to the Sea of Goldyndol, but is also on the route called "The Serrian Way" which leads to Namaliel.

Troll-horde, also, "trollwise" does not specify trolls as identified by the encyclopediast Guy of Xaragia, but rather in the Nord-tongue is a general term for humanoid monsters from beneath the earth or which stalk the night. The troll-horde which formed under Mulcifer were mostly horgoth and bolgoth, a few trolls and giants, some grey elves and evil men.

Ulthork (Ulthor, Ulthuring): The great kingdom of men which became the seat of order and civilization in the northern regions after the waning of the Regulian Principate. Bordered by the Sea of Goldyndol, its principle city, Yrbath, relies on the fishing industry. Maceon planted the Ammouric faith in old Ulthor in the time of his passing, and it has not weakened since then, as it has in the other kingdoms of the upper world. Ulthoran minuscule is the principle script of the fourth age.

The Ulthorings were great kings, such as Argoth the Good. It became a province of the Regulian Principate in the third age but finally broke ties with Regulis when the Red Ascetic came to power. The rangers of Ulthor protect many places in Illystra sacred to their faith, such as Mt. Arguzinial and Vesulum, and The Edolunt Riders, still patrol the civil lands of the old empire.

Ultima Thule: The classical name for the Nathycanthe, (Nathycanis) land of the Bifrost mountains, whose principal castle is Ael-Lot Upon the Sea. The King of Ael Lot also rules all of the Hothic islands to the north as well as the entire island of Kiluria.

Urguard: A powerful city-state of Itruria with massive walls of Atlantean architecture. The notorious and chaotic gold-mining city specializes in the gladitorial entertainments and is a highway for those entering the Underdyrth. They have fought many wars with Authapis.

Vale of Chimera: the principle passage through the Antelynk Range to the Eastern dry lands. The trek is dangerous, and the only known inhabitant of the Vale is Old Budderham (q.v.), who also looks after and feeds the (now tame) Chimera that dwells in the Orange-shroom Cave overlooking the valley.

Valaghir Mountains: The great mountains that rose south from Hyrcanum as far as the desert of Luz and the north bounds of the Kingdom of Atalur. These mountains separate the Sea of Ymmin from the Sea of Shirvav. They are grey in color and very high capped by snow on some peaks. No law governs these lands and the Edolunt Riders do not pass through them. There is only one road through the Mountains which was cut out by the Atlanteans ages ago. This

"Pass of Dariel" shows great wood and stone bridges that are aloft high in the cool mountain air and still are sturdy. The pass south ends at the Bronze Gates of Hermius which separates the isthmus in halves. The great Bronze Gates of Hermius were built in the second age when the great Conqueror heard that the people of Atalur and Gohha were being raided each year by barbarian horsemen from the North.

Valraph(s): Antiquated usage also employs plural, *Valraphim.* 1) Originally an oath-bound chivalric order of half-elves. Old epics lost to human memory recounted their heroic exploits, deeds which must be attributed to the sterling mix of fairy blood with human, infusing the best qualities of each. 2) In common speech the name is typically applied to the entire race of elven hybrids. It is recounted in the eldark myths how a marriage between a male human and a female elf resulted in a new race which was given the name *valraphim,* half-elves. That is misinformation spread by the Nystoli. The ingenious alchemist Rebus Pecequiohr had found a way to manipulate the genetic spindle. Having captured and performed cruel experiments on a particular elf, they needed a standing army of super-human warriors (since the run of the mill mercenaries refused to work for the accursed wizards). So he designed the human-elven hybrids known as valraphs and trained them from infancy in war. The valraph army however was too small in size to defeat the Mahark Barbarians. Many valraphs escaped the destruction of their home Nystol and settled their own kingdom Ayrs.

NB: In later times the old chivalric order of Valraphim was re-established by those questing for *The Black Books,* but when dwarves and other races were admitted into the order, the name could no longer be simultaneously applied only to the race of half-elves, who do not appreciate the title "half-elves." Hence, when the ancient plural *Valraphim* is used, the speaker refers to the old chivalric order, but when small case and common termination *valraph(s),* no capitalization is used as the race is indicated.

Vastess Desert: A designation which includes The Dry Blood Sea, Kithom, Cathon, the Yezez desert, the Deadly Hills, the Plain of Kanats, and part of the Orcodon Peninsula.

Vastess Sea: The Vastess Ocean-sea is also includes the Tethys Sea in its furthest known extent. It is called the *Intermundian Sea* of the upper world because its waters flow between the worlds. It is said that the name "intermundian" was first applied to those waters of the Vastess Sea which spill into the *mare infernum,* which Plato titled "Tartarus" in his cosmology; for by way of these vast flowing waterways many strange travelers have brought us rare and precious tomes: Moses, Homer, Plato, Hermes, Macrobius, Dante, and a few others. It has also been called "Ocean," and although it is not fresh water as the Okeanos of the epics, it does have strange, warm, fresh water currents that flow from the Hyperboric Sea in the North. The Vastess Sea has many dangers, and few men have ever returned who have beyond the horizon sailed.

Vath, Isle of: An oasis-city carved into a rock-island in The Dry Blood Sea. Its original inhabitants were possibly Vri, but Hycmen fugitives from Gohha took it over at the end of the third age. The hycmen who did not follow Noshar went and dwelt in tents near the lake of Asphyl. These were mostly put to the sword under the Pharaoh Paphsis or died of starvation in the following years when the Urash failed to flood and the lake dried up. Some fled to the deserts of the west under the judge, Vathar. These were known as the Vathim, and surviving they later carved out the underground city, Vath, on one of the great rock-isles in the desert, but it is now nearly uninhabited.

Veil, Cult of the: A strain of Arian heresy which became a fanatical cult of such great popularity it destabilized all Arraf and threatened to destroy by means of unholy war the Ammouric monarchies of the West. The patriarchs called for Crusades against the powerful and dangerous Veil-Knights. These dark warriors founded their power on an unholy communion of strict discipline mixed with fanatic religious enthusiasm. They made vows of absolute loyalty to Lord Synostocs of Atalur, namely to conquer all the western kingdoms or die trying. So a subsequent generation of crusaders again had to go east to protect Vesulum against the threat. The Ammouric knights held the city and pushed back the Veil.

Vesulum (Vorsalir): It was shortly before the Great Burning of Nyzium that a virtuous king rose up among the tent-dwelling Kutaal, a certain King Hsarhgoh the Righteous, (in the West called "King Argoth the Good"). This king realized fulfillment come in great prophecy concerning Kutaal: *"Your peoples shall be great Warriors and deliver the lands."* This did not refer to warriors of bow and horse, he perceived, but rather Spiritual Warriors. He thus convinced the High Patriarch of Illystra to establish a spiritual stronghold in a little cliff-village hidden away in the lower *canyons of Hermius*, known as Vesulum. Vesulum became a training ground for kings and a place of study for *selvas* (priests). Certain areas were established for prayer with guidelines requiring spiritual clean-ness. Many great monks, priests, and clerics have come from this land. Aetholus, the famous explorer, writes, "The entire city is of cliff-dwelling architecture, with ornate spires, seraphic statues, and elaborate porches, all carved out of an elevated side of the canyon, extending for nigh two furlongs and having apartments and towers of several stories, and in some places a total of perhaps seven cubits rising...its inhabitants are ruled over by not a king, but rather a queen, whose handmaidens have required their own separated dwellings. The virgins must be apart from all others, for the city is sacred, and no marriages are permitted within its precinct. It is said that they guard a great relic, the holy lance. It remains the only city that can rival wicked Nystol (Nyzium) in spiritual power." Although no Ammouric monastery was ever established there, it did boast the greatest library of sacred works from the ancient world. The city remained pure from corruption and heresy until the usurpation of the cult-master Shahi Nuzzib.

Voethius: A Regulian author of a history of Nyzium based on various eyewitness accounts detailing precisely the corruption of ethics among the arcane colleges which led to the triumph of summoning and demonolatry, and which led ultimately to the Hypostatic Rift and demise of the mortal magics in the world.

Vorsalir (norths-tongue, Vesulum the holy city)

Washir River: The great trading river of the Chyldishire forests which flows into the city Regulis and into the Vastess Sea.

Waffin leaf (also *Swaph* in the south) a giant swamp plant useful for creating huge tomes.

Weeping Brotherhood (the greatest monastery on the Furth continent, located in the Dry Blood Dunes, at the Vathic Rock Islands, a day's pilgrimage from Vath itself. It is renowned for its library, which features twelve books and scrolls rescued from Nystol. Only Whigg has a comparable collection. It is rumoured however that Heretics have seized control of the monastery and have destroyed many books.

Warlock: see note

Whigg: A small but significant fortress-town in the Nine Feudatories. Its library was once highly respected and is now strictly guarded by the Friars of Whigg, theological rivals of the Monks of Whitehaven.

Whitehawk: the emblem of Christiandom in the civil lands, an emblem first used for those who took up the crusading campaigns in the fourth age. The title was soon to designate all the Christian lands, but was also used loosely for the entire continent, including all non-Christian furthlands in the East, whereas all such lands would be the Ammouric inheritance anyway, it being their divinely sanctioned duty to free those peoples from the demon-gods and bring their inhabitants into civil and religious obedience. Includes all the intermundane principalities as well.

Xilmuria: A primordial land of unknown location, but perhaps it was Kargiwall (Ardeheim, Ardevium) when lush in the 2nd age, before the land was covered with the iron sands of the *Yahoros*: a city-state upon the plains of Kithom, neath the Andolyn mountains. Yahoros was founded by Aels in the third age having migrated from the Aelic paeninsula. Later the men of Yahoros conquered the island of Kiluria, St. Aldamar, because the coveted the fishing. They swore fealty to the High king of the Aels in Ael Lot.

Yaa, Chasm of: Believed to be located somewhere west of Anshan.

Yrbath, Irbath: The principal city under the Ulthurings Dynasty of Maceonid kings. After the eld city Ulthor was destroyed in the third age during the *Bellum Diabolicum*, the people of the kingdom rebuilt Yrbath on the sea instead of the city Ulthor. It has grown more powerful and resplendent than any would have thought. This city specializes in fishing and whaling, and hosts the invincible Ulthuring Fleet.

Yezez Desert: The desert between the Canyon of Hermius and the Antelynk Mountains. It stretches south and bends down into Garmsir. It is a place of great dangers.

Yule Queen: The patroness of bards in the old pagan world, perhaps a *nephilid*, who is rumoured to still bless the world with poetry. Ariandol's castles are found in the underworld, havens for bold adventurers who would tell or learn tales of great exploit. She exports her mead to all lands. It is said that she was courted by the overbold man Duke Ikonn, and to have kept the Erl king captivated for centuries (She is named Arva in elvish).

Zabul (Zabol, Nzulg): see *Nzul*

Zenops: an ancient wizard of great mischief, who built a famous colossal tower to rival Nystol.

Zorrogoh: A remote city on the southern coasts of Illystra. Zorrogoh is cut of by the jungles north of it and lives primarily from the sea trade, like Gandolon. Zorrogoh is the last stop for ships sailing east to Sippar and Anshan

H.G Potter parish priest; writer, and illustrator. MA Greek & Latin. teacher of ancient civilizations, classical literature, and mythology.

After ordination in 2009 he at last finished the epic *Never Leave Your Monastery* in 2019 and now has completed this much older collection of short stories which was originally begun in 1986.

Sub-Arctic zone

CRACH MTNS

Northern Warm Sea

THE GREAT NORTHERN FORESTS

Durgoth

Ael Lot

HROTHIC SEA

Hroth

PLATHONS

AVRS

Kath

ARMSIL

Axecut

Calleth L.

swamps of Kath

THE HORGWALL

PLAIN OF GEDERON

ARDAHEIM

ARTA

HYRKANTH

St. Aldemarz

Lokren

Bifrost Mtns

NATHYKANTH

iceflows

Dove Lake

Wyrmhole

Hurven -guard

Kargiwall

tower of Icloharius

Mt. Onager

IRONPORT

Hordingbay

Whitehaven

Timoh region

Whigg

Arkt

Ösring

SEA OF GOLDINDOL

URBATH

THE NINE FEUDATORIES

Washir R.

ULTHOR

SEA OF YMEIR

Isle of HARPIES

VASTESS OCEAN SEA

Ruins of OLD ALLAPIS

Forest

Lesser mtns.

TYRNOPOLIS

Zenop's tower

semi-arid

KITHOM

Namaliel

REGULUM

AIDEEN

AQUILAR

Echurias

Andolyn Mtns

Vesulum

CANYON OF HERMIUS

THE DRY BLOOD SEA

lake Asphyl

ATA

Duchy of GORRE

MAHANAXAR

Vale of Chymera

old Budder -ham

Nahoros

Azerdon

Yezez Desert

GARDAS RISE

Fort Guzaran

ISLE OF VATH

URUSCA

Thesprozia

ANCIENT RISES OF NYSTOL

SARDU PLATEAU

Monastery of ‡ The Weeping Brotherhood

URGUARD

AUTHAPIS

lower forests

STILLY HILLS

Kutaal

ISAURIA

-head of Echecrates

MULLIZH

Pyramid of THE SCULL

Uncharted

Forest Lamesh

The ACCURSED Sea

Gandolon

UNCHARTED

Orcodon

jungles

Pe

KANTH

Uncharted

H G R O T

Nzul

CRACKED

MOUNTAINS

Arc du Baffay

THE

THASOS

MAHARIM

Mt
ARGUNISOL?

Watch of
Ogodar

Niruz

CAPHTORIM

EPHRE

KNHVM

Chasm
of
Yaaz

UNCHARTED

Mt
Abaddon

SEA OF

GREAT CLIFFS

Mountains

Red squirrel
FOREST

SHIRVAV

XARTIZAN

XASEVR

Eight
Tigers
Monastery

ANSHAN

UNCHARTED

YARCUNE!

HERMOPOLIS

Ruins

YACESH

Dibon

dod

Lu

KALAR-
Maurob

Hills of Khalu-Kim

KALAR

Forbidden
passage

GHOSTLANDS
OF
SETET

WARLORD
KARKAR
Hur

NS
OF
ANATS

Urash Rv.

VALLEY OF MANY

SIPPAR

GOHHA

MAZES

stones
of Sippar

SARNAS

SUCCON

PYRAMIDS
of Dusk

Lotus
Forest

Karnang

don

Ruins of
Iquizan

Scopta

CHRONIAN
SEA

UNCHARTED

us Coast

Realms of

Whitehawk

www.ingramcontent.com/pod-product-compliance
Lightning Source LLC
Chambersburg PA
CBHW020836030726
47496CB00001B/249